OXFORD WORLD'S CLASSICS

STRANGE CASE OF
DR JEKYLL AND MR HYDE
AND OTHER TALES

ROBERT LOUIS STEVENSON, only child of Thomas Stevenson, engineer and lighthouse builder, and Margaret Balfour, daughter of a Scots minister, was born in Edinburgh in 1850. In 1871 he exchanged the study of engineering for the law. From 1876 he pursued a full-time literary career, beginning as an essayist and travel-writer with the publication of *An Inland Voyage* (1878), *Edinburgh: Picturesque Notes* (1878), *Travels with a Donkey in the Cévennes* (1879), and *Virginibus Puerisque* (1881). Stevenson is probably best remembered for *Treasure Island* (his first widespread success, 1883), *Kidnapped*, and *Dr Jekyll and Mr Hyde* (both published in 1886). Ill health and temperament prompted Stevenson to travel widely on the Continent and in the South Seas, where he settled in 1889–90 until his death in Samoa on 3 December 1894.

ROGER LUCKHURST is the author of *The Invention of Telepathy* (2002) and *Science Fiction* (2005) and co-editor of *The Fin de Siecle: A Reader in Cultural History c.1880–1900* (2000). He has edited *Late Victorian Gothic Tales* for the Oxford World's Classics series.

OXFORD WORLD'S CLASSICS

*For over 100 years Oxford World's Classics have brought
readers closer to the world's great literature. Now with over 700
titles—from the 4,000-year-old myths of Mesopotamia to the
twentieth century's greatest novels—the series makes available
lesser-known as well as celebrated writing.*

*The pocket-sized hardbacks of the early years contained
introductions by Virginia Woolf, T. S. Eliot, Graham Greene,
and other literary figures which enriched the experience of reading.
Today the series is recognized for its fine scholarship and
reliability in texts that span world literature, drama and poetry,
religion, philosophy and politics. Each edition includes perceptive
commentary and essential background information to meet the
changing needs of readers.*

OXFORD WORLD'S CLASSICS

ROBERT LOUIS STEVENSON

Strange Case of
Dr Jekyll and Mr Hyde
and Other Tales

Edited with an Introduction and Notes by
ROGER LUCKHURST

OXFORD
UNIVERSITY PRESS

OXFORD
UNIVERSITY PRESS

Great Clarendon Street, Oxford OX2 6DP

Oxford University Press is a department of the University of Oxford.
It furthers the University's objective of excellence in research, scholarship,
and education by publishing worldwide in

Oxford New York

Auckland Cape Town Dar es Salaam Hong Kong Karachi
Kuala Lumpur Madrid Melbourne Mexico City Nairobi
New Delhi Shanghai Taipei Toronto

With offices in

Argentina Austria Brazil Chile Czech Republic France Greece
Guatemala Hungary Italy Japan Poland Portugal Singapore
South Korea Switzerland Thailand Turkey Ukraine Vietnam

Oxford is a registered trade mark of Oxford University Press
in the UK and in certain other countries

Published in the United States
by Oxford University Press Inc., New York

Editorial matter © Roger Luckhurst 2006

British Library Cataloguing in Publication Data

Data available

Library of Congress Cataloging in Publication Data

Data available

Typeset in Ehrhardt
by RefineCatch Limited, Bungay, Suffolk
Printed in Great Britain by
Clays Ltd., St. Ives plc
ISBN 978-0-19-280597-3

3

CONTENTS

INTRODUCTION

[Readers who do not wish to learn details of the plot may prefer to treat the Introduction as an Epilogue]

What happens when a literary text becomes a modern myth, the names of its characters shorthand terms traded in the wider culture? The endless retellings in theatre, film, and television, the constant stream of rewritings and updatings, all take us further away from the original until it lies forgotten under the rubble of its imitators. *Jekyll and Hyde* immediately evokes chemistry sets and bubbling potions, werewolves and damsels in distress, Fredric March or Spencer Tracy acting histrionically, or the sensational tabloid story of the bland inoffensive neighbour unmasked as the latest serial killer. Everyone knows the story of Dr Jekyll and Mr Hyde, and what it is supposed to symbolize. But if you have never read Robert Louis Stevenson's *Strange Case of Dr Jekyll and Mr Hyde* try to forget everything you think you know, and start again with this deeply peculiar, perplexing, and backwards-told novella.

Robert Louis Stevenson

Robert Louis Stevenson (1850–94) was the literary star of his generation, one of the first writers to be turned into an international 'personality' by the vastly expanded popular press of the late nineteenth century. He was lauded across the world: the absent lodestone of literary London, but mobbed by crowds in America and Australia in the last decade of his life. He was an alluring yet enigmatic figure, perpetually described by his contemporaries in contradictory terms. He was a lifelong invalid (with a pulmonary disease that never received a definitive diagnosis) and was dependent on his parents well into his thirties, yet he also travelled ceaselessly to the extremes of the world, eventually dying in 1894 as the revered patriarch of a plantation on the Pacific island of Samoa. He was regarded as an innovative literary stylist who also produced boys' adventures, pirate romances, horror stories, children's poetry, and some truly terrible plays. He was an atheist obsessed with religious questions; a workaholic who wrote 'In Praise of Idlers'; a Tory who despised moralism and lived as a bohemian artist. Later critics have declared him the last Victorian or the first Modernist. As his friend Henry James put it, he was but 'linked dualities', 'a drenched yachtsman haunted with "style," a shameless Bohemian haunted with duty, and a victim at once of the personal hunger and instinct for adventure and of the critical, constructive, sedentary view of it'.[1]

Stevenson first became known as an essayist in the late 1870s, writing for the leading journals of the day in a concise, poised style that abandoned the bombast of Thomas Carlyle or John Ruskin. He was connected to an impressive network of London literary heavy-weights such as the editor Leslie Stephen (Virginia Woolf's father), the editor, poet, and his playwriting collaborator W. E. Henley, the scholars Edmund Gosse and Sidney Colvin, and the American émigré theorist of the 'art of the novel', Henry James. Andrew Lang, a critic who nurtured Rider Haggard and Rudyard Kipling to their fame, recalled unblushingly that Stevenson 'possessed, more than any man I ever met, the power of making other men fall in love with him'.[2] These men constantly implored Stevenson to produce the literary masterpiece that would secure his name. Instead, somewhat perversely, and more than occasionally railing against this pressure, Stevenson experimented with a bewildering variety of forms, from the travel narrative to the traditional seasonal ghost story. His first success came in the early 1880s, with the boys' adventure, *Treasure Island*, written initially as a family entertainment for his young step-son, serialized and then published in book form in 1883. It was to signal, for Andrew Lang, the start of a 'romance revival', a revital-izing riposte to the character studies of the so-called analytic novel that was associated with George Eliot and Henry James. Stevenson was to add his own essays to this debate (such as 'A Gossip on Romance', included in this edition). It was on the basis of this revival that some of the most famous writers of the late Victorian era found their form: Conan Doyle, H. G. Wells, Rider Haggard. Stevenson's second work to find public favour was *A Child's Garden of Verses* in

[1] Henry James, 'The Letters of Robert Louis Stevenson' (review, 1900), in *Henry James and Robert Louis Stevenson: A Record of Friendship and Criticism*, ed. Janet Adam Smith (London, 1948), 257.

[2] Andrew Lang, cited Claire Harman, *Robert Louis Stevenson: A Biography* (London, 2005), 213.

1885, a delightful evocation of childhood perspective and emotion, told in simple rousing stanzas.

The early reviews of *Jekyll and Hyde*, which appeared in early January 1886, just missing the Christmas market, were justifiably uncertain about how to treat Stevenson's latest work, since it came from a literary star and yet was marketed as a lowly and despised 'shilling shocker', 'a class of literature', *Academy* commented, 'familiarity with which has bred in the minds of most readers a certain measure of contempt'.[3] Stevenson veered constantly between high literary ambition and writing in commercial forms for market rates, and many of his critics were confused about where to place each work. Stevenson was himself unsure at times, and frequently misjudged things. *Prince Otto*, a novel on which he spent five years to secure his reputation as a 'serious' novelist, was not well received; *Jekyll and Hyde*, dreamt up, written, rewritten, and published all in under ten weeks, became his masterpiece. It was also a commercial success, selling 40,000 copies in England in six months, and innumerable tens of thousands of pirated copies in America, where the book was a popular sensation. This confusion over incompatible forms of high and low literary value was not unusual in the late Victorian era, as authors as diverse as Oscar Wilde, Arthur Conan Doyle, and Joseph Conrad sought to negotiate the new commercial forms and the increasing professionalization of literature (including newfangled things like literary agents and limited international copyright). The distinction of high and low literature, as we understand them in the modern sense, was still emergent, so that this was a moment when a lowly Gothic romance might conjoin unexpectedly with a species of psychological realism to produce a *Jekyll and Hyde*. But when these distinctions did harden in the twentieth century, Stevenson's eclectic body of work was to suffer badly.

Indeed, rarely has a reputation declined so steadily after death. Stevenson's wife, Fanny, and talentless stepson Lloyd Osbourne (with whom Stevenson collaborated on a number of later novels) benefited from the syndicate of publishers who put out no fewer than five collected editions of his work between 1894 and 1924 (when the copyright elapsed), raking in thousands of pounds yet slowly destroying Stevenson's achievement by issuing every last scrap of

---

[3] James Ashcroft Noble, review, *Academy*, 23 Jan. 1886, reprinted in Paul Maixner, *Robert Louis Stevenson: The Critical Heritage* (London, 1981), 203.

juvenilia, unfinished sketch, and first draft of poetry. Early editions
were edited by literary allies like Colvin and Gosse—both quietly
suppressed texts, and Colvin even rewrote passages. Later, Gosse
would complain of the exhausted scrapbooks of the 'Vailima' edition
that 'The Dead should be protected from their own carelessness.'[4]
Meanwhile, volumes of letters were produced, prompting the obses-
sively secretive Henry James to worry (privately, of course) 'whether
Louis's work itself doesn't *pay* somewhat for the so complete exhibition of the man and the life . . . The achieved legend and history
that has *him* for subject, has made so to speak, light of *their* subjects,
of their claim to represent him.'[5] This was an acute comment to
make to Stevenson's first biographer and cousin, Gerald Balfour, for
the general response to the book was to mock savagely the sanctifica-
tion of the author. Henley, who had broken with Stevenson over his
choice of wife, famously rejected the portrait of 'this Seraph in
chocolate, this barley-sugared effigy of a man'. Henley's memory
of his collaborator was, significantly, divided: 'there were two
Stevensons,' he said, and he preferred the rambunctious Edinburgh
bachelor called Lewis (not yet Frenchified to Louis) rather than the
internationally trademarked 'R. L. S.'[6] By 1914, the critical judgement of Frank Swinnerton was merciless. Stevenson was a lazy,
immature writer: 'with all his writing he took the road of least resistance, the road of limited horizons; because with all his desire for
romance . . . he was by physical delicacy made intellectually timid
and spiritually cautious.'[7] Stevenson had therefore become the victim of the posthumous management of his literary persona, and the
moderns buried him. Even Stevenson's superb rendition of the
mythology of the double in *Jekyll and Hyde* had escaped its textual
origins and entered the general collective imagination, but in doing
so it was often crudely stripped of its nuances and perplexities. We
now have to work quite hard to read the original in a proper set of
contexts.

---

[4] Edmund Gosse, cited by Andrew Nash, 'The Collected Editions of Robert Louis
Stevenson', in Andrew Nash (ed.), *The Culture of Collected Editions* (London, 2003),
111–27.

[5] Letter, Henry James to Graham Balfour (15 Nov. 1901), *Letters of Henry James*
(Cambridge, Mass., 1984), iv. 213.

[6] W. E. Henley, 'R. L. S.', *Pall Mall Magazine* (Dec. 1901), repr. in R. C. Terry (ed.),
Robert Louis Stevenson: Interviews and Recollections (Iowa City, 1996), 194 and 192.

[7] Frank Swinnerton, *R. L. Stevenson: A Critical Study* (London, 1914), 205.

Strange Case of Dr Jekyll and Mr Hyde

The origin of mythic figures usually resides in some misty prehistory. The origins of *Jekyll and Hyde* are themselves suitably murky. In the summer of 1885, Stevenson moved to Bournemouth, where his father had brought a house for his invalid son. Stevenson was often bedridden, taking morphine for pain, but also writing feverishly hard on the usual gamut of half-realized projects. Stevenson would later tell the story to journalists in 1887 and again in 'A Chapter on Dreams' that he was struggling to complete a tale about a double life, called 'The Travelling Companion', and had fallen into a feverish sleep: 'All I dreamed about Dr Jekyll,' he told the *Critic* interviewer, 'was that one man was being pressed into a cabinet, when he swallowed a drug and changed into another being. I awoke and said at once that I had found the missing link for which I had been looking so long, and before I again went to sleep almost every detail of the story, as it stands, was clear to me.'[8] With the shape of the story sketched out, he set to writing it in a frenzy. Lloyd Osbourne, the stepson who left unreliable memoirs, claimed that the novella was completed in three days, as if Stevenson had been in the white heat of Romantic inspiration. Fanny Stevenson also insisted on an active role in its composition. Gerald Balfour's biography placed Fanny as the first reader of the tale: she was harsh. 'I wrote pages of criticism pointing out that he had here a great moral allegory that the dream was obscuring.' If this sounds like a suspiciously retrospective reading, her view that the problem lay in the fact that 'Jekyll's nature was bad all through, and the Hyde change was worked only for the sake of disguise' sounds extremely plausible.[9] It was exactly the weakness of Stevenson's play, *Deacon Brodie: A Double Life*, that had failed once again on the London stage in July 1884. Whatever the nature of his wife's criticism, Stevenson's response was histrionic: he threw the whole manuscript on the fire and started again. He was to compose *Jekyll and Hyde* as we now have it probably over the next six weeks. It was produced so

---

[8] Stevenson interview, *Critic* (10 Sept. 1887), cited in J. A. Hammond (ed.), *Stevensoniana: An Anecdotal Life and Appreciation of Robert Louis Stevenson* (Edinburgh, 1907), 85.

[9] Fanny Stevenson, cited Claire Harman, *Robert Louis Stevenson: A Life* (London, 2005), 296.

fast—rushing for the Christmas market—that the final revisions were done in the margins of the proof copies.

The origin of the novella is therefore marked by strange splittings and doublings. *Jekyll and Hyde* has a shadow twin, consigned to the fire. There is that earlier version, 'The Travelling Companion', also lost to one of Stevenson's bonfires. These lost versions have tempted all sorts of speculation about just what Fanny felt the need to silence or revise. The existence of three fragments of the narrative in notebooks, with suggestively variant phrases, particularly of Dr Jekyll's 'Full Statement of the Case', has given further fuel to these speculations, making the text a stranger to itself through the kind of exorbitant interpretations critics have pursued. And behind all this is the kernel derived from a dream, making the book a product of an uneasy collaboration between the waking and the dreaming self, with neither quite in control of the final version. After all this, it is really no surprise that Longmans decided to issue two editions of the book on the same day, a cheap shilling edition and a slightly more well-heeled version, as if wanting to echo the strange double act of Dr Jekyll and Mr Hyde.

There is something very dreamlike about reading *Jekyll and Hyde*. It echoes with the half-remembered sonorous language of the Old Testament, bubbling up from Stevenson's fierce religious upbringing. Descriptions have a hallucinatory quality, where solitary men roam ugly streets that take on menacing attributes, evoked by inexplicable events or sudden eruptions of violence. Doubles proliferate everywhere: Jekyll and Hyde are discussed by Utterson and Enfield, Utterson and Lanyon, Poole and Utterson, dessicated men caught in joyless meetings, terrified by something they cannot utter. Dream logic allows people to change their aspect, to transform their very being. Perhaps the strangest thing is the way the story is structured: it starts out like a detective fiction but like a dream it gets distracted, seems to veer off course, and transmogrifies into something far more Gothic and unnerving. Rationally, we might expect a 'case' to be solved, or perhaps to be cured: we don't expect to be left in this unresolved metaphysical confusion.

In fact, the structure is the most ingeniously designed element of the book. It tells the story backwards, so that we work our way towards the confession of Dr Jekyll, which is revealed last. There are at least three narrators: Utterson, the nervous lawyer who plays detective to rescue Jekyll's reputation; Hastie Lanyon, the bluff materialist medic who is at first appalled by Jekyll's mystical turn and finally shocked to death by it; and Jekyll's own account. Yet there are several other interpolated narrators, too: the novella opens with Enfield's weirdly inconsequential story of the door, and the murder of Sir Danvers Carew is filtered through the newspaper reports of a maid's eyewitness account, itself told as if through the conventions of romantic fiction. The narrative moves from the outer edges of the secret to its final revelation. It unfolds like a sequence of Russian dolls nested inside each other. This is often literally the case: when Utterson opens a sealed envelope from his friend Lanyon, 'within there was another enclosure likewise sealed'. Again, when Utterson is called to Jekyll's house on the fateful last night, he finds another envelope with 'several enclosures'. Utterson cannot read this without racing home to read Lanyon's letter first: there is a constant sense of deferral, as if to get the dolls lined up in the right order.

This structure of the secret is repeated in the peculiar architecture of Jekyll's house. The town house on the respectable square backs onto an enclosed courtyard that contains an outbuilding: Denman's old laboratory. Within this there is the cabinet where Jekyll conducts his fateful experiments. Lanyon is given permission to break through these doors: he has the further task of breaking open a locked drawer in his desk to bring away Jekyll's chemicals. Utterson and Poole use an axe to break down the cabinet, only to find a body and sealed enclosures within sealed enclosures that contain the final truth. Stevenson undoubtedly borrowed this idea of texts within texts from the kinds of sensation fiction written by Wilkie Collins in the 1860s, melodramatic tales of the detection of extreme crimes unfolded across interlocking manuscripts. He also repeatedly invoked the *Arabian Night Entertainments*, that Arabic matrix of interconnected stories ostensibly told by Scheherazade to save herself from death— Stevenson had published his own *New Arabian Nights* and *An Island Night's Entertainments*.

The point of these nested stories is to situate Jekyll's final, impossible revelation in the world of the possible, a trick of embedding the supernatural in the everyday often used by late Victorian Gothic fictions. Yet for all this carefully constructed architecture of stories, *Jekyll and Hyde* does not end with a resounding resolution of the mystery. Indeed, the book finishes with an utterly puzzling sentence:

'Here then, as I lay down the pen and proceed to seal up my confession, I bring the life of that unhappy Henry Jekyll to an end.' This is, as Mark Currie has pointed out, not only an impossible attempt 'to narrate the end of narration', it also splits between first and third person, leaving one radically uncertain about who in the end is writing these words, for who is the 'I' in this utterance?[10] As the 'full statement' accelerates towards its doom, and the shuttle of identity between Jekyll and Hyde becomes more chaotic and uncontrolled, there are increasingly elaborate contortions like this, which cancel themselves out ('He, I say—I cannot say I'). These undermine any confidence in the confessional identity. Without any return to Utterson, to the scene in the cabinet, the book finishes with a troublesome metaphysical conundrum. It is more than possible to turn Stevenson's economical Gothic tale into a vertiginous, self-referential thing, as being about 'nothing other than the problems of narration'.[11] This is true, yet it is also possible to work to contextualize the book, and this at least can give a better grasp on how to situate the enduring enigma of those final pages.

The Psychology of the Double

'I thus drew steadily nearer to that truth, by whose partial discovery I have been doomed to such a dreadful shipwreck: that man is not truly one, but truly two.' Jekyll's statement tells us at last the secret which is usually the first and only thing known about the book: that Hyde is Jekyll's alter ego, his second self, his supernaturally generated evil twin. This confession only belatedly situates *Jekyll and Hyde* in a long tradition of texts featuring unnerving doublings and pairings. Indeed, the double had been a repeated theme in the Romantic movement and in Gothic fiction from their emergence in the late eighteenth century across Britain, Europe, and America. It was a particular obsession of the German Romantics: Goethe explored strange elective affinities and wrote about encountering his own double; Kleist, influenced by contemporary psychology, wrote plays like *Penthesilea* about alternating personalities; the great Gothic writer E. T. A. Hoffmann generated story after disordered

---

[10] Mark Currie, 'True Lies: Unreliable Identities in *Dr Jekyll and Mr Hyde*', *Postmodern Narrative Theory* (Basingstoke, 1998), 124.

[11] Currie, 'True Lies', 122.

story about doubling. This theme would continue as an obsession for writers long into the nineteenth century: the 1840s produced both Edgar Allan Poe's 'William Wilson' and Fyodor Dostoevsky's *The Double*. Stevenson's generation also produced another memorable cluster: *Jekyll and Hyde*, Guy de Maupassant's 'The Horla', Oscar Wilde's *The Picture of Dorian Gray*, Joseph Conrad's 'The Secret Sharer' or *Heart of Darkness*, and Henry James's 'The Jolly Corner'. The strange figure of the double, Karl Miller claims, 'stands at the start of that cultivation of uncertainty by which the literature of the modern world has come to be distinguished'.[12] Another way of saying this might be to suggest that the literature of the double became one of the privileged ways of exploring the mysteries of the modern self, a subjectivity marked less by rationality, order, and coherence than by dream, nightmare, and psychical multiplicity. From the Romantic era, the opening up of the vast interiors of the self seems to have made us strangers to ourselves: the double is the emblem of this self-estrangement.

The literature of the double has always existed in a symbiotic relation with psychology. The Romantics were fascinated by the weird phenomena associated with Mesmerism. In the 1780s, Franz Anton Mesmer claimed that he could cure patients in physical and mental distress by putting them into trance states and exerting an influence over them that he called 'animal magnetism'. Mesmerist and patient were found to be in an uncanny 'rapport' that was soon associated with the supernatural: patient and Mesmerist could read each other's minds; they could be psychically connected across vast distances. The twinning or pairing of minds was a consequence of treatment; soon, the figure of the evil Mesmerist entrancing and enslaving defenceless men and women entered into popular demonology and survived down to figures like Count Dracula or the Svengali of George du Maurier's 1894 novel *Trilby*. Although Mesmerism was discredited by numerous scientific bodies, it remained a quasi-scientific pursuit into the 1840s. It was taken up by English Romantics like Percy Shelley, and later Charles Dickens was an enthusiastic advocate and practitioner of the Mesmeric cure. Mesmer's claims of actual transfer of 'magnetic fluid' between people may have been wrong, but Mesmerism is now held to

---

[12] Karl Miller, *Doubles: Studies in Literary History* (Oxford, 1985), p. viii.

anticipate findings associated with hypnotism, which first began to
be given proper scientific legitimacy in the 1880s, just as Stevenson
was writing.[13]

The late nineteenth-century group of texts featuring doubles has
often been associated with the rise of psychoanalysis, a term coined
by Sigmund Freud in 1896. This is unsurprising, given that Freud
was steeped in German Romantic literature, and unusually used
literary texts in evidential ways to support his theories of mind. He
wrote extensively on Dostoevsky, and in his essay 'The Uncanny'
(1919) Freud analysed Hoffmann's hallucinatory tale of doubling,
'The Sandman'. Freud's interest in this tradition was the insistent
way in which the double appears first as a seductive, delightful companion, only to turn against its original and pursue a devilish persecution, frequently ending in death. This is the pattern of *Jekyll
and Hyde*; something like Dostoevsky's *The Double* is shrilly hysterical from the start about persecution. Freud's ideas were reliant on
his colleague Otto Rank, who published an essay on 'Der
Doppelgänger' in 1914. Rank suggested the double was a psychic
splitting of the self, initially projected as a kind of insurance against
the fear of death, but that soon turned into a punitive emblem of that
very death. 'So it happened', Rank argued, 'that the double, who
personifies narcissistic self-love, becomes an unequivocal rival in
sexual love; or else, originally created as a wish-defence against a
dreaded eternal destruction, he reappears in superstition as a messenger of death.'[14] Freud was able to relate these ideas to his view of
paranoia (where suppressed ideas are externalized, only to return as
threats and persecutions), thus providing a sophisticated framework
for reading the double.

Psychoanalytic readings of *Jekyll and Hyde* have been a large part
of the critical writing on the novel. Since Jekyll confesses that everyday restrictions of respectable society have prompted him to 'a profound duplicity', sexual repression is another obvious interpretative
route. That Hyde's murderous violence is directed at the elderly
patriarch Sir Danvers Carew, and that he shocks Lanyon to death

---

[13] For a history of Mesmerism in the nineteenth century, see Adam Crabtree, *From
Mesmer to Freud: Magnetic Sleep and the Roots of Psychological Healing* (New Haven,
1994). For its impact on English literary culture in the early Victorian period, see Fred
Kaplan, *Dickens and Mesmerism: The Hidden Springs of Fiction* (Princeton, 1975).

[14] Otto Rank, *The Double: A Psychoanalytic Study*, trans. Harry Tucker (London,
1989), 86.

and taunts Jekyll with his blasphemics and casual criminality, has also generated much speculation that Hyde is an emblem of a kind of Oedipal rage towards repressive father figures. Some are even tempted to read Stevenson's own repressed rage against the puritanical Thomas Stevenson here, too, with rage against fathers the abiding theme of his fiction.[15] *Jekyll and Hyde* therefore also involves a portrait of a band of elderly brothers trying to shore up their power against the affronts of the impudent Hyde, who becomes a monstrous embodiment of the crisis of patriarchy. Psychoanalysis has therefore clearly been a productive field of interpretation.[16]

Yet if we want to read Stevenson's double in a more accurately historical relation to psychology, we need to displace Freud and look to the moment just prior to the emergence of psychoanalysis, when a host of competing psychologies were assessing new evidences of the strange ability of the human mind to split and fragment. The 1870s and 1880s heralded the era of new kinds of dynamic psychology, and Stevenson's work did not merely *reflect* these developments, but actually helped *constitute* them.

In England, mental disorder was understood by Victorian 'alienists' through a strictly biological framework. Mental health was the continuous exercise of the will to produce psychological unity. Insanity was a disaggregation of the delicate apparatus of mind, and regarded as a decline from the pinnacle of civilized man. The mentally ill were, in effect, biological degenerates, moving lower down the evolutionary ladder with every symptom presented. On the continent, however, a new psychology was emerging that was fascinated by the extraordinary *potentials* exhibited in hysteria and other mental disorders. In 1876, Dr Eugène Azam published his sensational case history of Félida X, a patient who would spontaneously shift personality from her sullen and dysfunctional 'ordinary' self and into a secondary state that was more socially oriented and demurely feminine. The two states of consciousness did not appear to share the same memory or to be conscious of each other. Over the course of

---

[15] See, for instance, Alan Sandison, *Robert Louis Stevenson and the Appearance of Modernism: A Future Feeling* (Basingstoke, 1996).

[16] The most helpful essays in this field are Stephen Heath, 'Psychopathia Sexualis: Stevenson's Strange Case', *Critical Quarterly*, 28 (1986) and Jerrold E. Hogle, 'The Struggle for a Dichotomy: Abjection in Jekyll and his Interpreters', in William Veeder and Gordon Hirsch (eds.), *Dr Jekyll and Mr Hyde after One Hundred Years* (Chicago, 1988).

fifteen years, Azam watched this secondary state become the pre-dominant persona. This not only damaged the precious idea that mental health equated to an indissoluble unity of mind, it also wrecked any distinction of 'normal' and 'pathological' states, because Félida's secondary state was an improvement on her so-called ordinary self. Two years later, the pre-eminent neurologist of France, Jean-Martin Charcot, turned his attention to hysteria and to the alternating personalities that could be induced by hypnotism. Charcot's clinic at the Salpêtrière Hospital in Paris became a famous salon, his Tuesday lectures demonstrating the strange and sen-sational alternations produced by hypnosis on his stable of female hysterics (the gender politics of these demonstrations has been much discussed by feminist historians). In 1885, French doctors reported on another sensational case, a boy called Louis who had exhibited as many as five separate personalities, each with their own separate memory chains. Louis could jump between different mental ages or between states of abject hysteria, cunning criminality, and apparently normal boyhood at the appropriate trigger. As many as twenty lead-ing European psychologists experimented on him and the cultural historian Ian Hacking has proclaimed Louis Vivet the world's first 'multiple personality'.[17] By 1890, the technical term *dédouble-ment* or 'double consciousness' had become standard psychological terminology.[18]

Once again, like the Mesmerists a hundred years before, these experiments soon became linked to strange supernatural effects. People in trance appeared to have submerged selves with heightened memory and extraordinary powers of perception. These abilities shaded into the occult: many psychologists believed they had proved that entranced people exhibited telepathic powers; others saw little difference between 'artificial somnambulism' (trance) and the spir-itualist mediums who would fall into altered states to channel the voices of the dead. Soon, doubles were reinterpretable in the lan-guage of the new psychology but also in the jargon of psychical research, a new discipline founded in England in 1882, which

[17] Ian Hacking, *Rewriting the Soul: Multiple Personality and the Sciences of Memory* (Princeton, 1995).

[18] Alfred Binet, *On Double Consciousness* (1890), reissued in the series Significant Contributions to the History of Psychology 1750–1920 (Washington, DC, 1972).

theorized that doubles, phantasms, and ghosts might all be forms of projected psychic energy.

This context is important for Stevenson because his work became wrapped up in the ongoing theorizations of psychic splitting. It was not just that 'Jekyll and Hyde' became shorthand for multiple personality (as, for example, in Morton Prince's book-length case history, *The Dissociation of a Personality*, published in 1905). It was more that Stevenson provided a parallel case linking the mysterious fount of artistic genius to these new mental theories. The origins of *Jekyll and Hyde* in a dream became a source of fascination for many. He claimed that the story 'Olalla' had the same origins, and that several dream inspirations still remained to be turned into fictions. Stevenson wrote up these reflections in a slightly different way in the essay 'A Chapter on Dreams'. This spoke of a psyche populated by submerged Brownies, benign sprites that worked up literary raw materials in his subconscious mind as he slept. This essay was in turn incorporated into one of the most significant psychological theories produced in England at the end of the century: Frederic Myers's huge synthesis of psychological evidence and case histories, 'The Sub-liminal Consciousness', published in parts between 1891 and 1895. For Myers, Stevenson evidenced the profound creative possibilities of those mental capacities that existed below the threshold (therefore sub-liminal), beyond the narrow constraints of the conscious mind. Artistic genius lived on such flashes of insight produced by 'sub-liminal uprush'. In fact, Myers had written to Stevenson in February 1886, immediately after reading *Jekyll and Hyde*, in order to offer Stevenson a number of corrections to bring the novel into line with the latest psychological theories. This exchange flowered into an extensive reading of the novel, and Myers probably sent Stevenson his essay detailing the cases of Félida X and Louis V (which was likely to be the source of Fanny Stevenson's belief that *Jekyll and Hyde* had been partly inspired by 'a paper he had read in a French scientific journal on subconsciousness').[19] In 1892 Stevenson wrote again to Myers to pass on some more instances of psychic splitting during fever: the whole letter was included in the capacious pages of Myers's 'Subliminal Consciousness'.

It is important to know something about the new psychology of

[19] Fanny Stevenson, cited Claire Harman, *Robert Louis Stevenson* (London, 2005), 300.

the 1880s in order to get to grips not just with *Jekyll and Hyde* but also with Stevenson's other works, and with the way in which some of his contemporaries regarded his genius. This is why this edition includes both 'Olalla' and 'Markheim' (where the double is a benign rather than monstrous intrusion), as well as the essay 'A Chapter on Dreams'. There was a huge amount of contemporaneous writing on the psychology of the double, including work by Henry Maudsley and W. T. Stead, sampled in the appendices to this edition. Stead, one of the leading journalists of his day, also praised Stevenson's novel highly: 'What the public does not yet realize', Stead wrote in the wake of Stevenson's death, 'is that the story is more than an allegory. It is a setting forth in the form of an imaginary tale a foreshadowing of the most startling scientific discovery which will probably be fully established early in the twentieth century, viz., that the disintegration of personality is not merely possible but is of constant occurrence.'[20]

This material from psychology does not determine the final reading of the book, however. It situates the book at the juncture of various competing conceptions of subjectivity, but there is no single version to which it conforms. It is an artistic artefact, riven with ambiguity, not the psychological tract some of its readers wanted. Indeed, another context central to Stevenson's conception of the double remains untouched by this material: Scotland. Although set in London, it was the Edinburgh of his childhood and callow youth that Stevenson described as 'pre-eminently Gothic' and fatally divided: 'Half a capital and half a country town, the whole city leads a double existence; it has long trances of the one and flashes of the other . . . it is half alive and half a monumental marble.'[21] Probably the single most important literary precursor for *Jekyll and Hyde* was James Hogg's *Confessions of a Justified Sinner*, published in Edinburgh in 1824. Hogg's novel initially focuses on the persecution and murder of a man by his outcast brother. Yet the murderer's confession itself reveals another double and another devilish persecution. Robert Wringham is accused of an escalating series of heinous crimes that he ascribes to Gil-Martin, an intimate friend

[20] W. T. Stead, 'Robert Louis Stevenson: The Man of Dreams', *Borderland*, 2 (Jan. 1895), 17.
[21] Stevenson, 'Edinburgh: Picturesque Notes' (1879), in *The Lantern-Bearer and Other Essays* (London, 1988), 89.

who begins to take over his life, his physical likeness, and eventually his mind. In terms echoed by Jekyll's confession, Wringham agonizes that 'I was a being incomprehensible to myself. Either I had a second self . . . or else my body was at times possessed by a spirit over which it had no control.'[22] The significant element of Hogg's novel is that it sees the double as the product of the peculiarly Scottish twist given to the beliefs of the Protestant Calvinist sect. Calvinism, in the version carried to Scotland in the sixteenth century by John Knox, held that God's covenant of grace was extended only to those who were chosen, and that salvation was predestined for this Elect. Election to the covenant was confirmed by elders and clergy of the church, who conducted searching examinations of professed believers. It was a legalistic procedure, but also one that prompted 'an intense preoccupation with the subjective'.[23] In Hogg's novel, because Wringham is cast out as an illegitimate son of a pastor, he agonizes for years over his spiritual status. The moment he is assigned grace his double appears, arguing that any act is permissible, however monstrous, now that he is a 'justified' man.

Stevenson wrote extensively about the fearsome Calvinist instruction he was given as a child, mainly from his nanny and nurse, Alison Cunningham, but also from his parents. He suffered repeated nightmares of hellfire and damnation and warred with his father, who reacted in exorbitant ways to his son's loss of faith. This upbringing no doubt led to Stevenson's delicious embrace of the double life as an Edinburgh student, the respectful son by day, the bohemian womanizer in slum brothels by night. Stevenson was also fascinated from childhood with the eighteenth-century Edinburgh figure Deacon Brodie, who had led a double life, a civic man of virtue who secretly ran a criminal gang that terrorized Edinburgh. With Henley, Stevenson laboured for years over various versions of their play, *Deacon Brodie, or the Double Life*. The only virtue in reading the laboured script now is to realize that the narrative structure of *Jekyll and Hyde* marks a huge advance. The Gothic form further allowed Stevenson to connect to a long tradition of the Scottish Gothic that overlaid religious anxiety with the psychic splitting that was the metaphorical transcription of colonial occupation, since Scotland

[22] James Hogg, *Confessions of a Justified Sinner*, ed. John Carey (Oxford, 1969), 183.
[23] M. Charles Bell, *Calvin and Scottish Theology: The Doctrine of Assurance* (Edinburgh, 1985), 183.

was 'a place where a foreign body was violently installed in the very heart of the country'.[24]

The strictures of the Shorter Catechism, Stevenson later said, provoked inevitable counter-reaction: 'you generally take to drink; your youth, as far as I can find out, is a time of louder war against society . . . than if you had been born, for instance, in England.'[25] This religious view nevertheless left a strong mark on his incomplete essay, 'Lay Morals', written in 1878 and which anticipated some of Jekyll's formulations: 'It follows that man is twofold at least; that he is not a rounded and autonomous empire; but that in the same body with him there dwell other powers, tributary but independent.' He would suggest, however, that puritanical restriction, the injunction to 'starve my appetites', would lead to dangerous disaggregation. 'We shall not live alternately with our opposing tendencies in continual see-saw of passion and disgust,' he said: 'The soul demands unity of purpose, not the dismemberment of man.'[26] The lesson Jekyll takes from his own early double life appears to be the diametric opposite of this, as he seeks to amplify rather than resolve duality. Nevertheless, Stevenson responded to one complaint that the ethics of *Jekyll and Hyde* were enigmatic by apologizing for 'the old Scotch Presbyterian preoccupation about these problems; itself morbid.' Sounding distinctly modern, he confessed, 'Ethics are my veiled mistress; I love them, but know not what they are.'[27] Despite this, Stevenson's contemporaries, certainly from the pulpits, quickly adopted *Jekyll and Hyde* as an allegory of sin and temptation. This was because, as one attempt to reappropriate Stevenson for religious orthodoxy suggested, the book 'was a modern echo of St. Paul's words to the Romans, in which the apostle describes himself as leading the double life of unwilling sin and unfulfilled desire for holiness'.[28] Although the reading of the book as a religious allegory is often dismissed as simplistic, the peculiarly Scottish twist on

[24] David Punter, 'Scottish and Irish Gothic', in Jerrold E. Hogle (ed.), *The Cambridge Companion to Gothic Fiction* (Cambridge, 2002), 110.

[25] Stevenson, *The Silverado Squatters*, cited David Daiches, 'Stevenson and Scotland', in Jenni Calder (ed.), *Stevenson and Victorian Scotland* (Edinburgh, 1981), 21.

[26] Stevenson, 'Lay Morals' (1878), *Lay Morals and Other Ethical Papers*, vol. xxii, Skerryvore Edition of *Complete Works* (London, 1925), 180, 184, 185.

[27] Stevenson, letter to Edward Purcell (27 Feb. 1887), *The Letters of Robert Louis Stevenson*, ed. Bradford A. Booth and Ernest Mehew, vol. v (New Haven, 1994–8), 212–13.

[28] James Kelman, *The Faith of Robert Louis Stevenson* (Edinburgh, 1903), 220–1.

puritanism undoubtedly played an important role in generating the dynamic of Dr Jekyll and Mr Hyde.

For all these psychological and religious readings of the double, however, it must be recalled that one of Stevenson's narrative innovations is to delay the knowledge that Jekyll and Hyde are the same person until the penultimate chapter, Lanyon's broken and horrified report. Nearly every adaptation since T. R. Sullivan's stage play opened in Boston in 1887 (moving on to New York and London) has abandoned this innovation and betrayed the secret in an early transformation scene, fixing the cultural cliché of Jekyll downing a potion and contorting into the monstrous Hyde. This has erased much of the ambiguity and frisson of reading the book for the first time. For its first readers, uncluttered by expectation, the structure of delay would have prompted a host of speculations over the exact nature of the relationship between the respectable doctor and the low-life who has the run of his house and has been named his heir. In important ways, then, the unease of the book comes not just from the supernaturalism of the double but from the ambiguity of this mysterious relationship. To understand all the resonances of *Jekyll and Hyde*, readers need to see it as more than just an instance of the Gothic tradition of doubling: it also helps to know something about London in the 1880s.

Wider Contexts: Crime, Sex, Class, and Urbanism in the 1880s

In the opening chapter of *Jekyll and Hyde* Enfield recounts the uneasy story of Hyde's nocturnal journey, the stamping on a child, his near lynching by a crowd, and his escape by paying off the parents with a handsome cheque drawn in the name of Henry Jekyll. Why does Utterson receive this story with such alarm? It is not Hyde's acts that trouble him, but the unnatural relation further revealed between the eminent doctor and the obnoxious back-door visitor. Enfield's story in fact triggers a whole set of overlapping anxieties that were occupying London opinion in the mid-1880s.

Enfield confidently judges the meaning of the events he has related to his gloomy kinsman: 'Black mail, I suppose; an honest man paying through the nose for some of the capers of his youth. Black Mail House is what I call that place with the door, in consequence.' The extent of the blackmailing of middle- and upper-class men by working-class gangs had been revealed in 1885 by Michael Davitt, an Irish revolutionary who had been imprisoned by the British state and become a prison reformer. Davitt's *Leaves from a Prison Diary* opened with a categorization of the criminal classes, and described blackmailers as 'the most infamous of criminals'. The basic trick was 'the bounce', by which gullible men were entrapped in compromising positions, usually lured by women and accused by men playing the affronted husband. 'The number of aged and highly respectable men in wealthy and professional circles who are under this punishment, in London alone, would astonish society if it could be ascertained,' Davitt reported.[29] Hyde may be one of this despised category of men, but he is also blackmailed himself by Enfield to cover up his violence towards the girl. Perhaps then he is more of a perpetrator than a mere blackmailer. Readers have long been puzzled by this incident: the poet Gerard Manley Hopkins wrote to Robert Bridges: 'The trampling scene is perhaps a convention: he was thinking of something unsuitable for fiction.'[30] Hopkins is as oblique as the text at this point: what might it hide? For audiences in early 1886, at least two possibilities were likely to have been in mind.

In July 1885 the *Pall Mall Gazette*, under the campaigning editorship of W. T. Stead, published a sensational exposé of child prostitution in London, ending with the editor arranging for the purchase of three young virgin girls in a London brothel. 'The Maiden Tribute of Modern Babylon' achieved its immediate aims: Stead wanted to raise the age of consent (for girls) from 13 to 16, reviving a proposal that had recently been dropped from government legislation. Stead showed the power of the press, and the Establishment responded by prosecuting the editor for the illegal procuring of a child and he was given a prison sentence. The exposé and the subsequent trial took place in the summer and autumn of 1885, when Stevenson was composing *Jekyll and Hyde*. 'The Maiden Tribute' fully anticipated the novel in the way it invoked a Gothic, hellish London (indeed, Judith Walkowitz has examined how Stead's reportage incorporates aspects of melodrama and Gothic). 'The maw of the London

---

[29] Michael Davitt, *Leaves from a Prison Diary* (London, 1885), 131. Davitt was later to be savagely parodied by Joseph Conrad in his portrait of anarchist-revolutionaries in London, *The Secret Agent* (1907).

[30] Gerard Manley Hopkins, letter (28 Oct. 1886), *Selected Letters*, ed. Catherine Phillips (Oxford, 1990), 243.

minotaur is insatiable,' Stead thundered, 'and none that go into the secret recesses of his lair return again.'[31] The report focused its disgust not just on those who procured girls, but the medical doctors who were paid to examine girls to ensure their virginity. This venom against doctors had also been the target of an early feminist success: the repeal of the Contagious Diseases Act, which had allowed authorities in certain areas of the city to enforce medical examination of any woman suspected of being a prostitute and therefore a disease risk. Stead and his fellow evangelists (such as his friend Josephine Butler) spoke with outrage at this violation of womanhood, and insisted on the need to contain male desire instead. As he trawled the streets and brothels of London, moving from Oxford Circus to the Mile End Road in the East End, Stead reported rumours of a monstrous libertine who 'may be said to be an absolute incarnation of brutal lust . . . Here in London, moving about clad as respectably in broad cloth and fine linen as any bishop, with no foul shape or semblance of brute beast to mark him off from the rest of his fellows, is Dr ——.'

The trampled girl on a back street described provocatively by Stevenson as containing 'shop fronts . . . with an air of invitations, like rows of smiling saleswomen' might speak to this fevered context of imperilled girls and lusting libertines. Yet the brilliance of the novel is to poise itself ambiguously between multiple possibilities. Hopkins's gnomic comment about hidden codes in the book takes on a different aspect now we know that Hopkins was writing passionately about his love of men and the male body (as a Jesuit priest, this was largely redirected through religious language). 'Black Mail House' might have invoked something very different for Hopkins and other male readers. As Michael Davitt reported, the lowest of the low blackmail tricks was called 'the Common Bounce', where young men are trained 'to follow such men—always, alas! old men— as they believe to be "game," and endeavour to entice them to some out-of-the-way place, where the scoundrel who is watching pounces on the victim, and, under threat of giving him into custody upon the most abominable of all charges, obtains a sum of money.'[32] Angus

---

[31] 'The Maiden Tribute of Modern Babylon' appeared in the *Pall Mall Gazette* from 4 July 1885 onwards. Citations come from the twopenny complete text issued separately on 10 July.

[32] Davitt, *Leaves from a Prison Diary*, 132.

McLaren's study, *Sexual Blackmail*, suggests that blackmail was inextricably associated from the late eighteenth century onwards with that 'most abominable' crime—the charge of sodomy. An additional consequence of Stead's campaign to revise the age of consent for girls was that the bill, the Criminal Law Amendment Act, also had a late clause added to it by the radical MP Henry Labouchère. This outlawed 'acts of gross indecency' between men, and was the law invoked to prosecute Oscar Wilde in 1895. One might abruptly ask: is Hyde, then, Jekyll's bit of rough? Is this why Enfield and Utterson agree never to speak of the incident, and why this elderly band of bachelor men are so concerned for Jekyll's reputation? Is this why Utterson sweats over his own unnamed desires, feverishly imagining Hyde stealing to Jekyll's bedroom at night?

There has been a substantial body of 'Queer Theory' criticism that has consistently identified *Jekyll and Hyde* as an exemplary text that demonstrates how the Gothic theme of the double works through what Eve Kosofsky Sedgwick calls 'homosexual panic', where the desire of men for men is a possible meaning at once invited but also brutally suppressed by a text.[33] The structure of delayed revelation now takes on a different motivation: the half-uttered fears of Jekyll's friends over his relationship with Hyde allow the possibility of sexual dissidence to emerge, and the belated supernatural explanation silences those illicit speculations. It also gives a completely different interpretation to Stevenson's reputation amongst his fellow male writers, that 'power of making other men fall in love with him,' as Andrew Lang put it. In sequences that read impossibly camply now, Henry James's praise for Stevenson was that 'His books are for the most part without women, and it is not women who most fall in love with them. But Mr Stevenson does not need, as we may say, a petticoat to inflame him.'[34] Whilst James's sexuality has remained opaque (although his life was full of homoerotic friendships), Stevenson also had a friend in John Addington Symonds who was an ardent campaigner for the legal recognition of homosexuality. His response to *Jekyll and Hyde* was frank and horrified, and worth quoting at length:

[33] See Eve Kosofsky Sedgwick, *Between Men: English Literature and Male Homosexual Desire* (New York, 1985).

[34] James, 'Robert Louis Stevenson', in *Henry James and Robert Louis Stevenson*, 127.

It is indeed a dreadful book, most dreadful because of a certain moral callousness, a want of sympathy, a shutting out of hope . . . The fact is, that, viewed as an allegory, it touches one too closely. Most of us at some epoch in our lives have been upon the verge of developing a Mr Hyde. Physical and biological Science on a hundred lines is reducing individual freedom to zero, and weakening the sense of responsibility. I doubt whether the artist should lend his genius to this grim argument. Your Dr Jekyll seems to me capable of loosening the last threads of self-control in one who should read it while wavering between his better and coarse self.[35]

Symonds's point is a general one, that Stevenson risks a biological determinism that extinguishes any chance of moral decision or voluntary exercise of will. This view emerges, though, from Symonds's attempts to resist the belief of doctors and sexologists that homosexuality was a monstrous, degenerate state of being. For Symonds, Stevenson's Gothic story had risked putting art at the service of scientific determinism. There was perhaps an echo of this, too, in the jokey comments of that more notorious homosexual of the late Victorian era, Oscar Wilde. Wilde complained in 'The Decay of Lying' about a general rise of a modern vice, 'a morbid and unhealthy faculty of truth-telling'. His example? 'Even Mr Robert Louis Stevenson, that delightful master of delicate and fanciful prose, is tainted with this modern vice. . . . The transformation of Dr Jekyll reads dangerously like an experiment out of the *Lancet*.'[36] The language of pathology hovers near this brittle inversion of fantasy and morbid psychology.

Symonds offered a private response: the most significant thing about the posthumous history of *Jekyll and Hyde* in its myriad adaptations is that nearly every one, from 1887 onwards, invents central women characters absent from the original. Jekyll is commonly engaged to be married, in that transitional state of manhood—often to Agnes Carew, daughter of the MP killed in Hyde's murderous rage. In one way this merely places the tale more easily within melodramatic structures of stage and film, but it can also be regarded as an attempt to heterosexualize the novel—to do the work of filling out

[35] Letter, John Addington Symonds to Stevenson (3 Mar. 1886), *The Letters of John Addington Symonds*, ed. Herbert M. Schueller, 3 vols. (Detroit, 1969), iii. 120–1.

[36] Oscar Wilde, 'The Decay of Lying', *The Complete Works of Oscar Wilde* (London, 1986), 973.

the unnerving gaps and silences of the book with an acceptable, even rather mundane, array of sins.

Whilst some shadings beyond the homosocial and into the homo-sexual are possibly discernible in *Jekyll and Hyde*, more recent research in late nineteenth-century history of sexuality has rather cast doubt on the more confident assertions of the queer readings of the book proposed by Wayne Koestenbaum, Elaine Showalter, and others. H. G. Cocks has shown that the Labouchère Amendment produced little comment or change in behaviour and did not sub-stantially change the law or produce any notable increase in prosecu-tions after 1885. There was no sudden upsurge of 'homosexual panic'. Homosexuality was not the great 'unnamed' crime, but was 'named openly, publicly and repeatedly' throughout the nineteenth century in the criminal courts.[37] Perhaps the risk is that these read-ings impose a modern obsession with sexuality as the hidden truth of every self and every text. Victorians thought somewhat differently; and not all secrets, after all, are sexual. In 1887, Stevenson's sense of sheer disappointment that Hyde has already come to be regarded as 'a mere voluptuary' is palpable: 'There is no harm in a voluptuary,' he wrote, 'no harm whatever—in what prurient fools call "immoral-ity." ' Hyde, he claimed, was 'no more sexual than another,' and dismissed as impoverished 'this poor wish to have a woman, that they make such a cry about'.[38] Although Stevenson can never be fully in control of the meanings of his work (not least because of those toiling Brownies in his subliminal consciousness), such comments do invite us to go back to the drawing-board, and think again, one last time, about any other possible meanings of his protean double.

One of the most influential aspects of *Jekyll and Hyde* is the fevered way in which it imagines London. It is a hallucinatory place, never clearly navigable, the streets even in daylight 'like a district of some city in a nightmare'. The singular location of Jekyll's house is also weird: an imposing town house in a West End square that seems to have a back door that leads directly into a disreputable, lower-class area of the kind usually associated with slums of the East End. This physical split reinforces the division of personality: London becomes

[37] H. G. Cocks, *Nameless Offences: Homosexual Desire in the Nineteenth Century* (New York, 2003), 4. This is supported by the findings of Matt Cook, *London and the Culture of Homosexuality 1885–1914* (Cambridge, 2003).

[38] Letter, Stevenson to John Paul Bocock (mid-Nov. 1887), *Letters*, vi. 56.

a psychic topography. This was to have a major influence on the late Victorian Gothic: Oscar Wilde's Dorian Gray, Arthur Machen's Helen Vaughan, and Bram Stoker's Count Dracula all bring the primitive, marginal, and monstrous into the civilized imperial metropolis. But what the evident class difference between Jekyll and Hyde also picks up on is the urban crisis that beset London in the mid-1880s. Stead's exposé of London prostitution followed in the wake of two important studies of extreme poverty in London published in 1883, Andrew Mearns's *The Bitter Cry of Outcast London* and George Sims's *How the Poor Live*. Without some kind of social amelioration of poverty, these and other writers predicted major social unrest, particularly as newly enfranchised working-class men were imbibing the new radical politics of anarchism, socialism, and Marxism. Less than a month after *Jekyll and Hyde* was published, a political meeting about unemployment in Trafalgar Square erupted into violence, the rioters attacking the gentleman's clubs of Pall Mall and St James's. In early February 1886, the West End, shrouded in fog for days, was gripped with panicky rumours that gangs of roughs were marching on the centre from the slums of Bethnal Green in the East and Southwark in the South. This panic petered out, but in November 1887 Trafalgar Square was again the site of a major riot, in which the police killed a demonstrator in their violent suppression of a meeting of the tiny Social Democratic Federation. 'Bloody Sunday', as it became known, became the focus of renewed political and trade union agitation.[39]

Jekyll and Hyde became linked to this anxiety about violent class war through another famous London event at this time. Richard Mansfield's celebrated performances as both Jekyll and Hyde in the stage play of the book finally transferred from America to London, opening in late July 1888 at the Lyceum Theatre. Days later, the first murder of a prostitute in Whitechapel began an autumn in which the five killings by 'Jack the Ripper' gripped the London population. Very soon, journalists made the link: 'There certainly seems to be a tolerably realistic impersonification of Mr Hyde at large in Whitechapel,' the *Pall Mall Gazette* commented, adding: 'The Savage of Civilisation whom we are raising by the hundred thousand

---

[39] The classic account of these events remains Gareth Stedman Jones, *Outcast London: A Study in the Relationship between Classes in Victorian Society* (Harmondsworth, 1984), 281–314.

in our slums is quite as capable of bathing his hands in blood as any Sioux who ever scalped a foe.'[40] The associations with the stage version of *Jekyll and Hyde* were so strong that Mansfield decided to withdraw the production in the midst of the murders in October 1888, with some suggesting that Mansfield himself had become a suspect in the crimes, so convincing was his stage transformation into the murderous Hyde. This is a bizarre conjunction, not least because Stevenson's work always showed an obsession with the popular tradition of gruesome penny paper reports on famous murderers and their hangings. Stevenson borrowed all the details for 'The Body Snatcher' from Edinburgh's popular memory of the crimes of Burke and Hare in the 1820s, men who murdered fifteen times to supply the private anatomy schools that had grown up around the university. The unsolved 'Ripper' crimes have produced endless speculation about possible murderers, but the two favoured at the time showed how the crime was situated in London's class tensions. As the *Pall Mall Gazette* comment suggests, one was to see the crime as the product of the feral slums, the ritualistic elements of the crime pointing to the large Jewish immigrant population of Whitechapel (Jews were widely believed to sacrifice Christian babies, after all). The other version relied on the conventions of melodrama: the crimes were perpetrated by some crazed surgeon or aristocrat intent on punishing working-class prostitutes. Doctors became distrusted figures in the East End at this time.[41]

Jekyll and Hyde was an instantly available metaphor for these crimes because the book took some of its energy from London's violent class wars. The language in which Hyde is portrayed in the book—'apelike' and 'troglodytic'—owes something to the description of the degenerate urban poor, 'a stunted, puny race' in the words of one contemporary.[42] Indeed, a whole critical industry around the late Victorian Gothic has promised that the discourse of urban degeneration is the determining framework through which to

---

[40] *Pall Mall Gazette* (8 Sept. 1888), cited in L. Perry Curtis Jr., *Jack the Ripper and the London Press* (New Haven, 2001), 126.

[41] See Andrew Smith, *Victorian Demons: Medicine, Masculinity and the Gothic at the Fin de Siècle* (Manchester, 2004).

[42] James Cantlie, *Degeneration amongst Londoners* (London, 1885), 39.

read the text, and this is worth pursuing.[43] Stevenson was certainly
familiar with the discourse of racial degeneration, as evidenced by
the didactic conclusion of 'Olalla', a story which he composed in the
same winter as *Jekyll and Hyde*. However, this again risks ignoring
the protean way in which the text escapes reductive decoding. It is
improbable that Hyde can be solely reduced to the demonic figure of
middle-class panic, because the bohemian Stevenson despised this
class of professionals. He portrays them in Utterson and his joyless
friends as 'dry, dull and dead-alive', as he put it of office-bound
professionals in his essay 'The Education of an Engineer'.[44] It is
Jekyll he identifies as the monstrous hypocrite, not Hyde. Some of
his first readers in fact strongly admired Hyde. Frederic Myers's
detailed commentary on the character of Hyde defends him against
'jaded voluptuaries' like Jekyll: 'Mr Hyde's whole career forbids us
to insult him by classing him with these men,' he rather surprisingly
commented.[45] Andrew Lang probably agreed, given his view of the
primal energies of the romance: 'Not for nothing did Nature leave us
all savages under our white skins.'[46] Hyde in this instance might act
as the emblem of the lowly vitality of popular literature against the
frigid civilities of the novel.

Edwin Eigner complained as early as 1966 that *Jekyll and Hyde* had
been 'allegorised almost out of existence' by the huge quantity of
commentary it had generated.[47] This has multiplied many times over
since literary scholars afforded value to the Gothic genre and revived
their interest in Stevenson's career. This introduction may have felt
overwhelming, given the multiplicity of readings it has thrown out.
But this also carries its own lesson. The Gothic is not rational but is

[43] The best of these are Daniel Pick, *Faces of Degeneration: A European Disorder c.1848–c.1918* (Cambridge, 1989) and Robert Mighall, *A Geography of Victorian Gothic Fiction: Mapping History's Nightmares* (Oxford, 1999), as well Mighall's Penguin edition of *Jekyll and Hyde* (Harmondsworth, 2002).

[44] Stevenson, 'The Education of an Engineer' (1888), in R. L. Stevenson, *The Lantern-Bearers and Other Essays*, ed. Jeremy Treglown (London, 1988), 257–8, at p. 256.

[45] Frederic Myers, 'Further Meditations on the Character of the Late Mr Hyde', in Maixner, *Critical Heritage*, 220.

[46] Andrew Lang, 'Realism and Romance' (1888), in Sally Ledger and Roger Luckhurst (eds.), *The Fin de Siècle: A Reader in Cultural History c.1880–1900* (Oxford, 2000), 102.

[47] Edwin M. Eigner, *Robert Louis Stevenson and the Romantic Tradition* (Princeton, 1966), 148.

frenzied, disordered, and dreamlike. Dreams, Freud suggested, worked principally by condensation (compressing many elements into one) and displacement (repressed thoughts taking on disguised forms). A dream was like a rebus or picture-puzzle, and, because of this, Freud warned 'it is never in fact possible to be sure that a dream has been completely interpreted'.[48] The most enduring Gothic texts have a similar dynamic of condensation and displacement. The lure is always to seek the final, authoritative interpretation of such texts. The better reader is the one who enters the dream-logic of the Gothic knowing its capacities to twist and turn and to elicit then collapse or invert meanings. A text like *Jekyll and Hyde* is over-determined by multiple and often contradictory elements: its final meaning will always be running ahead of us, ducking round the corner like Mr Hyde, forever just out of reach.

[48] Sigmund Freud, *The Interpretation of Dreams* (1900), Penguin Freud Library 4 (Harmondsworth: 1976), 381.

NOTE ON THE TEXTS

Strange Case of Dr Jekyll and Mr Hyde was published on 9 January 1886, just too late for the Christmas market, when supernatural stories were traditionally released. It was issued in two formats by Longmans, one with paper wrappers for a shilling and one bound in cloth for 1s. 6d. This text is taken from the cloth first edition (London: Longmans, 1886).

'The Body Snatcher' first appeared in the *Pall Mall Gazette 'Extra'* Christmas special for 1884. Unusually, Stevenson did not collect this in any book of short stories, and it was not reprinted during his lifetime. This version is taken from the Tusitala collected edition of Stevenson's works, volume xi (London: William Heinemann, 1923–7).

'Markheim' first appeared in *Unwin's Christmas Annual*, 1885. It was then collected in *The Merry Men and Other Tales and Fables* (London: Chatto & Windus, 1887).

'Olalla' first appeared in the Christmas edition of *Court and Society Review*, 1885 and was included in *The Merry Men and Other Tales* (London: Chatto & Windus, 1887).

'A Gossip on Romance' was first printed in *Longman's Magazine*, 1 (November 1882), 69–79.

'A Chapter on Dreams' was published in *Scribner's Magazine*, 3 (January 1888), and reprinted in *Across the Plains* (1892).

SELECT BIBLIOGRAPHY

Bibliography, Biography, and Letters

Calder, Jenni, *RLS: A Life Study* (Edinburgh, 1980).

Hammerton, J. A., *Stevensoniana: An Anecdotal Life and Appreciation of Robert Louis Stevenson* (Edinburgh, 1907).

Harman, Claire, *Robert Louis Stevenson: A Biography* (London, 2005).

The Letters of Robert Louis Stevenson, ed. Bradford A. Booth and Ernest Mehew, 8 vols. (New Haven, 1994–8).

McLynn, Frank, *Robert Louis Stevenson* (London, 1994).

Swearingen, Roger G., *The Prose Writings of Robert Louis Stevenson: A Guide* (London, 1980).

Stevenson Criticism

Arata, Stephen D., 'The Sedulous Ape: Atavism, Professionalism and Stevenson's *Jekyll and Hyde*', Criticism, 37: 2 (1995), 233–59.

Beattie, Hilary J., 'Father and Son: The Origins of *Strange Case of Dr Jekyll and Mr Hyde*', *The Psychoanalytic Study of the Child*, 56 (2001), 317–60.

Block, E. Jr. (ed.), 'James Sully, Evolutionist Psychology and Late Victorian Gothic Fiction', *Victorian Studies*, 25: 4 (1986), 363–86.

Calder, Jenni (ed.), *Stevenson and Victorian Scotland* (Edinburgh, 1981).

Currie, Mark, 'True Lies: Unreliable Identities in *Dr Jekyll and Mr Hyde*', *Postmodern Narrative Theory* (Basingstoke, 1998), 117–34.

Egan, Joseph J., ' "Markheim": A Drama of Moral Psychology', *Nineteenth-Century Fiction*, 20: 4 (1966), 377–84.

Eigner, Edwin M., *Robert Louis Stevenson and the Romantic Tradition* (Princeton, 1966).

Gossman, Ann, 'On the Knocking at the Gate in "Markheim" ', *Nineteenth-Century Fiction*, 17: 1 (1962), 73–6.

Heath, Stephen, 'Psychopathia Sexualis: Stevenson's *Strange Case*', *Critical Quarterly*, 28 (1986), 93–108.

Knowlton, Edgar C., 'A Russian Influence on Stevenson', *Modern Philology*, 14 (1916), 449–54.

Koestenbaum, Wayne, *Double Talk: The Erotics of Male Literary Collaboration* (London, 1989).

Maixner, Paul, *Robert Louis Stevenson: The Critical Heritage* (London, 1981).

Nash, Andrew, ' "The Dead Should Be Protected from their own Carelessness": The Collected Editions of Robert Louis Stevenson', in Nash (ed.), *The Culture of Collected Editions* (Basingstoke, 2003), 111–27.

Pinkston, C. Alex, Jr., 'The Stage Premiere of *Dr Jekyll and Mr Hyde*', Nineteenth Century Theatre Research, 14 (1986), 21–43.

Rose, Brian A., *Jekyll and Hyde Adapted: Dramatizations of a Cultural Anxiety* (Westport, Conn., 1996).

Rosner, Mary, ' "A Total Subversion of Character": Dr Jekyll's Moral Insanity', *Victorian Newsletter*, 93 (Spring 1998), 27–31.

Sandison, Alan, *Robert Louis Stevenson and the Appearance of Modernism: A Future Feeling* (Basingstoke, 1996).

Swinnerton, Frank, *Robert Louis Stevenson: A Critical Study* (London, 1914).

Veeder, William, and Hirsch, Gordon (eds.), *Dr Jekyll and Mr Hyde after One Hundred Years* (Chicago, 1988).

The Double

Binet, Alfred, *On Double Consciousness* (1890), reissued in Significant Contributions to the History of Psychology 1750–1920 series (Washington, 1972).

Coates, Paul, *The Double and the Other: Identity as Ideology in Post-Romantic Fiction* (London, 1988).

Freud, Sigmund, 'The Uncanny' (1919), *Penguin Freud Library*, vol. xiv (Harmondsworth, 1985), 335–76.

Hacking, Ian, *Rewriting the Soul: Multiple Personality and the Sciences of Memory* (Princeton, 1995).

Miller, Karl, *Doubles: Studies in Literary History* (Oxford, 1985).

Prince, Morton, *The Dissociation of a Personality* (1905; Oxford, 1978).

Rank, Otto, *The Double: A Psychoanalytic Study* (1914), trans. Harry Tucker Jr. (London, 1989).

Tymms, Ralph, *Doubles in Literary Psychology* (Cambridge, 1949).

The Gothic

Botting, Fred, *Gothic* (London, 1996).

Brantlinger, Patrick, 'Imperial Gothic: Atavism and the Occult in the British Adventure Novel 1880–1914', in *Rule of Darkness: British Literature and Imperialism 1830–1914* (New York, 1988).

Dryden, Linda, *The Modern Gothic and Literary Doubles: Stevenson, Wilde and Wells* (Basingstoke, 2003).

Duncan, Ian, 'Walter Scott, James Hogg and Scottish Gothic', in David Punter (ed.), *A Companion to the Gothic* (Oxford, 2000), 70–80.

Halberstam, Judith, *Skin Shows: Gothic Horror and the Technology of Monsters* (Durham, 1995).

Hurley, Kelly, *The Gothic Body: Sexuality, Materialism, and Degeneration at the Fin de Siècle* (Cambridge, 1996).

Malchow, H. L., *Gothic Images of Race in Nineteenth-Century Britain* (Berkeley, 1996).

Mighall, Robert, *A Geography of Victorian Gothic Fiction: Mapping History's Nightmares* (Oxford, 1999).

Miles, Robert, *Gothic Writing: A Genealogy 1750–1820* (London, 1993).

Punter, David, 'Scottish and Irish Gothic', in Jerold E. Hogle, *The Cambridge Companion to Gothic Fiction* (Cambridge, 2002).

—— (ed.), *A Companion to the Gothic* (Oxford, 2000).

Robbins, Ruth, and Wolfreys, Julian (eds.), *Victorian Gothic: Literary and Cultural Manifestations in the Nineteenth Century* (Basingstoke, 2000).

Smith, Andrew, *Victorian Demons: Medicine, Masculinity and the Gothic at the Fin de Siècle* (Manchester, 2004).

Historical, Literary, and Scientific Contexts

Beckson, Karl, *London in the 1890s* (New York, 1992).

Bourne-Taylor, Jenny, and Shuttleworth, Sally (eds.), *Embodied Selves: An Anthology of Psychological Texts 1830–1890* (Oxford, 1998).

Cocks, H. G., *Nameless Offences: Homosexual Desire in the Nineteenth Century* (New York, 2003).

Curtis, L. Perry, *Jack the Ripper and the London Press* (New Haven, 2001).

Jones, Gareth Stedman, *Outcast London: A Study in the Relationship between the Classes in Victorian Society* (Harmondsworth, 1984).

Keating, Peter, *The Haunted Study: A Social History of the English Novel 1875–1914* (London, 1991).

Ledger, Sally, and Luckhurst, Roger (eds.), *The Fin de Siècle: A Reader in Cultural History c.1880–1900* (Oxford, 2000).

Luckhurst, Roger, *The Invention of Telepathy* (Oxford, 2002).

Petrow, Stefan, *Policing Morals: The Metropolitan Police and the Home Office 1870–1914* (Oxford, 1994).

Pick, Daniel, *Faces of Degeneration: A European Disorder c.1848–c.1918* (Cambridge, 1989).

Showalter, Elaine, *Sexual Anarchy: Gender and Culture at the Fin de Siècle* (London, 1991).

Stokes, John (ed.), *Fin de Siècle/Fin du Globe: Fears and Fantasies of the Late Nineteenth Century* (Basingstoke, 1992).

Turner, Frank M., *Between Science and Religion: The Reaction to Scientific Naturalism in Late Victorian England* (New Haven, 1974).

Walkowitz, Judith, *City of Dreadful Delight: Narratives of Sexual Danger in Late-Victorian London* (London, 1992).

Further Reading in Oxford World's Classics

Brown, Charles Brockden, *Wieland/Carwin, the Biloquist*, ed. Emory Elliott.

Corelli, Marie, *The Sorrows of Satan*, ed. Peter Keating.

Doyle, Arthur Conan, *The Hound of the Baskervilles*, ed. W. W. Robson.

Hogg, James, *The Private Memoirs and Confessions of a Justified Sinner*, ed. John Carey.

James, M. R., *Casting the Runes and Other Ghost Stories*, ed. Michael Cox.

Late Victorian Gothic Tales, ed. Roger Luckhurst.

Le Fanu, J. Sheridan, *In a Glass Darkly*, ed. Robert Tracy.

Poe, Edgar Allan, *Selected Tales*, ed. David Van Leer.

Tales of Terror from Blackwood's Magazine, ed. Chris Baldick and Robert Morrison.

Wilde, Oscar, *The Picture of Dorian Gray*, ed. Isobel Murray.

A CHRONOLOGY OF
ROBERT LOUIS STEVENSON

1850   Born Robert Lewis Balfour Stevenson, November 1850, only
        son of Thomas Stevenson and Margaret Isabella Balfour. The
        Stevensons have been a family of Scottish engineers and light-
        house builders since the 1790s; the son is expected to follow the
        family trade. Early childhood dominated by the strict Calvinist
        religious views of RLS's nurse, Alison Cummingham. Sickly
        child.

1866   First publication is *The Pentland Rising*, in a private printing of
        100 copies, strictly controlled by his anxious father.

1867   Enrols at Edinburgh University to study engineering. About
        this time changes his name from 'Lewis' to 'Louis', and begins
        to explore a bohemian student lifestyle, referring obliquely to
        his 'precocious depravity' in later reminiscences. Meets
        Charles Baxter, who becomes lifelong friend and eventually
        acts as RLS's lawyer and agent.

1871   Abandons engineering, and after being refused support by
        father for a literary life, studies law.

1873   Confesses to parents he has lost his religious faith, causing
        major distress. Illness sends him south to Suffolk. Meets
        Frances Sitwell, with whom he forms an intense (platonic)
        attachment. Meets Sidney Colvin, writer and art critic who
        helps shape RLS's literary career. In south of France for
        health, RLS's essay 'Ordered South' establishes his persona as
        an invalid literary sensitive. Meets Andrew Lang, important
        critic, reviewer, fellow Scot, and later to laud RLS as the
        reviver of the romance form against the enervation of the
        novel.

1874   Enters literary London society, joining the Savile Club.

1875   Meets W. E. Henley, poet and fellow invalid, in Edinburgh
        (introduced by the influential critic and editor, Leslie
        Stephen). Finally completes law degree, but never practises.
        Begins publishing essays in *Vanity Fair* and *Academy*.

1876   At artists' colony at Barbizon, meets Fanny Osbourne, a
        bohemian American woman travelling alone with her two
        surviving children, ostensibly studying art in Europe.

1878   RLS has first adult works published: *Edinburgh: Picturesque*

Notes and the travel book, *An Inland Voyage*. Writes stories for *New Arabian Nights*, published in the journal *London*. Leaves 'Lay Morals' incomplete.

1879   *Travels with a Donkey* published. Journeys to San Francisco to meet Fanny Osbourne, travelling by steerage across the Atlantic and then by train across America (a journey later published as *The Amateur Emigrant*).

1880   RLS has first haemorrhage in his lungs. This was treated as tuberculosis, but RLS was never to secure a fixed diagnosis for his lung disease. After Fanny Osbourne secures divorce, RLS marries her in San Francisco in May. Publication of *Deacon Brodie: A Double Life*, written in collaboration with W. E. Henley. The two spend the next few years revising and restaging this play without success.

1881   Writes *Treasure Island*, initially to entertain stepson, Lloyd Osbourne, then as serial in children's magazine. Publication of essays, *Virginibus Puerisque*, which secures his reputation as the finest literary stylist of his generation. Writes the classic horror tale in Scottish dialect, 'Thrawn Janet'. In London, the majority of his friends take a violent dislike to Fanny Osbourne, and this begins RLS's progressive isolation from the literary scene.

1881–2   Advised to winter in Davos, the Swiss health resort. Here meets important literary critic (and later advocate for the legalization of homosexuality) John Addington Symonds, who lives permanently in the resort.

1883   Publishes *The Silverado Squatters*, an account of his honeymoon stay with Fanny Osbourne in a disused silver mine in the Californian hills. *Treasure Island* appears and is RLS's first major success.

1884   2 July, Henley and Stevenson's much-revised *Deacon Brodie* opens at Prince's Theatre in London. Short run, but enough to continue to collaborate on two further plays with Henley. Fanny Osbourne also now collaborating with RLS, contributing two stories for *The Dynamiter*. RLS writes first version of 'Markheim'. Also writes 'A Humble Remonstrance', his important essay on the literary power of the romance form, partly in response to Henry James's essay 'The Art of Fiction'.

1885   Moves to Bournemouth, for health reasons, to a house bought by his father. Begins close friendship with Henry James, whose sister is also an invalid in Bournemouth. RLS also reads first book by H. Rider Haggard, *King Solomon's Mines*. Stevenson publishes *A Child's Garden of Verses* (another popular success), *Prince Otto*, and *More New Arabian Nights*. In July, Stead's exposé of child prostitution in London, 'A Maiden Tribute of Modern Babylon', published. It prompts a revival of the Criminal Law Amendment Act to raise the legal age of consent to sex to 16 in girls, and outlaw 'acts of gross indecency' between men. September–December, RLS writes and rewrites *Strange Case of Dr Jekyll and Mr Hyde* and 'Olalla'.

1886   January, publication of *Dr Jekyll and Mr Hyde*. In six months sells 40,000 copies. It is also phenomenally successful in America, although pirated copies deprive RLS of royalties. Exchange of letters about *Dr Jekyll and Mr Hyde* with psychologist Frederic Myers begins. Writes *Kidnapped*.

1887   Death of Stevenson's father in May. RLS oversees funeral, then sails for America in July, never to return to Britain. A celebrity author on arrival in New York, offered many publishing deals. His early responses to journalists on the writing of *Dr Jekyll and Mr Hyde* prompt him to write 'A Chapter on Dreams'. Publishes *The Merry Men*, a collection of short stories including 'Markheim' and 'Olalla'.

1888   Late July, T. R. Sullivan's stage adaptation of *Jekyll and Hyde* opens at the Lyceum Theatre in London, with Richard Mansfield in the leading role. In August, the first murder in the sequence of 'Jack the Ripper' killings takes place in Whitechapel, East London. After four murders, Mansfield suspends the production of *Jekyll and Hyde* in October, partly for his own safety as his famous stage transformation from Jekyll to Hyde makes him a suspect. The novella and the murders remain inextricably connected in the mythology of late Victorian London. RLS publishes *The Black Arrow*, *The Misadventures of John Nicholson*, and essays for *Scribner's Magazine*. Henry James writes glowing appreciation of RLS in *Century Magazine*, but RLS and Henley become estranged—Henley believes Fanny Osbourne has plagiarized a short story. The dispute is bitter, and will result in Henley's attack on RLS's character in 1901. Scribner's commissions RLS to write travel book on voyage to the South Seas. Sails in June. Long stop in Tahiti, then six months in Hawaii.

1889   Buys estate at Upolu in Samoa—an island at the centre of colonial struggle between Germany, England, and America.

Writes ten letters to *The Times* over the situation in these years (Oscar Wilde is to comment 'romantic surroundings are the worst surroundings possible for a romantic writer. In Gower Street, Stevenson could have written a new *Trois Mousquetaires*. In Samoa he wrote letters to *The Times* about Germans'). Publishes *The Master of Ballantrae* and his first collaboration with his stepson, Lloyd Osbourne, *The Wrong Box*, which receives very poor reviews.

1890   Serious haemorrhage leads RLS and Fanny to decide he must remain in tropical climate for health. Finally publishes his book, *In the South Seas*, and collection of poems, *Ballads*.

1891   Oscar Wilde, *The Picture of Dorian Gray*.

1892   Essays, *Across the Plains*; contribution to Samoan politics, *A Footnote on History*; further fictional collaboration with Lloyd Osbourne, *The Wrecker*.

1893   Stories, *An Island Night's Entertainments* published. Suffers serious writer's block, whilst Fanny Osbourne descends into severe mental disorder.

1894   Publishes novel *The Ebb-Tide* and is working to complete *Weir of Hermiston*. 3 December, dies of cerebral haemorrhage and buried in elaborate tribal ceremony on Samoa. Arthur Machen publishes the Stevenson-influenced Gothic novel, *The Great God Pan*.

1894–6   The private subscription collected 'Edinburgh' edition of RLS's works, edited by Baxter and Colvin, makes £10,000 profit for RLS's estate. Five further collected editions appear between 1894 and 1924 (when the thirty-year copyright on RLS's works ends) and make thousands of pounds.

1895   Arrest and prosecution of Oscar Wilde for 'acts of gross indecency'. Conrad's first novel, *Almayer's Folly*.

1901   December, W. E. Henley's attack on Graham Balfour's biography of Stevenson, attacking 'this Seraph in Chocolate'. Modernist authors begin to define themselves against the style of RLS, and ensure the prolonged eclipse of his literary standing.

STRANGE CASE OF
DR JEKYLL AND MR HYDE

TO

KATHARINE DE MATTOS*

It's ill to loose the bands that God decreed to bind;
Still will we be the children of the heather and the wind.
Far away from home, O it's still for you and me
That the broom is blowing bonnie in the north countrie.*

CONTENTS

MR UTTERSON the lawyer was a man of a rugged countenance, that was never lighted by a smile; cold, scanty and embarrassed in discourse; backward in sentiment; lean, long, dusty, dreary and yet somehow lovable. At friendly meetings, and when the wine was to his taste, something eminently human beaconed from his eye; something indeed which never found its way into his talk, but which spoke not only in these silent symbols of the after-dinner face, but more often and loudly in the acts of his life. He was austere with himself; drank gin when he was alone, to mortify a taste for vintages; and though he enjoyed the theatre, had not crossed the doors of one for twenty years. But he had an approved tolerance for others; sometimes wondering, almost with envy, at the high pressure of spirits involved in their misdeeds; and in any extremity inclined to help rather than to reprove. 'I incline to Cain's heresy,'* he used to say quaintly: 'I let my brother go to the devil in his own way.' In this character, it was frequently his fortune to be the last reputable acquaintance and the last good influence in the lives of down-going men. And to such as these, so long as they came about his chambers, he never marked a shade of change in his demeanour.

No doubt the feat was easy to Mr Utterson; for he was undemonstrative at the best, and even his friendships seemed to be founded in a similar catholicity of good-nature. It is the mark of a modest man to accept his friendly circle ready-made from the hands of opportunity; and that was the lawyer's way. His friends were those of his own blood or those whom he had known the longest; his affections, like ivy, were the growth of time, they implied no aptness in the object. Hence, no doubt, the bond that united him to Mr Richard Enfield, his distant kinsman, the well-known man about town.* It was a nut to crack for many, what these two could see in each other or what subject they could find in common. It was reported by those who encountered them in their Sunday walks, that they said nothing, looked singularly dull, and would hail with obvious relief the appearance of a friend. For all that, the two men put the greatest store by these excursions, counted them the chief jewel of each week, and not only set aside occasions of pleasure, but even resisted the calls of business, that they might enjoy them uninterrupted.

It chanced on one of these rambles that their way led them down a by-street in a busy quarter of London. The street was small and what is called quiet, but it drove a thriving trade on the week-days. The inhabitants were all doing well, it seemed, and all emulously hoping to do better still, and laying out the surplus of their gains in coquetry; so that the shop fronts stood along that thoroughfare with an air of invitation, like rows of smiling saleswomen. Even on Sunday, when it veiled its more florid charms and lay comparatively empty of passage, the street shone out in contrast to its dingy neighbourhood, like a fire in a forest; and with its freshly painted shutters, well-polished brasses, and general cleanliness and gaiety of note, instantly caught and pleased the eye of the passenger.

Two doors from one corner, on the left hand going east, the line was broken by the entry of a court; and just at that point, a certain sinister block of building thrust forward its gable on the street. It was two storeys high; showed no window, nothing but a door on the lower storey and a blind forehead of discoloured wall on the upper; and bore in every feature, the marks of prolonged and sordid negligence. The door, which was equipped with neither bell nor knocker, was blistered and distained. Tramps slouched into the recess and struck matches on the panels; children kept shop upon the steps; the schoolboy had tried his knife on the mouldings; and for close on a generation, no one had appeared to drive away these random visitors or to repair their ravages.

Mr Enfield and the lawyer were on the other side of the by-street; but when they came abreast of the entry, the former lifted up his cane and pointed.

'Did you ever remark that door?' he asked; and when his companion had replied in the affirmative, 'It is connected in my mind,' added he, 'with a very odd story.'

'Indeed?' said Mr Utterson, with a slight change of voice, 'and what was that?'

'Well, it was this way,' returned Mr Enfield: 'I was coming home from some place at the end of the world, about three o'clock of a black winter morning, and my way lay through a part of town where there was literally nothing to be seen but lamps. Street after street, and all the folks asleep—street after street, all lighted up as if for a procession and all as empty as a church—till at last I got into that state of mind when a man listens and listens and begins to long for the sight of a policeman. All at once, I saw two figures: one a little man who was stumping along eastward at a good walk, and the other a girl of maybe eight or ten who was running as hard as she was able down a cross street. Well, sir, the two ran into one another naturally enough at the corner; and then came the horrible part of the thing; for the man trampled calmly over the child's body and left her screaming on the ground. It sounds nothing to hear,* but it was hellish to see. It wasn't like a man; it was like some damned Juggernaut.* I gave a view halloa,* took to my heels, collared my gentleman, and brought him back to where there was already quite a group about the screaming child. He was perfectly cool and made no resistance, but gave me one look, so ugly that it brought out the sweat on me like running. The people who had turned out were the girl's own family; and pretty soon, the doctor, for whom she had been sent, put in his appearance. Well, the child was not much the worse, more frightened, according to the Sawbones;* and there you might have supposed would be an end to it. But there was one curious circumstance. I had taken a loathing to my gentleman at first sight. So had the child's family, which was only natural. But the doctor's case was what struck me. He was the usual cut and dry apothecary, of no particular age and colour, with a strong Edinburgh accent, and about as emotional as a bagpipe. Well, sir, he was like the rest of us; every time he looked at my prisoner, I saw that Sawbones turn sick and white with the desire to kill him. I knew what was in his mind, just as he knew what was in mine; and killing being out of the question, we did the next best. We told the man we could and would make such a scandal out of this, as should make his name stink from one end of London to the other. If he had any friends or any credit, we undertook that he should lose them. And all the time, as we were pitching it in red hot, we were keeping the women off him as best we could, for they were as wild as harpies.* I never saw a circle of such hateful faces; and there was the man in the middle, with a kind of black, sneering coolness—frightened too, I could see that—but carrying it off, sir, really like Satan. "If you choose to make capital out of this accident," said he, "I am naturally helpless. No gentleman but wishes to avoid a scene," says he. "Name your figure." Well, we screwed him up to a hundred pounds for the child's family; he would have clearly liked to stick out; but there was something about the lot of us that meant mischief, and at last he struck. The next thing was to get the money; and where do you think he carried us but to that place with the door?—whipped out a key, went in, and presently came back with the matter of ten pounds in gold and a cheque for the balance on Coutts's,* drawn payable to bearer and signed with a name that I can't mention, though it's one of the points of my story, but it was a name at least very well known and often printed. The figure was stiff; but the signature was good for more than that, if it was only genuine. I took the liberty of pointing out to my gentleman that the whole business looked apocryphal, and that a man does not, in real life, walk into a cellar door at four in the morning and come out of it with another man's cheque for close upon a hundred pounds. But he was quite easy and sneering. "Set your mind at rest," says he, "I will stay with you till the banks open and cash the cheque myself." So we all set off, the doctor, and the child's father, and our friend and myself, and passed the rest of the night in my chambers; and next day, when we had breakfasted, went in a body to the bank. I gave in the cheque myself, and said I had every reason to believe it was a forgery. Not a bit of it. The cheque was genuine.'

'Tut-tut,' said Mr Utterson.

'I see you feel as I do,' said Mr Enfield. 'Yes, it's a bad story. For my man was a fellow that nobody could have to do with, a really damnable man; and the person that drew the cheque is the very pink of the proprieties, celebrated too, and (what makes it worse) one of your fellows who do what they call good. Black mail, I suppose; an honest man paying through the nose for some of the capers of his youth. Black Mail House* is what I call that place with the door, in consequence. Though even that, you know, is far from explaining all,' he added, and with the words fell into a vein of musing.

From this he was recalled by Mr Utterson asking rather suddenly: 'And you don't know if the drawer of the cheque lives there?'

'A likely place isn't it?' returned Mr Enfield. 'But I happen to have noticed his address; he lives in some square or other.'

'And you never asked about—the place with the door?' said Mr Utterson.

'No, sir: I had a delicacy,' was the reply. 'I feel very strongly about putting questions; it partakes too much of the style of the day of judgment. You start a question, and it's like starting a stone. You sit quietly on the top of a hill; and away the stone goes, starting others; and presently some bland old bird (the last you would have thought of) is knocked on the head in his own back garden and the family have to change their name. No, sir, I make it a rule of mine: the more it looks like Queer Street,* the less I ask.'

'A very good rule, too,' said the lawyer.

'But I have studied the place for myself,' continued Mr Enfield. 'It seems scarcely a house. There is no other door, and nobody goes in or out of that one but, once in a great while, the gentleman of my adventure. There are three windows looking on the court on the first floor; none below; the windows are always shut but they're clean. And then there is a chimney which is generally smoking; so somebody must live there. And yet it's not so sure; for the buildings are so packed together about that court, that it's hard to say where one ends and another begins.'

The pair walked on again for a while in silence; and then 'Enfield,' said Mr Utterson, 'that's a good rule of yours.'

'Yes, I think it is,' returned Enfield.

'But for all that,' continued the lawyer, 'there's one point I want to ask: I want to ask the name of that man who walked over the child.'

'Well,' said Mr Enfield, 'I can't see what harm it would do. It was a man of the name of Hyde.'

'Hm,' said Mr Utterson. 'What sort of a man is he to see?'

'He is not easy to describe. There is something wrong with his appearance; something displeasing, something downright detestable. I never saw a man I so disliked, and yet I scarce know why. He must be deformed somewhere; he gives a strong feeling of deformity, although I couldn't specify the point. He's an extraordinary looking man, and yet I really can name nothing out of the way. No, sir; I can make no hand of it; I can't describe him. And it's not want of memory; for I declare I can see him this moment.'

Mr Utterson again walked some way in silence and obviously under a weight of consideration. 'You are sure he used a key?' he inquired at last.

'My dear sir . . .' began Enfield, surprised out of himself.

'Yes, I know,' said Utterson; 'I know it must seem strange. The fact is, if I do not ask you the name of the other party, it is because I know it already. You see, Richard, your tale has gone home. If you have been inexact in any point, you had better correct it.'

'I think you might have warned me,' returned the other with a touch of sullenness. 'But I have been pedantically exact, as you call it. The fellow had a key; and what's more, he has it still. I saw him use it, not a week ago.'

Mr Utterson sighed deeply but said never a word; and the young man presently resumed. 'Here is another lesson to say nothing,' said he. 'I am ashamed of my long tongue. Let us make a bargain never to refer to this again.'

'With all my heart,' said the lawyer. 'I shake hands on that, Richard.'

THAT evening, Mr Utterson came home to his bachelor house in sombre spirits and sat down to dinner without relish. It was his custom of a Sunday, when this meal was over, to sit close by the fire, a volume of some dry divinity on his reading desk, until the clock of the neighbouring church rang out the hour of twelve, when he would go soberly and gratefully to bed. On this night, however, as soon as the cloth was taken away, he took up a candle and went into his business room. There he opened his safe, took from the most private part of it a document endorsed on the envelope as Dr Jekyll's Will, and sat down with a clouded brow to study its contents. The will was holograph, for Mr Utterson, though he took charge of it now that it was made, had refused to lend the least assistance in the making of it; it provided not only that, in case of the decease of Henry Jekyll, M.D., D.C.L., LL.D., F.R.S.,* &c., all his possessions were to pass into the hands of his 'friend and bene-factor Edward Hyde,' but that in case of Dr Jekyll's 'disappearance or unexplained absence for any period exceeding three calendar months,' the said Edward Hyde should step into the said Henry Jekyll's shoes without further delay and free from any burthen or obligation, beyond the payment of a few small sums to the members of the doctor's household. This document had long been the law-yer's eyesore.* It offended him both as a lawyer and as a lover of the sane and customary sides of life, to whom the fanciful was the immodest. And hitherto it was his ignorance of Mr Hyde that had swelled his indignation; now, by a sudden turn, it was his know-ledge. It was already bad enough when the name was but a name of which he could learn no more. It was worse when it began to be clothed upon with detestable attributes; and out of the shifting, insubstantial mists that had so long baffled his eye, there leaped up the sudden, definite presentment of a fiend.

'I thought it was madness,' he said, as he replaced the obnoxious paper in the safe, 'and now I begin to fear it is disgrace.'

With that he blew out his candle, put on a great coat and set forth in the direction of Cavendish Square,* that citadel of medicine, where his friend, the great Dr Lanyon, had his house and received his crowding patients. 'If anyone knows, it will be Lanyon,' he had thought.

The solemn butler knew and welcomed him; he was subjected to no stage of delay, but ushered direct from the door to the dining-room where Dr Lanyon sat alone over his wine. This was a hearty, healthy, dapper, red-faced gentleman, with a shock of hair pre-maturely white, and a boisterous and decided manner. At sight of Mr Utterson, he sprang up from his chair and welcomed him with both hands. The geniality, as was the way of the man, was somewhat theatrical to the eye; but it reposed on genuine feeling. For these two were old friends, old mates both at school and college, both thorough respecters of themselves and of each other, and, what does not always follow, men who thoroughly enjoyed each other's company.

After a little rambling talk, the lawyer led up to the subject which so disagreeably preoccupied his mind.

'I suppose, Lanyon,' said he, 'you and I must be the two oldest friends that Henry Jekyll has?'

'I wish the friends were younger,' chuckled Dr Lanyon. 'But I suppose we are. And what of that? I see little of him now.'

'Indeed?' said Utterson. 'I thought you had a bond of common interest.'

'We had,' was the reply. 'But it is more than ten years since Henry Jekyll became too fanciful for me. He began to go wrong, wrong in mind; and though of course I continue to take an interest in him for old sake's sake as they say, I see and I have seen devilish little of the man. Such unscientific balderdash,' added the doctor, flushing suddenly purple, 'would have estranged Damon and Pythias.'*

This little spirt of temper was somewhat of a relief to Mr Utterson. 'They have only differed on some point of science,' he thought; and being a man of no scientific passions (except in the matter of con-veyancing) he even added: 'It is nothing worse than that!' He gave his friend a few seconds to recover his composure, and then approached the question he had come to put. 'Did you ever come across a protégé of his—one Hyde?' he asked.

'Hyde?' repeated Lanyon. 'No. Never heard of him. Since my time.'

That was the amount of information that the lawyer carried back with him to the great, dark bed on which he tossed to and fro, until the small hours of the morning began to grow large. It was a night of little ease to his toiling mind, toiling in mere darkness and besieged by questions.

Six o'clock struck on the bells of the church that was so conveniently near to Mr Utterson's dwelling, and still he was digging at the problem. Hitherto it had touched him on the intellectual side alone; but now his imagination also was engaged or rather enslaved; and as he lay and tossed in the gross darkness of the night and the curtained room, Mr Enfield's tale went by before his mind in a scroll of lighted pictures. He would be aware of the great field of lamps of a nocturnal city; then of the figure of a man walking swiftly; then of a child running from the doctor's; and then these met, and that human Juggernaut trod the child down and passed on regardless of her screams. Or else he would see a room in a rich house, where his friend lay asleep, dreaming and smiling at his dreams; and then the door of that room would be opened, the curtains of the bed plucked apart, the sleeper recalled, and lo! there would stand by his side a figure to whom power was given, and even at that dead hour, he must rise and do its bidding. The figure in these two phases haunted the lawyer all night; and if at any time he dozed over, it was but to see it glide more stealthily through sleeping houses, or move the more swiftly and still the more swiftly, even to dizziness, through wider labyrinths of lamplighted city, and at every street corner crush a child and leave her screaming. And still the figure had no face by which he might know it; even in his dreams, it had no face, or one that baffled him and melted before his eyes; and thus it was that there sprang up and grew apace in the lawyer's mind a singularly strong, almost an inordinate, curiosity to behold the features of the real Mr Hyde. If he could but once set eyes on him, he thought the mystery would lighten and perhaps roll altogether away, as was the habit of mysterious things when well examined. He might see a reason for his friend's strange preference or bondage (call it which you please) and even for the startling clauses of the will. And at least it would be a face worth seeing: the face of a man who was without bowels of mercy: a face which had but to show itself to raise up, in the mind of the unimpressionable Enfield, a spirit of enduring hatred.

From that time forward, Mr Utterson began to haunt the door in the by-street of shops. In the morning before office hours, at noon when business was plenty and time scarce, at night under the face of the fogged city moon, by all lights and at all hours of solitude or concourse, the lawyer was to be found on his chosen post.

'If he be Mr Hyde,' he had thought, 'I shall be Mr Seek.'

And at last his patience was rewarded. It was a fine dry night; frost in the air; the streets as clean as a ballroom floor; the lamps, unshaken by any wind, drawing a regular pattern of light and shadow. By ten o'clock, when the shops were closed, the by-street was very solitary and, in spite of the low growl of London from all round, very silent. Small sounds carried far; domestic sounds out of the houses were clearly audible on either side of the roadway; and the rumour of the approach of any passenger preceded him by a long time. Mr Utterson had been some minutes at his post, when he was aware of an odd, light footstep drawing near. In the course of his nightly patrols, he had long grown accustomed to the quaint effect with which the footfalls of a single person, while he is still a great way off, suddenly spring out distinct from the vast hum and clatter of the city. Yet his attention had never before been so sharply and decisively arrested; and it was with a strong, superstitious prevision of success that he withdrew into the entry of the court.

The steps drew swiftly nearer, and swelled out suddenly louder as they turned the end of the street. The lawyer, looking forth from the entry, could soon see what manner of man he had to deal with. He was small and very plainly dressed, and the look of him, even at that distance, went somehow strongly against the watcher's inclination. But he made straight for the door, crossing the roadway to save time; and as he came, he drew a key from his pocket like one approaching home.

Mr Utterson stepped out and touched him on the shoulder as he passed. 'Mr Hyde, I think?'

Mr Hyde shrank back with a hissing intake of the breath. But his fear was only momentary; and though he did not look the lawyer in the face, he answered coolly enough: 'That is my name. What do you want?'

'I see you are going in,' returned the lawyer. 'I am an old friend of Dr Jekyll's—Mr Utterson of Gaunt Street*—you must have heard my name; and meeting you so conveniently, I thought you might admit me.'

'You will not find Dr Jekyll; he is from home,' replied Mr Hyde, blowing in the key. And then suddenly, but still without looking up, 'How did you know me?' he asked.

'On your side,' said Mr Utterson, 'will you do me a favour?'

'With pleasure,' replied the other. 'What shall it be?'

'Will you let me see your face?' asked the lawyer.

Mr Hyde appeared to hesitate, and then, as if upon some sudden reflection, fronted about with an air of defiance; and the pair stared at each other pretty fixedly for a few seconds. 'Now I shall know you again,' said Mr Utterson. 'It may be useful.'

'Yes,' returned Mr Hyde, 'it is as well we have met; and *à propos*, you should have my address.' And he gave a number of a street in Soho.

'Good God!' thought Mr Utterson, 'can he too have been thinking of the will?' But he kept his feelings to himself and only grunted in acknowledgement of the address.

'And now,' said the other, 'how did you know me?'

'By description,' was the reply.

'Whose description?'

'We have common friends,' said Mr Utterson.

'Common friends?' echoed Mr Hyde, a little hoarsely. 'Who are they?'

'Jekyll, for instance,' said the lawyer.

'He never told you,' cried Mr Hyde, with a flush of anger. 'I did not think you would have lied.'

'Come,' said Mr Utterson, 'that is not fitting language.'

The other snarled aloud into a savage laugh; and the next moment, with extraordinary quickness, he had unlocked the door and disappeared into the house.

The lawyer stood awhile when Mr Hyde had left him, the picture of disquietude. Then he began slowly to mount the street, pausing every step or two and putting his hand to his brow like a man in mental perplexity. The problem he was thus debating as he walked, was one of a class that is rarely solved. Mr Hyde was pale and dwarfish, he gave an impression of deformity without any nameable malformation, he had a displeasing smile, he had borne himself to the lawyer with a sort of murderous mixture of timidity and boldness, and he spoke with a husky, whispering and somewhat broken voice; all these were points against him, but not all of these together could explain the hitherto unknown disgust, loathing and fear with which Mr Utterson regarded him. 'There must be something else,' said the perplexed gentleman. 'There *is* something more, if I could find a name for it. God bless me, the man seems hardly human! Something troglodytic,* shall we say? or can it be the old story of Dr Fell?* or is it the mere radiance of a foul soul that thus transpires through, and transfigures, its clay continent? The last, I think; for O my poor old Harry Jekyll, if ever I read Satan's signature upon a face, it is on that of your new friend.'

Round the corner from the by-street, there was a square of ancient, handsome houses, now for the most part decayed from their high estate and let in flats and chambers to all sorts and conditions of men:* map-engravers, architects, shady lawyers and the agents of obscure enterprises. One house, however, second from the corner, was still occupied entire; and at the door of this, which wore a great air of wealth and comfort, though it was now plunged in darkness except for the fan-light, Mr Utterson stopped and knocked. A well-dressed, elderly servant opened the door.

'Is Dr Jekyll at home, Poole?' asked the lawyer.

'I will see, Mr Utterson,' said Poole, admitting the visitor, as he spoke, into a large, low-roofed, comfortable hall, paved with flags, warmed (after the fashion of a country house) by a bright, open fire, and furnished with costly cabinets of oak. 'Will you wait here by the fire, sir? or shall I give you a light in the dining-room?'

'Here, thank you,' said the lawyer, and he drew near and leaned on the tall fender. This hall, in which he was now left alone, was a pet fancy of his friend the doctor's; and Utterson himself was wont to speak of it as the pleasantest room in London. But tonight there was a shudder in his blood; the face of Hyde sat heavy on his memory; he felt (what was rare with him) a nausea and distaste of life; and in the gloom of his spirits, he seemed to read a menace in the flickering of the firelight on the polished cabinets and the uneasy starting of the shadow on the roof. He was ashamed of his relief, when Poole presently returned to announce that Dr Jekyll was gone out.

'I saw Mr Hyde go in by the old dissecting room door, Poole,' he said. 'Is that right, when Dr Jekyll is from home?'

'Quite right, Mr Utterson, sir,' replied the servant. 'Mr Hyde has a key.'

'Your master seems to repose a great deal of trust in that young man, Poole,' resumed the other musingly.

'Yes, sir, he do indeed,' said Poole. 'We have all orders to obey him.'

'I do not think I ever met Mr Hyde?' asked Utterson.

'O, dear no, sir. He never *dines* here,' replied the butler. 'Indeed we see very little of him on this side of the house; he mostly comes and goes by the laboratory.'

'Well, good night, Poole.'

'Good night, Mr Utterson.'

And the lawyer set out homeward with a very heavy heart. 'Poor Harry Jekyll,' he thought, 'my mind misgives me he is in deep waters! He was wild when he was young; a long while ago to be sure; but in the law of God, there is no statute of limitations. Ay, it must be that; the ghost of some old sin, the cancer of some concealed disgrace: punishment coming, *pede claudo*,* years after memory has forgotten and self-love condoned the fault.' And the lawyer, scared by the thought, brooded awhile on his own past, groping in all the corners of memory, lest by chance some Jack-in-the-Box of an old iniquity should leap to light there. His past was fairly blameless; few men could read the rolls of their life with less apprehension; yet he was humbled to the dust by the many ill things he had done, and raised up again into a sober and fearful gratitude by the many that he had come so near to doing, yet avoided. And then by a return on his former subject, he conceived a spark of hope. 'This Master Hyde, if he were studied,' thought he, 'must have secrets of his own: black secrets, by the look of him; secrets compared to which poor Jekyll's worst would be like sunshine. Things cannot continue as they are. It turns me cold to think of this creature stealing like a thief to Harry's bedside; poor Harry, what a wakening! And the danger of it; for if this Hyde suspects the existence of the will, he may grow impatient to inherit. Ay, I must put my shoulder to the wheel—if Jekyll will but let me,' he added, 'if Jekyll will only let me.' For once more he saw before his mind's eye, as clear as a transparency, the strange clauses of the will.

DR JEKYLL WAS QUITE AT EASE

A FORTNIGHT later, by excellent good fortune, the doctor gave one of his pleasant dinners to some five or six old cronies, all intelligent, reputable men and all judges of good wine; and Mr Utterson so contrived that he remained behind after the others had departed. This was no new arrangement, but a thing that had befallen many scores of times. Where Utterson was liked, he was liked well. Hosts loved to detain the dry lawyer, when the light-hearted and the loose-tongued had already their foot on the threshold; they liked to sit awhile in his unobtrusive company, practising for solitude, sobering their minds in the man's rich silence after the expense and strain of gaiety. To this rule, Dr Jekyll was no exception; and as he now sat on the opposite side of the fire—a large, well-made, smooth-faced man of fifty, with something of a slyish cast perhaps, but every mark of capacity and kindness—you could see by his looks that he cherished for Mr Utterson a sincere and warm affection.

'I have been wanting to speak to you, Jekyll,' began the latter. 'You know that will of yours?'

A close observer might have gathered that the topic was distasteful; but the doctor carried it off gaily. 'My poor Utterson,' said he, 'you are unfortunate in such a client. I never saw a man so distressed as you were by my will; unless it were that hide-bound pedant, Lanyon, at what he called my scientific heresies. O, I know he's a good fellow—you needn't frown—an excellent fellow, and I always mean to see more of him; but a hide-bound pedant for all that; an ignorant, blatant pedant. I was never more disappointed in any man than Lanyon.'

'You know I never approved of it,' pursued Utterson, ruthlessly disregarding the fresh topic.

'My will? Yes, certainly, I know that,' said the doctor, a trifle sharply. 'You have told me so.'

'Well, I tell you so again,' continued the lawyer. 'I have been learning something of young Hyde.'

The large handsome face of Dr Jekyll grew pale to the very lips, and there came a blackness about his eyes. 'I do not care to hear more,' said he. 'This is a matter I thought we had agreed to drop.'

'What I heard was abominable,' said Utterson.

'It can make no change. You do not understand my position,' returned the doctor, with a certain incoherency of manner. 'I am painfully situated, Utterson; my position is a very strange—a very strange one. It is one of those affairs that cannot be mended by talking.'

'Jekyll,' said Utterson, 'you know me: I am a man to be trusted. Make a clean breast of this in confidence; and I make no doubt I can get you out of it.'

'My good Utterson,' said the doctor, 'this is very good of you, this is downright good of you, and I cannot find words to thank you in. I believe you fully; I would trust you before any man alive, ay, before myself, if I could make the choice; but indeed it isn't what you fancy; it is not so bad as that; and just to put your good heart at rest, I will tell you one thing: the moment I choose, I can be rid of Mr Hyde. I give you my hand upon that; and I thank you again and again; and I will just add one little word, Utterson, that I'm sure you'll take in good part: this is a private matter, and I beg of you to let it sleep.'

Utterson reflected a little looking in the fire.

'I have no doubt you are perfectly right,' he said at last, getting to his feet.

'Well, but since we have touched upon this business, and for the last time I hope,' continued the doctor, 'there is one point I should like you to understand. I have really a very great interest in poor Hyde. I know you have seen him; he told me so; and I fear he was rude. But I do sincerely take a great, a very great interest in that young man; and if I am taken away, Utterson, I wish you to promise me that you will bear with him and get his rights for him. I think you would, if you knew all; and it would be a weight off my mind if you would promise.'

'I can't pretend that I shall ever like him,' said the lawyer.

'I don't ask that,' pleaded Jekyll, laying his hand upon the other's arm; 'I only ask for justice; I only ask you to help him for my sake, when I am no longer here.'

Utterson heaved an irrepressible sigh. 'Well,' said he. 'I promise.'

NEARLY a year later, in the month of October 18—, London was startled by a crime of singular ferocity and rendered all the more notable by the high position of the victim. The details were few and startling. A maid servant living alone in a house not far from the river, had gone upstairs to bed about eleven. Although a fog rolled over the city in the small hours, the early part of the night was cloudless, and the lane, which the maid's window overlooked, was brilliantly lit by the full moon. It seems she was romantically given, for she sat down upon her box, which stood immediately under the window, and fell into a dream of musing. Never (she used to say, with streaming tears, when she narrated that experience) never had she felt more at peace with all men or thought more kindly of the world. And as she so sat she became aware of an aged and beautiful gentleman with white hair, drawing near along the lane; and advancing to meet him, another and very small gentleman, to whom at first she paid less attention. When they had come within speech (which was just under the maid's eyes) the older man bowed and accosted the other with a very pretty manner of politeness. It did not seem as if the subject of his address were of great importance; indeed, from his pointing, it sometimes appeared as if he were only inquiring his way; but the moon shone on his face as he spoke, and the girl was pleased to watch it, it seemed to breathe such an innocent and old-world kindness of disposition, yet with something high too, as of a well-founded self-content. Presently her eye wandered to the other, and she was surprised to recognise in him a certain Mr Hyde, who had once visited her master and for whom she had conceived a dislike. He had in his hand a heavy cane, with which he was trifling; but he answered never a word, and seemed to listen with an ill-contained impatience. And then all of a sudden he broke out in a great flame of anger, stamping with his foot, brandishing the cane, and carrying on (as the maid described it) like a madman. The old gentleman took a step back, with the air of one very much surprised and a trifle hurt; and at that Mr Hyde broke out of all bounds and clubbed him to the earth. And next moment, with ape-like fury, he was trampling his victim under foot, and hailing down a storm of blows, under which the bones were audibly shattered and the body jumped upon the roadway. At the horror of these sights and sounds,* the maid fainted.

It was two o'clock when she came to herself and called for the police. The murderer was gone long ago; but there lay his victim in the middle of the lane, incredibly mangled. The stick with which the deed had been done, although it was of some rare and very tough and heavy wood, had broken in the middle under the stress of this insensate cruelty; and one splintered half had rolled in the neigh-bouring gutter—the other, without doubt, had been carried away by the murderer. A purse and a gold watch were found upon the victim; but no cards or papers, except a sealed and stamped envelope, which he had been probably carrying to the post, and which bore the name and address of Mr Utterson.

This was brought to the lawyer the next morning, before he was out of bed; and he had no sooner seen it, and been told the circum-stances, than he shot out a solemn lip. 'I shall say nothing till I have seen the body,' said he; 'this may be very serious. Have the kindness to wait while I dress.' And with the same grave countenance he hurried through his breakfast and drove to the police station, whither the body had been carried. As soon as he came into the cell, he nodded.

'Yes,' said he, 'I recognise him. I am sorry to say that this is Sir Danvers Carew.'

'Good God, sir,' exclaimed the officer, 'is it possible?' And the next moment his eye lighted up with professional ambition. 'This will make a deal of noise,' he said. 'And perhaps you can help us to the man.' And he briefly narrated what the maid had seen; and showed the broken stick.

Mr Utterson had already quailed at the name of Hyde; but when the stick was laid before him, he could doubt no longer: broken and battered as it was, he recognised it for one that he had himself presented many years before to Henry Jckyll.

'Is this Mr Hyde a person of small stature?' he inquired.

'Particularly small and particularly wicked-looking, is what the maid calls him,' said the officer.

Mr Utterson reflected; and then, raising his head, 'If you will come with me in my cab,' he said, 'I think I can take you to his house.'

It was by this time about nine in the morning, and the first fog of the season. A great chocolate-coloured pall lowered over heaven, but the wind was continually charging and routing these embattled vapours; so that as the cab crawled from street to street, Mr Utterson beheld a marvellous number of degrees and hues of twilight; for here it would be dark like the back-end of evening; and there would be a glow of a rich, lurid brown, like the light of some strange conflagration; and here, for a moment, the fog would be quite broken up, and a haggard shaft of daylight would glance in between the swirling wreaths. The dismal quarter of Soho* seen under these changing glimpses, with its muddy ways, and slatternly passengers, and its lamps, which had never been extinguished or had been kindled afresh to combat this mournful reinvasion of darkness, seemed, in the lawyer's eyes, like a district of some city in a nightmare. The thoughts of his mind, besides, were of the gloomiest dye; and when he glanced at the companion of his drive, he was conscious of some touch of that terror of the law and the law's officers, which may at times assail the most honest.

As the cab drew up before the address indicated, the fog lifted a little and showed him a dingy street, a gin palace, a low French eating house, a shop for the retail of penny numbers and twopenny salads, many ragged children huddled in the doorways, and many women of many different nationalities passing out, key in hand, to have a morning glass;* and the next moment the fog settled down again upon that part, as brown as umber, and cut him off from his blackguardly surroundings. This was the home of Henry Jekyll's favourite; of a man who was heir to quarter of a million sterling.

An ivory-faced and silvery-haired old woman opened the door. She had an evil face, smoothed by hypocrisy; but her manners were excellent. Yes, she said, this was Mr Hyde's, but he was not at home; he had been in that night very late, but had gone away again in less than an hour; there was nothing strange in that; his habits were very irregular, and he was often absent; for instance, it was nearly two months since she had seen him till yesterday.

'Very well then, we wish to see his rooms,' said the lawyer; and when the woman began to declare it was impossible, 'I had better tell you who this person is,' he added. 'This is Inspector Newcomen of Scotland Yard.'

A flash of odious joy appeared upon the woman's face. 'Ah!' said she, 'he is in trouble! What has he done?'

Mr Utterson and the inspector exchanged glances. 'He don't seem a very popular character,' observed the latter. 'And now, my good woman, just let me and this gentleman have a look about us.'

In the whole extent of the house, which but for the old woman remained otherwise empty, Mr Hyde had only used a couple of rooms; but these were furnished with luxury and good taste. A closet was filled with wine; the plate was of silver, the napery elegant; a good picture hung upon the walls,* a gift (as Utterson supposed) from Henry Jekyll, who was much of a connoisseur; and the carpets were of many plies and agreeable in colour. At this moment, however, the rooms bore every mark of having been recently and hurriedly ransacked; clothes lay about the floor, with their pockets inside out; lockfast drawers stood open; and on the hearth there lay a pile of gray ashes, as though many papers had been burned. From these embers the inspector disinterred the butt end of a green cheque book, which had resisted the action of the fire; the other half of the stick was found behind the door; and as this clinched his suspicions, the officer declared himself delighted. A visit to the bank, where several thousand pounds were found to be lying to the murderer's credit, completed his gratification.

'You may depend upon it, sir,' he told Mr Utterson: 'I have him in my hand. He must have lost his head, or he never would have left the stick or, above all, burned the cheque book. Why, money's life to the man. We have nothing to do but wait for him at the bank, and get out the handbills.'

This last, however, was not so easy of accomplishment; for Mr Hyde had numbered few familiars—even the master of the servant maid had only seen him twice; his family could nowhere be traced; he had never been photographed; and the few who could describe him differed widely, as common observers will. Only on one point, were they agreed; and that was the haunting sense of unexpressed deformity with which the fugitive impressed his beholders.

IT was late in the afternoon, when Mr Utterson found his way to Dr Jekyll's door, where he was at once admitted by Poole, and carried down by the kitchen offices and across a yard which had once been a garden, to the building which was indifferently known as the laboratory or the dissecting rooms. The doctor had bought the house from the heirs of a celebrated surgeon; and his own tastes being rather chemical than anatomical, had changed the destination of the block at the bottom of the garden. It was the first time that the lawyer had been received in that part of his friend's quarters; and he eyed the dingy windowless structure with curiosity, and gazed round with a distasteful sense of strangeness as he crossed the theatre, once crowded with eager students and now lying gaunt and silent, the tables laden with chemical apparatus, the floor strewn with crates and littered with packing straw, and the light falling dimly through the foggy cupola. At the further end, a flight of stairs mounted to a door covered with red baize; and through this, Mr Utterson was at last received into the doctor's cabinet. It was a large room, fitted round with glass presses, furnished, among other things, with a cheval-glass and a business table, and looking out upon the court by three dusty windows barred with iron. The fire burned in the grate; a lamp was set lighted on the chimney shelf, for even in the houses the fog began to lie thickly; and there, close up to the warmth, sat Dr Jekyll, looking deadly sick. He did not rise to meet his visitor, but held out a cold hand and bade him welcome in a changed voice.

'And now,' said Mr Utterson, as soon as Poole had left them, 'you have heard the news?'

The doctor shuddered. 'They were crying it in the square,' he said. 'I heard them in my dining room.'

'One word,' said the lawyer. 'Carew was my client, but so are you, and I want to know what I am doing. You have not been mad enough to hide this fellow?'

'Utterson, I swear to God,' cried the doctor, 'I swear to God I will never set eyes on him again. I bind my honour to you that I am done with him in this world. It is all at an end. And indeed he does not

want my help; you do not know him as I do; he is safe, he is quite
safe; mark my words, he will never more be heard of.'

The lawyer listened gloomily; he did not like his friend's feverish
manner. 'You seem pretty sure of him,' said he; 'and for your sake,
I hope you may be right. If it came to a trial, your name might
appear.'

'I am quite sure of him,' replied Jekyll; 'I have grounds for certainty that I cannot share with anyone. But there is one thing on
which you may advise me. I have—I have received a letter; and I am
at a loss whether I should show it to the police. I should like to leave
it in your hands, Utterson; you would judge wisely I am sure; I have
so great a trust in you.'

'You fear, I suppose, that it might lead to his detection?' asked the
lawyer.

'No,' said the other. 'I cannot say that I care what becomes of
Hyde; I am quite done with him. I was thinking of my own character,
which this hateful business has rather exposed.'

Utterson ruminated awhile; he was surprised at his friend's selfishness, and yet relieved by it. 'Well,' said he, at last, 'let me see the
letter.'

The letter was written in an odd, upright hand and signed
'Edward Hyde': and it signified, briefly enough, that the writer's
benefactor, Dr Jekyll, whom he had long so unworthily repaid for a
thousand generosities, need labour under no alarm for his safety as
he had means of escape on which he placed a sure dependence. The
lawyer liked this letter well enough; it put a better colour on the
intimacy than he had looked for; and he blamed himself for some of
his past suspicions.

'Have you the envelope?' he asked.

'I burned it,' replied Jekyll, 'before I thought what I was about.
But it bore no postmark. The note was handed in.'

'Shall I keep this and sleep upon it?' asked Utterson.

'I wish you to judge for me entirely,' was the reply. 'I have lost
confidence in myself.'

'Well, I shall consider,' returned the lawyer. 'And now one word
more: it was Hyde who dictated the terms in your will about that
disappearance?'

The doctor seemed seized with a qualm of faintness; he shut his
mouth tight and nodded.

'I knew it,' said Utterson. 'He meant to murder you. You have had a fine escape.'

'I have had what is far more to the purpose,' returned the doctor solemnly: 'I have had a lesson—O God, Utterson, what a lesson I have had!' And he covered his face for a moment with his hands.

On his way out, the lawyer stopped and had a word or two with Poole. 'By the by,' said he, 'there was a letter handed in today: what was the messenger like?' But Poole was positive nothing had come except by post; 'and only circulars by that,' he added.

This news sent off the visitor with his fears renewed. Plainly the letter had come by the laboratory door; possibly, indeed, it had been written in the cabinet; and if that were so, it must be differently judged, and handled with the more caution. The newsboys, as he went, were crying themselves hoarse along the footways: 'Special edition. Shocking murder of an M.P.' That was the funeral oration of one friend and client; and he could not help a certain apprehension lest the good name of another should be sucked down in the eddy of the scandal. It was, at least, a ticklish decision that he had to make; and self-reliant as he was by habit, he began to cherish a longing for advice. It was not to be had directly; but perhaps, he thought, it might be fished for.

Presently after, he sat on one side of his own hearth, with Mr Guest, his head clerk, upon the other, and midway between, at a nicely calculated distance from the fire, a bottle of a particular old wine that had long dwelt unsunned in the foundations of his house. The fog still slept on the wing above the drowned city, where the lamps glimmered like carbuncles; and through the muffle and smother of these fallen clouds, the procession of the town's life was still rolling in through the great arteries with a sound as of a mighty wind. But the room was gay with firelight. In the bottle the acids were long ago resolved; the imperial dye had softened with time, as the colour grows richer in stained windows; and the glow of hot autumn afternoons on hillside vineyards, was ready to be set free and to disperse the fogs of London. Insensibly the lawyer melted. There was no man from whom he kept fewer secrets than Mr Guest; and he was not always sure that he kept as many as he meant. Guest had often been on business to the doctor's; he knew Poole; he could scarce have failed to hear of Mr Hyde's familiarity about the house; he might draw conclusions: was it not as well, then, that he should scc a letter which put that mystery to rights? and above all since Guest, being a great student and critic of handwriting, would consider the step natural and obliging? The clerk, besides, was a man of counsel; he would scarce read so strange a document without dropping a remark; and by that remark Mr Utterson might shape his future course.

'This is a sad business about Sir Danvers,' he said.

'Yes, sir, indeed. It has elicited a great deal of public feeling,' returned Guest. 'The man, of course, was mad.'

'I should like to hear your views on that,' replied Utterson. 'I have a document here in his handwriting; it is between ourselves, for I scarce know what to do about it; it is an ugly business at the best. But there it is; quite in your way: a murderer's autograph.'

Guest's eyes brightened, and he sat down at once and studied it with passion. 'No, sir,' he said; 'not mad; but it is an odd hand.'

'And by all accounts a very odd writer,' added the lawyer.

Just then the servant entered with a note.

'Is that from Doctor Jekyll, sir?' inquired the clerk. 'I thought I knew the writing. Anything private, Mr. Utterson?'

'Only an invitation to dinner. Why? do you want to see it?'

'One moment. I thank you, sir;' and the clerk laid the two sheets of paper alongside and sedulously compared their contents. 'Thank you, sir,' he said at last, returning both; 'it's a very interesting autograph.'

There was a pause, during which Mr Utterson struggled with himself. 'Why did you compare them, Guest?' he inquired suddenly.

'Well, sir,' returned the clerk, 'there's a rather singular resemblance; the two hands are in many points identical:* only differently sloped.'

'Rather quaint,' said Utterson.

'It is, as you say, rather quaint,' returned Guest.

'I wouldn't speak of this note, you know,' said the master.

'No, sir,' said the clerk. 'I understand.'

But no sooner was Mr Utterson alone that night, than he locked the note into his safe where it reposed from that time forward. 'What!' he thought. 'Henry Jekyll forge for a murderer!' And his blood ran cold in his veins.

REMARKABLE INCIDENT OF
DOCTOR LANYON

TIME ran on; thousands of pounds were offered in reward, for the death of Sir Danvers was resented as a public injury; but Mr Hyde had disappeared out of the ken of the police as though he had never existed. Much of his past was unearthed, indeed, and all disreputable: tales came out of the man's cruelty, at once so callous and violent, of his vile life, of his strange associates, of the hatred that seemed to have surrounded his career; but of his present whereabouts, not a whisper. From the time he had left the house in Soho on the morning of the murder, he was simply blotted out; and gradually, as time drew on, Mr Utterson began to recover from the hotness of his alarm, and to grow more at quiet with himself. The death of Sir Danvers was, to his way of thinking, more than paid for by the disappearance of Mr Hyde. Now that that evil influence had been withdrawn, a new life began for Dr Jekyll. He came out of his seclusion, renewed relations with his friends, became once more their familiar guest and entertainer; and whilst he had always been known for charities, he was now no less distinguished for religion. He was busy, he was much in the open air, he did good; his face seemed to open and brighten, as if with an inward consciousness of service; and for more than two months, the doctor was at peace.

On the 8th of January Utterson had dined at the doctor's with a small party; Lanyon had been there; and the face of the host had looked from one to the other as in the old days when the trio were inseparable friends. On the 12th, and again on the 14th, the door was shut against the lawyer. 'The doctor was confined to the house,' Poole said, 'and saw no one.' On the 15th, he tried again, and was again refused; and having now been used for the last two months to see his friend almost daily, he found this return of solitude to weigh upon his spirits. The fifth night, he had in Guest to dine with him; and the sixth he betook himself to Doctor Lanyon's.

There at least he was not denied admittance; but when he came in, he was shocked at the change which had taken place in the doctor's appearance. He had his death-warrant written legibly upon his face. The rosy man had grown pale; his flesh had fallen away; he was visibly balder and older; and yet it was not so much these tokens of a swift physical decay that arrested the lawyer's notice, as a look in the eye and quality of manner that seemed to testify to some deep-seated terror of the mind. It was unlikely that the doctor should fear death; and yet that was what Utterson was tempted to suspect. 'Yes,' he thought; 'he is a doctor, he must know his own state and that his days are counted; and the knowledge is more than he can bear.' And yet when Utterson remarked on his ill-looks, it was with an air of great firmness that Lanyon declared himself a doomed man.

'I have had a shock,' he said, 'and I shall never recover. It is a question of weeks. Well, life has been pleasant; I liked it; yes, sir, I used to like it. I sometimes think if we knew all, we should be more glad to get away.'

'Jekyll is ill, too,' observed Utterson. 'Have you seen him?'

But Lanyon's face changed, and he held up a trembling hand. 'I wish to see or hear no more of Doctor Jekyll,' he said in a loud, unsteady voice. 'I am quite done with that person; and I beg that you will spare me any allusion to one whom I regard as dead.'

'Tut-tut,' said Mr Utterson; and then after a considerable pause, 'Can't I do anything?' he inquired. 'We are three very old friends, Lanyon; we shall not live to make others.'

'Nothing can be done,' returned Lanyon; 'ask himself.'

'He will not see me,' said the lawyer.

'I am not surprised at that,' was the reply. 'Some day, Utterson, after I am dead, you may perhaps come to learn the right and wrong of this. I cannot tell you. And in the meantime, if you can sit and talk with me of other things, for God's sake, stay and do so; but if you cannot keep clear of this accursed topic, then, in God's name, go, for I cannot bear it.'

As soon as he got home, Utterson sat down and wrote to Jekyll, complaining of his exclusion from the house, and asking the cause of this unhappy break with Lanyon; and the next day brought him a long answer, often very pathetically worded, and sometimes darkly mysterious in drift. The quarrel with Lanyon was incurable. 'I do not blame our old friend,' Jekyll wrote, 'but I share his view that we must never meet. I mean from henceforth to lead a life of extreme seclusion; you must not be surprised, nor must you doubt my friendship, if my door is often shut even to you. You must suffer me to go my own dark way. I have brought on myself a punishment and a danger that I cannot name. If I am the chief of sinners, I am the chief of sufferers also. I could not think that this earth contained a place for sufferings and terrors so unmanning; and you can do but one thing, Utterson, to lighten this destiny, and that is to respect my silence.' Utterson was amazed; the dark influence of Hyde had been withdrawn, the doctor had returned to his old tasks and amities; a week ago, the prospect had smiled with every promise of a cheerful and an honoured age; and now in a moment, friendship, and peace of mind and the whole tenor of his life were wrecked. So great and unprepared a change pointed to madness; but in view of Lanyon's manner and words, there must lie for it some deeper ground.

A week afterwards Dr Lanyon took to his bed, and in something less than a fortnight he was dead. The night after the funeral, at which he had been sadly affected, Utterson locked the door of his business room, and sitting there by the light of a melancholy candle, drew out and set before him an envelope addressed by the hand and sealed with the seal of his dead friend. 'PRIVATE: for the hands of J. G. Utterson ALONE and in case of his predecease *to be destroyed unread*,' so it was emphatically superscribed; and the lawyer dreaded to behold the contents. 'I have buried one friend today,' he thought: 'what if this should cost me another?' And then he condemned the fear as a disloyalty, and broke the seal. Within there was another enclosure, likewise sealed, and marked upon the cover as 'not to be opened till the death or disappearance of Dr Henry Jekyll.' Utterson could not trust his eyes. Yes, it was disappearance; here again, as in the mad will which he had long ago restored to its author, here again were the idea of a disappearance and the name of Henry Jekyll bracketed. But in the will, that idea had sprung from the sinister suggestion of the man Hyde; it was set there with a purpose all too plain and horrible. Written by the hand of Lanyon, what should it mean? A great curiosity came on the trustee, to disregard the prohibition and dive at once to the bottom of these mysteries; but professional honour and faith to his dead friend were stringent obligations; and the packet slept in the inmost corner of his private safe.

It is one thing to mortify curiosity, another to conquer it; and it may be doubted if, from that day forth, Utterson desired the society of his surviving friend with the same eagerness. He thought of him kindly; but his thoughts were disquieted and fearful. He went to call indeed; but he was perhaps relieved to be denied admittance;

perhaps, in his heart, he preferred to speak with Poole upon the doorstep and surrounded by the air and sounds of the open city, rather than to be admitted into that house of voluntary bondage, and to sit and speak with its inscrutable recluse. Poole had, indeed, no very pleasant news to communicate. The doctor, it appeared, now more than ever confined himself to the cabinet over the laboratory, where he would sometimes even sleep; he was out of spirits, he had grown very silent, he did not read; it seemed as if he had something on his mind. Utterson became so used to the unvarying character of these reports, that he fell off little by little in the frequency of his visits.

INCIDENT AT THE WINDOW

IT chanced on Sunday, when Mr Utterson was on his usual walk with Mr Enfield, that their way lay once again through the by-street; and that when they came in front of the door, both stopped to gaze on it.

'Well,' said Enfield, 'that story's at an end at least. We shall never see more of Mr Hyde.'

'I hope not,' said Utterson. 'Did I ever tell you that I once saw him, and shared your feeling of repulsion?'

'It was impossible to do the one without the other,' returned Enfield. 'And by the way what an ass you must have thought me, not to know that this was a back way to Dr Jekyll's! It was partly your own fault that I found it out, even when I did.'

'So you found it out, did you?' said Utterson. 'But if that be so, we may step into the court and take a look at the windows. To tell you the truth, I am uneasy about poor Jekyll; and even outside, I feel as if the presence of a friend might do him good.'

The court was very cool and a little damp, and full of premature twilight, although the sky, high up overhead, was still bright with sunset. The middle one of the three windows was half way open; and sitting close beside it, taking the air with an infinite sadness of mien, like some disconsolate prisoner, Utterson saw Dr Jekyll.

'What! Jekyll!' he cried. 'I trust you are better.'

'I am very low, Utterson,' replied the doctor drearily, 'very low. It will not last long, thank God.'

'You stay too much indoors,' said the lawyer. 'You should be out, whipping up the circulation like Mr Enfield and me. (This is my cousin—Mr Enfield—Dr Jekyll.) Come now; get your hat and take a quick turn with us.'

'You are very good,' sighed the other. 'I should like to very much; but no, no, no, it is quite impossible; I dare not. But indeed, Utterson, I am very glad to see you; this is really a great pleasure; I would ask you and Mr Enfield up, but the place is really not fit.'

'Why then,' said the lawyer, good-naturedly, 'the best thing we can do is to stay down here and speak with you from where we are.'

'That is just what I was about to venture to propose,' returned the doctor with a smile. But the words were hardly uttered, before the smile was struck out of his face and succeeded by an expression of such abject terror and despair, as froze the very blood of the two gentlemen below. They saw it but for a glimpse, for the window was instantly thrust down; but that glimpse had been sufficient, and they turned and left the court without a word. In silence, too, they traversed the by-street; and it was not until they had come into a neighbouring thoroughfare, where even upon a Sunday there were still some stirrings of life, that Mr Utterson at last turned and looked at his companion. They were both pale; and there was an answering horror in their eyes.

'God forgive us, God forgive us,' said Mr Utterson.

But Mr Enfield only nodded his head very seriously, and walked on once more in silence.

MR UTTERSON was sitting by his fireside one evening after dinner, when he was surprised to receive a visit from Poole.

'Bless me, Poole, what brings you here?' he cried; and then taking a second look at him, 'What ails you?' he added, 'is the doctor ill?'

'Mr Utterson,' said the man, 'there is something wrong.'

'Take a seat, and here is a glass of wine for you,' said the lawyer. 'Now, take your time, and tell me plainly what you want.'

'You know the doctor's ways, sir,' replied Poole, 'and how he shuts himself up. Well, he's shut up again in the cabinet; and I don't like it, sir—I wish I may die if I like it. Mr Utterson, sir, I'm afraid.'

'Now, my good man,' said the lawyer, 'be explicit. What are you afraid of?'

'I've been afraid for about a week,' returned Poole, doggedly disregarding the question, 'and I can bear it no more.'

The man's appearance amply bore out his words; his manner was altered for the worse; and except for the moment when he had first announced his terror, he had not once looked the lawyer in the face. Even now, he sat with the glass of wine untasted on his knee, and his eyes directed to a corner of the floor. 'I can bear it no more,' he repeated.

'Come,' said the lawyer, 'I see you have some good reason, Poole; I see there is something seriously amiss. Try to tell me what it is.'

'I think there's been foul play,' said Poole, hoarsely.

'Foul play!' cried the lawyer, a good deal frightened and rather inclined to be irritated in consequence. 'What foul play? What does the man mean?'

'I daren't say, sir,' was the answer; 'but will you come along with me and see for yourself?'

Mr Utterson's only answer was to rise and get his hat and great coat; but he observed with wonder the greatness of the relief that appeared upon the butler's face, and perhaps with no less, that the wine was still untasted when he set it down to follow.

It was a wild, cold, seasonable night of March, with a pale moon, lying on her back as though the wind had tilted her, and a flying wrack of the most diaphanous and lawny texture. The wind made talking difficult, and flecked the blood into the face. It seemed to have swept the streets unusually bare of passengers, besides; for Mr Utterson thought he had never seen that part of London so deserted. He could have wished it otherwise; never in his life had he been conscious of so sharp a wish to see and touch his fellow-creatures; for struggle as he might, there was borne in upon his mind a crushing anticipation of calamity. The square, when they got there, was all full of wind and dust, and the thin trees in the garden were lashing themselves along the railing. Poole, who had kept all the way a pace or two ahead, now pulled up in the middle of the pavement, and in spite of the biting weather, took off his hat and mopped his brow with a red pocket-handkerchief. But for all the hurry of his coming, these were not the dews of exertion that he wiped away, but the moisture of some strangling anguish; for his face was white and his voice, when he spoke, harsh and broken.

'Well, sir,' he said, 'here we are, and God grant there be nothing wrong.'

'Amen, Poole,' said the lawyer.

Thereupon the servant knocked in a very guarded manner; the door was opened on the chain; and a voice asked from within, 'Is that you, Poole?'

'It's all right,' said Poole. 'Open the door.'

The hall, when they entered it, was brightly lighted up; the fire was built high; and about the hearth the whole of the servants, men and women, stood huddled together like a flock of sheep. At the sight of Mr Utterson, the housemaid broke into hysterical whimpering; and the cook, crying out 'Bless God! it's Mr Utterson,' ran forward as if to take him in her arms.

'What, what? Are you all here?' said the lawyer peevishly. 'Very irregular, very unseemly; your master would be far from pleased.'

'They're all afraid,' said Poole.

Blank silence followed, no one protesting; only the maid lifted up her voice and now wept loudly.

'Hold your tongue!' Poole said to her, with a ferocity of accent that testified to his own jangled nerves; and indeed, when the girl had so suddenly raised the note of her lamentation, they had all started and turned towards the inner door with faces of dreadful expectation. 'And now,' continued the butler, addressing the knife-boy, 'reach me a candle, and we'll get this through hands* at once.' And then he begged Mr Utterson to follow him, and led the way to the back garden.

'Now, sir,' said he, 'you come as gently as you can. I want you to hear, and I don't want you to be heard. And see here, sir, if by any chance he was to ask you in, don't go.'

Mr Utterson's nerves, at this unlooked-for termination, gave a jerk that nearly threw him from his balance; but he recollected his courage and followed the butler into the laboratory building and through the surgical theatre, with its lumber of crates and bottles, to the foot of the stair. Here Poole motioned him to stand on one side and listen; while he himself, setting down the candle and making a great and obvious call on his resolution, mounted the steps and knocked with a somewhat uncertain hand on the red baize of the cabinet door.

'Mr Utterson, sir, asking to see you,' he called; and even as he did so, once more violently signed to the lawyer to give ear.

A voice answered from within: 'Tell him I cannot see anyone,' it said complainingly.

'Thank you, sir,' said Poole, with a note of something like triumph in his voice; and taking up his candle, he led Mr Utterson back across the yard and into the great kitchen, where the fire was out and the beetles were leaping on the floor.

'Sir,' he said, looking Mr Utterson in the eyes, 'was that my master's voice?'

'It seems much changed,' replied the lawyer, very pale, but giving look for look.

'Changed? Well, yes, I think so,' said the butler. 'Have I been twenty years in this man's house, to be deceived about his voice? No, sir; master's made away with; he was made away with, eight days ago, when we heard him cry out upon the name of God; and *who's* in there instead of him, and *why* it stays there, is a thing that cries to Heaven, Mr Utterson!'

'This is a very strange tale, Poole; this is rather a wild tale, my man,' said Mr Utterson, biting his finger. 'Suppose it were as you suppose, supposing Dr Jekyll to have been—well, murdered, what could induce the murderer to stay? That won't hold water; it doesn't commend itself to reason.'

'Well, Mr Utterson, you are a hard man to satisfy, but I'll do it yet,' said Poole. 'All this last week (you must know) him, or it, or

whatever it is that lives in that cabinet, has been crying night and day
for some sort of medicine and cannot get it to his mind. It was
sometimes his way—the master's, that is—to write his orders on a
sheet of paper and throw it on the stair. We've had nothing else this
week back; nothing but papers, and a closed door, and the very meals
left there to be smuggled in when nobody was looking. Well, sir,
every day, ay, and twice and thrice in the same day, there have been
orders and complaints, and I have been sent flying to all the wholesale chemists in town. Every time I brought the stuff back, there
would be another paper telling me to return it, because it was not
pure, and another order to a different firm. This drug is wanted
bitter bad, sir, whatever for.'

'Have you any of these papers?' asked Mr Utterson.

Poole felt in his pocket and handed out a crumpled note, which
the lawyer, bending nearer to the candle, carefully examined. Its
contents ran thus: 'Dr Jekyll presents his compliments to Messrs
Maw. He assures them that their last sample is impure and quite
useless for his present purpose. In the year 18—, Dr J. purchased a
somewhat large quantity from Messrs M. He now begs them to
search with the most sedulous care, and should any of the same
quality be left, to forward it to him at once. Expense is no consideration. The importance of this to Dr J. can hardly be exaggerated.' So
far the letter had run composedly enough, but here with a sudden
splutter of the pen, the writer's emotion had broken loose. 'For
God's sake,' he had added, 'find me some of the old.'

'This is a strange note,' said Mr Utterson; and then sharply, 'How
do you come to have it open?'

'The man at Maw's was main angry, sir, and he threw it back to me
like so much dirt,' returned Poole.

'This is unquestionably the doctor's hand, do you know?' resumed
the lawyer.

'I thought it looked like it,' said the servant rather sulkily; and
then, with another voice, 'But what matters hand of write,' he said.
'I've seen him!'

'Seen him?' repeated Mr Utterson. 'Well?'

'That's it!' said Poole. 'It was this way. I came suddenly into the
theatre from the garden. It seems he had slipped out to look for this
drug or whatever it is; for the cabinet door was open, and there he
was at the far end of the room digging among the crates. He looked

up when I came in, gave a kind of cry, and whipped upstairs into the cabinet. It was but for one minute that I saw him, but the hair stood upon my head like quills. Sir, if that was my master, why had he a mask upon his face? If it was my master, why did he cry out like a rat, and run from me? I have served him long enough. And then . . .' the man paused and passed his hand over his face.

'These are all very strange circumstances,' said Mr Utterson, 'but I think I begin to see daylight. Your master, Poole, is plainly seized with one of those maladies that both torture and deform the sufferer; hence, for aught I know, the alteration of his voice; hence the mask and his avoidance of his friends; hence his eagerness to find this drug, by means of which the poor soul retains some hope of ultimate recovery—God grant that he be not deceived! There is my explanation; it is sad enough, Poole, ay, and appalling to consider; but it is plain and natural, hangs well together and delivers us from all exorbitant alarms.'

'Sir,' said the butler, turning to a sort of mottled pallor, 'that thing was not my master, and there's the truth. My master'—here he looked round him and began to whisper—'is a tall fine build of a man, and this was more of a dwarf.' Utterson attempted to protest. 'O, sir,' cried Poole, 'do you think I do not know my master after twenty years? do you think I do not know where his head comes to in the cabinet door, where I saw him every morning of my life? No, sir, that thing in the mask was never Doctor Jekyll—God knows what it was, but it was never Doctor Jekyll; and it is the belief of my heart that there was murder done.'

'Poole,' replied the lawyer, 'if you say that, it will become my duty to make certain. Much as I desire to spare your master's feelings, much as I am puzzled by this note which seems to prove him to be still alive, I shall consider it my duty to break in that door.'

'Ah, Mr Utterson, that's talking!' cried the butler.

'And now comes the second question,' resumed Utterson: 'Who is going to do it?'

'Why, you and me, sir,' was the undaunted reply.

'That is very well said,' returned the lawyer; 'and whatever comes of it, I shall make it my business to see you are no loser.'

'There is an axe in the theatre,' continued Poole; 'and you might take the kitchen poker for yourself.'

The lawyer took that rude but weighty instrument into his hand,

and balanced it. 'Do you know Poole,' he said, looking up, 'that you and I are about to place ourselves in a position of some peril?'

'You may say so, sir, indeed,' returned the butler.

'It is well, then, that we should be frank,' said the other. 'We both think more than we have said; let us make a clean breast. This masked figure that you saw, did you recognise it?'

'Well, sir, it went so quick, and the creature was so doubled up, that I could hardly swear to that,' was the answer. 'But if you mean, was it Mr Hyde?—why, yes, I think it was! You see, it was much of the same bigness; and it had the same quick light way with it; and then who else could have got in by the laboratory door? You have not forgot, sir, that at the time of the murder he had still the key with him? But that's not all. I don't know, Mr Utterson, if ever you met this Mr Hyde?'

'Yes,' said the lawyer, 'I once spoke with him.'

'Then you must know as well as the rest of us that there was something queer about that gentleman—something that gave a man a turn—I don't know rightly how to say it, sir, beyond this: that you felt it in your marrow kind of cold and thin.'

'I own I felt something of what you describe,' said Mr Utterson.

'Quite so, sir,' returned Poole. 'Well, when that masked thing like a monkey jumped from among the chemicals and whipped into the cabinet, it went down my spine like ice. O, I know it's not evidence, Mr Utterson; I'm book-learned enough for that; but a man has his feelings, and I give you my bible-word it was Mr Hyde!'

'Ay, ay,' said the lawyer. 'My fears incline to the same point. Evil, I fear, founded—evil was sure to come—of that connection. Ay, truly, I believe you; I believe poor Harry is killed; and I believe his murderer (for what purpose, God alone can tell) is still lurking in his victim's room. Well, let our name be vengeance. Call Bradshaw.'

The footman came at the summons, very white and nervous.

'Pull yourself together, Bradshaw,' said the lawyer. 'This suspense, I know, is telling upon all of you; but it is now our intention to make an end of it. Poole, here, and I are going to force our way into the cabinet. If all is well, my shoulders are broad enough to bear the blame. Meanwhile, lest anything should really be amiss, or any malefactor seek to escape by the back, you and the boy must go round the corner with a pair of good sticks, and take your post at the laboratory door. We give you ten minutes, to get to your stations.'

As Bradshaw left, the lawyer looked at his watch. 'And now, Poole, let us get to ours,' he said; and taking the poker under his arm, he led the way into the yard. The scud had banked over the moon, and it was now quite dark. The wind, which only broke in puffs and draughts into that deep well of building, tossed the light of the candle to and fro about their steps, until they came into the shelter of the theatre, where they sat down silently to wait. London hummed solemnly all around; but nearer at hand, the stillness was only broken by the sound of a footfall moving to and fro along the cabinet floor.

'So it will walk all day, sir,' whispered Poole; 'ay, and the better part of the night. Only when a new sample comes from the chemist, there's a bit of a break. Ah, it's an ill-conscience that's such an enemy to rest! Ah, sir, there's blood foully shed in every step of it! But hark again, a little closer—put your heart in your ears Mr Utterson, and tell me, is that the doctor's foot?'

The steps fell lightly and oddly, with a certain swing, for all they went so slowly; it was different indeed from the heavy creaking tread of Henry Jekyll. Utterson sighed. 'Is there never anything else?' he asked.

Poole nodded. 'Once,' he said. 'Once I heard it weeping!'

'Weeping? how that?' said the lawyer, conscious of a sudden chill of horror.

'Weeping like a woman or a lost soul,' said the butler. 'I came away with that upon my heart, that I could have wept too.'

But now the ten minutes drew to an end. Poole disinterred the axe from under a stack of packing straw; the candle was set upon the nearest table to light them to the attack; and they drew near with bated breath to where that patient foot was still going up and down, up and down, in the quiet of the night.

'Jekyll,' cried Utterson, with a loud voice, 'I demand to see you.' He paused a moment, but there came no reply. 'I give you fair warning, our suspicions are aroused, and I must and shall see you,' he resumed; 'if not by fair means, then by foul—if not of your consent, then by brute force!'

'Utterson,' said the voice, 'for God's sake, have mercy!'

'Ah, that's not Jekyll's voice—it's Hyde's!' cried Utterson. 'Down with the door, Poole.'

Poole swung the axe over his shoulder; the blow shook the building, and the red baize door leaped against the lock and hinges. A dismal screech, as of mere animal terror, rang from the cabinet. Up went the axe again, and again the panels crashed and the frame bounded; four times the blow fell; but the wood was tough and the fittings were of excellent workmanship; and it was not until the fifth, that the lock burst in sunder and the wreck of the door fell inwards on the carpet.

The besiegers, appalled by their own riot and the stillness that had succeeded, stood back a little and peered in. There lay the cabinet before their eyes in the quiet lamplight, a good fire glowing and chattering on the hearth, the kettle singing its thin strain, a drawer or two open, papers neatly set forth on the business table, and nearer the fire, the things laid out for tea: the quietest room, you would have said, and, but for the glazed presses full of chemicals, the most commonplace that night in London.

Right in the midst there lay the body of a man sorely contorted and still twitching. They drew near on tiptoe, turned it on its back and beheld the face of Edward Hyde. He was dressed in clothes far too large for him, clothes of the doctor's bigness; the cords of his face still moved with a semblance of life, but life was quite gone; and by the crushed phial in the hand and the strong smell of kernels that hung upon the air, Utterson knew that he was looking on the body of a self-destroyer.*

'We have come too late,' he said sternly, 'whether to save or punish. Hyde is gone to his account; and it only remains for us to find the body of your master.'

The far greater proportion of the building was occupied by the theatre, which filled almost the whole ground storey and was lighted from above, and by the cabinet, which formed an upper storey at one end and looked upon the court. A corridor joined the theatre to the door on the by-street; and with this, the cabinet communicated separately by a second flight of stairs. There were besides a few dark closets and a spacious cellar. All these they now thoroughly examined. Each closet needed but a glance, for all were empty and all, by the dust that fell from their doors, had stood long unopened. The cellar, indeed, was filled with crazy lumber, mostly dating from the times of the surgeon who was Jekyll's predecessor; but even as they opened the door, they were advertised of the uselessness of further search, by the fall of a perfect mat of cobweb which had for years sealed up the entrance. Nowhere was there any trace of Henry Jekyll, dead or alive.

Poole stamped on the flags of the corridor. 'He must be buried here,' he said, hearkening to the sound.

'Or he may have fled,' said Utterson, and he turned to examine the door in the by-street. It was locked; and lying near by on the flags, they found the key, already stained with rust.

'This does not look like use,' observed the lawyer.

'Use!' echoed Poole. 'Do you not see, sir, it is broken? much as if a man had stamped on it.'

'Ay,' continued Utterson, 'and the fractures, too, are rusty.' The two men looked at each other with a scare. 'This is beyond me, Poole,' said the lawyer. 'Let us go back to the cabinet.'

They mounted the stair in silence, and still with an occasional awestruck glance at the dead body, proceeded more thoroughly to examine the contents of the cabinet. At one table, there were traces of chemical work, various measured heaps of some white salt being laid on glass saucers, as though for an experiment in which the unhappy man had been prevented.

'That is the same drug that I was always bringing him,' said Poole; and even as he spoke, the kettle with a startling noise boiled over.

This brought them to the fireside, where the easy chair was drawn cosily up, and the tea things stood ready to the sitter's elbow, the very sugar in the cup. There were several books on a shelf; one lay beside the tea things open, and Utterson was amazed to find it a copy of a pious work, for which Jekyll had several times expressed a great esteem, annotated, in his own hand, with startling blasphemies.

Next, in the course of their review of the chamber, the searchers came to the cheval glass,* into whose depths they looked with an involuntary horror. But it was so turned as to show them nothing but the rosy glow playing on the roof, the fire sparkling in a hundred repetitions along the glazed front of the presses, and their own pale and fearful countenances stooping to look in.

'This glass have seen some strange things, sir,' whispered Poole.

'And surely none stranger than itself,' echoed the lawyer in the same tones. 'For what did Jekyll'—he caught himself up at the word with a start, and then conquering the weakness: 'what could Jekyll want with it?' he said.

'You may say that!' said Poole.

Next they turned to the business table. On the desk among the neat array of papers, a large envelope was uppermost, and bore, in the doctor's hand, the name of Mr Utterson. The lawyer unsealed it, and several enclosures fell to the floor. The first was a will, drawn in the same eccentric terms as the one which he had returned six months before, to serve as a testament in case of death and as a deed of gift in case of disappearance; but in place of the name of Edward Hyde, the lawyer, with indescribable amazement, read the name of Gabriel John Utterson. He looked at Poole, and then back at the paper, and last of all at the dead malefactor stretched upon the carpet.

'My head goes round,' he said. 'He has been all these days in possession; he had no cause to like me; he must have raged to see himself displaced; and he has not destroyed this document.'

He caught up the next paper; it was a brief note in the doctor's hand and dated at the top. 'O Poole!' the lawyer cried, 'he was alive and here this day. He cannot have been disposed of in so short a space, he must be still alive, he must have fled! And then, why fled? and how? and in that case, can we venture to declare this suicide? O, we must be careful. I foresee that we may yet involve your master in some dire catastrophe.'

'Why don't you read it, sir?' asked Poole.

'Because I fear,' replied the lawyer solemnly. 'God grant I have no cause for it!' And with that he brought the paper to his eyes and read as follows.

'My dear Utterson,—When this shall fall into your hands, I shall have disappeared, under what circumstances I have not the penetration to foresee, but my instinct and all the circumstances of my nameless situation tell me that the end is sure and must be early. Go then, and first read the narrative which Lanyon warned me he was to place in your hands; and if you care to hear more, turn to the confession of

'Your unworthy and unhappy friend,
'HENRY JEKYLL.'

'There was a third enclosure?' asked Utterson.

'Here, sir,' said Poole, and gave into his hands a considerable packet sealed in several places.

The lawyer put it in his pocket. 'I would say nothing of this paper.

If your master has fled or is dead, we may at least save his credit. It is now ten; I must go home and read these documents in quiet; but I shall be back before midnight, when we shall send for the police.'

They went out, locking the door of the theatre behind them; and Utterson, once more leaving the servants gathered about the fire in the hall, trudged back to his office to read the two narratives in which this mystery was now to be explained.

DOCTOR LANYON'S NARRATIVE

ON the ninth of January, now four days ago, I received by the evening delivery a registered envelope, addressed in the hand of my colleague and old school-companion, Henry Jekyll. I was a good deal surprised by this; for we were by no means in the habit of correspondence; I had seen the man, dined with him, indeed, the night before; and I could imagine nothing in our intercourse that should justify the formality of registration. The contents increased my wonder; for this is how the letter ran:

'10th December, 18—

'Dear Lanyon,—You are one of my oldest friends; and although we may have differed at times on scientific questions, I cannot remember, at least on my side, any break in our affection. There was never a day when, if you had said to me, "Jekyll, my life, my honour, my reason, depend upon you," I would not have sacrificed my fortune or my left hand* to help you. Lanyon, my life, my honour, my reason, are all at your mercy; if you fail me tonight, I am lost. You might suppose, after this preface, that I am going to ask you for something dishonourable to grant. Judge for yourself.

'I want you to postpone all other engagements for tonight—ay, even if you were summoned to the bedside of an emperor; to take a cab, unless your carriage should be actually at the door; and with this letter in your hand for consultation, to drive straight to my house. Poole, my butler, has his orders; you will find him waiting your arrival with a locksmith. The door of my cabinet is then to be forced; and you are to go in alone; to open the glazed press (letter E) on the left hand, breaking the lock if it be shut; and to draw out, *with all its contents as they stand*, the fourth drawer from the top or (which is the same thing) the third from the bottom. In my extreme distress of mind, I have a morbid fear of misdirecting you; but even if I am in error, you may know the right drawer by its contents: some powders, a phial and a paper book. This drawer I beg of you to carry back with you to Cavendish Square exactly as it stands.

'That is the first part of the service: now for the second. You should be back, if you set out at once on the receipt of this, long before midnight; but I will leave you that amount of margin, not only in the fear of one of those obstacles that can neither be prevented nor foreseen, but because an hour when your servants are in bed is to be preferred for what will then remain to do. At midnight, then, I have to ask you to be alone in your consulting room, to admit with your own hand into the house a man who will present himself in my name, and to place in his hands the drawer that you will have brought with you from my cabinet. Then you will have played your part and earned my gratitude completely. Five minutes, afterwards, if you insist upon an explanation, you will have understood that these arrangements are of capital importance; and that by the neglect of one of them, fantastic as they must appear, you might have charged your conscience with my death or the shipwreck of my reason.

'Confident as I am that you will not trifle with this appeal, my heart sinks and my hand trembles at the bare thought of such a possibility. Think of me at this hour, in a strange place, labouring under a blackness of distress that no fancy can exaggerate, and yet well aware that, if you will but punctually serve me, my troubles will roll away like a story that is told. Serve me, my dear Lanyon, and save

'Your friend,

H. J.

'P.S. I had already sealed this up when a fresh terror struck upon my soul. It is possible that the post office may fail me, and this letter not come into your hands until tomorrow morning. In that case, dear Lanyon, do my errand when it shall be most convenient for you in the course of the day; and once more expect my messenger at midnight. It may then already be too late; and if that night passes without event, you will know that you have seen the last of Henry Jekyll.'

Upon the reading of this letter, I made sure my colleague was insane; but till that was proved beyond the possibility of doubt, I felt bound to do as he requested. The less I understood of this farrago, the less I was in a position to judge of its importance; and an appeal so worded could not be set aside without a grave responsibility. I rose accordingly from table, got into a hansom, and drove straight to Jekyll's house. The butler was awaiting my arrival; he had received by the same post as mine a registered letter of instruction, and had sent at once for a locksmith and a carpenter. The tradesmen came while we were yet speaking; and we moved in a body to old Dr Denman's surgical theatre, from which (as you are doubtless aware) Jekyll's private cabinet is most conveniently entered. The door was very strong, the lock excellent; the carpenter avowed he would have great trouble and have to do much damage, if force were to be used; and the locksmith was near despair. But this last was a handy fellow, and after two hours' work, the door stood open. The press marked E was unlocked; and I took out the drawer, had it filled up with straw and tied in a sheet, and returned with it to Cavendish Square.

Here I proceeded to examine its contents. The powders were neatly enough made up, but not with the nicety of the dispensing chemist; so that it was plain they were of Jekyll's private manufacture; and when I opened one of the wrappers, I found what seemed to me a simple, crystalline salt of a white colour. The phial, to which I next turned my attention, might have been about half-full of a blood-red liquor, which was highly pungent to the sense of smell and seemed to me to contain phosphorus and some volatile ether. At the other ingredients, I could make no guess. The book was an ordinary version book* and contained little but a series of dates. These covered a period of many years, but I observed that the entries ceased nearly a year ago and quite abruptly. Here and there a brief remark was appended to a date, usually no more than a single word: 'double' occurring perhaps six times in a total of several hundred entries; and once very early in the list and followed by several marks of exclamation, 'total failure!!!' All this, though it whetted my curiosity, told me little that was definite. Here were a phial of some tincture, a paper of some salt, and the record of a series of experiments that had led (like too many of Jekyll's investigations) to no end of practical usefulness. How could the presence of these articles in my house affect either the honour, the sanity, or the life of my flighty colleague? If his messenger could go to one place, why could he not go to another? And even granting some impediment, why was this gentleman to be received by me in secret? The more I reflected, the more convinced I grew that I was dealing with a case of cerebral disease; and though I dismissed my servants to bed, I loaded an old revolver that I might be found in some posture of self-defence.

Twelve o'clock had scarce rung out over London, ere the knocker sounded very gently on the door. I went myself at the summons, and found a small man crouching against the pillars of the portico.

'Are you come from Dr Jekyll?' I asked.

He told me 'yes' by a constrained gesture; and when I had bidden him enter, he did not obey me without a searching backward glance into the darkness of the square. There was a policeman not far off, advancing with his bull's eye* open; and at the sight, I thought my visitor started and made greater haste.

These particulars struck me, I confess, disagreeably; and as I followed him into the bright light of the consulting room, I kept my
hand ready on my weapon. Here, at last, I had a chance of clearly
seeing him. I had never set eyes on him before, so much was certain.
He was small, as I have said; I was struck besides with the shocking
expression of his face, with his remarkable combination of great
muscular activity and great apparent debility of constitution, and—
last but not least—with the old, subjective disturbance caused by his
neighbourhood. This bore some resemblance to incipient rigor,* and
was accompanied by a marked sinking of the pulse. At the time, I set
it down to some idiosyncratic, personal distaste, and merely wondered at the acuteness of the symptoms; but I have since had reason
to believe the cause to lie much deeper in the nature of man, and to
turn on some nobler hinge than the principle of hatred.

This person (who had thus, from the first moment of his entrance,
struck in me what I can only describe as a disgustful curiosity) was
dressed in a fashion that would have made an ordinary person laugh-
able: his clothes, that is to say, although they were of rich and sober
fabric, were enormously too large for him in every measurement—
the trousers hanging on his legs and rolled up to keep them from the
ground, the waist of the coat below his haunches, and the collar
sprawling wide upon his shoulders. Strange to relate, this ludicrous
accoutrement was far from moving me to laughter. Rather, as there
was something abnormal and misbegotten in the very essence of the
creature that now faced me—something seizing, surprising and
revolting—this fresh disparity seemed but to fit in with and to re-
inforce it; so that to my interest in the man's nature and character,
there was added a curiosity as to his origin, his life, his fortune and
status in the world.

These observations, though they have taken so great a space to be
set down in, were yet the work of a few seconds. My visitor was,
indeed, on fire with sombre excitement.

'Have you got it?' he cried. 'Have you got it?' And so lively was his
impatience that he even laid his hand upon my arm and sought to
shake me.

I put him back, conscious at his touch of a certain icy pang along
my blood. 'Come, sir,' said I. 'You forget that I have not yet the
pleasure of your acquaintance. Be seated, if you please.' And I
showed him an example, and sat down myself in my customary seat

and with as fair an imitation of my ordinary manner to a patient, as the lateness of the hour, the nature of my preoccupations, and the horror I had of my visitor, would suffer me to muster.

'I beg your pardon, Dr Lanyon,' he replied civilly enough. 'What you say is very well founded; and my impatience has shown its heels to my politeness. I come here at the instance of your colleague, Dr Henry Jekyll, on a piece of business of some moment; and I understood . . .' he paused and put his hand to his throat, and I could see, in spite of his collected manner, that he was wrestling against the approaches of the hysteria—'I understood, a drawer . . .'

But here I took pity on my visitor's suspense, and some perhaps on my own growing curiosity.

'There it is, sir,' said I, pointing to the drawer, where it lay on the floor behind a table and still covered with the sheet.

He sprang to it, and then paused, and laid his hand upon his heart; I could hear his teeth grate with the convulsive action of his jaws; and his face was so ghastly to see that I grew alarmed both for his life and reason.

'Compose yourself,' said I.

He turned a dreadful smile to me, and as if with the decision of despair, plucked away the sheet. At sight of the contents, he uttered one loud sob of such immense relief that I sat petrified. And the next moment, in a voice that was already fairly well under control, 'Have you a graduated glass?' he asked.

I rose from my place with something of an effort and gave him what he asked.

He thanked me with a smiling nod, measured out a few minims of the red tincture and added one of the powders. The mixture, which was at first of a reddish hue, began, in proportion as the crystals melted, to brighten in colour, to effervesce audibly, and to throw off small fumes of vapour. Suddenly and at the same moment, the ebullition ceased and the compound changed to a dark purple, which faded again more slowly to a watery green. My visitor, who had watched these metamorphoses with a keen eye, smiled, set down the glass upon the table, and then turned and looked upon me with an air of scrutiny.

'And now,' said he, 'to settle what remains. Will you be wise? will you be guided? will you suffer me to take this glass in my hand and to go forth from your house without further parley? or has the greed of curiosity too much command of you? Think before you answer, for it shall be done as you decide. As you decide, you shall be left as you were before, and neither richer nor wiser, unless the sense of service rendered to a man in mortal distress may be counted as a kind of riches of the soul. Or, if you shall so prefer to choose, a new province of knowledge and new avenues to fame and power shall be laid open to you, here, in this room, upon the instant; and your sight shall be blasted by a prodigy to stagger the unbelief of Satan.'*

'Sir,' said I, affecting a coolness that I was far from truly possessing, 'you speak enigmas, and you will perhaps not wonder that I hear you with no very strong impression of belief. But I have gone too far in the way of inexplicable services to pause before I see the end.'

'It is well,' replied my visitor. 'Lanyon, you remember your vows: what follows is under the seal of our profession.* And now, you who have so long been bound to the most narrow and material views, you who have denied the virtue of transcendental medicine, you who have derided your superiors—behold!'

He put the glass to his lips and drank at one gulp. A cry followed; he reeled, staggered, clutched at the table and held on, staring with injected eyes, gasping with open mouth; and as I looked there came, I thought, a change—he seemed to swell—his face became suddenly black and the features seemed to melt and alter—and the next moment, I had sprung to my feet and leaped back against the wall, my arm raised to shield me from that prodigy, my mind submerged in terror.

'O God!' I screamed, and 'O God!' again and again; for there before my eyes—pale and shaken, and half fainting, and groping before him with his hands, like a man restored from death—there stood Henry Jekyll!

What he told me in the next hour, I cannot bring my mind to set on paper. I saw what I saw, I heard what I heard, and my soul sickened at it; and yet now when that sight has faded from my eyes, I ask myself if I believe it, and I cannot answer. My life is shaken to its roots; sleep has left me; the deadliest terror sits by me at all hours of the day and night; I feel that my days are numbered, and that I must die; and yet I shall die incredulous. As for the moral turpitude that man unveiled to me, even with tears of penitence, I cannot, even in memory, dwell on it without a start of horror. I will say but one thing, Utterson, and that (if you can bring your mind to credit it) will be more than enough. The creature who crept into my house that night was, on Jekyll's own confession, known by the name of Hyde and hunted for in every corner of the land as the murderer of Carew.

HASTIE LANYON.

HENRY JEKYLL'S FULL STATEMENT
OF THE CASE

I was born in the year 18— to a large fortune, endowed besides with excellent parts, inclined by nature to industry, fond of the respect of the wise and good among my fellow-men, and thus, as might have been supposed, with every guarantee of an honourable and distinguished future.* And indeed the worst of my faults was a certain impatient gaiety of disposition,* such as has made the happiness of many, but such as I found it hard to reconcile with my imperious desire to carry my head high, and wear a more than commonly grave countenance before the public. Hence it came about that I concealed my pleasures; and that when I reached years of reflection, and began to look round me and take stock of my progress and position in the world, I stood already committed to a profound duplicity of life. Many a man would have even blazoned such irregularities as I was guilty of; but from the high views that I had set before me, I regarded and hid them with an almost morbid sense of shame. It was thus rather the exacting nature of my aspirations than any particular degradation in my faults, that made me what I was and, with even a deeper trench than in the majority of men, severed in me those provinces of good and ill which divide and compound man's dual nature. In this case, I was driven to reflect deeply and inveterately on that hard law of life, which lies at the root of religion and is one of the most plentiful springs of distress. Though so profound a double-dealer, I was in no sense a hypocrite; both sides of me were in dead earnest; I was no more myself when I laid aside restraint and plunged in shame, than when I laboured, in the eye of day, at the furtherance of knowledge or the relief of sorrow and suffering. And it chanced that the direction of my scientific studies, which led wholly towards the mystic and the transcendental,* reacted and shed a strong light on this consciousness of the perennial war among my members.* With every day, and from both sides of my intelligence, the moral and the intellectual, I thus drew steadily nearer to that truth, by whose partial discovery I have been doomed to such a dreadful shipwreck: that man is not truly one, but truly two. I say two, because the state of my own knowledge does not pass beyond that point. Others will follow, others will outstrip me on the same lines; and I hazard the guess that man will be ultimately known for a mere polity of multifarious, incongruous and independent denizens. I for my part, from the nature of my life, advanced infallibly in one direction and in one direction only. It was on the moral side, and in my own person, that I learned to recognise the thorough and primitive duality of man; I saw that, of the two natures that contended in the field of my consciousness, even if I could rightly be said to be either, it was only because I was radically both; and from an early date, even before the course of my scientific discoveries had begun to suggest the most naked possibility of such a miracle, I had learned to dwell with pleasure, as a beloved daydream, on the thought of the separation of these elements. If each, I told myself, could but be housed in separate identities, life would be relieved of all that was unbearable; the unjust might go his way, delivered from the aspirations and remorse of his more upright twin; and the just could walk steadfastly and securely on his upward path, doing the good things in which he found his pleasure, and no longer exposed to disgrace and penitence by the hands of this extraneous evil. It was the curse of mankind that these incongruous faggots were thus bound together—that in the agonised womb of consciousness, these polar twins should be continuously struggling. How, then, were they dissociated?

I was so far in my reflections when, as I have said, a side light began to shine upon the subject from the laboratory table. I began to perceive more deeply than it has ever yet been stated, the trembling immateriality, the mist-like transience, of this seemingly so solid body in which we walk attired. Certain agents I found to have the power to shake and to pluck back that fleshly vestment, even as a wind might toss the curtains of a pavilion. For two good reasons, I will not enter deeply into this scientific branch of my confession. First, because I have been made to learn that the doom and burthen of our life is bound forever on man's shoulders, and when the attempt is made to cast it off, it but returns upon us with more unfamiliar and more awful pressure. Second, because as my narrative will make alas! too evident, my discoveries were incomplete. Enough, then, that I not only recognised my natural body for the mere aura and effulgence of certain of the powers that made up my spirit, but managed to compound a drug by which these powers should be dethroned from their supremacy, and a second form and countenance substituted, none the less natural to me because they were the expression, and bore the stamp, of lower elements in my soul.

I hesitated long before I put this theory to the test of practice. I knew well that I risked death; for any drug that so potently controlled and shook the very fortress of identity, might by the least scruple of an overdose or at the least inopportunity in the moment of exhibition, utterly blot out that immaterial tabernacle which I looked to it to change. But the temptation of a discovery so singular and profound, at last overcame the suggestions of alarm. I had long since prepared my tincture; I purchased at once, from a firm of wholesale chemists, a large quantity of a particular salt which I knew, from my experiments, to be the last ingredient required; and late one accursed night, I compounded the elements, watched them boil and smoke together in the glass, and when the ebullition had subsided, with a strong glow of courage, drank off the potion.

The most racking pangs succeeded: a grinding in the bones, deadly nausea, and a horror of the spirit that cannot be exceeded at the hour of birth or death. Then these agonies began swiftly to subside, and I came to myself as if out of a great sickness. There was something strange in my sensations, something indescribably new and, from its very novelty, incredibly sweet. I felt younger, lighter, happier in body; within I was conscious of a heady recklessness, a current of disordered sensual images running like a mill race in my fancy, a solution of the bonds of obligation, an unknown but not an innocent freedom of the soul. I knew myself, at the first breath of this new life, to be more wicked, tenfold more wicked, sold a slave to my original evil; and the thought, in that moment, braced and delighted me like wine. I stretched out my hands, exulting in the freshness of these sensations; and in the act, I was suddenly aware that I had lost in stature.

There was no mirror, at that date, in my room; that which stands beside me as I write, was brought there later on and for the very purpose of these transformations. The night, however, was far gone into the morning—the morning, black as it was, was nearly ripe for the conception of the day—the inmates of my house were locked in the most rigorous hours of slumber; and I determined, flushed as I was with hope and triumph, to venture in my new shape as far as to my bedroom. I crossed the yard, wherein the constellations looked down upon me, I could have thought, with wonder, the first creature of that sort that their unsleeping vigilance had yet disclosed to them; I stole through the corridors, a stranger in my own house; and coming to my room, I saw for the first time the appearance of Edward Hyde.

I must here speak by theory alone, saying not that which I know, but that which I suppose to be most probable. The evil side of my nature, to which I had now transferred the stamping efficacy, was less robust and less developed than the good which I had just deposed. Again, in the course of my life, which had been, after all, nine tenths a life of effort, virtue and control, it had been much less exercised and much less exhausted. And hence, as I think, it came about that Edward Hyde was so much smaller, slighter and younger than Henry Jekyll. Even as good shone upon the countenance of the one, evil was written broadly and plainly on the face of the other. Evil besides (which I must still believe to be the lethal side of man) had left on that body an imprint of deformity and decay. And yet when I looked upon that ugly idol in the glass, I was conscious of no repugnance, rather of a leap of welcome. This, too, was myself. It seemed natural and human. In my eyes it bore a livelier image of the spirit, it seemed more express and single, than the imperfect and divided countenance, I had been hitherto accustomed to call mine. And in so far I was doubtless right. I have observed that when I wore the semblance of Edward Hyde, none could come near to me at first without a visible misgiving of the flesh. This, as I take it, was because all human beings, as we meet them, are commingled out of good and evil: and Edward Hyde, alone in the ranks of mankind, was pure evil.

I lingered but a moment at the mirror: the second and conclusive experiment had yet to be attempted; it yet remained to be seen if I had lost my identity beyond redemption and must flee before daylight from a house that was no longer mine; and hurrying back to my cabinet, I once more prepared and drank the cup, once more suffered the pangs of dissolution, and came to myself once more with the character, the stature and the face of Henry Jekyll.

That night I had come to the fatal cross roads. Had I approached my discovery in a more noble spirit, had I risked the experiment while under the empire of generous or pious aspirations, all must have been otherwise, and from these agonies of death and birth, I

had come forth an angel instead of a fiend. The drug had no dis-
criminating action; it was neither diabolical nor divine; it but shook
the doors of the prisonhouse of my disposition; and like the captives
of Philippi,* that which stood within ran forth. At that time my virtue
slumbered; my evil, kept awake by ambition, was alert and swift to
seize the occasion; and the thing that was projected was Edward
Hyde. Hence, although I had now two characters as well as two
appearances, one was wholly evil, and the other was still the old
Henry Jekyll, that incongruous compound of whose reformation and
improvement I had already learned to despair. The movement was
thus wholly toward the worse.

Even at that time, I had not yet conquered my aversion to the
dryness of a life of study. I would still be merrily disposed at times;
and as my pleasures were (to say the least) undignified, and I was not
only well known and highly considered, but growing towards the
elderly man, this incoherency of my life was daily growing more
unwelcome. It was on this side that my new power tempted me until
I fell in slavery. I had but to drink the cup, to doff at once the body of
the noted professor, and to assume, like a thick cloak, that of Edward
Hyde. I smiled at the notion; it seemed to me at the time to be
humorous; and I made my preparations with the most studious care.
I took and furnished that house in Soho, to which Hyde was tracked
by the police; and engaged as housekeeper a creature whom I well
knew to be silent and unscrupulous. On the other side, I announced
to my servants that a Mr Hyde (whom I described) was to have full
liberty and power about my house in the square; and to parry mis-
haps, I even called and made myself a familiar object, in my second
character. I next drew up that will to which you so much objected; so
that if anything befell me in the person of Doctor Jekyll, I could
enter on that of Edward Hyde without pecuniary loss. And thus
fortified, as I supposed, on every side, I began to profit by the strange
immunities of my position.

Men have before hired bravos* to transact their crimes, while their
own person and reputation sat under shelter. I was the first that ever
did so for his pleasures. I was the first that could thus plod in the
public eye with a load of genial respectability, and in a moment, like a
schoolboy, strip off these lendings and spring headlong into the sea
of liberty. But for me, in my impenetrable mantle, the safety was
complete. Think of it—I did not even exist! Let me but escape into

my laboratory door, give me but a second or two to mix and swallow the draught that I had always standing ready; and whatever he had done, Edward Hyde would pass away like the stain of breath upon a mirror; and there in his stead, quietly at home, trimming the midnight lamp in his study, a man who could afford to laugh at suspicion, would be Henry Jekyll.

The pleasures which I made haste to seek in my disguise were, as I have said, undignified; I would scarce use a harder term. But in the hands of Edward Hyde, they soon began to turn towards the monstrous. When I would come back from these excursions, I was often plunged into a kind of wonder at my vicarious depravity. This familiar that I called out of my own soul, and sent forth alone to do his good pleasure, was a being inherently malign and villainous; his every act and thought centered on self; drinking pleasure with bestial avidity from any degree of torture to another; relentless like a man of stone. Henry Jekyll stood at times aghast before the acts of Edward Hyde; but the situation was apart from ordinary laws, and insidiously relaxed the grasp of conscience. It was Hyde, after all, and Hyde alone, that was guilty. Jekyll was no worse; he woke again to his good qualities seemingly unimpaired; he would even make haste, where it was possible, to undo the evil done by Hyde. And thus his conscience slumbered.

Into the details of the infamy at which I thus connived (for even now I can scarce grant that I committed it) I have no design of entering; I mean but to point out the warnings and the successive steps with which my chastisement approached. I met with one accident which, as it brought on no consequence, I shall no more than mention. An act of cruelty to a child aroused against me the anger of a passer by, whom I recognised the other day in the person of your kinsman; the doctor and the child's family joined him; there were moments when I feared for my life; and at last, in order to pacify their too just resentment, Edward Hyde had to bring them to the door, and pay them in a cheque drawn in the name, of Henry Jekyll. But this danger was easily eliminated from the future, by opening an account at another bank in the name of Edward Hyde himself; and when, by sloping my own hand backward,* I had supplied my double with a signature, I thought I sat beyond the reach of fate.

Some two months before the murder of Sir Danvers, I had been out for one of my adventures, had returned at a late hour, and woke

the next day in bed with somewhat odd sensations. It was in vain I
looked about me; in vain I saw the decent furniture and tall proportions of my room in the square; in vain that I recognised the pattern
of the bed curtains and the design of the mahogany frame; something still kept insisting that I was not where I was, that I had not
wakened where I seemed to be, but in the little room in Soho where I
was accustomed to sleep in the body of Edward Hyde. I smiled to
myself, and, in my psychological way, began lazily to inquire into the
elements of this illusion, occasionally, even as I did so, dropping back
into a comfortable morning doze. I was still so engaged when, in one
of my more wakeful moments, my eye fell upon my hand. Now the
hand of Henry Jekyll (as you have often remarked) was professional
in shape and size: it was large, firm, white and comely. But the hand
which I now saw, clearly enough, in the yellow light of a mid-
London morning, lying half shut on the bed clothes, was lean,
corded, knuckly, of a dusky pallor and thickly shaded with a swart
growth of hair. It was the hand of Edward Hyde.

I must have stared upon it for near half a minute, sunk as I was in
the mere stupidity of wonder, before terror woke up in my breast as
sudden and startling as the crash of cymbals; and bounding from my
bed, I rushed to the mirror. At the sight that met my eyes, my blood
was changed into something exquisitely thin and icy. Yes, I had gone
to bed Henry Jekyll, I had awakened Edward Hyde. How was this to
be explained? I asked myself; and then, with another bound of terror—how was it to be remedied? It was well on in the morning; the
servants were up; all my drugs were in the cabinet—a long journey,
down two pair of stairs, through the back passage, across the open
court and through the anatomical theatre, from where I was then
standing horror-struck. It might indeed be possible to cover my face;
but of what use was that, when I was unable to conceal the alteration
in my stature? And then with an overpowering sweetness of relief, it
came back upon my mind that the servants were already used to the
coming and going of my second self. I had soon dressed, as well as I
was able, in clothes of my own size: had soon passed through the
house, where Bradshaw stared and drew back at seeing Mr Hyde at
such an hour and in such a strange array; and ten minutes later,
Dr Jekyll had returned to his own shape and was sitting down, with a
darkened brow, to make a feint of breakfasting.

Small indeed was my appetite. This inexplicable incident, this reversal of my previous experience, seemed, like the Babylonian finger on the wall,* to be spelling out the letters of my judgment; and I began to reflect more seriously than ever before on the issues and possibilities of my double existence. That part of me which I had the power of projecting, had lately been much exercised and nourished; it had seemed to me of late as though the body of Edward Hyde had grown in stature, as though (when I wore that form) I were conscious of a more generous tide of blood; and I began to spy a danger that, if this were much prolonged, the balance of my nature might be permanently overthrown, the power of voluntary change be forfeited, and the character of Edward Hyde become irrevocably mine. The power of the drug had not been always equally displayed. Once, very early in my career, it had totally failed me; since then I had been obliged on more than one occasion to double, and once, with infinite risk of death, to treble the amount; and these rare uncertainties had cast hitherto the sole shadow on my contentment. Now, however, and in the light of that morning's accident, I was led to remark that whereas, in the beginning, the difficulty had been to throw off the body of Jekyll, it had of late, gradually but decidedly transferred itself to the other side. All things therefore seemed to point to this: that I was slowly losing hold of my original and better self, and becoming slowly incorporated with my second and worse.

Between these two, I now felt I had to choose. My two natures had memory in common, but all other faculties were most unequally shared between them. Jekyll (who was composite) now with the most sensitive apprehensions, now with a greedy gusto, projected and shared in the pleasures and adventures of Hyde; but Hyde was indifferent to Jekyll, or but remembered him as the mountain bandit remembers the cavern in which he conceals himself from pursuit. Jekyll had more than a father's interest; Hyde had more than a son's indifference. To cast in my lot with Jekyll, was to die to those appetites which I had long secretly indulged and had of late begun to pamper. To cast it in with Hyde, was to die to a thousand interests and aspirations, and to become, at a blow and forever, despised and friendless. The bargain might appear unequal; but there was still another consideration in the scales; for while Jekyll would suffer smartingly in the fires of abstinence, Hyde would be not even conscious of all that he had lost. Strange as my circumstances were, the terms of this debate are as old and commonplace as man; much the

same inducements and alarms cast the die for any tempted and trembling sinner; and it fell out with me, as it falls with so vast a majority
of my fellows, that I chose the better part and was found wanting in
the strength to keep to it.

Yes, I preferred the elderly and discontented doctor, surrounded
by friends and cherishing honest hopes; and bade a resolute farewell
to the liberty, the comparative youth, the light step, leaping pulses
and secret pleasures, that I had enjoyed in the disguise of Hyde. I
made this choice perhaps with some unconscious reservation, for
I neither gave up the house in Soho, nor destroyed the clothes of
Edward Hyde, which still lay ready in my cabinet. For two months,
however, I was true to my determination; for two months, I led a life
of such severity as I had never before attained to, and enjoyed the
compensations of an approving conscience. But time began at last to
obliterate the freshness of my alarm; the praises of conscience began
to grow into a thing of course; I began to be tortured with throes and
longings, as of Hyde struggling after freedom; and at last, in an hour
of moral weakness, I once again compounded and swallowed the
transforming draught.

I do not suppose that, when a drunkard reasons with himself upon
his vice, he is once out of five hundred times affected by the dangers
that he runs through his brutish, physical insensibility; neither had I,
long as I had considered my position, made enough allowance for the
complete moral insensibility and insensate readiness to evil, which
were the leading characters of Edward Hyde. Yet it was by these that
I was punished. My devil had been long caged, he came out roaring.*
I was conscious, even when I took the draught, of a more unbridled,
a more furious propensity to ill. It must have been this, I suppose,
that stirred in my soul that tempest of impatience with which I
listened to the civilities of my unhappy victim; I declare at least,
before God, no man morally sane* could have been guilty of that
crime upon so pitiful a provocation; and that I struck in no more
reasonable spirit than that in which a sick child may break a play-
thing. But I had voluntarily stripped myself of all those balancing
instincts, by which even the worst of us continues to walk with some
degree of steadiness among temptations; and in my case, to be
tempted, however slightly, was to fall.

Instantly the spirit of hell awoke in me and raged. With a trans-
port of glee, I mauled the unresisting body, tasting delight from

every blow; and it was not till weariness had begun to succeed, that I was suddenly, in the top fit of my delirium, struck through the heart by a cold thrill of terror. A mist dispersed; I saw my life to be forfeit; and fled from the scene of these excesses, at once glorying and trembling, my lust of evil gratified and stimulated, my love of life screwed to the topmost peg. I ran to the house in Soho, and (to make assurance doubly sure) destroyed my papers; thence I set out through the lamplit streets, in the same divided ecstasy of mind, gloating on my crime, light-headedly devising others in the future, and yet still hastening and still hearkening in my wake for the steps of the avenger. Hyde had a song upon his lips as he compounded the draught, and as he drank it, pledged the dead man. The pangs of transformation had not done tearing him, before Henry Jekyll, with streaming tears of gratitude and remorse, had fallen upon his knees and lifted his clasped hands to God. The veil of self-indulgence was rent* from head to foot, I saw my life as a whole: I followed it up from the days of childhood, when I had walked with my father's hand, and through the self-denying toils of my professional life, to arrive again and again, with the same sense of unreality, at the damned horrors of the evening. I could have screamed aloud; I sought with tears and prayers to smother down the crowd of hideous images and sounds with which my memory swarmed against me; and still, between the petitions, the ugly face of my iniquity stared into my soul. As the acuteness of this remorse began to die away, it was succeeded by a sense of joy. The problem of my conduct was solved. Hyde was thenceforth impossible; whether I would or not, I was now confined to the better part of my existence; and O, how I rejoiced to think it! with what willing humility, I embraced anew the restrictions of natural life! with what sincere renunciation, I locked the door by which I had so often gone and come, and ground the key under my heel!

The next day, came the news that the murder had been overlooked, that the guilt of Hyde was patent to the world, and that the victim was a man high in public estimation. It was not only a crime, it had been a tragic folly. I think I was glad to know it; I think I was glad to have my better impulses thus buttressed and guarded by the terrors of the scaffold. Jekyll was now my city of refuge; let but Hyde peep out an instant, and the hands of all men would be raised to take and slay him.

I resolved in my future conduct to redeem the past; and I can say with honesty that my resolve was fruitful of some good. You know yourself how earnestly in the last months of last year, I laboured to relieve suffering; you know that much was done for others, and that the days passed quietly, almost happily for myself. Nor can I truly say that I wearied of this beneficent and innocent life; I think instead that I daily enjoyed it more completely; but I was still cursed with my duality of purpose; and as the first edge of my penitence wore off, the lower side of me, so long indulged, so recently chained down, began to growl for license. Not that I dreamed of resuscitating Hyde; the bare idea of that would startle me to frenzy: no, it was in my own person, that I was once more tempted to trifle with my conscience; and it was as an ordinary secret sinner, that I at last fell before the assaults of temptation.

There comes an end to all things; the most capacious measure is filled at last; and this brief condescension to my evil finally destroyed the balance of my soul. And yet I was not alarmed; the fall seemed natural, like a return to the old days before I had made my discovery. It was a fine, clear, January day, wet under foot where the frost had melted, but cloudless overhead; and the Regent's park was full of winter chirruppings and sweet with Spring odours. I sat in the sun on a bench; the animal within me licking the chops of memory; the spiritual side a little drowsed, promising subsequent penitence, but not yet moved to begin. After all, I reflected I was like my neighbours; and then I smiled, comparing myself with other men, comparing my active goodwill with the lazy cruelty of their neglect. And at the very moment of that vainglorious thought, a qualm came over me, a horrid nausea and the most deadly shuddering. These passed away, and left me faint; and then as in its turn the faintness subsided, I began to be aware of a change in the temper of my thoughts, a greater boldness, a contempt of danger, a solution of the bonds of obligation. I looked down; my clothes hung formlessly on my shrunken limbs; the hand that lay on my knee was corded and hairy. I was once more Edward Hyde. A moment before I had been safe of all men's respect, wealthy, beloved—the cloth laying for me in the dining room at home; and now I was the common quarry of mankind, hunted, houseless, a known murderer, thrall to the gallows.

My reason wavered, but it did not fail me utterly. I have more than once observed that, in my second character, my faculties seemed sharpened to a point and my spirits more tensely elastic; thus it came about that, where Jekyll perhaps might have succumbed, Hyde rose to the importance of the moment. My drugs were in one of the presses of my cabinet; how was I to reach them? That was the problem that (crushing my temples in my hands) I set myself to solve. The laboratory door I had closed. If I sought to enter by the house, my own servants would consign me to the gallows. I saw I must employ another hand, and thought of Lanyon. How was he to be reached? how persuaded? Supposing that I escaped capture in the streets, how was I to make my way into his presence? and how should I, an unknown and displeasing visitor, prevail on the famous physician to rifle the study of his colleague, Dr Jekyll? Then I remembered that of my original character, one part remained to me: I could write my own hand; and once I had conceived that kindling spark, the way that I must follow became lighted up from end to end.

Thereupon, I arranged my clothes as best I could, and summoning a passing hansom, drove to an hotel in Portland street, the name of which I chanced to remember. At my appearance (which was indeed comical enough, however tragic a fate these garments covered) the driver could not conceal his mirth. I gnashed my teeth upon him with a gust of devilish fury; and the smile withered from his face—happily for him—yet more happily for myself, for in another instant I had certainly dragged him from his perch. At the inn, as I entered, I looked about me with so black a countenance as made the attendants tremble; not a look did they exchange in my presence; but obsequiously took my orders, led me to a private room, and brought me wherewithal to write. Hyde in danger of his life was a creature new to me: shaken with inordinate anger, strung to the pitch of murder, lusting to inflict pain. Yet the creature was astute; mastered his fury with a great effort of the will; composed his two important letters, one to Lanyon and one to Poole; and that he might receive actual evidence of their being posted, sent them out with directions that they should be registered.

Thenceforward, he sat all day over the fire in the private room; gnawing his nails; there he dined, sitting alone with his fears, the waiter visibly quailing before his eye; and thence, when the night was fully come, he set forth in the corner of a closed cab, and was driven to and fro about the streets of the city. He, I say—I cannot say, I. That child of Hell had nothing human; nothing lived in him but fear and hatred. And when at last, thinking the driver had begun to grow suspicious, he discharged the cab and ventured on foot, attired in his misfitting clothes, an object marked out for observation, into the midst of the nocturnal passengers, these two base passions raged within him like a tempest. He walked fast, hunted by his fears, chattering to himself, skulking through the less frequented thoroughfares, counting the minutes that still divided him from midnight. Once a woman spoke to him, offering, I think, a box of lights. He smote her in the face, and she fled.

When I came to myself at Lanyon's, the horror of my old friend perhaps affected me somewhat: I do not know; it was at least but a drop in the sea to the abhorrence with which I looked back upon these hours. A change had come over me. It was no longer the fear of the gallows, it was the horror of being Hyde that racked me. I received Lanyon's condemnation partly in a dream; it was partly in a dream that I came home to my own house and got into bed. I slept after the prostration of the day, with a stringent and profound slumber which not even the nightmares that wrung me could avail to break. I awoke in the morning shaken, weakened, but refreshed. I still hated and feared the thought of the brute that slept within me, and I had not of course forgotten the appalling dangers of the day before; but I was once more at home, in my own house and close to my drugs; and gratitude for my escape shone so strong in my soul that it almost rivalled the brightness of hope.

I was stepping leisurely across the court after breakfast, drinking the chill of the air with pleasure, when I was seized again with those indescribable sensations that heralded the change; and I had but the time to gain the shelter of my cabinet, before I was once again raging and freezing with the passions of Hyde. It took on this occasion a double dose to recall me to myself; and alas, six hours after, as I sat looking sadly in the fire, the pangs returned, and the drug had to be re-administered. In short, from that day forth it seemed only by a great effort as of gymnastics, and only under the immediate stimulation of the drug, that I was able to wear the countenance of Jekyll. At all hours of the day and night, I would be taken with the premonitory shudder; above all, if I slept, or even dozed for a moment in my chair, it was always as Hyde that I awakened. Under the strain of this continually impending doom and by the sleeplessness to which I now condemned myself, ay, even beyond what I had thought possible to man, I became, in my own person, a creature eaten up and emptied by fever, languidly weak both in body and mind, and solely occupied by one thought: the horror of my other self.* But when I slept, or when the virtue of the medicine wore off, I would leap almost without transition (for the pangs of transformation grew daily less marked) into the possession of a fancy brimming with images of terror, a soul boiling with causeless hatreds, and a body that seemed not strong enough to contain the raging energies of life. The powers of Hyde seemed to have grown with the sickliness of Jekyll. And certainly the hate that now divided them was equal on each side. With Jekyll, it was a thing of vital instinct. He had now seen the full deformity of that creature that shared with him some of the phenomena of consciousness, and was co-heir with him to death: and beyond these links of community, which in themselves made the most poignant part of his distress, he thought of Hyde, for all his energy of life, as of something not only hellish but inorganic. This was the shocking thing; that the slime of the pit seemed to utter cries and voices; that the amorphous dust gesticulated and sinned; that what was dead, and had no shape, should usurp the offices of life. And this again, that that insurgent horror was knit to him closer than a wife, closer than an eye; lay caged in his flesh, where he heard it mutter and felt it struggle to be born; and at every hour of weakness, and in the confidence of slumber, prevailed against him, and deposed him out of life. The hatred of Hyde for Jekyll, was of a different order. His terror of the gallows drove him continually to commit temporary suicide, and return to his subordinate station of a part instead of a person; but he loathed the necessity, he loathed the despondency into which Jekyll was now fallen, and he resented the dislike with which he was himself regarded. Hence the apelike tricks that he would play me, scrawling in my own hand blasphemies on the pages of my books, burning the letters and destroying the portrait of my father; and indeed, had it not been for his fear of death, he would long ago have ruined himself in order to involve me in the ruin. But his love of life is wonderful; I go further: I, who sicken and freeze at the mere thought of him, when I recall the abjection and passion of this attachment, and when I know how he fears my power to cut him off by suicide, I find it in my heart to pity him.

It is useless, and the time awfully fails me, to prolong this description; no one has ever suffered such torments, let that suffice; and yet even to these, habit brought—no, not alleviation—but a certain

callousness of soul, a certain acquiescence of despair; and my punishment might have gone on for years, but for the last calamity which
has now fallen, and which has finally severed me from my own face
and nature. My provision of the salt, which had never been renewed
since the date of the first experiment, began to run low. I sent out for
a fresh supply, and mixed the draught; the ebullition followed, and
the first change of colour, not the second; I drank it and it was
without efficiency. You will learn from Poole how I have had London
ransacked; it was in vain; and I am now persuaded that my first
supply was impure, and that it was that unknown impurity which
lent efficacy to the draught.

About a week has passed, and I am now finishing this statement
under the influence of the last of the old powders. This, then, is the
last time, short of a miracle, that Henry Jekyll can think his own
thoughts or see his own face (now how sadly altered!) in the glass.
Nor must I delay too long to bring my writing to an end; for if my
narrative has hitherto escaped destruction, it has been by a combination of great prudence and great good luck. Should the throes of
change take me in the act of writing it, Hyde will tear it in pieces; but
if some time shall have elapsed after I have laid it by, his wonderful
selfishness and circumscription to the moment will probably save it
once again from the action of his apelike spite. And indeed the doom
that is closing on us both, has already changed and crushed him.
Half an hour from now, when I shall again and forever reindue that
hated personality, I know how I shall sit shuddering and weeping in
my chair, or continue, with the most strained and fearstruck ecstasy
of listening, to pace up and down this room (my last earthly refuge)
and give ear to every sound of menace. Will Hyde die upon the
scaffold? or will he find the courage to release himself at the last
moment? God knows; I am careless; this is my true hour of death,
and what is to follow concerns another than myself. Here then, as I
lay down the pen and proceed to seal up my confession, I bring the
life of that unhappy Henry Jekyll to an end.

THE BODY SNATCHER

EVERY night in the year, four of us sat in the small parlour of the George at Debenham—the undertaker, and the landlord, and Fettes, and myself. Sometimes there would be more; but blow high, blow low, come rain or snow or frost, we four would be each planted in his own particular armchair. Fettes was an old drunken Scotsman, a man of education obviously, and a man of some property, since he lived in idleness. He had come to Debenham years ago, while still young, and by a mere continuance of living had grown to be an adopted towns-man. His blue camlet cloak* was a local antiquity, like the church spire. His place in the parlour at the George, his absence from church, his old, crapulous, disreputable vices, were all things of course in Debenham. He had some vague Radical opinions and some fleeting infidelities, which he would now and again set forth and emphasise with tottering slaps upon the table. He drank rum—five glasses regularly every evening; and for the greater portion of his nightly visit to the George sat, with his glass in his right hand, in a state of melancholy alcoholic saturation. We called him the Doctor, for he was supposed to have some special knowledge of medicine, and had been known, upon a pinch, to set a fracture or reduce a dislocation; but, beyond these slight particulars, we had no know-ledge of his character and antecedents.

One dark winter night—it had struck nine some time before the landlord joined us—there was a sick man in the George, a great neighbouring proprietor suddenly struck down with apoplexy on his way to Parliament; and the great man's still greater London doctor had been telegraphed to his bedside. It was the first time that such a thing had happened in Debenham, for the railway was but newly open, and we were all proportionately moved by the occurrence.

'He's come,' said the landlord, after he had filled and lighted his pipe.

'He?' said I. 'Who?—not the doctor?'

'Himself,' replied our host.

'What is his name?'

'Dr Macfarlane,' said the landlord.

Fettes was far through his third tumbler, stupidly fuddled, now nodding over, now staring mazily around him; but at the last word he seemed to awaken, and repeated the name 'Macfarlane' twice, quietly enough the first time, but with sudden emotion at the second.

'Yes,' said the landlord, 'that's his name, Dr Wolfe Macfarlane.'

Fettes became instantly sober; his eyes awoke, his voice became clear, loud, and steady, his language forcible and earnest. We were all startled by the transformation, as if a man had risen from the dead.

'I beg your pardon,' he said; 'I am afraid I have not been paying much attention to your talk. Who is this Wolfe Macfarlane?' And then, when he had heard the landlord out, 'It cannot be, it cannot be,' he added; 'and yet I would like well to see him face to face.'

'Do you know him, Doctor?' asked the undertaker, with a gasp.

'God forbid!' was the reply. 'And yet the name is a strange one; it were too much to fancy two. Tell me, landlord, is he old?'

'Well,' said the host, 'he's not a young man, to be sure, and his hair is white; but he looks younger than you.'

'He is older, though; years older. But,' with a slap upon the table, 'it's the rum you see in my face—rum and sin. This man, perhaps, may have an easy conscience and a good digestion. Conscience! Hear me speak. You would think I was some good, old, decent Christian, would you not? But no, not I; I never canted. Voltaire might have canted* if he'd stood in my shoes; but the brains'—with a rattling fillip on his bald head—'the brains were clear and active, and I saw and made no deductions.'

'If you know this doctor,' I ventured to remark, after a somewhat awful pause, 'I should gather that you do not share the landlord's good opinion.'

Fettes paid no regard to me.

'Yes,' he said, with sudden decision, 'I must see him face to face.'

There was another pause, and then a door was closed rather sharply on the first floor, and a step was heard upon the stair.

'That's the doctor,' cried the landlord. 'Look sharp, and you can catch him.'

It was but two steps from the small parlour to the door of the old George Inn; the wide oak staircase landed almost in the street; there was room for a Turkey rug and nothing more between the threshold and the last round of the descent; but this little space was every evening brilliantly lit up, not only by the light upon the stair and the great signal-lamp below the sign, but by the warm radiance of the bar-room window. The George thus brightly advertised itself to passers-by in the cold street. Fettes walked steadily to the spot, and we, who were hanging behind, beheld the two men meet, as one of them had phrased it, face to face. Dr Macfarlane was alert and vigorous. His white hair set off his pale and placid, although energetic, countenance. He was richly dressed in the finest of broadcloth and the whitest of linen, with a great gold watch-chain, and studs and spectacles of the same precious material. He wore a broad-folded tie, white and speckled with lilac, and he carried on his arm a comfortable driving-coat of fur. There was no doubt but he became his years, breathing, as he did, of wealth and consideration; and it was a surprising contrast to see our parlour sot—bald, dirty, pimpled, and robed in his old camlet cloak—confront him at the bottom of the stairs.

'Macfarlane!' he said somewhat loudly, more like a herald than a friend.

The great doctor pulled up short on the fourth step, as though the familiarity of the address surprised and somewhat shocked his dignity.

'Toddy Macfarlane!' repeated Fettes.

The London man almost staggered. He stared for the swiftest of seconds at the man before him, glanced behind him with a sort of scare, and then in a startled whisper, 'Fettes!' he said, 'you!'

'Ay,' said the other, 'me! Did you think I was dead, too? We are not so easy shut of our acquaintance.'

'Hush, hush!' exclaimed the doctor. 'Hush, hush! this meeting is so unexpected—I can see you are unmanned. I hardly knew you, I confess, at first; but I am overjoyed—overjoyed to have this opportunity. For the present it must be how-d'ye-do and goodbye in one, for my fly* is waiting, and I must not fail the train; but you shall—let me see—yes—you shall give me your address, and you can count on early news of me. We must do something for you, Fettes. I fear you are out at elbows; but we must see to that for auld lang syne, as once we sang at suppers.'

'Money!' cried Fettes; 'money from you! The money that I had from you is lying where I cast it in the rain.'

Dr Macfarlane had talked himself into some measure of superiority and confidence, but the uncommon energy of this refusal cast him back into his first confusion.

A horrible, ugly look came and went across his almost venerable countenance. 'My dear fellow,' he said, 'be it as you please; my last thought is to offend you. I would intrude on none. I will leave you my address, however—'

'I do not wish it—I do not wish to know the roof that shelters you,' interrupted the other. 'I heard your name; I feared it might be you; I wished to know if, after all, there were a God; I know now that there is none. Begone!'

He still stood in the middle of the rug, between the stair and doorway; and the great London physician, in order to escape, would be forced to step to one side. It was plain that he hesitated before the thought of this humiliation. White as he was, there was a dangerous glitter in his spectacles; but, while he still paused uncertain, he became aware that the driver of his fly was peering in from the street at this unusual scene, and caught a glimpse at the same time of our little body from the parlour, huddled by the corner of the bar. The presence of so many witnesses decided him at once to flee. He crouched together, brushing on the wainscot, and made a dart like a serpent, striking for the door. But his tribulation was not yet entirely at an end, for even as he was passing Fettes clutched him by the arm and these words came in a whisper, and yet painfully distinct, 'Have you seen it again?'

The great rich London doctor cried out aloud with a sharp, throttling cry; he dashed his questioner across the open space, and, with his hands over his head, fled out of the door like a detected thief. Before it had occurred to one of us to make a movement the fly was already rattling toward the station. The scene was over like a dream, but the dream had left proofs and traces of its passage. Next day the servant found the fine gold spectacles broken on the threshold, and that very night we were all standing breathless by the barroom window, and Fettes at our side, sober, pale, and resolute in look.

'God protect us, Mr Fettes!' said the landlord, coming first into possession of his customary senses. 'What in the universe is all this? These are strange things you have been saying.'

Fettes turned toward us; he looked us each in succession in the face. 'See if you can hold your tongues,' said he. 'That man

Macfarlane is not safe to cross; those that have done so already have repented it too late.'

And then, without so much as finishing his third glass, far less waiting for the other two, he bade us goodbye and went forth, under the lamp of the hotel, into the black night.

We three turned to our places in the parlour, with the big red fire and four clear candles; and, as we recapitulated what had passed, the first chill of our surprise soon changed into a glow of curiosity. We sat late; it was the latest session I have known in the old George. Each man, before we parted, had his theory that he was bound to prove; and none of us had any nearer business in this world than to track out the past of our condemned companion, and surprise the secret that he shared with the great London doctor. It is no great boast, but I believe I was a better hand at worming out a story than either of my fellows at the George; and perhaps there is now no other man alive who could narrate to you the following foul and unnatural events.

In his young days Fettes studied medicine in the schools of Edinburgh. He had talent of a kind, the talent that picks up swiftly what it hears and readily retails it for its own. He worked little at home; but he was civil, attentive, and intelligent in the presence of his masters. They soon picked him out as a lad who listened closely and remembered well; nay, strange as it seemed to me when I first heard it, he was in those days well favoured, and pleased by his exterior. There was, at that period, a certain extramural teacher of anatomy, whom I shall here designate by the letter K. His name was subsequently too well known. The man who bore it skulked through the streets of Edinburgh in disguise, while the mob that applauded at the execution of Burke called loudly for the blood of his employer. But Mr K—— was then at the top of his vogue;* he enjoyed a popularity due partly to his own talent and address, partly to the incapacity of his rival, the university professor. The students, at least, swore by his name, and Fettes believed himself, and was believed by others, to have laid the foundations of success when he had acquired the favour of this meteorically famous man. Mr K—— was a *bon vivant* as well as an accomplished teacher; he liked a sly illusion no less than a careful preparation. In both capacities Fettes enjoyed and deserved his notice, and by the second year of his attendance he held the half-regular position of second demonstrator or sub-assistant in his class.

In this capacity the charge of the theatre and lecture-room devolved in particular upon his shoulders. He had to answer for the cleanliness of the premises and the conduct of the other students, and it was a part of his duty to supply, receive, and divide the various subjects. It was with a view to this last—at that time very delicate—affair that he was lodged by Mr K—— in the same wynd,* and at last in the same building, with the dissecting-rooms. Here, after a night of turbulent pleasures, his hand still tottering, his sight still misty and confused, he would be called out of bed in the black hours before the winter dawn by the unclean and desperate interlopers who supplied the table. He would open the door to these men, since infamous throughout the land. He would help them with their tragic burden, pay them their sordid price, and remain alone, when they were gone, with the unfriendly relics of humanity. From such a scene he would return to snatch another hour or two of slumber, to repair the abuses of the night, and refresh himself for the labours of the day.

Few lads could have been more insensible to the impressions of a life thus passed among the ensigns of mortality. His mind was closed against all general considerations. He was incapable of interest in the fate and fortunes of another, the slave of his own desires and low ambitions. Cold, light, and selfish in the last resort, he had that modicum of prudence, miscalled morality which keeps a man from inconvenient drunkenness or punishable theft. He coveted, besides, a measure of consideration from his masters and his fellow-pupils, and he had no desire to fail conspiciously in the external parts of life. Thus he made it his pleasure to gain some distinction in his studies, and day after day rendered unimpeachable eye-service to his employer, Mr K——. For his day of work he indemnified himself by nights of roaring, blackguardly enjoyment; and when that balance had been struck, the organ that he called his conscience declared itself content.

The supply of subjects was a continual trouble to him as well as to his master. In that large and busy class, the raw material of the anatomists kept perpetually running out; and the business thus rendered necessary was not only unpleasant in itself, but threatened dangerous consequences to all who were concerned. It was the policy of Mr K—— to ask no questions in his dealings with the trade. 'They bring the body, and we pay the price,' he used to say, dwelling on the alliteration—'*quid pro quo*'.* And, again, and somewhat

profanely, 'Ask no questions,' he would tell his assistants, 'for conscience' sake.' There was no understanding that the subjects were
provided by the crime of murder. Had that idea been broached to
him in words, he would have recoiled in horror; but the lightness of
his speech upon so grave a matter was, in itself, an offence against
good manners, and a temptation to the men with whom he dealt.
Fettes, for instance, had often remarked to himself upon the singular
freshness of the bodies. He had been struck again and again by the
hang-dog, abominable looks of the ruffians who came to him before
the dawn; and, putting things together clearly in his private
thoughts, he perhaps attributed a meaning too immoral and too cat-
egorical to the unguarded counsels of his master. He understood his
duty, in short, to have three branches: to take what was brought, to
pay the price, and to avert the eye from any evidence of crime.

One November morning this policy of silence was put sharply to
the test. He had been awake all night with a racking toothache—
pacing his room like a caged beast or throwing himself in fury on his
bed—and had fallen at last into that profound, uneasy slumber that
so often follows on a night of pain, when he was awakened by the
third or fourth angry repetition of the concerted signal. There was a
thin, bright moonshine; it was bitter cold, windy, and frosty; the
town had not yet awakened, but an indefinable stir already preluded
the noise and business of the day. The ghouls* had come later than
usual, and they seemed more than usually eager to be gone. Fettes,
sick with sleep, lighted them upstairs. He heard their grumbling
Irish voices through a dream; and as they stripped the sack from
their sad merchandise he leaned dozing, with his shoulder propped
against the wall; he had to shake himself to find the men their money.
As he did so his eyes lighted on the dead face. He started; he took
two steps nearer, with the candle raised.

'God Almighty!' he cried. 'That is Jane Galbraith!'

The men answered nothing, but they shuffled nearer the door.

'I know her, I tell you,' he continued. 'She was alive and hearty
yesterday. It's impossible she can be dead; it's impossible you should
have got this body fairly.'

'Sure, sir, you're mistaken entirely,' said one of the men.

But the other looked Fettes darkly in the eyes, and demanded the
money on the spot.

It was impossible to misconceive the threat or to exaggerate the danger. The lad's heart failed him. He stammered some excuses, counted out the sum, and saw his hateful visitors depart. No sooner were they gone than he hastened to confirm his doubts. By a dozen unquestionable marks he identified the girl he had jested with the day before.* He saw, with horror, marks upon her body that might well betoken violence. A panic seized him, and he took refuge in his room. There he reflected at length over the discovery that he had made; considered soberly the bearing of Mr K——'s instructions and the danger to himself of interference in so serious a business, and at last, in sore perplexity, determined to wait for the advice of his immediate superior, the class assistant.

This was a young doctor, Wolfe Macfarlane, a high favourite among all the reckless students, clever, dissipated, and unscrupulous to the last degree. He had travelled and studied abroad. His manners were agreeable and a little forward. He was an authority on the stage, skilful on the ice or the links with skate or golf-club; he dressed with nice audacity, and, to put the finishing touch upon his glory, he kept a gig and a strong trotting-horse. With Fettes he was on terms of intimacy; indeed, their relative positions called for some community of life; and when subjects were scarce the pair would drive far into the country in Macfarlane's gig, visit and desecrate some lonely graveyard, and return before dawn with their booty to the door of the dissecting-room.

On that particular morning Macfarlane arrived somewhat earlier than his wont. Fettes heard him, and met him on the stairs, told him his story, and showed him the cause of his alarm. Macfarlane examined the marks on her body.

'Yes,' he said with a nod, 'it looks fishy.'

'Well, what should I do?' asked Fettes.

'Do?' repeated the other. 'Do you want to do anything? Least said soonest mended, I should say.'

'Someone else might recognise her,' objected Fettes. 'She was as well known as the Castle Rock.'

'We'll hope not,' said Macfarlane, 'and if anybody does—well, you didn't, don't you see, and there's an end. The fact is, this has been going on too long. Stir up the mud, and you'll get K—— into the most unholy trouble; you'll be in a shocking box yourself. So will I, if you come to that. I should like to know how any one of us would look, or what the devil we should have to say for ourselves, in any

Christian witness-box. For me, you know, there's one thing certain—that, practically speaking, all our subjects have been murdered.'

'Macfarlane!' cried Fettes.

'Come now!' sneered the other. 'As if you hadn't suspected it yourself!'

'Suspecting is one thing—'

'And proof another. Yes, I know; and I'm as sorry as you are this should have come here,' tapping the body with his cane. 'The next best thing for me is not to recognise it; and,' he added coolly, 'I don't. You may, if you please. I don't dictate, but I think a man of the world would do as I do; and, I may add, I fancy that is what K—— would look for at our hands. The question is, Why did he choose us two for his assistants? And I answer, Because he didn't want old wives.'

This was the tone of all others to affect the mind of a lad like Fettes. He agreed to imitate Macfarlane. The body of the unfortunate girl was duly dissected, and no one remarked or appeared to recognise her.

One afternoon, when his day's work was over, Fettes dropped into a popular tavern and found Macfarlane sitting with a stranger. This was a small man, very pale and dark, with coal-black eyes. The cut of his features gave a promise of intellect and refinement which was but feebly realised in his manners, for he proved, upon a nearer acquaintance, coarse, vulgar, and stupid. He exercised, however, a very remarkable control over Macfarlane; issued orders like the Great Bashaw;* became inflamed at the least discussion or delay, and commented rudely on the servility with which he was obeyed. This most offensive person took a fancy to Fettes on the spot, plied him with drinks, and honoured him with unusual confidences on his past career. If a tenth part of what he confessed were true, he was a very loathsome rogue; and the lad's vanity was tickled by the attention of so experienced a man.

'I'm a pretty bad fellow myself,' the stranger remarked, 'but Macfarlane is the boy—Toddy Macfarlane I call him. Toddy, order your friend another glass.' Or it might be, 'Toddy, you jump up and shut the door.' 'Toddy hates me,' he said again. 'Oh, yes, Toddy, you do!'

'Don't you call me that confounded name,' growled Macfarlane.

'Hear him! Did you ever see the lads play knife? He would like to do that all over my body,' remarked the stranger.

'We medicals have a better way than that,' said Fettes. 'When we dislike a dead friend of ours, we dissect him.'

Macfarlane looked up sharply, as though this jest were scarcely to his mind.

The afternoon passed. Gray, for that was the stranger's name, invited Fettes to join them at dinner, ordered a feast so sumptuous that the tavern was thrown into commotion, and when all was done commanded Macfarlane to settle the bill. It was late before they separated; the man Gray was incapably drunk. Macfarlane, sobered by his fury, chewed the cud of the money he had been forced to squander and the slights he had been obliged to swallow. Fettes, with various liquors singing in his head, returned home with devious footsteps and a mind entirely in abeyance. Next day Macfarlane was absent from the class, and Fettes smiled to himself as he imagined him still squiring the intolerable Gray from tavern to tavern. As soon as the hour of liberty had struck, he posted from place to place in quest of his last night's companions. He could find them, however, nowhere; so returned early to his rooms, went early to bed, and slept the sleep of the just.

At four in the morning he was awakened by the well-known signal. Descending to the door, he was filled with astonishment to find Macfarlane with his gig, and in the gig one of those long and ghastly packages with which he was so well acquainted.

'What?' he cried. 'Have you been out alone? How did you manage?'

But Macfarlane silenced him roughly, bidding him turn to business. When they had got the body upstairs and laid it on the table, Macfarlane made at first as if he were going away. Then he paused and seemed to hesitate; and then, 'You had better look at the face,' said he, in tones of some constraint. 'You had better,' he repeated, as Fettes only stared at him in wonder.

'But where, and how, and when did you come by it?' cried the other.

'Look at the face,' was the only answer.

Fettes was staggered; strange doubts assailed him. He looked from the young doctor to the body, and then back again. At last, with a start, he did as he was bidden. He had almost expected the sight that met his eyes, and yet the shock was cruel. To see, fixed in the rigidity of death and naked on that coarse layer of sackcloth, the man whom he had left well clad and full of meat and sin upon the threshold of a tavern, awoke, even in the thoughtless Fettes, some of the terrors of the conscience. It was a *cras tibi** which re-echoed in his soul, that two whom he had known should have come to lie upon these icy tables. Yet these were only secondary thoughts. His first concern regarded Wolfe. Unprepared for a challenge so momentous, he knew not how to look his comrade in the face. He durst not meet his eye, and he had neither words nor voice at his command.

It was Macfarlane himself who made the first advance. He came up quietly behind and laid his hand gently but firmly on the other's shoulder.

'Richardson,' said he, 'may have the head.'

Now, Richardson was a student who had long been anxious for that portion of the human subject to dissect. There was no answer, and the murderer resumed: 'Talking of business, you must pay me; your accounts, you see, must tally.'

Fettes found a voice, the ghost of his own: 'Pay you!' he cried. 'Pay you for that?'

'Why, yes, of course you must. By all means and on every possible account, you must,' returned the other. 'I dare not give it for nothing, you dare not take it for nothing; it would compromise us both. This is another case like Jane Galbraith's. The more things are wrong, the more we must act as if all were right. Where does old K—— keep his money?'

'There,' answered Fettes hoarsely, pointing to a cupboard in the corner.

'Give me the key, then,' said the other calmly, holding out his hand.

There was an instant's hesitation, and the die was cast. Macfarlane could not suppress a nervous twitch, the infinitesimal mark of an immense relief, as he felt the key between his fingers. He opened the cupboard, brought out pen and ink and a paper-book that stood in one compartment, and separated from the funds in a drawer a sum suitable to the occasion.

'Now, look here,' he said, 'there is the payment made—first proof of your good faith: first step to your security. You have now to clinch it by a second. Enter the payment in your book, and then you for your part may defy the devil.'

The next few seconds were for Fettes an agony of thought; but in balancing his terrors it was the most immediate that triumphed. Any future difficulty seemed almost welcome if he could avoid a present quarrel with Macfarlane. He set down the candle which he had been carrying all this time, and with a steady hand entered the date, the nature, and the amount of the transaction.

'And now,' said Macfarlane, 'it's only fair that you should pocket the lucre. I've had my share already. By-the-by, when a man of the world falls into a bit of luck, has a few shillings extra in his pocket— I'm ashamed to speak of it, but there's a rule of conduct in the case. No treating, no purchase of expensive class-books, no squaring of old debts; borrow, don't lend.'

'Macfarlane,' began Fettes, still somewhat hoarsely, 'I have put my neck in a halter to oblige you.'

'To oblige me?' cried Wolfe. 'Oh, come! You did, as near as I can see the matter, what you downright had to do in self-defence. Suppose I got into trouble, where would you be? This second little matter flows clearly from the first. Mr Gray is the continuation of Miss Galbraith. You can't begin and then stop. If you begin, you must keep on beginning; that's the truth. No rest for the wicked.'

A horrible sense of blackness and the treachery of fate seized hold upon the soul of the unhappy student.

'My God!' he cried, 'but what have I done? and when did I begin? To be made a class assistant—in the name of reason, where's the harm in that? Service wanted the position; Service might have got it. Would *he* have been where *I* am now?'

'My dear fellow,' said Macfarlane, 'what a boy you are! What harm *has* come to you? What harm *can* come to you if you hold your tongue? Why, man, do you know what this life is? There are two squads of us—the lions and the lambs. If you're a lamb, you'll come to lie upon these tables like Gray or Jane Galbraith; if you're a lion, you'll live and drive a horse like me, like K——, like all the world with any wit or courage. You're staggered at the first. But look at K——! My dear fellow, you're clever, you have pluck. I like you, and K—— likes you. You were born to lead the hunt; and I tell you, on my honour and my experience of life, three days from now you'll laugh at all these scarecrows like a High School boy at a farce.'

And with that Macfarlane took his departure and drove off up the wynd in his gig to get under cover before daylight. Fettes was thus left alone with his regrets. He saw the miserable peril in which he stood involved. He saw, with inexpressible dismay, that there was no limit to his weakness, and that, from concession to concession, he had fallen from the arbiter of Macfarlane's destiny to his paid and helpless accomplice. He would have given the world to have been a little braver at the time, but it did not occur to him that he might still be brave. The secret of Jane Galbraith and the cursed entry in the day-book closed his mouth.

Hours passed; the class began to arrive; the members of the unhappy Gray were dealt out to one and to another, and received without remark. Richardson was made happy with the head; and, before the hour of freedom rang, Fettes trembled with exultation to perceive how far they had already gone toward safety.

For two days he continued to watch, with an increasing joy, the dreadful process of disguise.

On the third day Macfarlane made his appearance. He had been ill, he said; but he made up for lost time by the energy with which he directed the students. To Richardson in particular he extended the most valuable assistance and advice, and that student, encouraged by the praise of the demonstrator, burned high with ambitious hopes, and saw the medal already in his grasp.

Before the week was out Macfarlane's prophecy had been fulfilled. Fettes had outlived his terrors and had forgotten his baseness. He began to plume himself upon his courage, and had so arranged the story in his mind that he could look back on these events with an unhealthy pride. Of his accomplice he saw but little. They met, of course, in the business of the class; they received their orders together from Mr K——. At times they had a word or two in private, and Macfarlane was from first to last particularly kind and jovial. But it was plain that he avoided any reference to their common secret; and even when Fettes whispered to him that he had cast in his lot with the lions and forsworn the lambs, he only signed to him smilingly to hold his peace.

At length an occasion arose which threw the pair once more into a closer union. Mr K—— was again short of subjects; pupils were eager, and it was a part of this teacher's pretensions to be always well supplied. At the same time there came the news of a burial in the rustic graveyard of Glencorse. Time has little changed the place in question. It stood then, as now, upon a cross-road, out of call of human habitations, and buried fathoms deep in the foliage of six cedar-trees. The cries of the sheep upon the neighbouring hills, the streamlets upon either hand, one loudly singing among pebbles, the other dripping furtively from pond to pond, the stir of the wind in mountainous old flowering chestnuts, and once in seven days the voice of the bell and the old tunes of the precentor,* were the only sounds that disturbed the silence around the rural church. The Resurrection Man—to use a by-name of the period—was not to be deterred by any of the sanctities of customary piety. It was part of his trade to despise and desecrate the scrolls and trumpets of old tombs, the paths worn by the feet of worshippers and mourners, and the offerings and the inscriptions of bereaved affection. To rustic neighbourhoods where love is more than commonly tenacious, and where some bonds of blood or fellowship unite the entire society of a parish, the body snatcher, far from being repelled by natural respect, was attracted by the ease and safety of the task. To bodies that had been laid in earth, in joyful expectation of a far different awakening, there came that hasty, lamp-lit, terror-haunted resurrection of the spade and mattock. The coffin was forced, the cerements torn, and the melancholy relics, clad in sackcloth, after being rattled for hours on moonless by-ways, were at length exposed to uttermost indignities before a class of gaping boys.

Somewhat as two vultures may swoop upon a dying lamb, Fettes and Macfarlane were to be let loose upon a grave in that green and quiet resting-place. The wife of a farmer, a woman who had lived for sixty years, and been known for nothing but good butter and a godly conversation, was to be rooted from her grave at midnight and carried, dead and naked, to that far-away city that she had always honoured with her Sunday's best; the place beside her family was to be empty till the crack of doom; her innocent and almost venerable members to be exposed to that last curiosity of the anatomist.

Late one afternoon the pair set forth, well wrapped in cloaks and furnished with a formidable bottle. It rained without remission—a cold, dense, lashing rain. Now and again there blew a puff of wind, but these sheets of falling water kept it down. Bottle and all, it was a sad and silent drive as far as Penicuik, where they were to spend the evening. They stopped once, to hide their implements in a thick bush not far from the churchyard, and once again at the Fisher's Tryst, to have a toast before the kitchen fire and vary their nips of whisky with a glass of ale. When they reached their journey's end the gig was housed, the horse was fed and comforted, and the two young doctors in a private room sat down to the best dinner and the best wine the house afforded. The lights, the fire, the beating rain upon the window, the cold, incongruous work that lay before them, added zest to their enjoyment of the meal. With every glass their cordiality increased. Soon Macfarlane handed a little pile of gold to his companion.

'A compliment,' he said. 'Between friends these little d——d accommodations ought to fly like pipe-lights.'

Fettes pocketed the money, and applauded the sentiment to the echo. 'You are a philosopher,' he cried. 'I was an ass till I knew you. You and K—— between you, by the Lord Harry! but you'll make a man of me.'

'Of course we shall,' applauded Macfarlane. 'A man? I tell you, it required a man to back me up the other morning. There are some big, brawling, forty-year-old cowards who would have turned sick at the look of the d——d thing; but not you—you kept your head. I watched you.'

'Well, and why not?' Fettes thus vaunted himself. 'It was no affair of mine. There was nothing to gain on the one side but disturbance, and on the other I could count on your gratitude, don't you see?' And he slapped his pocket till the gold pieces rang.

Macfarlane somehow felt a certain touch of alarm at these unpleasant words. He may have regretted that he had taught his young companion so successfully, but he had no time to interfere, for the other noisily continued in this boastful strain:

'The great thing is not to be afraid. Now, between you and me, I don't want to hang—that's practical; but for all cant, Macfarlane, I was born with a contempt. Hell, God, devil, right, wrong, sin, crime, and all the old gallery of curiosities—they may frighten boys, but men of the world, like you and me, despise them. Here's to the memory of Gray!'

It was by this time growing somewhat late. The gig, according to order, was brought round to the door with both lamps brightly shining, and the young men had to pay their bill and take the road. They announced that they were bound for Peebles, and drove in that direction till they were clear of the last houses of the town; then, extinguishing the lamps, returned upon their course, and followed a by-road toward Glencorse. There was no sound but that of their own passage, and the incessant, strident pouring of the rain. It was pitch dark; here and there a white gate or a white stone in the wall guided them for a short space across the night; but for the most part it was at a foot pace, and almost groping, that they picked their way through that resonant blackness to their solemn and isolated destination. In the sunken woods that traverse the neighbourhood of the burying-ground the last glimmer failed them, and it became necessary to kindle a match and reillumine one of the lanterns of the gig. Thus, under the dripping trees, and environed by huge and moving shadows, they reached the scene of their unhallowed labours.

They were both experienced in such affairs, and powerful with the spade; and they had scarce been twenty minutes at their task before they were rewarded by a dull rattle on the coffin lid. At the same moment, Macfarlane, having hurt his hand upon a stone, flung it carelessly above his head. The grave, in which they now stood almost to the shoulders, was close to the edge of the plateau of the grave-yard; and the gig lamp had been propped, the better to illuminate their labours, against a tree, and on the immediate verge of the steep bank descending to the stream. Chance had taken a sure aim with the stone. Then came a clang of broken glass; night fell upon them; sounds alternately dull and ringing announced the bounding of the lantern down the bank, and its occasional collision with the trees. A stone or two, which it had dislodged in its descent, rattled behind it into the profundities of the glen; and then silence, like night, resumed its sway; and they might bend their hearing to its utmost pitch, but naught was to be heard except the rain, now marching to the wind, now steadily falling over miles of open country.

They were so nearly at an end of their abhorred task that they judged it wisest to complete it in the dark. The coffin was exhumed and broken open; the body inserted in the dripping sack and carried between them to the gig; one mounted to keep it in its place, and the other, taking the horse by the mouth, groped along by wall and bush until they reached the wider road by the Fisher's Tryst. Here was a faint, diffused radiancy, which they hailed like daylight; by that they pushed the horse to a good pace and began to rattle along merrily in the direction of the town.

They had both been wetted to the skin during their operations, and now, as the gig jumped among the deep ruts, the thing that stood propped between them fell now upon one and now upon the other.

At every repetition of the horrid contact each instinctively repelled it with the greater haste; and the process, natural although it was, began to tell upon the nerves of the companions. Macfarlane made some ill-favoured jest about the farmer's wife, but it came hollowly from his lips, and was allowed to drop in silence. Still their unnatural burden bumped from side to side; and now the head would be laid, as if in confidence, upon their shoulders, and now the drenching sack-cloth would flap icily about their faces. A creeping chill began to possess the soul of Fettes. He peered at the bundle, and it seemed somehow larger than at first. All over the country-side, and from every degree of distance, the farm dogs accompanied their passage with tragic ululations; and it grew and grew upon his mind that some unnatural miracle had been accomplished, that some nameless change had befallen the dead body, and that it was in fear of their unholy burden that the dogs were howling.

'For God's sake,' said he, making a great effort to arrive at speech, 'for God's sake, let's have a light!'*

Seemingly Macfarlane was affected in the same direction; for though he made no reply, he stopped the horse, passed the reins to his companion, got down, and proceeded to kindle the remaining lamp. They had by that time got no farther than the cross-road down to Auchenclinny. The rain still poured as though the deluge were returning, and it was no easy matter to make a light in such a world of wet and darkness. When at last the flickering blue flame had been transferred to the wick and began to expand and clarify, and shed a wide circle of misty brightness round the gig, it became possible for the two young men to see each other and the thing they had along with them. The rain had moulded the rough sacking to the outlines of the body underneath; the head was distinct from the trunk, the shoulders plainly modelled; something at once spectral and human riveted their eyes upon the ghastly comrade of their drive.

For some time Macfarlane stood motionless, holding up the lamp. A nameless dread was swathed, like a wet sheet, about the body, and tightened the white skin upon the face of Fettes; a fear that was meaningless, a horror of what could not be, kept mounting to his brain. Another beat of the watch, and he had spoken. But his comrade forestalled him.

'That is not a woman,' said Macfarlane, in a hushed voice.

'It was a woman when we put her in,' whispered Fettes.

'Hold that lamp,' said the other. 'I must see her face.'

And as Fettes took the lamp his companion untied the fastenings of the sack and drew down the cover from the head. The light fell very clear upon the dark, well-moulded features and smooth-shaven cheeks of a too familiar countenance, often beheld in dreams of both of these young men. A wild yell rang up into the night; each leaped from his own side into the roadway: the lamp fell, broke, and was extinguished; and the horse, terrified by this unusual commotion, bounded and went off toward Edinburgh at a gallop, bearing along with it, sole occupant of the gig, the body of the dead and long-dissected Gray.

MARKHEIM

'YES,' said the dealer, 'our windfalls are of various kinds. Some customers are ignorant, and then I touch a dividend on my superior knowledge. Some are dishonest,' and here he held up the candle, so that the light fell strongly on his visitor, 'and in that case,' he continued, 'I profit by my virtue.'

Markheim* had but just entered from the daylight streets, and his eyes had not yet grown familiar with the mingled shine and darkness in the shop. At these pointed words, and before the near presence of the flame, he blinked painfully and looked aside.

The dealer chuckled. 'You come to me on Christmas Day,' he resumed, 'when you know that I am alone in my house, put up my shutters, and make a point of refusing business. Well, you will have to pay for that; you will have to pay for my loss of time, when I should be balancing my books; you will have to pay, besides, for a kind of manner that I remark in you today very strongly. I am the essence of discretion, and ask no awkward questions; but when a customer cannot look me in the eye, he has to pay for it.' The dealer once more chuckled; and then, changing to his usual business voice, though still with a note of irony, 'You can give, as usual, a clear account of how you came into the possession of the object?' he continued. 'Still your uncle's cabinet? A remarkable collector, sir!'

And the little pale, round-shouldered dealer stood almost on tiptoe, looking over the top of his gold spectacles, and nodding his head with every mark of disbelief. Markheim returned his gaze with one of infinite pity, and a touch of horror.

'This time,' said he, 'you are in error. I have not come to sell, but to buy. I have no curios to dispose of; my uncle's cabinet is bare to the wainscot; even were it still intact, I have done well on the Stock Exchange, and should more likely add to it than otherwise, and my errand today is simplicity itself. I seek a Christmas present for a lady,' he continued, waxing more fluent as he struck into the speech he had prepared; 'and certainly I owe you every excuse for thus disturbing you upon so small a matter. But the thing was neglected yesterday; I must produce my little compliment at dinner; and, as you very well know, a rich marriage is not a thing to be neglected.'

There followed a pause, during which the dealer seemed to weigh this statement incredulously. The ticking of many clocks among the curious lumber of the shop, and the faint rushing of the cabs in a near thoroughfare, filled up the interval of silence. 'Well, sir,' said the dealer, 'be it so. You are an old customer after all; and if, as you say, you have the chance of a good marriage, far be it from me to be an obstacle. Here is a nice thing for a lady now,' he went on, 'this hand-glass—fifteenth century, warranted; comes from a good collection, too; but I reserve the name, in the interests of my customer, who was just like yourself, my dear sir, the nephew and sole heir of a remarkable collector.'

The dealer, while he thus ran on in his dry and biting voice, had stooped to take the object from its place; and, as he had done so, a shock had passed through Markheim, a start both of hand and foot, a sudden leap of many tumultuous passions to the face. It passed as swiftly as it came, and left no trace beyond a certain trembling of the hand that now received the glass.

'A glass,' he said hoarsely, and then paused, and repeated it more clearly. 'A glass? For Christmas? Surely not?'

'And why not?' cried the dealer. 'Why not a glass?'

Markheim was looking upon him with an indefinable expression. 'You ask me why not?' he said. 'Why, look here—look in it—look at yourself! Do you like to see it? No! nor I—nor any man.'

The little man had jumped back when Markheim had so suddenly confronted him with the mirror; but now, perceiving there was nothing worse on hand, he chuckled. 'Your future lady, sir, must be pretty hard-favoured,' said he.

'I ask you,' said Markheim, 'for a Christmas present, and you give me this—this damned reminder of years, and sins and follies—this hand-conscience! Did you mean it? Had you a thought in your mind? Tell me. It will be better for you if you do. Come, tell me about yourself. I hazard a guess now, that you are in secret a very charitable man?'

The dealer looked closely at his companion. It was very odd, Markheim did not appear to be laughing; there was something in his face like an eager sparkle of hope, but nothing of mirth.

'What are you driving at?' the dealer asked.

'Not charitable?' returned the other gloomily. 'Not charitable; not pious; not scrupulous; unloving, unbeloved; a hand to get money, a safe to keep it. Is that all? Dear God, man, is that all?'

'I will tell you what it is,' began the dealer, with some sharpness, and then broke off again into a chuckle. 'But I see this is a love match of yours, and you have been drinking the lady's health.'

'Ah!' cried Markheim, with a strange curiosity. 'Ah, have you been in love? Tell me about that.'

'I,' cried the dealer. 'I in love! I never had the time, nor have I the time today for all this nonsense. Will you take the glass?'

'Where is the hurry?' returned Markheim. 'It is very pleasant to stand here talking; and life is so short and insecure that I would not hurry away from any pleasure—no, not even from so mild a one as this. We should rather cling, cling to what little we can get, like a man at a cliff's edge. Every second is a cliff, if you think upon it—a cliff a mile high—high enough, if we fall, to dash us out of every feature of humanity. Hence it is best to talk pleasantly. Let us talk of each other: why should we wear this mask? Let us be confidential. Who knows, we might become friends?'

'I have just one word to say to you,' said the dealer. 'Either make your purchase, or walk out of my shop!'

'True, true,' said Markheim. 'Enough fooling. To business. Show me something else.'

The dealer stooped once more, this time to replace the glass upon the shelf, his thin blond hair falling over his eyes as he did so. Markheim moved a little nearer, with one hand in the pocket of his greatcoat; he drew himself up and filled his lungs; at the same time many different emotions were depicted together on his face—terror, horror, and resolve, fascination and a physical repulsion; and through a haggard lift of his upper lip, his teeth looked out.

'This, perhaps, may suit,' observed the dealer: and then, as he began to re-arise, Markheim bounded from behind upon his victim. The long, skewer-like dagger flashed and fell. The dealer struggled like a hen, striking his temple on the shelf, and then tumbled on the floor in a heap.

Time had some score of small voices in that shop, some stately and slow, as was becoming to their great age; others garrulous and hurried. All these told out the seconds in an intricate chorus of tickings. Then the passage of a lad's feet, heavily running on the pavement, broke in upon these smaller voices and startled Markheim into the consciousness of his surroundings. He looked about him awfully. The candle stood on the counter, its flame solemnly wagging in a draught; and by that inconsiderable movement, the whole room was filled with noiseless bustle and kept heaving like a sea: the tall shadows nodding, the gross blots of darkness swelling and dwindling as with respiration, the faces of the portraits and the china gods changing and wavering like images in water. The inner door stood ajar, and peered into that leaguer of shadows with a long slit of daylight like a pointing finger.

From these fear-stricken rovings, Markheim's eyes returned to the body of his victim, where it lay both humped and sprawling, incredibly small and strangely meaner than in life. In these poor, miserly clothes, in that ungainly attitude, the dealer lay like so much sawdust. Markheim had feared to see it, and lo! it was nothing. And yet, as he gazed, this bundle of old clothes and pool of blood began to find eloquent voices. There it must lie; there was none to work the cunning hinges or direct the miracle of locomotion—there it must lie till it was found. Found! ay, and then? Then would this dead flesh lift up a cry that would ring over England, and fill the world with the echoes of pursuit. Ay, dead or not, this was still the enemy. 'Time was that when the brains were out,' he thought; and the first word struck into his mind. Time, now that the deed was accomplished—time, which had closed for the victim, had become instant and momentous for the slayer.

The thought was yet in his mind, when, first one and then another, with every variety of pace and voice—one deep as the bell from a cathedral turret, another ringing on its treble notes the prelude of a waltz—the clocks began to strike the hour of three in the afternoon.

The sudden outbreak of so many tongues in that dumb chamber staggered him. He began to bestir himself, going to and fro with the candle, beleaguered by moving shadows, and startled to the soul by chance reflections. In many rich mirrors, some of home design, some from Venice or Amsterdam, he saw his face repeated and repeated, as it were an army of spies; his own eyes met and detected him; and the sound of his own steps, lightly as they fell, vexed the surrounding quiet. And still, as he continued to fill his pockets, his mind accused him, with a sickening iteration, of the thousand faults of his design.

He should have chosen a more quiet hour; he should have prepared an alibi; he should not have used a knife; he should have been more cautious, and only bound and gagged the dealer, and not killed him; he should have been more bold, and killed the servant also; he should have done all things otherwise: poignant regrets, weary, incessant toiling of the mind to change what was unchangeable, to plan what was now useless, to be the architect of the irrevocable past. Meanwhile, and behind all this activity, brute terrors, like the scurrying of rats in a deserted attic, filled the more remote chambers of his brain with riot; the hand of the constable would fall heavy on his shoulder, and his nerves would jerk like a hooked fish; or he beheld, in galloping defile, the dock, the prison, the gallows, and the black coffin.

Terror of the people in the street sat down before his mind like a besieging army. It was impossible, he thought, but that some rumour of the struggle must have reached their ears and set on edge their curiosity; and now, in all the neighbouring houses, he divined them sitting motionless and with uplifted ear—solitary people, condemned to spend Christmas dwelling alone on memories of the past, and now startingly recalled from that tender exercise; happy family parties, struck into silence round the table, the mother still with raised finger: every degree and age and humour, but all, by their own hearths, prying and hearkening and weaving the rope that was to hang him. Sometimes it seemed to him he could not move too softly; the clink of the tall Bohemian goblets rang out loudly like a bell; and alarmed by the bigness of the ticking, he was tempted to stop the clocks. And then, again, with a swift transition of his terrors, the very silence of the place appeared a source of peril, and a thing to strike and freeze the passer-by; and he would step more boldly, and bustle aloud among the contents of the shop, and imitate, with elaborate bravado, the movements of a busy man at ease in his own house.

But he was now so pulled about by different alarms that, while one portion of his mind was still alert and cunning, another trembled on the brink of lunacy. One hallucination in particular took a strong hold on his credulity. The neighbour hearkening with white face beside his window, the passer-by arrested by a horrible surmise on the pavement—these could at worst suspect, they could not know; through the brick walls and shuttered windows only sounds could penetrate. But here, within the house, was he alone? He knew he was;

he had watched the servant set forth sweethearting, in her poor best, 'out for the day' written in every ribbon and smile. Yes, he was alone, of course; and yet, in the bulk of empty house above him, he could surely hear a stir of delicate footing—he was surely conscious, inexplicably conscious of some presence. Ay, surely; to every room and corner of the house his imagination followed it; and now it was a faceless thing, and yet had eyes to see with; and again it was a shadow of himself; and yet again behold the image of the dead dealer, reinspired with cunning and hatred.

At times, with a strong effort, he would glance at the open door which still seemed to repel his eyes. The house was tall, the skylight small and dirty, the day blind with fog; and the light that filtered down to the ground storey was exceedingly faint, and showed dimly on the threshold of the shop. And yet, in that strip of doubtful brightness, did there not hang wavering a shadow?

Suddenly, from the street outside, a very jovial gentleman began to beat with a staff on the shop door, accompanying his blows with shouts and railleries in which the dealer was continually called upon by name. Markheim, smitten into ice, glanced at the dead man. But no! he lay quite still; he was fled away far beyond earshot of these blows and shoutings; he was sunk beneath seas of silence; and his name, which would once have caught his notice above the howling of a storm, had become an empty sound. And presently the jovial gentleman desisted from his knocking and departed.

Here was a broad hint to hurry what remained to be done, to get forth from this accusing neighbourhood, to plunge into a bath of London multitudes, and to reach, on the other side of day, that haven of safety and apparent innocence—his bed. One visitor had come: at any moment another might follow and be more obstinate. To have done the deed, and yet not to reap the profit, would be too abhorrent a failure. The money, that was now Markheim's concern; and as a means to that, the keys.

He glanced over his shoulder at the open door, where the shadow was still lingering and shivering; and with no conscious repugnance of the mind, yet with a tremor of the belly, he drew near the body of his victim. The human character had quite departed. Like a suit half-stuffed with bran, the limbs lay scattered, the trunk doubled, on the floor; and yet the thing repelled him. Although so dingy and inconsiderable to the eye, he feared it might have more significance to the touch. He took the body by the shoulders, and turned it on its back. It was strangely light and supple, and the limbs, as if they had been broken, fell into the oddest postures. The face was robbed of all expression; but it was as pale as wax, and shockingly smeared with blood about one temple. That was, for Markheim, the one displeasing circumstance. It carried him back, upon the instant, to a certain fair-day in a fishers' village: a grey day, a piping wind, a crowd upon the street, the blare of brasses, the booming of drums, the nasal voice of a ballad-singer; and a boy going to and fro, buried overhead in the crowd and divided between interest and fear, until, coming out upon the chief place of concourse, he beheld a booth and a great screen with pictures, dismally designed, garishly coloured: Brownrigg with her apprentice; the Mannings with their murdered guest; Weare in the death-grip of Thurtell;* and a score besides of famous crimes. The thing was as clear as an illusion; he was once again that little boy; he was looking once again, and with the same sense of physical revolt, at these vile pictures; he was still stunned by the thumping of the drums. A bar of that day's music returned upon his memory; and at that, for the first time, a qualm came over him, a breath of nausea, a sudden weakness of the joints, which he must instantly resist and conquer.

He judged it more prudent to confront than to flee from these considerations; looking the more hardily in the dead face, bending his mind to realise the nature and greatness of his crime. So little a while ago that face had moved with every change of sentiment, that pale mouth had spoken, that body had been all on fire with governable energies; and now, and by his act, that piece of life had been arrested, as the horologist, with interjected finger, arrests the beating of the clock. So he reasoned in vain; he could rise to no more remorseful consciousness; the same heart which had shuddered before the painted effigies of crime, looked on its reality unmoved. At best, he felt a gleam of pity for one who had been endowed in vain with all those faculties that can make the world a garden of enchantment, one who had never lived and who was now dead. But of penitence, no, not a tremor.

With that, shaking himself clear of these considerations, he found the keys and advanced towards the open door of the shop. Outside, it had begun to rain smartly; and the sound of the shower upon the roof had banished silence. Like some dripping cavern, the chambers of the house were haunted by an incessant echoing, which filled the ear and mingled with the ticking of the clocks. And, as Markheim approached the door, he seemed to hear, in answer to his own cautious tread, the steps of another foot withdrawing up the stair. The shadow still palpitated loosely on the threshold. He threw a ton's weight of resolve upon his muscles, and drew back the door.

The faint, foggy daylight glimmered dimly on the bare floor and stairs; on the bright suit of armour posted, halbert in hand,* upon the landing; and on the dark wood-carvings, and framed pictures that hung against the yellow panels of the wainscot. So loud was the beating of the rain through all the house that, in Markheim's ears, it began to be distinguished into many different sounds. Footsteps and sighs, the tread of regiments marching in the distance, the chink of money in the counting, and the creaking of doors held stealthily ajar, appeared to mingle with the patter of the drops upon the cupola and the gushing of the water in the pipes. The sense that he was not alone grew upon him to the verge of madness. On every side he was haunted and begirt by presences. He heard them moving in the upper chambers; from the shop, he heard the dead man getting to his legs; and as he began with a great effort to mount the stairs, feet fled quietly before him and followed stealthily behind. If he were but deaf, he thought, how tranquilly he would possess his soul! And then again, and hearkening with ever fresh attention, he blessed himself for that unresting sense which held the outposts and stood a trusty sentinel upon his life. His head turned continually on his neck; his eyes, which seemed starting from their orbits, scouted on every side, and on every side were half-rewarded as with the tail of something nameless vanishing. The four-and-twenty steps to the first floor were four-and-twenty agonies.

On that first storey, the doors stood ajar, three of them like three ambushes, shaking his nerves like the throats of cannon. He could never again, he felt, be sufficiently immured and fortified from men's observing eyes; he longed to be home, girt in by walls, buried among bedclothes, and invisible to all but God. And at that thought he wondered a little, recollecting tales of other murderers and the fear they were said to entertain of heavenly avengers. It was not so, at least, with him. He feared the laws of nature, lest, in their callous and immutable procedure, they should preserve some damning evidence of his crime. He feared tenfold more, with a slavish, superstitious terror, some scission in the continuity of man's experience, some wilful illegality of nature. He played a game of skill, depending on the rules, calculating consequence from cause; and what if nature, as the defeated tyrant overthrew the chess-board, should break the mould of their succession? The like had befallen Napoleon (so writers said) when the winter changed the time of its appearance. The like might befall Markheim: the solid walls might become transparent and reveal his doings like those of bees in a glass hive; the stout planks might yield under his foot like quicksands and detain him in their clutch; ay, and there were soberer accidents that might destroy him: if, for instance, the house should fall and imprison him beside the body of his victim; or the house next door should fly on fire, and the firemen invade him from all sides. These things he feared; and, in a sense, these things might be called the hands of God reached forth against sin. But about God Himself he was at ease; his act was doubtless exceptional, but so were his excuses, which God knew; it was there, and not among men, that he felt sure of justice.

When he had got safe into the drawing-room, and shut the door behind him, he was aware of a respite from alarms. The room was quite dismantled, uncarpeted besides, and strewn with packing-cases and incongruous furniture; several great pier-glasses,* in which he beheld himself at various angles, like an actor on a stage; many pictures, framed and unframed, standing, with their faces to the wall; a fine Sheraton sideboard, a cabinet of marquetry, and a great old bed, with tapestry hangings. The windows opened to the floor; but by great good fortune the lower part of the shutters had been closed, and this concealed him from the neighbours. Here, then, Markheim drew in a packing-case before the cabinet, and began to search among the keys. It was a long business, for there were many; and it was irksome, besides; for, after all, there might be nothing in the cabinet, and time was on the wing. But the closeness of the occupation sobered him. With the tail of his eye he saw the door— even glanced at it from time to time directly, like a besieged commander pleased to verify the good estate of his defences. But in truth he was at peace. The rain falling in the street sounded natural and pleasant. Presently, on the other side, the notes of a piano were wakened to the music of a hymn, and the voices of many children took up the air and words. How stately, how comfortable was the melody! How fresh the youthful voices! Markheim gave ear to it smilingly, as he sorted out the keys; and his mind was thronged with answerable ideas and images; church-going children and the pealing of the high organ; children afield, bathers by the brookside, ramblers on the brambly common, kite-flyers in the windy and cloud-navigated sky; and then, at another cadence of the hymn, back again to church, and the somnolence of summer Sundays, and the high genteel voice of the parson (which he smiled a little to recall) and the painted Jacobean tombs, and the dim lettering of the Ten Commandments in the chancel.

And as he sat thus, at once busy and absent, he was startled to his feet. A flash of ice, a flash of fire, a bursting gush of blood, went over him, and then he stood transfixed and thrilling. A step mounted the stair slowly and steadily, and presently a hand was laid upon the knob, and the lock clicked, and the door opened.

Fear held Markheim in a vice. What to expect he knew not, whether the dead man walking, or the official ministers of human justice, or some chance witness blindly stumbling in to consign him to the gallows. But when a face was thrust into the aperture, glanced round the room, looked at him, nodded and smiled as if in friendly recognition, and then withdrew again, and the door closed behind it, his fear broke loose from his control in a hoarse cry. At the sound of this the visitant returned.

'Did you call me?' he asked pleasantly, and with that he entered the room and closed the door behind him.

Markheim stood and gazed at him with all his eyes. Perhaps there was a film upon his sight, but the outlines of the newcomer seemed to change and waver like those of the idols in the wavering candle-light of the shop; and at times he thought he knew him; and at times he thought he bore a likeness to himself; and always, like a lump of living terror, there lay in his bosom the conviction that this thing was not of the earth and not of God.

And yet the creature had a strange air of the commonplace, as he stood looking on Markheim with a smile; and when he added: 'You are looking for the money, I believe?' it was in the tones of everyday politeness.

Markheim made no answer.

'I should warn you,' resumed the other, 'that the maid has left her sweetheart earlier than usual and will soon be here. If Mr Markheim be found in this house, I need not describe to him the consequences.'

'You know me?' cried the murderer.

The visitor smiled. 'You have long been a favourite of mine,' he said; 'and I have long observed and often sought to help you.'

'What are you?' cried Markheim: 'the devil?'

'What I may be,' returned the other, 'cannot affect the service I propose to render you.'

'It can,' cried Markheim; 'it does! Be helped by you? No, never; not by you! You do not know me yet; thank God, you do not know me!'

'I know you,' replied the visitant, with a sort of kind severity or rather firmness. 'I know you to the soul.'

'Know me!' cried Markheim. 'Who can do so? My life is but a travesty and slander on myself. I have lived to belie my nature. All men do; all men are better than this disguise that grows about and stifles them. You see each dragged away by life, like one whom bravos* have seized and muffled in a cloak. If they had their own control—if you could see their faces, they would be altogether different, they would shine out for heroes and saints! I am worse than most; myself is more overlaid; my excuse is known to me and God. But, had I the time, I could disclose myself.'

'To me?' inquired the visitant.

'To you before all,' returned the murderer. 'I supposed you were intelligent. I thought—since you exist—you would prove a reader of the heart. And yet you would propose to judge me by my acts! Think of it; my acts! I was born and I have lived in a land of giants; giants have dragged me by the wrists since I was born out of my mother— the giants of circumstance. And you would judge me by my acts! But can you not look within? Can you not understand that evil is hateful to me? Can you not see within me the clear writing of conscience, never blurred by any wilful sophistry, although too often disregarded? Can you not read me for a thing that surely must be common as humanity—the unwilling sinner?'

'All this is very feelingly expressed,' was the reply, 'but it regards me not. These points of consistency are beyond my province, and I care not in the least by what compulsion you may have been dragged away, so as you are but carried in the right direction. But time flies; the servant delays, looking in the faces of the crowd and at the pictures on the hoardings, but still she keeps moving nearer; and remember, it is as if the gallows itself was striding towards you through the Christmas streets! Shall I help you; I, who know all? Shall I tell you where to find the money?'

'For what price?' asked Markheim.

'I offer you the service for a Christmas gift,' returned the other.

Markheim could not refrain from smiling with a kind of bitter triumph. 'No,' said he, 'I will take nothing at your hands; if I were dying of thirst, and it was your hand that put the pitcher to my lips, I should find the courage to refuse. It may be credulous, but I will do nothing to commit myself to evil.'

'I have no objection to a death-bed repentance,' observed the visitant.

'Because you disbelieve their efficacy!' Markheim cried.

'I do not say so,' returned the other; 'but I look on these things from a different side, and when the life is done my interest falls. The man has lived to serve me, to spread black looks under colour of religion, or to sow tares in the wheat-field,* as you do, in a course of weak compliance with desire. Now that he draws so near to his deliverance, he can add but one act of service—to repent, to die smiling, and thus to build up in confidence and hope the more timorous of my surviving followers. I am not so hard a master. Try me. Accept my help. Please yourself in life as you have done hitherto; please yourself more amply, spread your elbows at the board; and when the night begins to fall and the curtains to be drawn, I tell you, for your greater comfort, that you will find it even easy to compound your quarrel with your conscience, and to make a truckling peace with God. I came but now from such a death-bed, and the room was full of sincere mourners, listening to the man's last words: and when I looked into that face, which had been set as a flint against mercy, I found it smiling with hope.'

'And do you, then, suppose me such a creature?' asked Markheim. 'Do you think I have no more generous aspirations than to sin, and sin, and sin, and, at the last, sneak into heaven? My heart rises at the thought. Is this, then, your experience of mankind? or is it because you find me with red hands that you presume such baseness? and is this crime of murder indeed so impious as to dry up the very springs of good?'

'Murder is to me no special category,' replied the other. 'All sins are murder, even as all life is war. I behold your race, like starving mariners on a raft, plucking crusts out of the hands of famine and feeding on each other's lives. I follow sins beyond the moment of their acting; I find in all that the last consequence is death; and to my eyes, the pretty maid who thwarts her mother with such taking graces on a question of a ball, drips no less visibly with human gore than such a murderer as yourself. Do I say that I follow sins? I follow virtues also; they differ not by the thickness of a nail, they are both scythes for the reaping angel of Death. Evil, for which I live, consists not in action but in character. The bad man is dear to me; not the bad act, whose fruits, if we could follow them far enough down the hurtling cataract of the ages, might yet be found more blessed than those of the rarest virtues. And it is not because you have killed a dealer, but because you are Markheim, that I offer to forward your escape.'

'I will lay my heart open to you,' answered Markheim. 'This crime on which you find me is my last. On my way to it I have learned many lessons; itself is a lesson, a momentous lesson. Hitherto I have been driven with revolt to what I would not; I was a bond-slave to poverty, driven and scourged. There are robust virtues that can stand in these temptations; mine was not so: I had a thirst of pleasure. But today, and out of this deed, I pluck both warning and riches—both the power and a fresh resolve to be myself. I become in all things a free actor in the world; I begin to see myself all changed, these hands the agents of good, this heart at peace. Something comes over me out of the past; something of what I have dreamed on Sabbath evenings to the sound of the church organ, of what I forecast when I shed tears over noble books, or talked, an innocent child, with my mother. There lies my life; I have wandered a few years, but now I see once more my city of destination.'

'You are to use this money on the Stock Exchange, I think?' remarked the visitor; 'and there, if I mistake not, you have already lost some thousands?'

'Ah,' said Markheim, 'but this time I have a sure thing.'

'This time, again, you will lose,' replied the visitor quietly.

'Ah, but I keep back the half!' cried Markheim.

'That also you will lose,' said the other.

The sweat started upon Markheim's brow. 'Well, then, what matter?' he exclaimed. 'Say it be lost, say I am plunged again in poverty, shall one part of me, and that the worse, continue until the end to override the better? Evil and good run strong in me, haling me both ways. I do not love the one thing, I love all. I can conceive great deeds, renunciations, martyrdoms; and though I be fallen to such a crime as murder, pity is no stranger to my thoughts. I pity the poor; who knows their trials better than myself? I pity and help them; I prize love, I love honest laughter; there is no good thing nor true thing on earth but I love it from my heart. And are my vices only to direct my life, and my virtues to lie without effect, like some passive lumber of the mind? Not so; good, also, is a spring of acts.'

But the visitant raised his finger. 'For six-and-thirty years that you have been in this world,' said he, 'through many changes of fortune and varieties of humour, I have watched you steadily fall. Fifteen years ago you would have started at a theft. Three years back you would have blenched at the name of murder. Is there any crime, is there any cruelty or meanness, from which you still recoil?—five years from now I shall detect you in the fact! Downward, downward, lies your way; nor can anything but death avail to stop you.'

'It is true,' Markheim said huskily, 'I have in some degree complied with evil. But it is so with all: the very saints, in the mere exercise of living, grow less dainty, and take on the tone of their surroundings.'

'I will propound to you one simple question,' said the other; 'and as you answer, I shall read to you your moral horoscope. You have grown in many things more lax; possibly you do right to be so; and at any account, it is the same with all men. But granting that, are you in any one particular, however trifling, more difficult to please with your own conduct, or do you go in all things with a looser rein?'

'In any one?' repeated Markheim, with an anguish of consideration. 'No,' he added, with despair, 'in none! I have gone down in all.'

'Then,' said the visitor, 'content yourself with what you are, for you will never change; and the words of your part on this stage are irrevocably written down.'

Markheim stood for a long while silent, and indeed it was the visitor who first broke the silence. 'That being so,' he said, 'shall I show you the money?'

'And grace?' cried Markheim.

'Have you not tried it?' returned the other. 'Two or three years ago, did I not see you on the platform of revival meetings, and was not your voice the loudest in the hymn?'

'It is true,' said Markheim; 'and I see clearly what remains for me by way of duty. I thank you for these lessons from my soul; my eyes are opened, and I behold myself at last for what I am.'

At this moment, the sharp note of the door-bell rang through the house; and the visitant, as though this were some concerted signal for which he had been waiting, changed at once in his demeanour.

'The maid!' he cried. 'She has returned, as I forewarned you, and there is now before you one more difficult passage. Her master, you must say, is ill; you must let her in, with an assured but rather serious countenance—no smiles, no overacting, and I promise you success! Once the girl within, and the door closed, the same dexterity that has already rid you of the dealer will relieve you of this last danger in your path. Thenceforward you have the whole evening—the whole night, if needful—to ransack the treasures of the house and to make good your safety. This is help that comes to you with the mask of danger. Up!' he cried; 'up, friend; your life hangs trembling in the scales: up, and act!'

Markheim steadily regarded his counsellor. 'If I be condemned to evil acts,' he said, 'there is still one door of freedom open—I can cease from action. If my life be an ill thing, I can lay it down. Though I be, as you say truly, at the beck of every small temptation, I can yet, by one decisive gesture, place myself beyond the reach of all. My love of good is damned to barrenness; it may, and let it be! But I have still my hatred of evil; and from that, to your galling disappointment, you shall see that I can draw both energy and courage.'

The features of the visitor began to undergo a wonderful and lovely change: they brightened and softened with a tender triumph, and, even as they brightened, faded and dislimned. But Markheim did not pause to watch or understand the transformation. He opened the door and went downstairs very slowly, thinking to himself. His past went soberly before him; he beheld it as it was, ugly and strenuous like a dream, random as chance-medley—a scene of defeat. Life, as he thus reviewed it, tempted him no longer; but on the farther side he perceived a quiet haven for his bark. He paused in the passage, and looked into the shop, where the candle still burned by the dead body. It was strangely silent. Thoughts of the dealer swarmed into his mind, as he stood gazing. And then the bell once more broke out into impatient clamour.

He confronted the maid upon the threshold with something like a smile.

'You had better go for the police,' said he: 'I have killed your master.'

OLALLA

'Now,' said the doctor, 'my part is done, and I may say, with some vanity, well done. It remains only to get you out of this cold and poisonous city, and to give you two months of a pure air* and an easy conscience. The last is your affair. To the first I think I can help you. It falls indeed rather oddly; it was but the other day the Padre came in from the country; and as he and I are old friends, although of contrary professions, he applied to me in a matter of distress among some of his parishioners. This was a family—but you are ignorant of Spain, and even the names of our grandees are hardly known to you; suffice it, then, that they were once great people, and are now fallen to the brink of destitution. Nothing now belongs to them but the residencia, and certain leagues of desert mountain, in the greater part of which not even a goat could support life. But the house is a fine old place, and stands at a great height among the hills, and most salubriously; and I had no sooner heard my friend's tale, than I remembered you. I told him I had a wounded officer, wounded in the good cause,* who was now able to make a change; and I proposed that his friends should take you for a lodger. Instantly the Padre's face grew dark, as I had maliciously foreseen it would. It was out of the question, he said. Then let them starve, said I, for I have no sympathy with tatterdemalion pride.* Thereupon we separated, not very content with one another; but yesterday, to my wonder, the Padre returned and made a submission: the difficulty, he said, he had found upon inquiry to be less than he had feared; or, in other words, these proud people had put their pride in their pocket. I closed with the offer; and, subject to your approval, I have taken rooms for you in the residencia. The air of these mountains will renew your blood; and the quiet in which you will there live is worth all the medicines in the world.'

'Doctor,' said I, 'you have been throughout my good angel, and your advice is a command. But tell me, if you please, something of the family with which I am to reside.'

'I am coming to that,' replied my friend; 'and, indeed, there is a difficulty in the way. These beggars are, as I have said, of very high descent and swollen with the most baseless vanity; they have lived for some generations in a growing isolation, drawing away, on either hand, from the rich who had now become too high for them, and from the poor, whom they still regarded as too low; and even today, when poverty forces them to unfasten their door to a guest, they cannot do so without a most ungracious stipulation. You are to remain, they say, a stranger; they will give you attendance, but they refuse from the first the idea of the smallest intimacy.'

I will not deny that I was piqued, and perhaps the feeling strengthened my desire to go, for I was confident that I could break down that barrier if I desired. 'There is nothing offensive in such a stipulation,' said I; 'and I even sympathise with the feeling that inspired it.'

'It is true they have never seen you,' returned the doctor politely; 'and if they knew you were the handsomest and the most pleasant man that ever came from England (where I am told that handsome men are common, but pleasant ones not so much so), they would doubtless make you welcome with a better grace. But since you take the thing so well, it matters not. To me, indeed, it seems discourteous. But you will find yourself the gainer. The family will not much tempt you. A mother, a son, and a daughter; an old woman said to be half-witted, a country lout, and a country girl, who stands very high with her confessor, and is, therefore,' chuckled the physician, 'most likely plain: there is not much in that to attract the fancy of a dashing officer.'

'And yet you say they are high-born,' I objected.

'Well, as to that, I should distinguish,' returned the doctor. 'The mother is; not so the children. The mother was the last representative of a princely stock, degenerate both in parts and fortune.* Her father was not only poor, he was mad: and the girl ran wild about the residencia till his death. Then, much of the fortune having died with him, and the family being quite extinct, the girl ran wilder than ever, until at last she married, Heaven knows whom, a muleteer some say, others a smuggler; while there are some who uphold there was no marriage at all, and that Felipe and Olalla are bastards. The union, such as it was, was tragically dissolved some years ago; but they live in such seclusion, and the country at that time was in so much disorder, that the precise manner of the man's end is known only to the priest—if even to him.'

'I begin to think I shall have strange experiences,' said I.

'I would not romance, if I were you,' replied the doctor; 'you will find, I fear, a very grovelling and commonplace reality. Felipe, for instance, I have seen. And what am I to say? He is very rustic, very cunning, very loutish, and, I should say, an innocent; the others are probably to match. No, no, señor commandante, you must seek congenial society among the great sights of our mountains; and in these at least, if you are at all a lover of the works of nature, I promise you will not be disappointed.'

The next day Felipe* came for me in a rough country cart, drawn by a mule; and a little before the stroke of noon, after I had said farewell to the doctor, the innkeeper, and different good souls who had befriended me during my sickness, we set forth out of the city by the Eastern gate, and began to ascend into the Sierra. I had been so long a prisoner, since I was left behind for dying after the loss of the convoy, that the mere smell of the earth set me smiling. The country through which we went was wild and rocky, partially covered with rough woods, now of the cork-tree, and now of the great Spanish chestnut, and frequently intersected by the beds of mountain torrents. The sun shone, the wind rustled joyously; and we had advanced some miles, and the city had already shrunk into an inconsiderable knoll upon the plain behind us, before my attention began to be diverted to the companion of my drive. To the eye, he seemed but a diminutive, loutish, well-made country lad, such as the doctor had described, mighty quick and active, but devoid of any culture; and this first impression was with most observers final. What began to strike me was his familiar, chattering talk; so strangely inconsistent with the terms on which I was to be received; and partly from his imperfect enunciation, partly from the sprightly incoherence of the matter, so very difficult to follow clearly without an effort of the mind. It is true I had before talked with persons of a similar mental constitution; persons who seemed to live (as he did) by the senses, taken and possessed by the visual object of the moment and unable to discharge their minds of that impression. His seemed to me (as I sat, distantly giving ear) a kind of conversation proper to drivers, who pass much of their time in a great vacancy of the intellect and threading the sights of a familiar country. But this was not the case of Felipe; by his own account, he was a home-keeper; 'I wish I was there now,' he said; and then, spying a tree by the wayside, he broke off to tell me that he had once seen a crow among its branches.

'A crow?' I repeated, struck by the ineptitude of the remark, and thinking I had heard imperfectly.

But by this time he was already filled with a new idea; hearkening with a rapt intentness, his head on one side, his face puckered; and he struck me rudely, to make me hold my peace. Then he smiled and shook his head.

'What did you hear?' I asked.

'O, it is all right,' he said; and began encouraging his mule with cries that echoed unhumanly up the mountain walls.

I looked at him more closely. He was superlatively well built, light, and lithe and strong; he was well featured; his yellow eyes were very large, though, perhaps, not very expressive; take him altogether, he was a pleasant-looking lad, and I had no fault to find with him, beyond that he was of a dusky hue, and inclined to hairyness; two characteristics that I disliked. It was his mind that puzzled, and yet attracted me. The doctor's phrase—an innocent—came back to me; and I was wondering if that were, after all, the true description, when the road began to go down into the narrow and naked chasm of a torrent. The waters thundered tumultuously in the bottom; and the ravine was filled full of the sound, the thin spray, and the claps of wind, that accompanied their descent. The scene was certainly impressive; but the road was in that part very securely walled in; the mule went steadily forward; and I was astonished to perceive the paleness of terror in the face of my companion. The voice of that wild river was inconstant, now sinking lower as if in weariness, now doubling its hoarse tones; momentary freshets seemed to swell its volume, sweeping down the gorge, raving and booming against the barrier walls; and I observed it was at each of these accessions to the clamour that my driver more particularly winced and blanched. Some thoughts of Scottish superstition and the river Kelpie* passed across my mind; I wondered if perchance the like were prevalent in that part of Spain; and turning to Felipe, sought to draw him out.

'What is the matter?' I asked.

'O, I am afraid,' he replied.

'Of what are you afraid?' I returned. 'This seems one of the safest places on this very dangerous road.'

'It makes a noise,' he said, with a simplicity of awe that set my doubts at rest.

The lad was but a child in intellect; his mind was like his body, active and swift, but stunted in development; and I began from that time forth to regard him with a measure of pity, and to listen at first with indulgence, and at last even with pleasure, to his disjointed babble.

By about four in the afternoon we had crossed the summit of the mountain line, said farewell to the western sunshine, and began to go down upon the other side, skirting the edge of many ravines and moving through the shadow of dusky woods. There rose upon all sides the voice of falling water, not condensed and formidable as in the gorge of the river, but scattered and sounding gaily and musically from glen to glen. Here, too, the spirits of my driver mended, and he began to sing aloud in a falsetto voice, and with a singular bluntness of musical perception, never true either to melody or key, but wandering at will, and yet somehow with an effect that was natural and pleasing, like that of the song of birds. As the dusk increased, I fell more and more under the spell of this artless warbling, listening and waiting for some articulate air, and still disappointed; and when at last I asked him what it was he sang—'Oh,' cried he, 'I am just singing!' Above all, I was taken with a trick he had of unweariedly repeating the same note at little intervals; it was not so monotonous as you would think, or, at least, not disagreeable; and it seemed to breathe a wonderful contentment with what is, such as we love to fancy in the attitude of trees, or the quiescence of a pool.

Night had fallen dark before we came out upon a plateau, and drew up a little after, before a certain lump of superior blackness which I could only conjecture to be the residencia. Here, my guide, getting down from the cart, hooted and whistled for a long time in vain; until at last an old peasant man came towards us from somewhere in the surrounding dark, carrying a candle in his hand. By the light of this I was able to perceive a great arched doorway of a Moorish character: it was closed by iron-studded gates, in one of the leaves of which Felipe opened a wicket. The peasant carried off the cart to some out-building; but my guide and I passed through the wicket, which was closed again behind us; and by the glimmer of the candle, passed through a court, up a stone stair, along a section of an open gallery, and up more stairs again, until we came at last to the door of a great and somewhat bare apartment. This room, which I understood was to be mine, was pierced by three windows, lined with some lustrous wood disposed in panels, and carpeted with the skins of many savage animals. A bright fire burned in the chimney, and shed abroad a changeful flicker; close up to the blaze there was drawn a table, laid for supper; and in the far end a bed stood ready. I was pleased by these preparations, and said so to Felipe; and he, with the same simplicity of disposition that I had already remarked in him, warmly re-echoed my praises. 'A fine room,' he said; 'a very fine room. And fire, too; fire is good; it melts out the pleasure in your bones. And the bed,' he continued, carrying over the candle in that direction—'see what fine sheets—how soft, how smooth, smooth'; and he passed his hand again and again over their texture, and then laid down his head and rubbed his cheeks among them with a grossness of content that somehow offended me. I took the candle from his hand (for I feared he would set the bed on fire) and walked back to the supper-table, where, perceiving a measure of wine, I poured out a cup and called to him to come and drink of it. He started to his feet at once and ran to me with a strong expression of hope; but when he saw the wine, he visibly shuddered.

'Oh, no,' he said, 'not that; that is for you. I hate it.'

'Very well, Señor,' said I; 'then I will drink to your good health, and to the prosperity of your house and family. Speaking of which,' I added, after I had drunk, 'shall I not have the pleasure of laying my salutations in person at the feet of the Señora, your mother?'

But at these words all the childishness passed out of his face, and was succeeded by a look of indescribable cunning and secrecy. He backed away from me at the same time, as though I were an animal about to leap or some dangerous fellow with a weapon, and when he had got near the door, glowered at me sullenly with contracted pupils. 'No,' he said at last, and the next moment was gone noiselessly out of the room; and I heard his footing die away downstairs as light as rainfall, and silence closed over the house.

After I had supped I drew up the table nearer to the bed and began to prepare for rest; but in the new position of the light, I was struck by a picture on the wall.* It represented a woman, still young. To judge by her costume and the mellow unity which reigned over the canvas, she had long been dead; to judge by the vivacity of the attitude, the eyes and the features, I might have been beholding in a mirror the image of life. Her figure was very slim and strong, and of just proportion; red tresses lay like a crown over her brow; her eyes, of a very golden brown, held mine with a look; and her face, which was perfectly shaped, was yet marred by a cruel, sullen, and sensual expression. Something in both face and figure, something exquisitely intangible, like the echo of an echo, suggested the features and bearing of my guide; and I stood awhile, unpleasantly attracted and wondering at the oddity of the resemblance. The common, carnal stock of that race, which had been originally designed for such high dames as the one now looking on me from the canvas, had fallen to baser uses, wearing country clothes, sitting on the shaft and holding the reins of a mule cart, to bring home a lodger. Perhaps an actual link subsisted; perhaps some scruple of the delicate flesh that was once clothed upon with the satin and brocade of the dead lady, now winced at the rude contact of Felipe's frieze.*

The first light of the morning shone full upon the portrait, and, as I lay awake, my eyes continued to dwell upon it with growing complacency; its beauty crept about my heart insidiously, silencing my scruples one after another; and while I knew that to love such a woman were to sign and seal one's own sentence of degeneration, I still knew that, if she were alive, I should love her. Day after day the double knowledge of her wickedness and of my weakness grew clearer. She came to be the heroine of many day-dreams, in which her eyes led on to, and sufficiently rewarded, crimes. She cast a dark shadow on my fancy; and when I was out in the free air of heaven, taking vigorous exercise and healthily renewing the current of my blood, it was often a glad thought to me that my enchantress was safe in the grave, her wand of beauty broken, her lips closed in silence, her philtre* spilt. And yet I had a half-lingering terror that she might not be dead after all, but re-arisen in the body of some descendant.

Felipe served my meals in my own apartment; and his resemblance to the portrait haunted me. At times it was not; at times, upon some change of attitude or flash of expression, it would leap out upon me like a ghost. It was above all in his ill-tempers that the likeness triumphed. He certainly liked me; he was proud of my notice, which he sought to engage by many simple and child-like devices; he loved to sit close before my fire, talking his broken talk or singing his odd, endless, wordless songs, and sometimes drawing his hand over my clothes with an affectionate manner of caressing that never failed to cause in me an embarrassment of which I was ashamed. But for all that, he was capable of flashes of causeless anger and fits of sturdy sullenness. At a word of reproof, I have seen him upset the dish of which I was about to eat, and this not surreptitiously, but with defiance; and similarly at a hint of inquisition. I was not unnaturally curious, being in a strange place and surrounded by strange people; but at the shadow of a question, he shrank back, lowering and dangerous. Then it was that, for a fraction of a second, this rough lad might have been the brother of the lady in the frame. But these humours were swift to pass; and the resemblance died along with them.

In these first days I saw nothing of anyone but Felipe, unless the portrait is to be counted; and since the lad was plainly of weak mind, and had moments of passion, it may be wondered that I bore his dangerous neighbourhood with equanimity. As a matter of fact, it was for some time irksome; but it happened before long that I obtained over him so complete a mastery as set my disquietude at rest.

It fell in this way. He was by nature slothful, and much of a vagabond, and yet he kept by the house, and not only waited upon my wants, but laboured every day in the garden or small farm to the south of the residencia. Here he would be joined by the peasant whom I had seen on the night of my arrival, and who dwelt at the far end of the enclosure, about half a mile away, in a rude outhouse; but it was plain to me that, of these two, it was Felipe who did most; and though I would sometimes see him throw down his spade and go to sleep among the very plants he had been digging, his constancy and energy were admirable in themselves, and still more so since I was well assured they were foreign to his disposition and the fruit of an ungrateful effort. But while I admired, I wondered what had called forth in a lad so shuttle-witted this enduring sense of duty. How was it sustained? I asked myself, and to what length did it prevail over his instincts? The priest was possibly his inspirer; but the priest came one day to the residencia. I saw him both come and go after an interval of close upon an hour, from a knoll where I was sketching, and all that time Felipe continued to labour undisturbed in the garden.

At last, in a very unworthy spirit, I determined to debauch the lad from his good resolutions, and, waylaying him at the gate, easily persuaded him to join me in a ramble. It was a fine day, and the woods to which I led him were green and pleasant and sweet-smelling and alive with the hum of insects. Here he discovered

himself in a fresh character, mounting up to heights of gaiety that
abashed me, and displaying an energy and grace of movement that
delighted the eye. He leaped, he ran round me in mere glee; he
would stop, and look and listen, and seem to drink in the world like a
cordial; and then he would suddenly spring into a tree with one
bound, and hang and gambol there like one at home. Little as he said
to me, and that of not much import, I have rarely enjoyed more
stirring company; the sight of his delight was a continual feast; the
speed and accuracy of his movements pleased me to the heart; and I
might have been so thoughtlessly unkind as to make a habit of these
walks, had not chance prepared a very rude conclusion to my pleasure. By some swiftness or dexterity the lad captured a squirrel in a
treetop. He was then some way ahead of me, but I saw him drop to
the ground and crouch there, crying aloud for pleasure like a child.
The sound stirred my sympathies, it was so fresh and innocent; but
as I bettered my pace to draw near, the cry of the squirrel knocked
upon my heart. I have heard and seen much of the cruelty of lads,
and above all of peasants; but what I now beheld struck me into a
passion of anger. I thrust the fellow aside, plucked the poor brute out
of his hands, and with swift mercy killed it. Then I turned upon the
torturer, spoke to him long out of the heat of my indignation, calling
him names at which he seemed to wither; and at length, pointing
toward the residencia, bade him begone and leave me, for I chose to
walk with men, not with vermin. He fell upon his knees, and, the
words coming to him with more clearness than usual, poured out a
stream of the most touching supplications, begging me in mercy to
forgive him, to forget what he had done, to look to the future. 'O, I
try so hard,' he said. 'O, commandante, bear with Felipe this once; he
will never be a brute again!' Thereupon, much more affected than I
cared to show, I suffered myself to be persuaded, and at last shook
hands with him and made it up. But the squirrel, by way of penance,
I made him bury; speaking of the poor thing's beauty, telling him
what pains it had suffered, and how base a thing was the abuse of
strength. 'See, Felipe,' said I, 'you are strong indeed; but in my
hands you are as helpless as that poor thing of the trees. Give me
your hand in mine. You cannot remove it. Now suppose that I were
cruel like you, and took a pleasure in pain. I only tighten my hold,
and see how you suffer.' He screamed aloud, his face stricken ashy
and dotted with needle-points of sweat; and when I set him free, he

fell to the earth and nursed his hand and moaned over it like a baby. But he took the lesson in good part; and whether from that, or from what I had said to him, or the higher notion he now had of my bodily strength, his original affection was changed into a dog-like, adoring fidelity.

Meanwhile I gained rapidly in health. The residencia stood on the crown of a stony plateau; on every side the mountains hemmed it about; only from the roof, where was a bartizan,* there might be seen, between two peaks, a small segment of plain, blue with extreme distance. The air in these altitudes moved freely and largely; great clouds congregated there, and were broken up by the wind and left in tatters on the hilltops; a hoarse, and yet faint rumbling of torrents rose from all round; and one could there study all the ruder and more ancient characters of nature in something of their pristine force. I delighted from the first in the vigorous scenery and changeful weather; nor less in the antique and dilapidated mansion where I dwelt. This was a large oblong, flanked at two opposite corners by bastion-like projections, one of which commanded the door, while both were loopholed for musketry. The lower storey was, besides, naked of windows, so that the building, if garrisoned, could not be carried without artillery. It enclosed an open court planted with pomegranate trees. From this a broad flight of marble stairs ascended to an open gallery, running all round and resting, towards the court, on slender pillars. Thence again, several enclosed stairs led to the upper storeys of the house, which were thus broken up into distinct divisions. The windows, both within and without, were closely shuttered; some of the stonework in the upper parts had fallen; the roof, in one place, had been wrecked in one of the flurries of wind which were common in these mountains; and the whole house, in the strong, beating sunlight, and standing out above a grove of stunted cork-trees, thickly laden and discoloured with dust, looked like the sleeping palace of the legend. The court, in particular, seemed the very home of slumber. A hoarse cooing of doves haunted about the eaves; the winds were excluded, but when they blew outside, the mountain dust fell here as thick as rain, and veiled the red bloom of the pomegranates; shuttered windows and the closed doors of numerous cellars, and the vacant arches of the gallery, enclosed it; and all day long the sun made broken profiles on the four sides, and paraded the shadow of the pillars on the gallery floor.

At the ground level there was, however, a certain pillared recess, which bore the marks of human habitation. Though it was open in front upon the court, it was yet provided with a chimney, where a wood fire would be always prettily blazing; and the tile floor was littered with the skins of animals.

It was in this place that I first saw my hostess. She had drawn one of the skins forward and sat in the sun, leaning against a pillar. It was her dress that struck me first of all, for it was rich and brightly coloured, and shone out in that dusty courtyard with something of the same relief as the flowers of the pomegranates. At a second look it was her beauty of person that took hold of me. As she sat back—watching me, I thought, though with invisible eyes—and wearing at the same time an expression of almost imbecile good-humour and contentment, she showed a perfectness of feature and a quiet nobility of attitude that were beyond a statue's. I took off my hat to her in passing, and her face puckered with suspicion as swiftly and lightly as a pool ruffles in the breeze; but she paid no heed to my courtesy. I went forth on my customary walk a trifle daunted, her idol-like impassivity haunting me; and when I returned, although she was still in much the same posture, I was half-surprised to see that she had moved as far as the next pillar, following the sunshine. This time, however, she addressed me with some trivial salutation, civilly enough conceived, and uttered in the same deep-chested, and yet indistinct and lisping tones, that had already baffled the utmost niceness of my hearing from her son. I answered rather at a venture; for not only did I fail to take her meaning with precision, but the sudden disclosure of her eyes disturbed me. They were unusually large, the iris golden like Felipe's, but the pupil at that moment so distended that they seemed almost black; and what affected me was not so much their size as (what was perhaps its consequence) the singular insignificance of their regard. A look more blankly stupid I have never met. My eyes dropped before it even as I spoke, and I went on my way upstairs to my own room, at once baffled and embarrassed. Yet, when I came there and saw the face of the portrait, I was again reminded of the miracle of family descent. My hostess was, indeed, both older and fuller in person; her eyes were of a different colour; her face, besides, was not only free from the ill-significance that offended and attracted me in the painting; it was devoid of either good or bad—a moral blank expressing literally

naught. And yet there was a likeness, not so much speaking as imma-
nent, not so much in any particular feature as upon the whole. It
should seem, I thought, as if when the master set his signature to
that grave canvas, he had not only caught the image of one smiling
and false-eyed woman, but stamped the essential quality of a race.

From that day forth, whether I came or went, I was sure to find
the Señora seated in the sun against a pillar, or stretched on a rug
before the fire; only at times she would shift her station to the top
round of the stone staircase, where she lay with the same noncha-
lance right across my path. In all these days, I never knew her to
display the least spark of energy beyond what she expended in
brushing and rebrushing her copious copper-coloured hair, or in
lisping out, in the rich and broken hoarseness of her voice, her
customary idle salutations to myself. These, I think, were her two
chief pleasures, beyond that of mere quiescence. She seemed always
proud of her remarks, as though they had been witticisms; and,
indeed, though they were empty enough, like the conversation of
many respectable persons, and turned on a very narrow range of
subjects, they were never meaningless or incoherent; nay, they had a
certain beauty of their own, breathing, as they did, of her entire
contentment. Now she would speak of the warmth, in which (like
her son) she greatly delighted; now of the flowers of the pomegranate trees, and now of the white doves and long-winged swallows that
fanned the air of the court. The birds excited her. As they raked the
eaves in their swift flight, or skimmed sidelong past her with a rush
of wind, she would sometimes stir, and sit a little up, and seem to
awaken from her doze of satisfaction. But for the rest of her days she
lay luxuriously folded on herself and sunk in sloth and pleasure.* Her
invincible content at first annoyed me, but I came gradually to find
repose in the spectacle, until at last it grew to be my habit to sit down
beside her four times in the day both coming and going, and to talk
with her sleepily, I scarce knew of what. I had come to like her dull,
almost animal neighbourhood; her beauty and her stupidity soothed
and amused me. I began to find a kind of transcendental good sense
in her remarks, and her unfathomable good-nature moved me to
admiration and envy. The liking was returned; she enjoyed my presence half-unconsciously, as a man in deep meditation may enjoy
the babbling of a brook. I can scarce say she brightened when I came,
for satisfaction was written on her face eternally, as on some foolish

statue's; but I was made conscious of her pleasure by some more intimate communication than the sight. And one day, as I sat within reach of her on the marble step, she suddenly shot forth one of her hands and patted mine. The thing was done, and she was back in her accustomed attitude, before my mind had received intelligence of the caress; and when I turned to look her in the face I could perceive no answerable sentiment. It was plain she attached no moment to the act, and I blamed myself for my own more uneasy consciousness.

The sight and (if I may so call it) the acquaintance of the mother confirmed the view I had already taken of the son. The family blood had been impoverished, perhaps by long inbreeding, which I knew to be a common error among the proud and the exclusive. No decline, indeed, was to be traced in the body, which had been handed down unimpaired in shapeliness and strength; and the faces of today were struck as sharply from the mint, as the face of two centuries ago that smiled upon me from the portrait. But the intelligence (that more precious heirloom) was degenerate; the treasure of ancestral memory ran low; and it had required the potent, plebeian crossing of a muleteer or mountain contrabandista to raise, what approached hebetude* in the mother, into the active oddity of the son. Yet of the two, it was the mother I preferred. Of Felipe, vengeful and placable, full of starts and shyings, inconstant as a hare, I could even conceive as a creature possibly noxious. Of the mother I had no thoughts but those of kindness. And indeed, as spectators are apt ignorantly to take sides, I grew something of a partisan in the enmity which I perceived to smoulder between them. True, it seemed mostly on the mother's part. She would sometimes draw in her breath as he came near, and the pupils of her vacant eyes would contract as if with horror or fear. Her emotions, such as they were, were much upon the surface and readily shared; and this latent repulsion occupied my mind, and kept me wondering on what grounds it rested, and whether the son was certainly in fault.

I had been about ten days in the residencia, when there sprang up a high and harsh wind, carrying clouds of dust. It came out of malarious lowlands, and over several snowy sierras. The nerves of those on whom it blew were strung and jangled; their eyes smarted with the dust; their legs ached under the burthen of their body; and the touch of one hand upon another grew to be odious. The wind, besides, came down the gullies of the hills and stormed about the house with a great, hollow buzzing and whistling that was wearisome to the ear and dismally depressing to the mind. It did not so much blow in gusts as with the steady sweep of a waterfall, so that there was no remission of discomfort while it blew. But higher up on the mountain, it was probably of a more variable strength, with accesses of fury; for there came down at times a far-off wailing, infinitely grievous to hear; and at times, on one of the high shelves or terraces, there would start up, and then disperse, a tower of dust, like the smoke of an explosion.

I no sooner awoke in bed than I was conscious of the nervous tension and depression of the weather, and the effect grew stronger as the day proceeded. It was in vain that I resisted; in vain that I set forth upon my customary morning's walk; the irrational, unchanging fury of the storm had soon beat down my strength and wrecked my temper; and I returned to the residencia, glowing with dry heat, and foul and gritty with dust. The court had a forlorn appearance; now and then a glimmer of sun fled over it; now and then the wind swooped down upon the pomegranates, and scattered the blossoms, and set the window shutters clapping on the wall. In the recess the Señora was pacing to and fro with a flushed countenance and bright eyes; I thought, too, she was speaking to herself, like one in anger. But when I addressed her with my customary salutation, she only replied by a sharp gesture and continued her walk. The weather had distempered even this impassive creature; and as I went on upstairs I was the less ashamed of my own discomposure.

All day the wind continued; and I sat in my room and made a feint of reading, or walked up and down, and listened to the riot overhead. Night fell and I had not so much as a candle. I began to long for some society, and stole down to the court. It was now plunged in the blue of the first darkness; but the recess was redly lighted by the fire. The wood had been piled high, and was crowned by a shock of flames, which the draught of the chimney brandished to and fro. In this strong and shaken brightness the Señora continued pacing from wall to wall with disconnected gestures, clasping her hands, stretching forth her arms, throwing back her head as in appeal to heaven. In these disordered movements the beauty and grace of the woman showed more clearly; but there was a light in her eye that struck on me unpleasantly; and when I had looked on awhile in silence, and seemingly unobserved, I turned tail as I had come, and groped my way back again to my own chamber.

By the time Felipe brought my supper and lights, my nerve was utterly gone; and, had the lad been such as I was used to seeing him, I should have kept him (even by force had that been necessary) to take off the edge from my distasteful solitude. But on Felipe, also, the wind had exercised its influence. He had been feverish all day; now that the night had come he was fallen into a low and tremulous humour that reacted on my own. The sight of his scared face, his starts and pallors and sudden hearkenings, unstrung me; and when he dropped and broke a dish, I fairly leaped out of my seat.

'I think we are all mad today,' said I, affecting to laugh.

'It is the black wind,' he replied dolefully. 'You feel as if you must do something, and you don't know what it is.'

I noted the aptness of the description; but, indeed, Felipe had sometimes a strange felicity in rendering into words the sensations of the body. 'And your mother, too,' said I; 'she seems to feel this weather much. Do you not fear she may be unwell?'

He stared at me a little, and then said, 'No,' almost defiantly; and the next moment, carrying his hand to his brow, cried out lamentably on the wind and the noise that made his head go round like a mill-wheel. 'Who can be well?' he cried; and, indeed, I could only echo his question, for I was disturbed enough myself.

I went to bed early, wearied with day-long restlessness, but the poisonous nature of the wind, and its ungodly and unintermittent uproar, would not suffer me to sleep. I lay there and tossed, my nerves and senses on the stretch. At times I would doze, dream horribly, and wake again; and these snatches of oblivion confused me as to time. But it must have been late on in the night, when I was suddenly startled by an outbreak of pitiable and hateful cries. I leaped from my bed, supposing I had dreamed; but the cries still continued to fill the house, cries of pain, I thought, but certainly of rage also, and so savage and discordant that they shocked the heart. It was no illusion; some living thing, some lunatic or some wild animal, was being foully tortured. The thought of Felipe and the squirrel flashed into my mind, and I ran to the door, but it had been locked from the outside; and I might shake it as I pleased, I was a fast prisoner. Still the cries continued. Now they would dwindle down into a moaning that seemed to be articulate, and at these times I made sure they must be human; and again they would break forth and fill the house with ravings worthy of hell. I stood at the door and gave ear to them, till at last they died away. Long after that, I still lingered and still continued to hear them mingle in fancy with the storming of the wind; and when at last I crept to my bed, it was with a deadly sickness and a blackness of horror on my heart.

It was little wonder if I slept no more. Why had I been locked in? What had passed? Who was the author of these indescribable and shocking cries? A human being? It was inconceivable. A beast? The cries were scarce quite bestial; and what animal, short of a lion or a tiger, could thus shake the solid walls of the residencia? And while I was thus turning over the elements of the mystery, it came into my mind that I had not yet set eyes upon the daughter of the house. What was more probable than that the daughter of the Señora, and the sister of Felipe, should be herself insane? Or, what more likely than that these ignorant and half-witted people should seek to manage an afflicted kinswoman by violence? Here was a solution; and yet when I called to mind the cries (which I never did without a shuddering chill) it seemed altogether insufficient: not even cruelty could wring such cries from madness. But of one thing I was sure: I could not live in a house where such a thing was half conceivable, and not probe the matter home and, if necessary, interfere.

The next day came, the wind had blown itself out, and there was nothing to remind me of the business of the night. Felipe came to my bedside with obvious cheerfulness; as I passed through the court, the Señora was sunning herself with her accustomed immobility; and when I issued from the gateway, I found the whole face of nature austerely smiling, the heavens of a cold blue, and sown with great cloud islands, and the mountain-sides mapped forth into provinces of light and shadow. A short walk restored me to myself, and renewed within me the resolve to plumb this mystery; and when, from the vantage of my knoll, I had seen Felipe pass forth to his labours in the garden, I returned at once to the residencia to put my design in practice. The Señora appeared plunged in slumber; I stood awhile and marked her, but she did not stir; even if my design were indiscreet, I had little to fear from such a guardian; and turning away, I mounted to the gallery and began my exploration of the house.

All morning I went from one door to another, and entered spacious and faded chambers, some rudely shuttered, some receiving their full charge of daylight, all empty and unhomely. It was a rich house, on which Time had breathed his tarnish and dust had scattered disillusion. The spider swung there; the bloated tarantula scampered on the cornices; ants had their crowded highways on the floor of halls of audience; the big and foul fly, that lives on carrion and is often the messenger of death, had set up his nest in the rotten woodwork, and buzzed heavily about the rooms. Here and there a stool or two, a couch, a bed, or a great carved chair remained behind, like islets on the bare floors, to testify of man's bygone habitation; and everywhere the walls were set with the portraits of the dead. I could judge, by these decaying effigies, in the house of what a great and what a handsome race I was then wandering. Many of the men wore orders on their breasts and had the port of noble offices;* the women were all richly attired; the canvases most of them by famous hands. But it was not so much these evidences of greatness that took hold upon my mind, even contrasted, as they were, with the present depopulation and decay of that great house. It was rather the parable of family life that I read in this succession of fair faces and shapely bodies. Never before had I so realised the miracle of the continued race, the creation and re-creation, the weaving and changing and handing down of fleshly elements. That a child should be born of its mother, that it should grow and clothe itself (we know not how) with humanity, and put on inherited looks, and turn its head with the manner of one ascendant, and offer its hand with the gesture of another, are wonders dulled for us by repetition. But in the singular unity of look, in the common features and common bearing, of all these painted generations on the walls of the residencia, the miracle started out and looked me in the face. And an ancient mirror falling opportunely in my way, I stood and read my own features a long while, tracing out on either hand the filaments of descent and the bonds that knit me with my family.

At last, in the course of these investigations, I opened the door of a chamber that bore the marks of habitation. It was of large proportions and faced to the north, where the mountains were most wildly figured. The embers of a fire smouldered and smoked upon the hearth, to which a chair had been drawn close. And yet the aspect of the chamber was ascetic to the degree of sternness; the chair was uncushioned; the floor and walls were naked; and beyond the books which lay here and there in some confusion, there was no instrument of either work or pleasure. The sight of books in the house of such a family exceedingly amazed me; and I began with a great hurry, and in momentary fear of interruption, to go from one to another and hastily inspect their character. They were of all sorts, devotional, historical, and scientific, but mostly of a great age and in the Latin tongue.* Some I could see to bear the marks of constant study; others had been torn across and tossed aside as if in petulance or disapproval. Lastly, as I cruised about that empty chamber, I espied some papers written upon with pencil on a table near the window. An unthinking curiosity led me to take one up. It bore a copy of verses, very roughly metred in the original Spanish, and which I may render somewhat thus—

> Pleasure approached with pain and shame,
> Grief with a wreath of lilies came.
> Pleasure showed the lovely sun;
> Jesu dear, how sweet it shone!
> Grief with her worn hand pointed on,
>   Jesu dear, to thee!

Shame and confusion at once fell on me; and, laying down the paper, I beat an immediate retreat from the apartment. Neither Felipe nor his mother could have read the books nor written these rough but feeling verses. It was plain I had stumbled with sacrilegious feet into the room of the daughter of the house. God knows, my own heart most sharply punished me for my indiscretion. The thought that I had thus secretly pushed my way into the confidence of a girl so strangely situated, and the fear that she might somehow come to hear of it, oppressed me like guilt. I blamed myself besides for my suspicions of the night before; wondered that I should ever have attributed those shocking cries to one of whom I now conceived as of a saint, spectral of mien, wasted with maceration, bound up in the practices of a mechanical devotion, and dwelling in a great isolation of soul with her incongruous relatives; and as I leaned on the balustrade of the gallery and looked down into the bright close of pomegranates and at the gaily dressed and somnolent woman, who just then stretched herself and delicately licked her lips as in the very sensuality of sloth, my mind swiftly compared the scene with the cold chamber looking northward on the mountains, where the daughter dwelt.

That same afternoon, as I sat upon my knoll, I saw the Padre enter the gates of the residencia. The revelation of the daughter's character had struck home to my fancy, and almost blotted out the horrors of the night before; but at sight of this worthy man the memory revived. I descended, then, from the knoll, and making a circuit among the woods, posted myself by the wayside to await his passage. As soon as he appeared I stepped forth and introduced myself as the lodger of the residencia. He had a very strong, honest countenance, on which it was easy to read the mingled emotions with which he regarded me, as a foreigner, a heretic, and yet one who had been wounded for the good cause.* Of the family at the residencia he spoke with reserve, and yet with respect. I mentioned that I had not yet seen the daughter, whereupon he remarked that that was as it should be, and looked at me a little askance. Lastly, I plucked up courage to refer to the cries that had disturbed me in the night. He heard me out in silence, and then stopped and partly turned about, as though to mark beyond doubt that he was dismissing me.

'Do you take tobacco powder?' said he, offering his snuff-box; and then, when I had refused, 'I am an old man,' he added, 'and I may be allowed to remind you that you are a guest.'

'I have, then, your authority,' I returned, firmly enough, although I flushed at the implied reproof, 'to let things take their course, and not to interfere?'

He said 'Yes,' and with a somewhat uneasy salute turned and left me where I was. But he had done two things: he had set my conscience at rest, and he had awakened my delicacy. I made a great effort, once more dismissed the recollections of the night, and fell once more to brooding on my saintly poetess. At the same time, I could not quite forget that I had been locked in, and that night when Felipe brought me my supper I attacked him warily on both points of interest.

'I never see your sister,' said I casually.

'Oh, no,' said he; 'she is a good, good girl,' and his mind instantly veered to something else.

'Your sister is pious, I suppose?' I asked in the next pause.

'Oh!' he cried, joining his hands with extreme fervour, 'a saint; it is she that keeps me up.'

'You are very fortunate,' said I, 'for the most of us, I am afraid, and myself among the number, are better at going down.'

'Señor,' said Felipe earnestly, 'I would not say that. You should not tempt your angel. If one goes down, where is he to stop?'

'Why, Felipe,' said I, 'I had no guess you were a preacher, and I may say a good one; but I suppose that is your sister's doing?'

He nodded at me with round eyes.

'Well, then,' I continued, 'she has doubtless reproved you for your sin of cruelty?'

'Twelve times!' he cried; for this was the phrase by which the odd creature expressed the sense of frequency. 'And I told her you had done so—I remembered that,' he added proudly—'and she was pleased.'

'Then, Felipe,' said I, 'what were those cries that I heard last night? for surely they were cries of some creature in suffering.'

'The wind,' returned Felipe, looking in the fire.

I took his hand in mine, at which, thinking it to be a caress, he smiled with a brightness of pleasure that came near disarming my resolve. But I trod the weakness down. 'The wind,' I repeated; 'and yet I think it was this hand,' holding it up, 'that had first locked me in.' The lad shook visibly, but answered never a word. 'Well,' said I, 'I am a stranger and a guest. It is not my part either to meddle or to judge in your affairs; in these you shall take your sister's counsel, which I cannot doubt to be excellent. But in so far as concerns my own I will be no man's prisoner, and I demand that key.' Half an hour later my door was suddenly thrown open, and the key tossed ringing on the floor.

A day or two after, I came in from a walk a little before the point of noon. The Señora was lying lapped in slumber on the threshold of the recess; the pigeons dozed below the eaves like snowdrifts; the house was under a deep spell of noontide quiet; and only a wandering and gentle wind from the mountain stole round the galleries, rustled among the pomegranates, and pleasantly stirred the shadows. Something in the stillness moved me to imitation, and I went very lightly across the court and up the marble staircase. My foot was on the topmost round, when a door opened, and I found myself face to face with Olalla. Surprise transfixed me; her loveliness struck to my heart; she glowed in the deep shadow of the gallery, a gem of colour; her eyes took hold upon mine and clung there, and bound us together like the joining of hands; and the moments we thus stood face to face, drinking each other in, were sacramental and the wedding of souls. I know not how long it was before I awoke out of a deep trance, and, hastily bowing, passed on into the upper stair. She did not move, but followed me with her great, thirsting eyes; and as I passed out of sight it seemed to me as if she paled and faded.

In my own room, I opened the window and looked out, and could not think what change had come upon that austere field of mountains that it should thus sing and shine under the lofty heaven. I had seen her—Olalla! And the stone crags answered, Olalla! and the dumb, unfathomable azure answered, Olalla! The pale saint of my dreams had vanished for ever; and in her place I beheld this maiden on whom God had lavished the richest colours and the most exuberant energies of life, whom He had made active as a deer, slender as a reed, and in whose great eyes He had lighted the torches of the soul. The thrill of her young life, strung like a wild animal's, had entered into me; the force of soul that had looked out from her eyes and conquered mine, mantled about my heart and sprang to my lips in singing. She passed through my veins: she was one with me.

I will not say that this enthusiasm declined; rather my soul held out in its ecstasy as in a strong castle, and was there besieged by cold and sorrowful considerations. I could not doubt but that I loved her at first sight, and already with a quivering ardour that was strange to my experience. What then was to follow? She was the child of an afflicted house, the Señora's daughter, the sister of Felipe; she bore it even in her beauty. She had the lightness and swiftness of the one, swift as an arrow, light as dew; like the other, she shone on the pale background of the world with the brilliancy of flowers. I could not call by the name of brother that half-witted lad, nor by the name of mother that immovable and lovely thing of flesh, whose silly eyes and perpetual simper now recurred to my mind like something hateful. And if I could not marry, what then? She was helplessly unprotected; her eyes, in that single and long glance which had been all our intercourse, had confessed a weakness equal to my own; but in my heart I knew her for the student of the cold northern chamber, and the writer of the sorrowful lines; and this was a knowledge to disarm a brute. To flee was more than I could find courage for; but I registered a vow of unsleeping circumspection.

As I turned from the window, my eyes alighted on the portrait. It had fallen dead, like a candle after sunrise; it followed me with eyes of paint. I knew it to be like, and marvelled at the tenacity of type in that declining race; but the likeness was swallowed up in difference. I remembered how it had seemed to me a thing unapproachable in the life, a creature rather of the painter's craft than of the modesty of nature, and I marvelled at the thought, and exulted in the image of Olalla. Beauty I had seen before, and not been charmed, and I had been often drawn to women, who were not beautiful except to me; but in Olalla all that I desired and had not dared to imagine was united.

I did not see her the next day, and my heart ached and my eyes longed for her, as men long for morning. But the day after, when I returned, about my usual hour, she was once more on the gallery, and our looks once more met and embraced. I would have spoken, I would have drawn near to her; but strongly as she plucked at my heart, drawing me like a magnet, something yet more imperious withheld me; and I could only bow and pass by; and she, leaving my salutation unanswered, only followed me with her noble eyes.

I had now her image by rote, and as I conned the traits in memory it seemed as if I read her very heart. She was dressed with something of her mother's coquetry and love of positive colour. Her robe, which I knew she must have made with her own hands, clung about her with a cunning grace. After the fashion of that country, besides, her bodice stood open in the middle, in a long slit, and here, in spite of the poverty of the house, a gold coin, hanging by a ribbon, lay on her brown bosom. These were proofs, had any been needed, of her inborn delight in life and her own loveliness. On the other hand, in her eyes that hung upon mine, I could read depth beyond depth of passion and sadness, lights of poetry and hope, blacknesses of despair, and thoughts that were above the earth. It was a lovely body, but the inmate, the soul, was more than worthy of that lodging. Should I leave this incomparable flower to wither unseen on these rough mountains? Should I despise the great gift offered me in the eloquent silence of her eyes? Here was a soul immured; should I not burst its prison? All side considerations fell off from me; were she the child of Herod I swore I should make her mine; and that very evening I set myself, with a mingled sense of treachery and disgrace, to captivate the brother. Perhaps I read him with more favourable eyes, perhaps the thought of his sister always summoned up the better qualities of that imperfect soul; but he had never seemed to be so amiable, and his very likeness to Olalla, while it annoyed, yet softened me.

A third day passed in vain—an empty desert of hours. I would not lose a chance, and loitered all afternoon in the court where (to give myself a countenance) I spoke more than usual with the Señora. God knows it was with a most tender and sincere interest that I now studied her; and even as for Felipe, so now for the mother, I was conscious of a growing warmth of toleration. And yet I wondered. Even while I spoke with her, she would doze off into a little sleep, and presently awake again without embarrassment; and this composure staggered me. And again, as I marked her make infinitesimal changes in her posture, savouring and lingering on the bodily pleasure of the movement, I was driven to wonder at this depth of passive sensuality. She lived in her body; and her consciousness was all sunk into and disseminated through her members, where it luxuriously dwelt. Lastly, I could not grow accustomed to her eyes. Each time she turned on me these great beautiful and meaningless orbs, wide open to the day, but closed against human inquiry—each time I had occasion to observe the lively changes of her pupils which expanded and contracted in a breath—I know not what it was came over me, I can find no name for the mingled feeling of disappointment, annoyance, and distaste that jarred along my nerves. I tried her on a variety of subjects, equally in vain; and at last led the talk to her daughter. But even there she proved indifferent; said she was pretty, which (as with children) was her highest word of commendation, but was plainly incapable of any higher thought; and when I remarked that Olalla seemed silent, merely yawned in my face and replied that speech was of no great use when you had nothing to say. 'People speak much, very much,' she added, looking at me with expanded pupils; and then again yawned, and again showed me a mouth that was as dainty as a toy. This time I took the hint, and, leaving her to her repose, went up into my own chamber to sit by the open window, looking on the hills and not beholding them, sunk in lustrous and deep dreams, and hearkening in fancy to the note of a voice that I had never heard.

I awoke on the fifth morning with a brightness of anticipation that seemed to challenge fate. I was sure of myself, light of heart and foot, and resolved to put my love incontinently to the touch of knowledge. It should lie no longer under the bonds of silence, a dumb thing, living by the eye only, like the love of beasts; but should now put on the spirit, and enter upon the joys of the complete human intimacy. I thought of it with wild hopes, like a voyager to El Dorado;* into that unknown and lovely country of her soul, I no longer trembled to adventure. Yet when I did indeed encounter her, the same force of passion descended on me and at once submerged my mind; speech seemed to drop away from me like a childish habit; and I but drew near to her as the giddy man draws near to the margin of a gulf. She drew back from me a little as I came; but her eyes did not waver from mine, and these lured me forward. At last, when I was already within reach of her, I stopped. Words were denied me; if I advanced I could but clasp her to my heart in silence; and all that was sane in me, all that was still unconquered, revolted against the thought of such an accost. So we stood for a second, all our life in our eyes, exchanging salvos of attraction and yet each resisting; and then, with a great effort of the will, and conscious at the same time of a sudden bitterness of disappointment, I turned and went away in the same silence.

What power lay upon me that I could not speak? And she, why was she also silent? Why did she draw away before me dumbly, with fascinated eyes? Was this love? or was it a mere brute attraction, mindless and inevitable, like that of the magnet for the steel? We had never spoken, we were wholly strangers; and yet an influence, strong as the grasp of a giant, swept us silently together. On my side, it filled me with impatience; and yet I was sure that she was worthy; I had seen her books, read her verses, and thus, in a sense, divined the soul of my mistress. But on her side, it struck me almost cold. Of me, she knew nothing but my bodily favour; she was drawn to me as stones fall to the earth; the laws that rule the earth conducted her, unconsenting, to my arms; and I drew back at the thought of such a bridal, and began to be jealous for myself. It was not thus that I desired to be loved. And then I began to fall into a great pity for the girl herself. I thought how sharp must be her mortification, that she, the student, the recluse, Felipe's saintly monitress, should have thus confessed an overweening weakness for a man with whom she had never exchanged a word. And at the coming of pity, all other thoughts were swallowed up; and I longed only to find and console and reassure her; to tell her how wholly her love was returned on my side, and how her choice, even if blindly made, was not unworthy.

The next day it was glorious weather; depth upon depth of blue

over-canopied the mountains; the sun shone wide; and the wind in
the trees and the many falling torrents in the mountains filled the air
with delicate and haunting music. Yet I was prostrated with sadness.
My heart wept for the sight of Olalla, as a child weeps for its mother.
I sat down on a boulder on the verge of the low cliffs that bound the
plateau to the north. Thence I looked down into the wooded valley
of a stream, where no foot came. In the mood I was in, it was even
touching to behold the place untenanted; it lacked Olalla; and I
thought of the delight and glory of a life passed wholly with her in
that strong air, and among these rugged and lovely surroundings, at
first with a whimpering sentiment, and then again with such a fiery
joy that I seemed to grow in strength and stature, like a Samson.

And then suddenly I was aware of Olalla drawing near. She
appeared out of a grove of cork-trees, and came straight towards me;
and I stood up and waited. She seemed in her walking a creature of
such life and fire and lightness as amazed me; yet she came quietly
and slowly. Her energy was in the slowness; but for inimitable
strength, I felt she would have run, she would have flown to me. Still,
as she approached, she kept her eyes lowered to the ground; and
when she had drawn quite near, it was without one glance that she
addressed me. At the first note of her voice I started. It was for this I
had been waiting; this was the last test of my love. And lo, her
enunciation was precise and clear, not lisping and incomplete like
that of her family; and the voice, though deeper than usual with
women, was still both youthful and womanly. She spoke in a rich
chord; golden contralto strains mingled with hoarseness, as the red
threads were mingled with the brown among her tresses. It was not
only a voice that spoke to my heart directly; but it spoke to me of her.
And yet her words immediately plunged me back upon despair.

'You will go away,' she said, 'today.'

Her example broke the bonds of my speech; I felt as lightened of a
weight, or as if a spell had been dissolved. I know not in what words I
answered; but, standing before her on the cliffs, I poured out the
whole ardour of my love, telling her that I lived upon the thought of
her, slept only to dream of her loveliness, and would gladly forswear
my country, my language, and my friends, to live for ever by her side.
And then, strongly commanding myself, I changed the note; I
reassured, I comforted her; I told her I had divined in her a pious
and heroic spirit, with which I was worthy to sympathise, and which

I longed to share and lighten. 'Nature,' I told her, 'was the voice of God, which men disobey at peril; and if we were thus dumbly drawn together, ay, even as by a miracle of love, it must imply a divine fitness in our souls; we must be made,' I said—'made for one another. We should be mad rebels,' I cried out—'mad rebels against God, not to obey this instinct.'

She shook her head. 'You will go today,' she repeated, and then with a gesture, and in a sudden, sharp note—'no, not today,' she cried, 'tomorrow!'

But at this sign of relenting, power came in upon me in a tide. I stretched out my arms and called upon her name; and she leaped to me and clung to me. The hills rocked about us, the earth quailed; a shock as of a blow went through me and left me blind and dizzy. And the next moment she had thrust me back, broken rudely from my arms, and fled with the speed of a deer among the cork-trees.

I stood and shouted to the mountains; I turned and went back towards the residencia, walking upon air. She sent me away, and yet I had but to call upon her name and she came to me. These were but the weaknesses of girls, from which even she, the strangest of her sex, was not exempted. Go? Not I, Olalla—O, not I, Olalla, my Olalla! A bird sang nearby; and in that season, birds were rare. It bade me be of good cheer. And once more the whole countenance of nature, from the ponderous and stable mountains down to the lightest leaf and the smallest darting fly in the shadow of the groves, began to stir before me and to put on the lineaments of life and wear a face of awful joy. The sunshine struck upon the hills, strong as a hammer on the anvil, and the hills shook; the earth, under that vigorous insolation, yielded up heady scents; the woods smouldered in the blaze. I felt the thrill of travail and delight run through the earth. Something elemental, something rude, violent, and savage, in the love that sang in my heart, was like a key to nature's secrets; and the very stones that rattled under my feet appeared alive and friendly. Olalla! Her touch had quickened, and renewed, and strung me up to the old pitch of concert with the rugged earth, to a swelling of the soul that men learn to forget in their polite assemblies. Love burned in me like rage; tenderness waxed fierce; I hated, I adored, I pitied, I revered her with ecstasy. She seemed the link that bound me in with dead things on the one hand, and with our pure and pitying

God upon the other: a thing brutal and divine, and akin at once to the innocence and to the unbridled forces of the earth.

My head thus reeling, I came into the courtyard of the residencia, and the sight of the mother struck me like a revelation. She sat there, all sloth and contentment, blinking under the strong sunshine, branded with a passive enjoyment, a creature set quite apart, before whom my ardour fell away like a thing ashamed. I stopped a moment, and, commanding such shaken tones as I was able, said a word or two. She looked at me with her unfathomable kindness; her voice in reply sounded vaguely out of the realm of peace in which she slumbered, and there fell on my mind, for the first time, a sense of respect for one so uniformly innocent and happy, and I passed on in a kind of wonder at myself, that I should be so much disquieted.

On my table there lay a piece of the same yellow paper I had seen in the north room; it was written on with pencil in the same hand, Olalla's hand, and I picked it up with a sudden sinking of alarm, and read, 'If you have any kindness for Olalla, if you have any chivalry for a creature sorely wrought, go from here today; in pity, in honour, for the sake of Him who died, I supplicate that you shall go.' I looked at this awhile in mere stupidity, then I began to awaken to a weariness and horror of life; the sunshine darkened outside on the bare hills, and I began to shake like a man in terror. The vacancy thus suddenly opened in my life unmanned me like a physical void. It was not my heart, it was not my happiness, it was life itself that was involved. I could not lose her. I said so, and stood repeating it. And then, like one in a dream, I moved to the window, put forth my hand to open the casement, and thrust it through the pane. The blood spurted from my wrist; and with an instantaneous quietude and command of myself, I pressed my thumb on the little leaping fountain and reflected what to do. In that empty room there was nothing to my purpose; I felt, besides, that I required assistance. There shot into my mind a hope that Olalla herself might be my helper, and I turned and went downstairs, still keeping my thumb upon the wound.

There was no sign of either Olalla or Felipe, and I addressed myself to the recess, whither the Señora had now drawn quite back and sat dozing close before the fire, for no degree of heat appeared too much for her.

'Pardon me,' said I, 'if I disturb you, but I must apply to you for help.'

She looked up sleepily and asked me what it was, and with the very words I thought she drew in her breath with a widening of the nostrils and seemed to come suddenly and fully alive.

'I have cut myself,' I said, 'and rather badly. See!' And I held out my two hands from which the blood was oozing and dripping.

Her great eyes opened wide, the pupils shrank into points; a veil seemed to fall from her face, and leave it sharply expressive and yet inscrutable. And as I still stood, marvelling a little at her disturbance, she came swiftly up to me, and stooped and caught me by the hand; and the next moment my hand was at her mouth, and she had bitten me to the bone.* The pang of the bite, the sudden spurting of blood, and the monstrous horror of the act, flashed through me all in one, and I beat her back; and she sprang at me again and again, with bestial cries, cries that I recognised, such cries as had awakened me on the night of the high wind. Her strength was like that of madness; mine was rapidly ebbing with the loss of blood; my mind besides was whirling with the abhorrent strangeness of the onslaught, and I was already forced against the wall, when Olalla ran betwixt us, and Felipe, following at a bound, pinned down his mother on the floor.

A trance-like weakness fell upon me; I saw, heard, and felt, but I was incapable of movement. I heard the struggle roll to and fro upon the floor, the yells of that catamount* ringing up to Heaven as she strove to reach me. I felt Olalla clasp me in her arms, her hair falling on my face, and, with the strength of a man, raise and half-drag, half-carry me upstairs into my own room, where she cast me down upon the bed. Then I saw her hasten to the door and lock it, and stand an instant listening to the savage cries that shook the residencia. And then, swift and light as a thought, she was again beside me, binding up my hand, laying it in her bosom, moaning and mourning over it with dove-like sounds. They were not words that came to her, they were sounds more beautiful than speech, infinitely touching, infinitely tender; and yet as I lay there, a thought stung to my heart, a thought wounded me like a sword, a thought, like a worm in a flower, profaned the holiness of my love. Yes, they were beautiful sounds, and they were inspired by human tenderness; but was their beauty human?

All day I lay there. For a long time the cries of that nameless female thing, as she struggled with her half-witted whelp, resounded through the house, and pierced me with despairing sorrow and disgust. They were the death-cry of my love; my love was murdered; it was not only dead, but an offence to me; and yet, think as I pleased, feel as I must, it still swelled within me like a storm of sweetness, and my heart melted at her looks and touch. This horror that had sprung out, this doubt upon Olalla, this savage and bestial strain that ran not only through the whole behaviour of her family, but found a place in the very foundations and story of our love— though it appalled, though it shocked and sickened me, was yet not of power to break the knot of my infatuation.

When the cries had ceased, there came a scraping at the door, by which I knew Felipe was without; and Olalla went and spoke to him—I know not what. With that exception, she stayed close beside me, now kneeling by my bed and fervently praying, now sitting with her eyes upon mine. So then, for these six hours I drank in her beauty, and silently perused the story in her face. I saw the golden coin hover on her breaths; I saw her eyes darken and brighten, and still speak no language but that of an unfathomable kindness; I saw the faultless face, and, through the robe, the lines of the faultless body. Night came at last, and in the growing darkness of the chamber, the sight of her slowly melted; but even then the touch of her smooth hand lingered in mine and talked with me. To lie thus in deadly weakness and drink in the traits of the beloved, is to reawake to love from whatever shock of disillusion. I reasoned with myself; and I shut my eyes on horrors, and again I was very bold to accept the worst. What mattered it, if that imperious sentiment survived; if her eyes still beckoned and attached me; if now, even as before, every fibre of my dull body yearned and turned to her? Late on in the night some strength revived in me, and I spoke:

'Olalla,' I said, 'nothing matters; I ask nothing; I am content; I love you.'

She knelt down awhile and prayed, and I devoutly respected her devotions. The moon had begun to shine in upon one side of each of the three windows, and make a misty clearness in the room, by which I saw her indistinctly. When she re-arose she made the sign of the cross.

'It is for me to speak,' she said, 'and for you to listen. I know; you can but guess. I prayed, how I prayed for you to leave this place. I begged it of you, and I know you would have granted me even this; or if not, O let me think so!'

'I love you,' I said.

'And yet you have lived in the world,' she said; after a pause, 'you are a man and wise; and I am but a child. Forgive me, if I seem to teach, who am as ignorant as the trees of the mountain; but those who learn much do but skim the face of knowledge; they seize the laws, they conceive the dignity of the design—the horror of the living fact fades from their memory. It is we who sit at home with evil who remember, I think, and are warned and pity. Go, rather, go now, and keep me in mind. So I shall have a life in the cherished places of your memory: a life as much my own, as that which I lead in this body.'

'I love you,' I said once more; and reaching out my weak hand, took hers, and carried it to my lips, and kissed it. Nor did she resist, but winced a little; and I could see her look upon me with a frown that was not unkindly, only sad and baffled. And then it seemed she made a call upon her resolution; plucked my hand towards her, herself at the same time leaning somewhat forward, and laid it on the beating of her heart. 'There,' she cried, 'you feel the very footfall of my life. It only moves for you; it is yours. But is it even mine? It is mine indeed to offer you, as I might take the coin from my neck, as I might break a live branch from a tree, and give it you. And yet not mine! I dwell, or I think I dwell (if I exist at all), somewhere apart, an impotent prisoner, and carried about and deafened by a mob that I disown. This capsule, such as throbs against the sides of animals, knows you at a touch for its master; ay, it loves you! But my soul, does my soul? I think not; I know not, fearing to ask. Yet when you spoke to me your words were of the soul; it is of the soul that you ask—it is only from the soul that you would take me.'

'Olalla,' I said, 'the soul and the body are one, and mostly so in love. What the body chooses, the soul loves; where the body clings, the soul cleaves; body for body, soul to soul, they come together at God's signal; and the lower part (if we can call aught low) is only the footstool and foundation of the highest.'

'Have you,' she said, 'seen the portraits in the house of my fathers? Have you looked at my mother or at Felipe? Have your eyes never rested on that picture that hangs by your bed? She who sat for it died ages ago; and she did evil in her life. But, look again: there is my hand to the least line, there are my eyes and my hair. What is mine, then, and what am I? If not a curve in this poor body of mine (which you love, and for the sake of which you dotingly dream that you love me), not a gesture that I can frame, not a tone of my voice, not any look from my eyes, no, not even now when I speak to him I love, but has belonged to others? Others, ages dead, have wooed other men with my eyes; other men have heard the pleading of the same voice that now sounds in your ears. The hands of the dead are in my bosom; they move me, they pluck me, they guide me; I am a puppet at their command; and I but re-inform features and attributes that have long been laid aside from evil in the quiet of the grave. Is it me you love, friend? or the race that made me? The girl who does not know and cannot answer for the least portion of herself? or the stream of which she is a transitory eddy, the tree of which she is the passing fruit? The race exists; it is old, it is ever young, it carries its eternal destiny in its bosom; upon it, like waves upon the sea, individual succeeds to individual, mocked with a semblance of self-control, but they are nothing. We speak of the soul, but the soul is in the race.'

'You fret against the common law,' I said. 'You rebel against the voice of God, which He has made so winning to convince, so imperious to command. Hear it, and how it speaks between us! Your hand clings to mine, your heart leaps at my touch, the unknown elements of which we are compounded awake and run together at a look; the clay of the earth remembers its independent life and yearns to join us; we are drawn together as the stars are turned about in space, or as the tides ebb and flow, by things older and greater than we ourselves.'

'Alas!' she said, 'what can I say to you? My fathers, eight hundred years ago, ruled all this province: they were wise, great, cunning, and cruel; they were a picked race of the Spanish; their flags led in war; the king called them his cousin; the people, when the rope was slung for them or when they returned and found their hovels smoking, blasphemed their name. Presently a change began. Man has risen; if he has sprung from the brutes, he can descend again to the same level. The breath of weariness blew on their humanity and the cords relaxed; they began to go down; their minds fell on sleep, their passions awoke in gusts, heady and senseless like the wind in the gutters of the mountains; beauty was still handed down, but no longer the guiding wit nor the human heart; the seed passed on, it was wrapped in flesh, the flesh covered the bones, but they were the bones and the flesh of brutes, and their mind was as the mind of flies. I speak to you as I dare; but you have seen for yourself how the wheel has gone backward with my doomed race. I stand, as it were, upon a little rising ground in this desperate descent, and see both before and behind, both what we have lost and to what we are condemned to go farther downward. And shall I—I that dwell apart in the house of the dead, my body, loathing its ways—shall I repeat the spell? Shall I bind another spirit, reluctant as my own, into this bewitched and tempest-broken tenement that I now suffer in? Shall I hand down this cursed vessel of humanity, charge it with fresh life as with fresh poison, and dash it, like a fire, in the faces of posterity? But my vow has been given; the race shall cease from off the earth. At this hour my brother is making ready; his foot will soon be on the stair; and you will go with him and pass out of my sight for ever. Think of me sometimes as one to whom the lesson of life was very harshly told, but who heard it with courage; as one who loved you indeed, but who hated herself so deeply that her love was hateful to her; as one who sent you away and yet would have longed to keep you for ever; who had no dearer hope than to forget you, and no greater fear than to be forgotten.'*

She had drawn towards the door as she spoke, her rich voice sounding softer and farther away; and with the last word she was gone, and I lay alone in the moonlit chamber. What I might have done had not I lain bound by my extreme weakness, I know not; but as it was there fell upon me a great and blank despair. It was not long before there shone in at the door the ruddy glimmer of a lantern, and Felipe coming, charged me without a word upon his shoulders, and carried me down to the great gate, where the cart was waiting. In the moonlight the hills stood out sharply, as if they were of cardboard; on the glimmering surface of the plateau, and from among the low trees which swung together and sparkled in the wind, the great black cube of the residencia stood out bulkily, its mass only broken by three dimly-lighted windows in the northern front above the gate. They were Olalla's windows, and as the cart jolted onwards I kept my eyes fixed upon them till, where the road dipped into a valley, they were lost to my view for ever. Felipe walked in silence beside the shafts, but from time to time he would check the mule and seem to look back upon me; and at length drew quite near and laid his hand upon my head. There was such kindness in the touch, and such a simplicity, as of the brutes, that tears broke from me like the bursting of an artery.

'Felipe,' I said, 'take me where they will ask no questions.'

He said never a word, but he turned his mule about, end for end, retraced some part of the way we had gone, and, striking into another path, led me to the mountain village, which was, as we say in Scotland, the kirk-town* of that thinly-peopled district. Some broken memories dwell in my mind of the day breaking over the plain, of the cart stopping, of arms that helped me down, of a bare room into which I was carried, and of a swoon that fell upon me like sleep.

The next day and the days following the old priest was often at my side with his snuff-box and prayer-book, and after a while, when I began to pick up strength, he told me that I was now on a fair way to recovery, and must as soon as possible hurry my departure; whereupon, without naming any reason, he took snuff and looked at me sideways. I did not affect ignorance; I knew he must have seen Olalla. 'Sir,' said I, 'you know that I do not ask in wantonness. What of that family?'

He said they were very unfortunate; that it seemed a declining race, and that they were very poor and had been much neglected.

'But she has not,' I said. 'Thanks, doubtless, to yourself, she is instructed and wise beyond the use of women.'

'Yes,' he said; 'the Señorita is well informed. But the family has been neglected.'

'The mother?' I queried.

'Yes, the mother too,' said the Padre, taking snuff. 'But Felipe is a well-intentioned lad.'

'The mother is odd?' I asked.

'Very odd,' replied the priest.

'I think, sir, we beat about the bush,' said I. 'You must know more of my affairs than you allow. You must know my curiosity to be justified on many grounds. Will you not be frank with me?'

'My son,' said the old gentleman, 'I will be very frank with you on matters within my competence; on those of which I know nothing it does not require much discretion to be silent. I will not fence with you, I take your meaning perfectly; and what can I say, but that we are all in God's hands, and that His ways are not as our ways? I have even advised with my superiors in the church, but they, too, were dumb. It is a great mystery.'

'Is she mad?' I asked.

'I will answer you according to my belief. She is not,' returned the Padre, 'or she was not. When she was young—God help me, I fear I neglected that wild lamb—she was surely sane; and yet, although it did not run to such heights, the same strain was already notable; it had been so before her in her father, ay, and before him, and this inclined me, perhaps, to think too lightly of it. But these things go on growing, not only in the individual but in the race.'

'When she was young,' I began, and my voice failed me for a moment, and it was only with a great effort that I was able to add, 'was she like Olalla?'

'Now God forbid!' exclaimed the Padre. 'God forbid that any man should think so slightingly of my favourite penitent. No, no; the Señorita (but for her beauty, which I wish most honestly she had less of) has not a hair's resemblance to what her mother was at the same age. I could not bear to have you think so; though, Heaven knows, it were, perhaps, better that you should.'

At this, I raised myself in bed, and opened my heart to the old man; telling him of our love and of her decision, owning my own horrors, my own passing fancies, but telling him that these were at an end; and with something more than a purely formal submission, appealing to his judgment.

He heard me very patiently and without surprise; and when I had done, he sat for some time silent. Then be began: 'The church,' and instantly broke off again to apologise. 'I had forgotten, my child, that you were not a Christian,' said he. 'And indeed, upon a point so highly unusual, even the church can scarce be said to have decided. But would you have my opinion? The Señorita is, in a matter of this kind, the best judge; I would accept her judgment.'

On the back of that he went away, nor was he thenceforward so assiduous in his visits; indeed, even when I began to get about again, he plainly feared and deprecated my society, not as in distaste but much as a man might be disposed to flee from the riddling sphinx. The villagers, too, avoided me; they were unwilling to be my guides upon the mountain. I thought they looked at me askance, and I made sure that the more superstitious crossed themselves on my approach.*
At first I set this down to my heretical opinions; but it began at length to dawn upon me that if I was thus redoubted it was because I had stayed at the residencia. All men despise the savage notions of

such peasantry; and yet I was conscious of a chill shadow that seemed to fall and dwell upon my love. It did not conquer, but I may not deny that it restrained my ardour.

Some miles westward of the village there was a gap in the sierra, from which the eye plunged direct upon the residencia; and thither it became my daily habit to repair. A wood crowned the summit; and just where the pathway issued from its fringes, it was overhung by a considerable shelf of rock, and that, in its turn, was surmounted by a crucifix of the size of life and more than usually painful in design. This was my perch; thence, day after day, I looked down upon the plateau, and the great old house, and could see Felipe, no bigger than a fly, going to and fro about the garden. Sometimes mists would draw across the view, and be broken up again by mountain winds; sometimes the plain slumbered below me in unbroken sunshine; it would sometimes be all blotted out by rain. This distant post, these interrupted sights of the place where my life had been so strangely changed, suited the indecision of my humour. I passed whole days there, debating with myself the various elements of our position; now leaning to the suggestions of love, now giving an ear to prudence, and in the end halting irresolute between the two.

One day, as I was sitting on my rock, there came by that way a somewhat gaunt peasant wrapped in a mantle. He was a stranger, and plainly did not know me even by repute; for, instead of keeping the other side, he drew near and sat down beside me, and we had soon fallen in talk. Among other things he told me he had been a muleteer, and in former years had much frequented these mountains; later on, he had followed the army with his mules, had realised a competence, and was now living retired with his family.

'Do you know that house?' I inquired at last, pointing to the residencia, for I readily wearied of any talk that kept me from the thought of Olalla.

He looked at me darkly and crossed himself.

'Too well,' he said, 'it was there that one of my comrades sold himself to Satan; the Virgin shield us from temptations! He has paid the price; he is now burning in the reddest place in Hell!'

A fear came upon me; I could answer nothing; and presently the man resumed, as if to himself: 'Yes,' he said, 'O yes, I know it. I have passed its doors. There was snow upon the pass, the wind was driving it; sure enough there was death that night upon the mountains, but there was worse beside the hearth. I took him by the arm, Señor, and dragged him to the gate; I conjured him, by all he loved and respected, to go forth with me; I went on my knees before him in the snow; and I could see he was moved by my entreaty. And just then she came out on the gallery, and called him by his name; and he turned, and there was she standing with a lamp in her hand and smiling on him to come back. I cried out aloud to God, and threw my arms about him, but he put me by, and left me alone. He had made his choice; God help us. I would pray for him, but to what end? there are sins that not even the Pope can loose.'

'And your friend,' I asked, 'what became of him?'

'Nay, God knows,' said the muleteer. 'If all be true that we hear, his end was like his sin, a thing to raise the hair.'

'Do you mean that he was killed?' I asked.

'Sure enough, he was killed,' returned the man. 'But how? Ay, how? But these are things that it is sin to speak of.'

'The people of that house . . .' I began.

But he interrupted me with a savage outburst. 'The people?' he cried. 'What people? There are neither men nor women in that house of Satan's! What? have you lived here so long, and never heard?' And here he put his mouth to my ear and whispered, as if even the fowls of the mountain might have overheard and been stricken with horror.

What he told me was not true, nor was it even original; being, indeed, but a new edition, vamped up again by village ignorance and superstition, of stories nearly as ancient as the race of man. It was rather the application that appalled me. In the old days, he said, the church would have burned out that nest of basilisks;* but the arm of the church was now shortened; his friend Miguel had been unpunished by the hands of men, and left to the more awful judgment of an offended God. This was wrong; but it should be so no more. The Padre was sunk in age; he was even bewitched himself; but the eyes of his flock were now awake to their own danger; and some day—ay, and before long—the smoke of that house should go up to heaven.

He left me filled with horror and fear. Which way to turn I knew not; whether first to warn the Padre, or to carry my ill-news direct to the threatened inhabitants of the residencia. Fate was to decide for me; for, while I was still hesitating, I beheld the veiled figure of a woman drawing near to me up the pathway. No veil could deceive my penetration; by every line and every movement I recognised Olalla; and keeping hidden behind a corner of the rock, I suffered her to gain the summit. Then I came forward. She knew me and paused, but did not speak; I, too, remained silent; and we continued for some time to gaze upon each other with a passionate sadness.

'I thought you had gone,' she said at length. 'It is all that you can do for me—to go. It is all I ever asked of you. And you still stay. But do you know, that every day heaps up the peril of death, not only on your head, but on ours? A report has gone about the mountain; it is thought you love me, and the people will not suffer it.'

I saw she was already informed of her danger, and I rejoiced at it. 'Olalla,' I said, 'I am ready to go this day, this very hour, but not alone.'

She stepped aside and knelt down before the crucifix to pray, and I stood by and looked now at her and now at the object of her adoration, now at the living figure of the penitent, and now at the ghastly, daubed countenance, the painted wounds, and the projected ribs of the image. The silence was only broken by the wailing of some large birds that circled sidelong, as if in surprise or alarm, about the summit of the hills. Presently Olalla rose again, turned towards me, raised her veil, and, still leaning with one hand on the shaft of the crucifix, looked upon me with a pale and sorrowful countenance.

'I have laid my hand upon the cross,' she said. 'The Padre says you are no Christian; but look up for a moment with my eyes, and behold the face of the Man of Sorrows. We are all such as He was—the inheritors of sin; we must all bear and expiate a past which was not ours; there is in all of us—ay, even in me—a sparkle of the divine. Like Him, we must endure for a little while, until morning returns bringing peace. Suffer me to pass on upon my way alone; it is thus that I shall be least lonely, counting for my friend Him who is the friend of all the distressed; it is thus that I shall be the most happy, having taken my farewell of earthly happiness, and willingly accepted sorrow for my portion.'

I looked at the face of the crucifix, and, though I was no friend to images, and despised that imitative and grimacing art of which it was a rude example, some sense of what the thing implied was carried home to my intelligence. The face looked down upon me with a painful and deadly contraction; but the rays of a glory encircled it, and reminded me that the sacrifice was voluntary. It stood there, crowning the rock, as it still stands on so many highway sides, vainly preaching to passers-by, an emblem of sad and noble truths; that pleasure is not an end, but an accident; that pain is the choice of the magnanimous; that it is best to suffer all things and do well. I turned and went down the mountain in silence; and when I looked back for the last time before the wood closed about my path, I saw Olalla still leaning on the crucifix.

A GOSSIP ON ROMANCE

In anything fit to be called by the name of reading, the process itself should be absorbing and voluptuous; we should gloat over a book, be rapt clean out of ourselves, and rise from the perusal, our mind filled with the busiest, kaleidoscopic dance of images, incapable of sleep or of continuous thought. The words, if the book be eloquent, should run thenceforward in our ears like the noise of breakers, or the story, if it be a story, repeat itself in a thousand coloured pictures to the eye. It was for this last pleasure that we read so closely, and loved our books so dearly, in the bright, troubled period of boyhood. Eloquence and thought, character and conversation, were but obstacles to brush aside as we dug blithely after a certain sort of incident, like a pig for truffles. For my part, I liked a story to begin with an old wayside inn where, 'towards the close of the year 17—,' several gentlemen in three-cocked hats were playing bowls. A friend of mine preferred the Malabar coast in a storm, with a ship beating to windward, and a scowling fellow of Herculean proportions striding along the beach: he, to be sure, was a pirate. This was further afield than my home-keeping fancy loved to travel, and designed altogether for a larger canvas than the tales that I affected. Give me a highwayman and I was full to the brim; a Jacobite would do,* but the highwayman was my favourite dish. I can still hear that merry clatter of the hoofs along the moonlit lane; night and the coming of day are still related in my mind with the doings of John Rann or Jerry Abershaw;* and the words 'postchaise,' the 'great North road,' 'ostler,' and 'nag' still sound in my ears like poetry. One and all, at least, and each with his particular fancy, we read story-books in childhood, not for eloquence or character or thought, but for some quality of the brute incident. That quality was not mere bloodshed or wonder. Although each of these was welcome in its place, the charm for the sake of which we read depended on something different from either. My elders used to read novels aloud; and I can still remember four different passages which I heard, before I was ten, with the same keen and lasting pleasure. One I discovered long afterwards to be the admirable opening of 'What will he Do with It':* it was no wonder I was pleased with that. The other three still remain unidentified. One is a little vague: it was about a dark, tall house at night, and people groping on the stairs by the light that escaped from the open door of a sick-room. In another, a lover left a ball, and went walking in a cool, dewy park, whence he could watch the lighted windows and the figures of the dancers as they moved. This was the most sentimental impression I think I had yet received, for a child is somewhat deaf to the sentimental. In the last, a poet, who had been tragically wrangling with his wife, walked forth on the sea-beach on a tempestuous night and witnessed the horrors of a wreck.* Different as they are, all these early favourites have a common note—they have all a touch of the romantic.

Drama is the poetry of conduct, romance the poetry of circumstance. The pleasure that we take in life is of two sorts—the active and the passive. Now we are conscious of a great command over our destiny; anon we are lifted up by circumstance, as by a breaking wave, and dashed we know not how into the future. Now we are pleased by our conduct, anon merely pleased by our surroundings. It would be hard to say which of these modes of satisfaction is the more effective, but the latter is surely the more constant. Conduct is three parts of life, but it is not all the four. There is a vast deal in life and letters both which is not immoral, but simply a-moral; which either does not regard the human will at all, or deals with it in obvious and healthy relations; where the interest turns, not upon what a man shall choose to do, but on how he manages to do it; not on the passionate slips and hesitations of the conscience, but on the problems of the body and of the practical intelligence, in clean, open-air adventure, the shock of arms, or the diplomacy of life. With such material as this it is impossible to build a play, for the serious theatre exists solely on moral grounds, and is a standing proof of the dissemination of the human conscience. But it is possible to build, upon this ground, the most joyous of verses, and the most lively, beautiful, and buoyant tales.

One thing in life calls for another; there is a fitness in events and places. The sight of a pleasant arbour puts it in our mind to sit there. One place suggests work, another idleness, a third early rising and long rambles in the dew. The effect of night, of any flowing water, of lighted cities, of the peep of day, of ships, of the open ocean, calls up in the mind an army of anonymous desires and pleasures. Something, we feel, should happen; we know not what, yet we proceed in quest of it. And many of the happiest hours of life fleet by us in this vain attendance of the genius of the place and moment. It is thus that tracts of young fir, and low rocks that reach into deep soundings, particularly torture and delight me. Something must have happened in such places, and perhaps ages back, to members of my race; and when I was a child I tried in vain to invent appropriate games for them, as I still try, just as vainly, to fit them with the proper story. Some places speak distinctly. Certain dank gardens cry aloud for a murder; certain old houses demand to be haunted; certain coasts are set apart for shipwreck. Other spots again seem to abide their destiny, suggestive and impenetrable, 'miching mallecho.'* The inn at Burford Bridge, with its arbours and green garden and silent, eddying river—though it is known already as the place where Keats finished his 'Endymion' and Nelson parted from his Emma—still seems to wait the coming of the appropriate legend. Within these ivied walls, behind these old green shutters, some further business smoulders, waiting for its hour. The old Hawes Inn at the Queen's Ferry is another. There it stands, apart from the town, beside the pier, in a climate of its own, half inland, half marine—in front, the ferry bubbling with the tide and the guardship swinging to her anchor; behind, the old garden with the trees. Americans seek it already for the sake of Lovel and Oldbuck, who dined there at the beginning of the 'Antiquary.'* But you need not tell me—that is not all; there is some story, unrecorded or not yet complete, which must express the meaning of that inn more fully. So it is with names and faces; so it is with incidents that are idle and inconclusive in themselves, and yet seem like the beginning of some quaint romance, which the all-careless author leaves untold. How many of these romances have we not seen determine at their birth; how many people have met us with a look of meaning in their eye, and sunk at once into idle acquaintances; to how many places have we not drawn near, with express intimations—'here my destiny awaits me'—and we have but dined there and passed by! I have lived both at the Hawes and Burford in a perpetual flutter, on the heels, as it seemed, of some adventure that should justify the place; but though the feeling had me to bed at night and called me again at morning in one unbroken round of pleasure and suspense, nothing befell me in either worth remark. The man or the hour had not yet come; but some day, I think, a boat shall put off from the Queen's Ferry, fraught with a dear cargo, and some frosty night a horseman, on a tragic errand, rattle with his whip upon the green shutters of the inn at Burford.

Now, this is one of the natural appetites with which any lively literature has to count. The desire for knowledge, I had almost added the desire for meat, is not more deeply seated than this demand for fit and striking incident. The dullest of clowns tells, or tries to tell, himself a story, as the feeblest of children uses invention in his play; and even as the imaginative grown person, joining in the game, at once enriches it with many delightful circumstances, the great creative writer shows us the realisation and the apotheosis of the day-dreams of common men. His stories may be nourished with the realities of life, but their true mark is to satisfy the nameless longings of the reader and to obey the ideal laws of the daydream. The right kind of thing should fall out in the right kind of place; the right kind of thing should follow; and not only the characters talk aptly and think naturally, but all the circumstances in a tale answer one to another like notes in music. The threads of a story come from time to time together and make a picture in the web; the characters fall from time to time into some attitude to each other or to nature, which stamps the story home like an illustration. Crusoe recoiling from the footprint, Achilles shouting over against the Trojans, Ulysses bending the great bow, Christian* running with his fingers in his ears, these are each culminating moments in the legend, and each has been printed on the mind's eye for ever. Other things we may forget; we may forget the words, although they are beautiful; we may forget the author's comment, although perhaps it was ingenious and true; but these epoch-making scenes, which put the last mark of truth upon a story and fill up, at one blow, our capacity for sympathetic pleasure, we so adopt into the very bosom of our mind that neither time nor tide can efface or weaken the impression. This, then, is the plastic part of literature: to embody character, thought, or emotion in some act or attitude that shall be remarkably striking to the mind's eye. This is the highest and hardest thing to do in words; the thing which, once accomplished, equally delights the schoolboy and the sage, and makes, in its own right, the quality of epics. Compared with this, all other purposes in literature, except the purely lyrical or the purely philosophic, are bastard in nature, facile of execution, and feeble in result. It is one thing to write about the inn at Burford, or to describe scenery with the word-painters; it is quite another to seize on the heart of the suggestion and make a country famous with a legend. It is one thing to remark and to dissect, with the most cutting logic, the complications of life, and of the human spirit; it is quite another to give them body and blood in the story of Ajax or of Hamlet. The first is literature, but the second is something besides, for it is likewise art.

English people of the present day are apt, I know not why, to look somewhat down on incident, and reserve their admiration for the clink of tea-spoons and the accents of the curate. It is thought clever to write a novel with no story at all, or at least with a very dull one. Reduced even to the lowest terms, a certain interest can be communicated by the art of narrative; a sense of human kinship stirred; and a kind of monotonous fitness, comparable to the words and air of 'Sandy's Mull,' preserved among the infinitesimal occurrences recorded. Some people work, in this manner, with even a strong touch. Mr Trollope's inimitable clergymen naturally arise to the mind in this connection. But even Mr Trollope* does not confine himself to chronicling small beer. Mr Crawley's collision with the Bishop's wife, Mr Melnotte dallying in the deserted banquet-room, are typical incidents, epically conceived, fitly embodying a crisis. If Rawdon Crawley's blow were not delivered, 'Vanity Fair' would cease to be a work of art.* That scene is the chief ganglion of the tale; and the discharge of energy from Rawdon's fist is the reward and consolation of the reader. The end of 'Esmond' is a yet wider excursion from the author's customary fields; the scene at Castlewood is pure Dumas; the great and wily English borrower has here borrowed from the great, unblushing French thief;* as usual, he has borrowed admirably well, and the breaking of the sword rounds off the best of all his books with a manly, martial note. But perhaps nothing can more strongly illustrate the necessity for marking incident than to compare the living fame of 'Robinson Crusoe' with the discredit of 'Clarissa Harlowe.'* 'Clarissa' is a book of a far more startling import, worked out, on a great canvas, with inimitable courage and unflagging art; it contains wit, character, passion, plot, conversations full of spirit and insight, letters sparkling with unstrained humanity; and if the death of the heroine be somewhat frigid and artificial, the last days of the hero strike the only note of what we now call Byronism, between the Elizabethans and Byron himself. And yet a little story of

a shipwrecked sailor, with not a tenth part of the style nor a thou-
sandth part of the wisdom, exploring none of the arcana of humanity
and deprived of the perennial interest of love, goes on from edition
to edition, ever young, while 'Clarissa' lies upon the shelves unread.
A friend of mine, a Welsh blacksmith, was twenty-five years old, and
could neither read nor write, when he heard a chapter of 'Robinson'
read aloud in a farm kitchen. Up to that moment he had sat content,
huddled in his ignorance; but he left that farm another man. There
were daydreams, it appeared, divine daydreams, written and printed
and bound, and to be bought for money and enjoyed at pleasure.
Down he sat that day, painfully learned to read Welsh, and returned
to borrow the book. It had been lost, nor could he find another copy
but one that was in English. Down he sat once more, learned
English, and at length, and with entire delight, read 'Robinson.' It is
like the story of a love-chase. If he had heard a letter from 'Clarissa,'
would he have been fired with the same chivalrous ardour? I wonder.
Yet 'Clarissa' has every quality that can be shown in prose, one alone
excepted: pictorial, or picture-making romance. While 'Robinson'
depends, for the most part and with the overwhelming majority of its
readers, on the charm of circumstance.

   In the highest achievements of the art of words, the dramatic and
the pictorial, the moral and romantic interest rise and fall together by
a common and organic law. Situation is animated with passion, passion clothed upon with situation. Neither exists for itself, but each
inheres indissolubly with the other. This is high art; and not only the
highest art possible in words, but the highest art of all, since it
combines the greatest mass and diversity of the elements of truth
and pleasure. Such are epics, and the few prose tales that have the
epic weight. But as from a school of works, aping the creative, incident and romance are ruthlessly discarded, so may character and
drama be omitted or subordinated to romance. There is one book,
for example, more generally loved than Shakespeare, that captivates
in childhood, and still delights in age—I mean the 'Arabian
Nights'*—where you shall look in vain for moral or for intellectual
interest. No human face or voice greets us among that wooden crowd
of kings and genies, sorcerers and beggarmen. Adventure, on the
most naked terms furnishes forth the entertainment and is found
enough. Dumas approaches perhaps nearest of any modern to these
Arabian authors in the purely material charm of his romances. The

early part of 'Monte Christo,' down to the finding of the treasure, is
a piece of perfect story-telling; the man never breathed who shared
these moving incidents without a tremor; and yet Faria is a thing of
packthread and Dantès little more than a name. The sequel is one
long-drawn error, gloomy, bloody, unnatural and dull; but as for
these early chapters, I do not believe there is another volume extant
where you can breathe the same unmingled atmosphere of romance.
It is very thin and light, to be sure, as on a high mountain; but it is
brisk and clear and sunny in proportion. I saw the other day, with
envy, an old and a very clever lady setting forth on a second or third
voyage into 'Monte Christo.' Here are stories, which powerfully
affect the reader, which can be reperused at any age, and where the
characters are no more than puppets. The bony fist of the showman
visibly propels them; their springs are an open secret; their faces are
of wood, their bellies filled with bran; and yet we thrillingly partake
of their adventures. And the point may be illustrated still further.
The last interview between Lucy and Richard Feverell* is pure
drama; more than that, it is the strongest scene, since Shakespeare,
in the English tongue. Their first meeting by the river, on the other
hand, is pure romance; it has nothing to do with character; it might
happen to any other boy and maiden, and be none the less delightful
for the change. And yet I think he would be a bold man who should
choose between these passages. Thus, in the same book, we may have
two scenes, each capital in its order: in the one, human passion, deep
calling unto deep, shall utter its genuine voice; in the second, according circumstances, like instruments in tune, shall build up a trivial
but desirable incident, such as we love to prefigure for ourselves; and
in the end, in spite of the critics, we may hesitate to give the preference to either. The one may ask more genius—I do not say it does;
but at least the other dwells as clearly in the memory.

True romantic art, again, makes a romance of all things. It reaches
into the highest abstraction of the ideal; it does not refuse the most
pedestrian realism. 'Robinson Crusoe' is as realistic as it is romantic;
both qualities are pushed to an extreme, and neither suffers. Nor
does romance depend upon the material importance of the incidents.
To deal with strong and deadly elements, banditti, pirates, war, and
murder, is to conjure with great names, and, in the event of failure,
to double the disgrace. The arrival of Haydn and Consuelo at the
Canon's villa is a very trifling incident;* yet we may read a dozen

boisterous stories from beginning to end, and not receive so fresh
and stirring an impression of adventure. It was the scene of Crusoe
at the wreck, if I remember rightly, that so bewitched my blacksmith.
Nor is the fact surprising. Every single article the castaway recovers
from the hulk is 'a joy for ever' to the man who reads of them. They
are the things he ought to find, and the bare enumeration stirs the
blood. I found a glimmer of the same interest the other day in a new
book, 'The Sailor's Sweetheart,' by Mr Clark Russell.* The whole
business of the brig 'Morning Star' is very rightly felt and spiritedly
written; but the clothes, the books, and the money satisfy the
reader's mind like things to eat. We are dealing here with the old cut-
and-dry, legitimate interest of treasure trove. But even treasure
trove can be made dull. There are few people who have not groaned
under the plethora of goods that fell to the lot of the 'Swiss Family
Robinson,' that dreary family.* They found article after article, creature after creature, from milk kine to pieces of ordnance, a whole
consignment; but no informing taste had presided over the selection,
there was no smack or relish in the invoice; and all these riches left
the fancy cold. The box of goods in Verne's 'Mysterious Island'* is
another case in point: there was no gusto and no glamour about that;
it might have come from a shop. But the two hundred and seventy-
eight Australian sovereigns on board the 'Morning Star' fell upon
me like a surprise that I had expected; whole vistas of secondary
stories, besides the one in hand, radiated forth from that discovery,
as they radiate from a striking particular in life; and I was made for
the moment as happy as a reader has the right to be.

To come at all at the nature of this quality of romance, we must
bear in mind the peculiarity of our attitude to any art. No art pro-
duces illusion; in the theatre, we never forget that we are in the
theatre; and while we read a story, we sit wavering between two
minds, now merely clapping our hands at the merit of the performance, now condescending to take an active part in fancy with the
characters. This last is the triumph of story-telling: when the reader
consciously plays at being the hero, the scene is a good scene. Now in
character-studies the pleasure that we take is critical; we watch, we
approve, we smile at incongruities, we are moved to sudden heats of
sympathy with courage, suffering, or virtue. But the characters are
still themselves; they are not us; the more clearly they are depicted,
the more widely do they stand away from us, the more imperiously

do they thrust us back into our place as a spectator. I cannot identify myself with Rawdon Crawley or with Eugene de Rastignac,* for I have scarce a hope or fear in common with them. It is not character, but incident, that wooes us out of our reserve. Something happens, as we desire to have it happen to ourselves; some situation, that we have long dallied with in fancy, is realised in the story with enticing and appropriate details. Then we forget the characters; then we push the hero aside; then we plunge into the tale in our own person and bathe in fresh experience; and then, and then only, do we say we have been reading a romance. It is not only pleasurable things that we imagine in our daydreams; there are lights in which we are willing to contemplate even the idea of our own death; ways in which it seems as if it would amuse us to be cheated, wounded, or calumniated. It is thus possible to construct a story, even of tragic import, in which every incident, detail, and trick of circumstance shall be welcome to the reader's thoughts. Fiction is to the grown man what play is to the child. It is there that he changes the atmosphere and tenor of his life. And when the game so chimes with his fancy that he can join in it with all his heart, when it pleases him with every turn, when he loves to recall it and dwells upon its recollection with entire delight, fiction is called romance.

Walter Scott is out and away the king of the romantics.* 'The Lady of the Lake' has no indisputable claim to be a poem beyond the inherent fitness and desirability of the tale. It is just such a story as a man would make up for himself, walking, in the best health and temper, through just such scenes as it is laid in. Hence it is that a charm dwells undefinable among these slovenly verses, as the unseen cuckoo fills the mountains with his note; hence, even after we have flung the book aside, the scenery and adventures remain present to the mind, a new and green possession, not unworthy of that beautiful name, 'The Lady of the Lake,' or that direct, romantic opening— one of the most spirited and poetical in literature—'The stag at eve had drunk his fill.' The same strength and the same weaknesses adorn and disfigure the novels. In that ill-written, ragged book, 'The Pirate,' the figure of Cleveland—cast up by the sea on the resounding foreland of Dunrossness—moving, with the blood on his hands and the Spanish words on his tongue, among the simple islanders— singing a serenade under the window of his Shetland mistress—is conceived in the very highest manner of romantic invention. The

words of his song, 'Through groves of palm,' sung in such a scene
and by such a lover, clench, as in a nutshell, the emphatic contrast
upon which the tale is built. In 'Guy Mannering,' again, every incident is delightful to the imagination; and the scene when Harry
Bertram lands at Ellangowan is a model instance of romantic
method.

' "I remember the tune well," ' he says, ' "though I cannot guess
what should at present so strongly recall it to my memory." He took
his flageolet from his pocket and played a simple melody. Apparently
the tune awoke the corresponding associations of a damsel. . . . She
immediately took up the song:—

> Are these the links of Forth, she said;
>   Or are they the crooks of Dee,
> Or the bonny woods of Warroch Head
>   That I so fain would see?

' "By heaven!" said Bertram, "it is the very ballad." '

On this quotation two remarks fall to be made. First, as an
instance of modern feeling for romance, this famous touch of the
flageolet and the old song is selected by Miss Braddon for omission.
Miss Braddon's idea of a story, like Mrs Todgers's idea of a wooden
leg, were something strange to have expounded.* As a matter of personal experience, Meg's appearance to old Mr Bertram on the road,
the ruins of Derncleugh, the scene of the flageolet, and the Dom-
inie's recognition of Harry, are the four strong notes that continue to
ring in the mind after the book is laid aside. The second point is still
more curious. The reader will observe a mark of excision in the
passage as quoted by me. Well, here is how it runs in the original: 'A
damsel, who, close behind a fine spring about half-way down the
descent, and which had once supplied the castle with water, was
engaged in bleaching linen.' A man who gave in such copy would be
discharged from the staff of a daily paper. Scott has forgotten to
prepare the reader for the presence of the 'damsel'; he has forgotten
to mention the spring and its relation to the ruin; and now, face to
face with his omission, instead of trying back and starting fair, crams
all this matter, tail foremost, into a single shambling sentence. It is
not merely bad English, or bad style; it is abominably bad narrative
besides.

Certainly the contrast is remarkable; and it is one that throws a strong light upon the subject of this paper. For here we have a man, of the finest creative instinct, touching with perfect certainty and charm the romantic junctures of his story; and we find him utterly careless, almost, it would seem, incapable, in the technical matter of style; and not only frequently weak, but frequently wrong, in points of drama. In character parts, indeed, and particularly in the Scotch, he was delicate, strong, and truthful; but the trite, obliterated features of too many of his heroes have already wearied two generations of readers. At times, his characters will speak with something far beyond propriety, with a true heroic note; but on the next page they will be wading wearily forward with an ungrammatical and undramatic rigmarole of words. The man who could conceive and write the character of Elspeth of the Craigburnfoot, as Scott has conceived and written it, had not only splendid romantic, but splendid tragic, gifts. How comes it, then, that he could so often fob us off with languid, inarticulate twaddle?

It seems to me that the explanation is to be found in the very quality of his surprising merits. As his books are play to the reader, so were they play to him. He conjured up the beautiful with delight, but he had hardly patience to describe it. He was a great daydreamer, a seer of fit and beautiful and humorous visions; but hardly a great artist; hardly, in the manful sense, an artist at all. He pleased himself, and so he pleases us. Of the pleasures of his art he tasted fully; but of its toils and vigils and distresses never man knew less. A great romantic—an idle child.

A CHAPTER ON DREAMS

THE past is all of one texture—whether feigned or suffered—whether acted out in three dimensions, or only witnessed in that small theatre of the brain which we keep brightly lighted all night long, after the jets are down, and darkness and sleep reign undisturbed in the remainder of the body. There is no distinction on the face of our experiences; one is vivid indeed, and one dull, and one pleasant, and another agonising to remember; but which of them is what we call true, and which a dream, there is not one hair to prove. The past stands on a precarious footing; another straw split in the field of metaphysic, and behold us robbed of it. There is scarce a family that can count four generations but lays a claim to some dormant title or some castle and estate: a claim not prosecutable in any court of law, but flattering to the fancy and a great alleviation of idle hours. A man's claim to his own past is yet less valid. A paper might turn up (in proper story-book fashion) in the secret drawer of an old ebony secretary, and restore your family to its ancient honours, and reinstate mine in a certain West Indian islet (not far from St Kitt's, as beloved tradition hummed in my young ears) which was once ours, and is now unjustly some one else's, and for that matter (in the state of the sugar trade) is not worth anything to anybody. I do not say that these revolutions are likely; only no man can deny that they are possible; and the past, on the other hand, is lost for ever: our old days and deeds, our old selves, too, and the very world in which these scenes were acted, all brought down to the same faint residuum as a last night's dream, to some incontinuous images, and an echo in the chambers of the brain. Not an hour, not a mood, not a glance of the eye, can we revoke; it is all gone, past conjuring. And yet conceive us robbed of it, conceive that little thread of memory that we trail behind us broken at the pocket's edge; and in what naked nullity should we be left! for we only guide ourselves, and only know ourselves, by these air-painted pictures of the past.

Upon these grounds, there are some among us who claim to have lived longer and more richly than their neighbours; when they lay asleep they claim they were still active; and among the treasures of memory that all men review for their amusement, these count in no second place the harvests of their dreams. There is one of this kind whom I have in my eye, and whose case is perhaps unusual enough to be described. He was from a child an ardent and uncomfortable dreamer.* When he had a touch of fever at night, and the room swelled and shrank, and his clothes, hanging on a nail, now loomed up instant to the bigness of a church, and now drew away into a horror of infinite distance and infinite littleness, the poor soul was very well aware of what must follow, and struggled hard against the approaches of that slumber which was the beginning of sorrows. But his struggles were in vain; sooner or later the night-hag would have him by the throat, and pluck him, strangling and screaming, from his sleep. His dreams were at times commonplace enough, at times very strange: at times they were almost formless, he would be haunted, for instance, by nothing more definite than a certain hue of brown, which he did not mind in the least while he was awake, but feared and loathed while he was dreaming; at times, again, they took on every detail of circumstance, as when once he supposed he must swallow the populous world, and awoke screaming with the horror of the thought. The two chief troubles of his very narrow existence— the practical and everyday trouble of school tasks and the ultimate and airy one of hell and judgment—were often confounded together into one appalling nightmare.* He seemed to himself to stand before the Great White Throne; he was called on, poor little devil, to recite some form of words, on which his destiny depended; his tongue stuck, his memory was blank, hell gaped for him; and he would awake, clinging to the curtain-rod with his knees to his chin.

These were extremely poor experiences, on the whole; and at that time of life my dreamer would have very willingly parted with his power of dreams. But presently, in the course of his growth, the cries and physical contortions passed away, seemingly for ever; his visions were still for the most part miserable, but they were more constantly supported; and he would awake with no more extreme symptom than a flying heart, a freezing scalp, cold sweats, and the speechless midnight fear. His dreams, too, as befitted a mind better stocked with particulars, became more circumstantial, and had more the air and continuity of life. The look of the world beginning to take hold on his attention, scenery came to play a part in his sleeping as well as in his waking thoughts, so that he would take long, uneventful journeys and see strange towns and beautiful places as he lay in bed. And, what is more significant, an odd taste that he had for the Georgian costume and for stories laid in that period of English history, began to rule the features of his dreams; so that he masqueraded there in a three-cornered hat, and was much engaged with Jacobite conspiracy* between the hour for bed and that for breakfast. About the same time, he began to read in his dreams—tales, for the most part, and for the most part after the manner of G. P. R. James,* but so incredibly more vivid and moving than any printed book, that he has ever since been malcontent with literature.

And then, while he was yet a student, there came to him a dream-adventure which he has no anxiety to repeat; he began, that is to say, to dream in sequence and thus to lead a double life—one of the day, one of the night—one that he had every reason to believe was the true one, another that he had no means of proving to be false. I should have said he studied, or was by way of studying, at Edinburgh College, which (it may be supposed) was how I came to know him. Well, in his dream-life, he passed a long day in the surgical theatre, his heart in his mouth, his teeth on edge, seeing monstrous mal-formations and the abhorred dexterity of surgeons. In a heavy, rainy, foggy evening he came forth into the South Bridge, turned up the High Street, and entered the door of a tall *land*,* at the top of which he supposed himself to lodge. All night long, in his wet clothes, he climbed the stairs, stair after stair in endless series, and at every second flight a flaring lamp with a reflector. All night long, he brushed by single persons passing downward—beggarly women of the street, great, weary, muddy labourers, poor scarecrows of men, pale parodies of women—but all drowsy and weary like himself, and all single, and all brushing against him as they passed. In the end, out of a northern window, he would see day beginning to whiten over the Firth, give up the ascent, turn to descend, and in a breath be back again upon the streets, in his wet clothes, in the wet, haggard dawn, trudging to another day of monstrosities and operations. Time went quicker in the life of dreams, some seven hours (as near as he can guess) to one; and it went, besides, more intensely, so that the gloom of these fancied experiences clouded the day, and he had not shaken off their shadow ere it was time to lie down and to renew them. I cannot tell how long it was that he endured this discipline; but it was long enough to leave a great black blot upon his memory, long enough to send him, trembling for his reason, to the doors of a certain doctor; whereupon with a simple draught he was restored* to the common lot of man.

The poor gentleman has since been troubled by nothing of the sort; indeed, his nights were for some while like other men's, now blank, now chequered with dreams, and these sometimes charming, sometimes appalling, but except for an occasional vividness, of no extraordinary kind. I will just note one of these occasions, ere I pass on to what makes my dreamer truly interesting. It seemed to him that he was in the first floor of a rough hill-farm. The room showed some poor efforts at gentility, a carpet on the floor, a piano, I think, against the wall; but, for all these refinements, there was no mistaking he was in a moorland place, among hillside people, and set in miles of heather. He looked down from the window upon a bare farmyard, that seemed to have been long disused. A great, uneasy stillness lay upon the world. There was no sign of the farm-folk or of any live stock, save for an old, brown, curly dog of the retriever breed, who sat close in against the wall of the house and seemed to be dozing. Sometimes about this dog disquieted the dreamer; it was quite a nameless feeling, for the beast looked right enough—indeed, he was so old and dull and dusty and broken-down, that he should rather have awakened pity; and yet the conviction came and grew upon the dreamer that this was no proper dog at all, but something hellish. A great many dozing summer flies hummed about the yard; and presently the dog thrust forth his paw, caught a fly in his open palm, carried it to his mouth like an ape, and looking suddenly up at the dreamer in the window, winked to him with one eye. The dream went on, it matters not how it went; it was a good dream as dreams go; but there was nothing in the sequel worthy of that devilish brown dog. And the point of interest for me lies partly in that very fact: that having found so singular an incident, my imperfect dreamer should prove unable to carry the tale to a fit end and fall back on indescribable noises and indiscriminate horrors. It would be different now; he knows his business better!

For, to approach at last the point: This honest fellow had long been in the custom of setting himself to sleep with tales, and so had his father before him; but these were irresponsible inventions, told for the teller's pleasure, with no eye to the crass public or the thwart reviewer: tales where a thread might be dropped, or one adventure quitted for another, on fancy's least suggestion. So that the little people* who manage man's internal theatre had not as yet received a very rigorous training, and played upon their stage like children who should have slipped into the house and found it empty, rather than like drilled actors performing a set piece to a huge hall of faces. But presently my dreamer began to turn his former amusement of story-telling to (what is called) account; by which I mean that he began to write and sell his tales. Here was he, and here were the little people who did that part of his business, in quite new conditions. The stories must now be trimmed and pared and set upon all fours, they must run from a beginning to an end and fit (after a manner) with the laws of life; the pleasure, in one word, had become a business; and that not only for the dreamer, but for the little people of his theatre. These understood the change as well as he. When he lay down to prepare himself for sleep, he no longer sought amusement, but printable and profitable tales; and after he had dozed off in his box-seat, his little people continued their evolutions with the same mercantile designs. All other forms of dream deserted him but two: he still occasionally reads the most delightful books, he still visits at times the most delightful places; and it is perhaps worthy of note that to these same places, and to one in particular, he returns at intervals of months and years, finding new field-paths, visiting new neighbours, beholding that happy valley under new effects of noon and dawn and sunset. But all the rest of the family of visions is quite lost to him: the common, mangled version of yesterday's affair, the raw-head-and-bloody-bones nightmare, rumoured to be the child of toasted cheese—these and their like are gone; and, for the most part, whether awake or asleep, he is simply occupied—he or his little people—in consciously making stories for the market. This dreamer (like many other persons) has encountered some trifling vicissitudes of fortune. When the bank begins to send letters and the butcher to linger at the back gate, he sets to belabouring his brains after a story, for that is his readiest money-winner; and, behold! at once the little people begin to bestir themselves in the same quest, and labour all night long, and all night long set before him truncheons of tales upon their lighted theatre. No fear of his being frightened now; the flying heart and the frozen scalp are things bygone; applause, grow-ing applause, growing interest, growing exultation in his own clev-erness (for he takes all the credit), and at last a jubilant leap to wakefulness, with the cry, 'I have it, that'll do!' upon his lips: with such and similar emotions he sits at these nocturnal dramas, with such outbreaks, like Claudius in the play,* he scatters the performance in the midst. Often enough the waking is a disappointment: he has been too deep asleep, as I explain the thing; drowsiness has gained his little people, they have gone stumbling and maundering through their parts; and the play, to the awakened mind, is seen to be a tissue of absurdities. And yet how often have these sleepless Brownies* done him honest service, and given him, as he sat idly taking his pleasure in the boxes, better tales than he could fashion for himself.

Here is one, exactly as it came to him. It seemed he was the son of a very rich and wicked man, the owner of broad acres and a most damnable temper. The dreamer (and that was the son) had lived much abroad, on purpose to avoid his parent; and when at length he returned to England, it was to find him married again to a young wife, who was supposed to suffer cruelly and to loathe her yoke. Because of this marriage (as the dreamer indistinctly understood) it was desirable for father and son to have a meeting; and yet both being proud and both angry, neither would condescend upon a visit. Meet they did accordingly, in a desolate, sandy country by the sea; and there they quarrelled, and the son, stung by some intolerable insult, struck down the father dead. No suspicion was aroused; the dead man was found and buried, and the dreamer succeeded to the broad estates, and found himself installed under the same roof with his father's widow, for whom no provision had been made. These two lived very much alone, as people may after a bereavement, sat down to table together, shared the long evenings, and grew daily better friends; until it seemed to him of a sudden that she was prying about dangerous matters, that she had conceived a notion of his guilt, that she watched him and tried him with questions. He drew back from her company as men draw back from a precipice suddenly discovered; and yet so strong was the attraction that he would drift again and again into the old intimacy, and again and again be startled back by some suggestive question or some inexplicable meaning in her eye. So they lived at cross purposes, a life full of broken dialogue, challenging glances, and suppressed passion; until, one day, he saw the woman slipping from the house in a veil, followed her to the station, followed her in the train to the seaside country, and out over the sandhills to the very place where the murder was done. There she began to grope among the bents, he watching her, flat upon his face; and presently she had something in her hand—I cannot remember what it was, but it was deadly evidence against the dreamer—and as she held it up to look at it, perhaps from the shock of the discovery, her foot slipped, and she hung at some peril on the brink of the tall sand-wreaths. He had no thought but to spring up and rescue her; and there they stood face to face, she with that deadly matter openly in her hand—his very presence on the spot another link of proof. It was plain she was about to speak, but this was more than he could bear—he could bear to be lost, but not to talk of it with his destroyer; and he cut her short with trivial conversation. Arm in arm, they returned together to the train, talking he knew not what, made the journey back in the same carriage, sat down to dinner, and passed the evening in the drawing-room as in the past. But suspense and fear drummed in the dreamer's bosom. 'She has not denounced me yet'—so his thoughts ran—'when will she denounce me? Will it be tomorrow?' And it was not tomorrow, nor the next day, nor the next; and their life settled back on the old terms, only that she seemed kinder than before, and that, as for him, the burthen of his suspense and wonder grew daily more unbearable, so that he wasted away like a man with a disease. Once, indeed, he broke all bounds of decency, seized an occasion when she was abroad, ransacked her room, and at last, hidden away among her jewels, found the damning evidence. There he stood, holding this thing, which was his life, in the hollow of his hand, and marvelling at her inconsequent behaviour, that she should seek, and keep, and yet not use it; and then the door opened, and behold herself. So, once more, they stood, eye to eye, with the evidence between them; and once more she raised to him a face brimming with some communication; and once more he shied away from speech and cut her off. But before he left the room, which he had turned upside down, he laid back his death-warrant where he had found it; and at that, her face lighted up. The next thing he heard, she was explaining to her maid, with some ingenious falsehood, the disorder of her things. Flesh and blood could bear the strain no longer; and I think it was the next morning (though chronology is always hazy in the theatre of the mind) that he burst from his reserve. They had been breakfasting together in one corner of a great, parqueted, sparely-furnished room of many windows; all the time of the meal she had tortured him with sly allusions; and no sooner were the servants gone, and these two protagonists alone together, than he leaped to his feet. She too sprang up, with a pale face; with a pale face, she heard him as he raved out his complaint: Why did she torture him so? she knew all, she knew he was no enemy to her; why did she not denounce him at once? what signified her whole behaviour? why did she torture him? and yet again, why did she torture him? And when he had done, she fell upon her knees, and with outstretched hands: 'Do you not understand?' she cried. 'I love you!'

Hereupon, with a pang of wonder and mercantile delight, the dreamer awoke. His mercantile delight was not of long endurance; for it soon became plain that in this spirited tale there were unmarketable elements; which is just the reason why you have it here so briefly told. But his wonder has still kept growing; and I think the reader's will also, if he consider it ripely. For now he sees why I speak of the little people as of substantive inventors and performers. To the end they had kept their secret. I will go bail for the dreamer (having excellent grounds for valuing his candour) that he had no guess whatever at the motive of the woman—the hinge of the whole well-invented plot—until the instant of that highly dramatic declaration. It was not his tale; it was the little people's! And observe: not only was the secret kept, the story was told with really guileful craftsmanship. The conduct of both actors is (in the cant phrase) psychologically correct, and the emotion aptly graduated up to the surprising climax. I am awake now, and I know this trade; and yet I cannot better it. I am awake, and I live by this business; and yet I could not outdo—could not perhaps equal—that crafty artifice (as of some old, experienced carpenter of plays, some Dennery or Sardou*) by which the same situation is twice presented and the two actors twice brought face to face over the evidence, only once it is in her hand, once in his—and these in their due order, the least dramatic first. The more I think of it, the more I am moved to press upon the world my question: Who are the Little People? They are near connections of the dreamer's, beyond doubt; they share in his financial worries and have an eye to the bank-book; they share plainly in his training; they have plainly learned like him to build the scheme of a considerate story and to arrange emotion in progressive order; only I think they have more talent; and one thing is beyond doubt, they can tell him a story piece by piece, like a serial, and keep him all the while in ignorance of where they aim. Who are they, then? and who is the dreamer?

Well, as regards the dreamer, I can answer that, for he is no less a person than myself;—as I might have told you from the beginning, only that the critics murmur over my consistent egotism;—and as I am positively forced to tell you now, or I could advance but little farther with my story. And for the Little People, what shall I say they are but just my Brownies, God bless them! who do one-half my work for me while I am fast asleep, and in all human likelihood, do the rest for me as well, when I am wide awake and fondly suppose I do it for myself. That part which is done while I am sleeping is the Brownies' part beyond contention; but that which is done when I am up and about is by no means necessarily mine, since all goes to show the Brownies have a hand in it even then. Here is a doubt that much concerns my conscience. For myself—what I call I, my conscious ego, the denizen of the pineal gland unless he has changed his residence since Descartes,* the man with the conscience and the variable bank-account, the man with the hat and the boots, and the privilege of voting and not carrying his candidate at the general elections—I am sometimes tempted to suppose he is no story-teller at all, but a creature as matter of fact as any cheesemonger or any cheese, and a realist bemired up to the ears in actuality; so that, by that account, the whole of my published fiction should be the single-handed product of some Brownie, some Familiar, some unseen collaborator, whom I keep locked in a back garret, while I get all the praise and he but a share (which I cannot prevent him getting) of the pudding. I am an excellent adviser, something like Molière's servant; I pull back and I cut down; and I dress the whole in the best words and sentences that I can find and make; I hold the pen, too; and I do the sitting at the table, which is about the worst of it; and when all is done, I make up the manuscript and pay for the registration; so that, on the whole, I have some claim to share, though not so largely as I do, in the profits of our common enterprise.

I can but give an instance or so of what part is done sleeping and what part awake, and leave the reader to share what laurels there are, at his own nod, between myself and my collaborators; and to do this I will first take a book that a number of persons have been polite enough to read, the *Strange Case of Dr Jekyll and Mr Hyde*. I had long been trying to write a story on this subject, to find a body, a vehicle, for that strong sense of man's double being which must at times come in upon and overwhelm the mind of every thinking creature. I had even written one, *The Travelling Companion*, which was returned by an editor on the plea that it was a work of genius and indecent, and which I burned the other day on the ground that it was not a work of genius, and that *Jekyll* had supplanted it. Then came one of those financial fluctuations to which (with an elegant modesty) I have hitherto referred in the third person. For two days I went about racking my brains for a plot of any sort; and on the second night I dreamed the scene at the window, and a scene afterward split in two, in which Hyde, pursued for some crime, took the powder and underwent the change in the presence of his pursuers. All the rest was made awake, and consciously, although I think I can trace in much of it the manner of my Brownies. The meaning of the tale is therefore mine, and had long pre-existed in my garden of Adonis,* and tried one body after another in vain; indeed, I do most of the morality, worse luck! and my Brownies have not a rudiment of what we call a conscience. Mine, too, is the setting, mine the characters. All that was given me was the matter of three scenes, and the central idea of a voluntary change becoming involuntary. Will it be thought ungenerous, after I have been so liberally ladling out praise to my unseen collaborators, if I here toss them over, bound hand and foot, into the arena of the critics? For the business of the powders, which so many have censured, is, I am relieved to say, not mine at all but the Brownies'. Of another tale, in case the reader should have glanced at it, I may say a word: the not very defensible story of *Olalla*. Here the court, the mother, the mother's niche, Olalla, Olalla's chamber, the meetings on the stair, the broken window, the ugly scene of the bite, were all given me in bulk and detail as I have tried to write them; to this I added only the external scenery (for in my dream I never was beyond the court), the portrait, the characters of Felipe and the priest, the moral, such as it is, and the last pages, such as, alas! they are. And I may even say that in this case the moral itself was given me; for it arose immediately on a comparison of the mother and the daughter, and from the hideous trick of atavism in the first. Sometimes a parabolic sense is still more undeniably present in a dream; sometimes I cannot but suppose my Brownies have been aping Bunyan,* and yet in no case with what would possibly be called a moral in a tract; never with the ethical narrowness; conveying hints instead of life's larger limitations and that sort of sense which we seem to perceive in the arabesque of time and space.

For the most part, it will be seen, my Brownies are somewhat fantastic, like their stories hot and hot, full of passion and the picturesque, alive with animating incident; and they have no prejudice against the supernatural. But the other day they gave me a surprise, entertaining me with a love-story, a little April comedy, which I ought certainly to hand over to the author of *A Chance Acquaintance*,* for he could write it as it should be written, and I am sure (although I mean to try) that I cannot.—But who would have supposed that a Brownie of mine should invent a tale for Mr Howells?

APPENDIX A

from HENRY MAUDSLEY, 'THE DISINTEGRATIONS OF THE "EGO"'

[THIS short sample is taken from section VI of part III of Maudsley's *Body and Will, Being an Essay concerning Will in its Metaphysical, Physiological and Pathological Aspects* (taken from the 1883 edition, the closest to the publication date of *Jekyll and Hyde*, 301–16). Henry Maudsley (1835–1918) was one of the most influential 'alienists' of his day: he was an asylum director in the 1860s before turning to private practice and a prolific writing career, beginning with *Physiology and Pathology of Mind* in 1867. He regarded mental illness as a disorder of biological heredity and dysfunctional will: he was a materialist suspicious of the religious or metaphysical language of 'soul'.]

In that exquisitely fine and intricately complex organisation which is the physical basis of mind every interest of the entire body, every organic energy, has direct or indirect representation: there is nothing in the outermost that is not, so to speak, represented in the innermost. Not one organ but all organs, not one structure but all structures, not one movement but all movements, not one feeling but all feelings; all vibrations of energy, of what sort soever, from all parts of the body, the nearest and the most remote, the meanest and most noble, conscious and infra-conscious;—stream into the unifying centre and make their felt or unfelt contributions to the outcome of conscious function. The brain is the central organ of the bodily synthesis, sympathy, and synergy, and the will at its best the supreme expression of that unity. Therefore it is that in will is contained character: not character of mind only, as commonly under-stood, but the character of every organ of the body, the consentient functions of which enter into the full expression of individuality.

That being so, it is made evident that disorganisation of the union of the supreme cerebral centres must be a more or less dissolution of the conscious self, the *ego*, according to the depth of the damage to the physiological unity. Even if any one organ of the body be defective, it is a breach in the supreme unity of consciousness, for it is a deprivation to the extent of its deficient energy, and a disturbance to the degree that its work is thrown upon other organs: it is like a horse in a team that does not do its exact share of the work uniformly. The constant feeling of personal identity on which metaphysicians lay so much stress as a fundamental intuition of consciousness, discerning in it the incontestable touch and proof of a spiritual *ego* which they cannot get into actual contact with in any other way, may be expected to be sometimes wavering and uncertain, in other cases divided and discordant, and in extreme cases extinguished. But that is a dismayful expectation to entertain concerning the 'I,' the '*ego*'—the *ens unum et semper cognitum in omnibus notitiis**—of which they thus protest we have more or less clear consciousness in every exercise of intelligence. Look frankly then at the facts and see what conclusion they warrant. Is there the least sign of a consciousness of his *ego* in the senseless, speechless, howling, slavering, dirty, defenceless, and utterly helpless idiot, whose defective cerebral centres are incapable of responding to such weak and imperfect impressions as his dull senses are able to convey, and incapable of any association of the few, dim and vague impressions that he does receive? No doubt his body, so long as it holds together by the ministering care of others, may be said to be an *ego* or self; but from the human standpoint what a self! It is not a mental *ego*, since the central organic mechanism in which the lower bodily energies should obtain higher representation, and mental organisation take place—the before-mentioned synthesis, sympathy, and synergy be effected—is either altogether wanting or hopelessly ill constructed. The miserable specimen of degeneracy does not and cannot therefore in the least know that he is a self, or feel that a human self is degraded in him. If the sure and certain proof of a soul existing independent of the organism, and the thereupon based sure and certain hope of a resurrection to life eternal, be the distinct and permanent consciousness of identity amongst all changes and chances of mortal structure, it is certainly a mighty pity that the proof should fail us in the very case in which its certitude is most needed, would be most consoling and assuring, and its success most triumphant.

The truth is that the manifold varieties of mental derangement yield examples of all degrees of lessening brightness of the consciousness of self down to its actual extinction, and of all sorts of derangement and confusion of it from the least unto the worst distraction. Always the difficulty in a particular case is to know exactly what the defect or confusion is, since it is not possible to enter into another person's mind, to realise his state of consciousness, and in that way to measure and appreciate its exact degree and quality.

It is a common event in one sort of mental disorder, especially at the beginning of it, for the person to complain that he is completely and painfully changed; that he is no longer himself, but feels himself unutterably strange; and that things around him, though wearing their usual aspect, yet somehow seem quite different. I am so changed that I feel as if I were not myself but another person; although I know it is an illusion, it is an illusion which I cannot shake off; all things appear strange to me and I cannot properly apprehend them even though they are really familiar;

they look a long way off and more like the figures of a dream than realities, and indeed it is just as if I were in a dream and my will paralysed. It is impossible to describe the feeling of unreality that I have about everything; I assure myself over and over again that I am myself, but still I cannot make impressions take their proper hold of me, and come into fit relations of familiarity with my true self; between my present self and my past self it seems as if an eternity of time and an infinity of space were interposed; the suffering that I endure is indescribable:—such is the kind of language by which these persons endeavour to express the profound change in themselves which they feel only too painfully but cannot describe adequately.

An interesting and very striking example of changed personal identity is furnished by a form of mental derangement which, as it revolves regularly through two alternating and opposite phases, was called by French writers circular insanity, but is better called alternating insanity. An attack of much mental excitement with great elation of thought, feeling, and conduct is followed by an opposite dark phase of depression, gloom, and apathy, each state lasting for weeks or months, and the usual succession of them recurring from time to time after longer or shorter intervals of sanity. Between the two states the contrast is as striking as could well be imagined: in the one the person is elated, exultant, self-confident, boastful and overflowing with energy; talks freely of private matters which he would never have mentioned in his sound state, and familiarly with those above and below him in station whom, when himself, he would not have thought of addressing; in like manner writes many and long letters full of details of opinions, affairs, and plans, to persons with whom he has a slight acquaintance only; spends money recklessly, though not reckless in that way by natural disposition; projects bold and sometimes wild schemes of adventure; is ready and pleased to harangue in public who never made a public speech before; is careless of social proprieties and even disregards moral reticences and restraints; listens to prudential advice but heeds it not, being inspired with an extraordinary feeling of well-being, of intellectual power, of unfettered thought and will. An actual disruption of the *ego* there is not, but there is an extraordinary exaltation of it, in fact an extreme moral rather than an intellectual alienation. The condition of things is much like that which goes before an ordinary outbreak of acute mania, when there is great mental exaltation without actual incoherence, alienation of character without alienation of intelligence, but it is not, like it, followed by turbulent degeneracy; for when the excitement passes off there supervenes the second phase, that of extreme mental despondency and moral prostration.

How changed the person now from what he was! As self-distrustful as before he was self-sufficient; as retiring as before he was obtrusive; as shy and silent as before he was loud and talkative; as diffident as before he was boastful; as impotent to think and act as before he was eager and energetic to plan and to do; as entirely oppressed with a dominating sense of mental and bodily incapacity as before he was possessed with an exultant feeling of exalted powers. To all intents and purposes he is a different person, another *ego*, at any rate so far as consciousness is concerned—subjectively though not objectively—since in all relations he feels, thinks, and acts quite differently. Not less marked than the mental transformation is the accompanying veritable bodily transfiguration in some cases; for during the exaltation there is a general animation of the bodily functions which makes the individual look, as he feels, years younger. The skin is more fresh and soft, its wrinkles are smoothened, the eyes bright, eager, and animated, the hair less grey than it perhaps was, the pulse more vigorous, the digestion stronger, the activity increased tenfold, and one who had ceased to be after the manner of women may become so again. During the sequent prostration the contrast is so great that he would hardly be known to be the same person by one who knew him only slightly; for every one of the foregoing signs of youth and vigour has given place to as marked a sign of age and want of vigour. In the one state he is as if he had drunk a draught of the elixir of life, in the other as if he had foretasted the apathy of death.

An interesting fact which cannot fail to attract attention is that during the exalted state of this alternating derangement the person does with almost exact automatic repetition the things that he did, and has the thoughts and feelings that he had, in former exalted states, and during the prostrate state that he thinks, feels and does exactly as he did in former prostrate states. In the one state, however, he has not a clear and exact remembrance of the events of the other; not probably that he forgets them entirely, but that he has only that sort of vague, hazy and incomplete remembrance which one has oftentimes of the events of a dream, or that a drunken man has, when sober, of his drunken feelings and doings. How indeed could he remember them clearly, since it is plain he would be compelled, in order to do so, to reproduce exactly in himself the one state when he was actually in the other? It is impossible therefore he should realise sincerely the experiences of the one during the other, though he may know as a matter of fact that they occurred to him, and, feeling some shame for what he remembers, and misgivings concerning what he does not remember, be unwilling to recall them and speak of them.

In spite, then, of aught which psychological theory appealing to its own internal oracle may urge to the contrary, it is incontestably proved by observation of instances that there are states of disordered consciousness which, being quite unlike states of normal consciousness, are not to be measured by them, and the events of which may be remembered only dimly, hazily felt rather than remembered, or completely forgotten. The lesson of them is the lesson which has been enforced over and over again on physiological grounds—namely, that the consciousness of self, the unity of the *ego*, is a consequence, not a cause; the expression of a full and harmonious function of the aggregate of differentiated mind-centres, not a mysterious metaphysical entity lying behind function and inspiring and guiding it; a subjective synthesis or unity based upon the objective synthesis or unity of the organism. As such, it may be obscured, deranged, divided, apparently transformed. For every breach of the unity of the united centres is a breach of it: subtract any one centre from the intimate physiological co-operation, the self is *pro tanto** weakened or mutilated; obstruct or derange the conducting function of the associating bonds between the various centres, so that they are dissociated or disunited, the self loses in corresponding degree its sense of continuity and unity; stimulate one or two centres or groups of centres to a morbid hypertrophy so that they absorb to them most of the mental nourishment and keep up a predominant and almost exclusive function, the personality appears to be transformed; strip off a whole layer of the highest centres—that highest superordinate organisation of them that ministers to abstract reasoning and moral feeling—you reduce man to the condition of one of the higher animals; take away all the supreme centres, you bring him to the state of a simply sentient creature; remove the centres of sense, you reduce him to a bare vegetative existence when, like a cabbage, he has an objective but no subjective *ego*. These are the conclusions which we are compelled to form when, not blinking facts, we observe nature sincerely and interpret it faithfully, going to plain experience for facts to inform our understandings, instead of invoking our own imaginations to utter oracles to us.

APPENDIX B

from FREDERIC MYERS,
'THE MULTIPLEX PERSONALITY'

[THIS essay first appeared in the leading monthly journal, the *Nineteenth Century*, in November 1886 (648–66). Frederic Myers (1843–1901) was a Cambridge classicist, poet, schools inspector, and an amateur psychologist who trained himself into being one of the leading psychologists of his time. Myers read emergent French and German dynamic theories of mind to contest the sort of materialism upheld by Maudsley, producing a very different conception of consciousness that embraced rather than pathologized the possibility of multiple strands of consciousness. This was part of his project to attempt to prove the existence of telepathy, a term Myers coined in 1882, as part of his work with the Society for Psychical Research. He was at the centre of literary society, and knew many of RLS's close friends. Myers's critical and psychological papers on *Jekyll and Hyde* are referred to in the Explanatory Notes; RLS also wrote to Myers on his experience of divided consciousness during his fevers, and this was used in Myers's synthesis of his theory of mind, 'The Subliminal Consciousness'.]

I purpose in this paper briefly to suggest certain topics for reflection, topics which will need to be more fully worked out elsewhere. My theme is the multiplex and mutable character of that which we know as the Personality of man, and the practical advantage which we may gain by discerning and working upon this as yet unrecognised modifiability. I shall begin by citing a few examples of hysterical transfer, of morbid disintegration; I shall then show that these spontaneous readjustments of man's being are not all of them pathological or retrogressive; nay, that the familiar changes of sleep and waking contain the hint of further alternations which may be beneficially acquired.

I begin, then, with one or two examples of the pitch to which the dissociation of memories, faculties, sensibilities may be carried, without resulting in mere insane chaos, mere demented oblivion. These cases as yet are few in number. It is only of late years—and it is mainly in France—that *savants** have recorded with due care those psychical lessons, deeper than any art of our own can teach us, which natural anomalies and aberrant instances afford.

Pre-eminent among the priceless living documents which nature thus offers to our study stand the singular personages known as Louis V. and

Félida X. Félida's name at least is probably familiar to most of my readers; but Louis V.'s case* is little known, and although some account of it has already been given in English, it will be needful to recall certain particulars in order to introduce the speculations which follow.

Louis V. began life (in 1863) as the neglected child of a turbulent mother. He was sent to a reformatory at ten years old, and there showed himself, as he has always done when his organisation has given him a chance, quiet, well-behaved, and obedient. Then at fourteen years old he had a great fright from a viper—a fright which threw him off his balance and started the series of psychical oscillations on which he has been tossed ever since. At first the symptoms were only physical, epilepsy* and hysterical paralysis of the legs; and at the asylum of Bonneval, whither he was next sent, he worked at tailoring steadily for a couple of months. Then suddenly he had a hystero-epileptic attack—fifty hours of convulsions and ecstasy—and when he awoke from it he was no longer paralysed, no longer acquainted with tailoring, and no longer virtuous. His memory was set back, so to say, to the moment of the viper's appearance, and he could remember nothing since. His character had become violent, greedy, and quarrelsome, and his tastes were radically changed. For instance, though he had before the attack been a total abstainer, he now not only drank his own wine but stole the wine of the other patients. He escaped from Bonneval, and after a few turbulent years, tracked by his occasional relapses into hospital or madhouse, he turned up once more at the Rochefort asylum in the character of a private of marines, convicted of theft but considered to be of unsound mind. And at Rochefort and La Rochelle, by great good fortune, he fell into the hands of three physicians—Professors Bourm and Burot, and Dr Mabille—able and willing to continue and extend the observations which Dr Camuset at Bonneval and Dr Jules Voisin at Bicêtre had already made on this most precious of *mauvais sujets** at earlier points in his chequered career.

He is now no longer at Rochefort, and Dr Burot informs me that his health has much improved, and that his peculiarities have in great part disappeared. I must, however, for clearness' sake, use the present tense in briefly describing his condition at the time when the long series of experiments were made.

The state into which he has gravitated is a very unpleasing one. There is paralysis and insensibility of the right side, and (as is often the case in right hemiplegia) the speech is indistinct and difficult. Nevertheless he is constantly haranguing any one who will listen to him, abusing his physicians, or preaching, with a monkey-like impudence rather than with reasoned clearness, radicalism in politics and atheism in religion. He makes bad jokes, and if any one pleases him he endeavours to caress him.

He remembers recent events during his residence at the Rochefort asylum, but only two scraps of his life before that date—namely, his vicious period at Bonneval and a part of his stay at Bicêtre.

Except this strangely fragmentary memory there is nothing very unusual in this condition, and in many asylums no experiments on it would have been attempted. Fortunately the physicians of Rochefort were familiar with the efficacy of the contact of metals in provoking transfer of hysterical hemiplegia from one side to the other.* They tried various metals in turn on Louis V. Lead, silver, and zinc had no effect. Copper produced a slight return of sensibility in the paralysed arm. But steel, applied to the right arm, transferred the whole insensibility to the left side of the body.

Inexplicable as such a phenomenon certainly is, it is sufficiently common (as French physicians hold) in hysterical cases to excite little surprise. What puzzled the doctors was the change of character which accompanied the change of sensibility. When Louis V. issued from the crisis of transfer, with its minute of anxious expression and panting breath, he was what might fairly be called a new man. The restless insolence, the savage impulsiveness, have wholly disappeared. The patient is now gentle, respectful, and modest. He can speak clearly now, but he only speaks when he is spoken to. If he is asked his views on religion and politics, he prefers to leave such matters to wiser heads than his own. It might seem that morally and intellectually the patient's cure had been complete.

But now ask him what he thinks of Rochefort; how he liked his regiment of marines. He will blankly answer that he knows nothing of Rochefort, and was never a soldier in his life. 'Where are you, then, and what is the date of to-day?' 'I am at Bicêtre; it is January 2, 1884; and I hope to see M. Voisin today, as I did yesterday.'

It is found, in fact, that he has now the memory of two short periods of life (different from those which he remembers when his *right* side is paralysed), periods during which, so far as can now be ascertained, his character was of this same decorous type and his paralysis was on the left side.

These two conditions are what are now termed his first and his second, out of a series of six or more through which he can be made to pass. For brevity's sake I will further describe his *fifth* state only.

If he is placed in an electric bath, or if a magnet be placed on his head, it looks at first sight as though a complete physical cure had been effected. All paralysis, all defect of sensibility, has disappeared. His movements are light and active, his expression gentle and timid. But ask him where he is, and you find that he has gone back to a boy of fourteen, that he is at St Urbain, his first reformatory, and that his memory embraces his years

of childhood, and stops short on the very day when he had the fright with
the viper. If he is pressed to recollect the incident of the viper a violent
epileptiform crisis puts a sudden end to this phase of his personality.

Is there, then, the reader may ask, any assignable law which governs
these strange revolutions? any reason why Louis V. should at one moment
seem a mere lunatic or savage, at another moment should rise into decorous manhood, at another should recover his physical soundness, but sink
backward in mind into the child? Briefly, and with many reserves and
technicalities perforce omitted, the view of the doctors who have watched
him is somewhat as follows: A sudden shock, falling on an unstable organisation, has effected in this boy a profounder severance between the functions of the right and left hemispheres of the brain than has perhaps ever
been observed before. We are accustomed, of course, to see the right side
of the body paralysed and insensible in consequence of injury to the left
hemisphere, which governs it, and *vice versâ*. And we are accustomed in
hysterical cases—cases where there is no actual traceable injury to either
hemisphere—to see the defects in sensation and motility shift rapidly—
shift, as I may say, at a touch—from one side of the body to the other. But
we cannot usually trace any corresponding change in the mode of func-
tioning of what we assume as the 'highest centres,' the centres which
determine those manifestations of intelligence, character, memory, on
which our *identity* mainly depends. Yet in some cases of *aphasia* and of
other forms of *asemia* (the loss of power over *signs*, spoken or written
words and the like) phenomena have occurred which have somewhat prepared us to find that the loss of power to use the left—which certainly is in
some ways the more developed—hemisphere may bring with it a retro-
gression in the higher characteristics of human life. And the singular
phenomenon of *automatic writing* seems often to depend on an obscure
action of the less-used hemisphere. Those who have followed these lines
of observation may be somewhat prepared to think it possible that in
Louis V.'s case the alternate predominance of right or left hemisphere
affects memory and character as well as motor and sensory innervation.
Inhibit his left brain (and right side) and he becomes, as one may say, not
only left-handed but *sinister*; he manifests himself through nervous
arrangements which have reached a lower degree of evolution. And he can
represent in memory those periods only when his personality had
assumed the same attitude, when he had crystallised about the same point.

Inhibit his right brain, and the higher qualities of character remain, like
the power of speech, intact. There is self-control; there is modesty; there
is the sense of duty—the qualities which man has developed as he has
risen from the savage level. But nevertheless he is only half himself.
Besides the hemiplegia, which is a matter of course, memory is truncated

too, and he can summon up only such fragments of the past as chance to have been linked with this one abnormal state, leaving unrecalled not only the period of sinister inward ascendency, but the normal period of childhood, before his *Wesen** was thus cloven in twain. And now if by some art we can restore the equipoise of the two hemispheres again, if we can throw him into a state in which no physical trace is left of the severance which has become for him a second nature, what may we expect to find as the psychical concomitant of this restored integrity? What we *do* find is a change in the patient which, in the glimpse of physical possibilities which it offers us, is among the most interesting of all. He is, if I may so say, born again; he becomes as a little child; he is set back in memory, character, knowledge, powers, to the days before this trouble came upon him or his worse self assumed its sway.

I have begun with the description of an extreme case, a case which to many of my readers may seem incredible in its *bizarrerie*. But though it is extreme it is not really isolated; it is approached from different sides by cases already known. The mere resumption of life at an earlier moment, for instance, is of course only an exaggeration of a phenomenon which frequently appears after cerebral injury. The trainer, stunned by the kick of a horse, completes his order to loosen the girths the moment that trepanning has been successfully performed. The old lady struck down at a card party, and restored to consciousness after long insensibility, surprises her weeping family by the inquiry, 'What are trumps?' But in these common cases there is but a morsel cut out of life; the personality reawakens as from sleep and is the same as of old. With Louis V. it is not thus; the memories of the successive stages are not lost but juxtaposed, as it were, in separate compartments; nor can one say what epochs are in truth intercalary, or in what central channel the stream of his being flows.

Self-severances profound as Louis V.'s are naturally to be sought mainly in the lunatic asylum. There indeed we find duplicated individuality in its grotesquer forms. We have the man who has always lost himself and insists on looking for himself under the bed. We have the man who maintains that there are two of him, and sends his plate a second time, remarking, 'I have had plenty, but the other fellow has not.' We have the man who maintains that he is himself and his brother too, and when asked how he can possibly be both at once, replies, 'Oh, by a different mother.'

Or sometimes the personality oscillates from one focus to another, and the rival impulses, which in us merely sway different moods, objectify themselves each in a *persona* of its own. An hysterical penitent believes herself one week to be 'Sœur Marthe des Cinq Plaies,' and the next week relapses into an imaginary 'Madame Poulmaire,' with tastes recalling a quite other than conventual model. Another patient seems usually sane enough, but at intervals he lets his beard grow, and is transformed into a swaggering lieutenant of artillery. The excess over, he shaves his beard and becomes once more a lucid though melancholy student of the early Fathers. Such changes of character, indeed, may be rapid and varied to any extent which the patient's experience of life will allow. In one well-known case a poor lady varied her history, her character, even her sex, from day to day. One day she would be an emperor's bride, the next an imprisoned statesman—

> Juvenis quondam, nunc femina, Cæneus,
> Rursus et in veterem fato revoluta figuram.*

Yet more instructive, though often sadder still, are the cases where the disintegration of personality has not reached the pitch of insanity, but has ended in a bewildered impotence, in the horror of a lifelong dream. Speaking generally, such cases fall under two main heads—those where the loss of control is mainly over *motor* centres, and the patient can feel but cannot act; and those where the loss of control is mainly over *sensory* centres, and the patient acts but cannot feel.

Inability to act just as we would wish to act is a trouble in which we most of us share. We probably have moods in which we can even sympathise with that provoking patient of Esquirol's* who, after an attack of monomania, recovered all those social gifts which made him the delight of his friends, but could no longer be induced to give five minutes' attention to the most urgent business. 'Your advice,' he said cordially to Esquirol, 'is thoroughly good. I should ask nothing better than to follow it, if you could further oblige me with the power to *will* what I please.' Sometimes the whole life is spent in the endeavour to perform trifling acts—as when a patient of M. Billod's spent nearly an hour in trying to make the flourish under his signature to a power of attorney; or tried in vain for three hours, with hat and gloves on, to leave his room and go out to a pageant which he much wished to see. Such cases need heroic treatment, and this gentleman had the luck to be caught and cured by the Revolution of 1848.

Still more mournful are the cases where it is mainly the sensory centres which lie, as it were, outside the personality; where thought and will remain intact, but the world around no longer stirs the wonted feelings, nor can reach the solitary soul. 'In all my acts one thing is lacking—the sense of effort that should accompany them, the sense of pleasure that they should yield.' 'All things,' said another sufferer, 'are immeasurably distant from me; they are covered with a heavy air.' 'Men seem to move round me,' said another, 'like moving shadows.' And gradually this sense of ghostly vacancy extends to the patient's own person. 'Each of my senses, each part of me, is separate from myself.' 'J'existe, mais en dehors de la vie réelle.'* It is as though Teiresias,* who alone kept his true life in unsubstantial Hades, should at last feel himself dream into a shade.

These instances have shown us the *retrogressive* change of personality, the dissolution into incoordinate elements of the polity of our being. We have seen the state of man like a city blockaded, like a great empire dying at the core. And of course a spontaneous, unguided disturbance in a machinery so complete is likely to alter it more often for the worse than for the better. Yet here we reach the very point which I most desire to urge in this paper. I mean that even these spontaneous, these unguided disturbances do sometimes effect a change which is a marked improvement. Apart from all direct experiment they show us that we are in fact capable of being reconstituted after an improved pattern, that we may be fused and recrystallised into greater clarity; or, let us say more modestly, that the shifting sand-heap of our being will sometimes suddenly settle itself into a new attitude of more assured equilibrium.

Among cases of this kind which have thus far been recorded, none is more striking than that of Dr Azam's often quoted patient, Félida X.

Many of my readers will remember that in her case the somnambulic life has become the normal life; the 'second state,' which appeared at first only in short, dream-like accesses, has gradually replaced the 'first state,' which now recurs but for a few hours at long intervals. But the point on which I wish to dwell is this: that Félida's second state is altogether *superior* to the first—physically superior, since the nervous pains which had troubled her from childhood have disappeared; and morally superior, inasmuch as her morose, self-centred disposition is exchanged for a cheerful activity which enables her to attend to her children and her shop much more effectively than when she was in the 'état bête,'* as she now calls what was once the only personality that she knew. In this case, then, which is now of nearly thirty years' standing, the spontaneous readjustment of nervous activities—the second state, no memory of which remains in the first state—has resulted in an improvement profounder than could have been anticipated from any moral or medical treatment that we know. The case shows us how often the word 'normal' means nothing more than 'what happens to exist.' For Félida's *normal* state was in fact her *morbid* state; and the new condition, which seemed at first a mere hysterical abnormality, has brought her to a life of bodily and mental sanity which makes her fully the equal of average women of her class.

One or two brief instances may indicate the moral and the physical benefits which hypnotisation is bringing within the range of practical medicine. And first I will cite one of the cases—rare as yet—where an insane person has been hypnotised with permanent benefit.

In the summer of 1884 there was at the Salpêtrière a young woman of a deplorable type. Jeanne Sch—— was a criminal lunatic, filthy in habits, violent in demeanour, and with a lifelong history of impurity and theft. M. Auguste Voisin, one of the physicians on the staff, undertook to hypnotise her on May 31, at a time when she could only be kept quiet by the strait jacket and 'bonnet d'irrigation,' or perpetual cold douche to the head. She would not—indeed, she could not—look steadily at the operator, but raved and spat at him. M. Voisin kept his face close to hers, and followed her eyes wherever she moved them. In about ten minutes a stertorous sleep ensued; and in five minutes more she passed into a sleep-waking state and began to talk incoherently. The process was repeated on many days, and gradually she became sane when in the trance, though she still raved when awake. Gradually too she became able to obey in waking hours commands impressed on her in the trance—first trivial orders (to sweep the room and so forth), then orders involving a marked change of behaviour. Nay, more; in the hypnotic state she voluntarily expressed repentance for her past life, made a confession which involved more evil than the police were cognisant of (though it agreed with facts otherwise known), and finally of her own impulse made good resolves for the future. Two years have now elapsed, and M. Voisin writes to me (July 31, 1886) that she is now a nurse in a Paris hospital and that her conduct is irreproachable. In this case, and in some recent cases of M. Voisin's, there may, of course, be matter for controversy as to the precise nature and the prognosis, apart from hypnotism, of the insanity which was cured. But my point is amply made out by the fact that this poor woman, whose history since the age of 13 had been one of reckless folly and vice, is now capable of the steady, self-controlled work of a nurse at a hospital, the reformed character having first manifested itself in the hypnotic state, partly in obedience to suggestion and partly as the natural result of the tranquillisation of morbid passions.

But here my paper must close. I will conclude it with a single reflection which may somewhat meet the fears of those who dislike any tamperings with our personality, who dread that this invading analysis may steal their very self away. All living things, it is said, strive towards their maximum of pleasure. In what hours, then, and under what conditions, do we find that human beings have attained to their intensest joy? Do not our thoughts in answer turn instinctively to scenes and moments when all personal pre-occupation, all care for individual interest, is lost in the sense of spiritual union, whether with one beloved soul, or with a mighty nation, or with 'the whole world and creatures of God'? We think of Dante with Beatrice, of Nelson at Trafalgar, of S. Francis on the Umbrian hill. And surely here, as in Galahad's cry* of 'If I lose myself I find myself,' we have a hint that much, very much, of what we are wont to regard as an integral part of us may drop away, and yet leave us with a consciousness of our own being which is more vivid and purer than before. This web of habits and appetencies, of lusts and fears, is not, perhaps, the ultimate manifestation of what in truth we are. It is the cloak which our rude forefathers have woven themselves against the cosmic storm; but we are already learning to shift and refashion it as our gentler weather needs, and if perchance it slip from us in the sunshine then something more ancient and more glorious is for a moment guessed within.

APPENDIX C

from W. T. STEAD, 'HAS MAN TWO MINDS OR ONE?'

[W. T. Stead (1849–1912) was a radical journalist and editor who helped invent the sensationalist New Journalism in the 1880s. His campaigns succeeded in pushing imperialist policy forward, raising the age of consent for girls to 16, and closing brothels. He was the most famous Englishman to die on the maiden voyage of the *Titanic*. This essay, subtitled 'Various Views on Multiple Personality', appeared in the second number of Stead's occult magazine, *Borderland* (October 1893, 170–3). The eccentricity of *Borderland* began the eclipse of his influence. The journal, which was a quarterly and designed to be a collation of available published material from Spiritualists, Theosophists, psychical researchers and others, ran from 1893 to 1897. This short essay is typical in largely transcribing a number of different theories of mind from different and largely incompatible sources. When RLS died in 1894, he was inducted into Stead's 'Gallery of Borderlanders', and Stead wrote a fulsome tribute to the 'psychical' Stevenson.]

My Own Experience

The fact that there is another side to the human personality, or rather the whole of the Ego is not manifested through the small portion of animated clay which acts as a two-legged telephone to communicate with its fellows seems to be pretty well established. The process of automatic handwriting by which some of my friends constantly report to me* day by day or week by week what they have been doing, is to my mind a constant proof that the Ego is much wider and greater than its conscious manifestation. In the course of my constant communications I have come upon some very curious and interesting confirmations of this theory.

Miss X.'s Communications

That is to say, my hand—writing what purports to come from Miss X*— will describe phenomena of which I know nothing, and give a psychical explanation describing, for instance, monitions and premonitions which have averted some threatened danger, quieted some alarm, or dismissed some pain. On reading the communication over to her, I have found again and again that the facts have been stated correctly, but that she herself, although knowing the result, had no conscious knowledge of the means by which the result reported correctly by me had been brought about. That is to say, Miss X.'s subliminal self is more sensitive to the influences of psychic forces than Miss X. is in her normal consciousness, and it reports to me not only the outward facts which Miss X. can confirm, but also the explanation of these facts of which Miss X. was ignorant. There is at least a *primâ facie* ground for accepting these statements in that they explain the occurrence of phenomena which Miss X. herself was unable to account for, and both the occurrence and the explanation were entirely unknown to me when my hand wrote them down.

Which Self Survives?

The system of automatic telepathy brings constantly into clear relief the difference between the conscious mind and the sub-conscious mind. In one of my friends the difference is so strongly developed that the influence which writes with my hand, continually complains of the influence of the body exercised on the mind. My conscious friend is very indignant with her subliminal consciousness, which is so very different from herself in sympathy, in aspiration, and in sentiment. Yet my friend recognises that the entity which writes with my hand is part of herself inasmuch as it will continually inform me of the full meaning of phenomena of which she is only partially conscious. It will, for instance, explain the origin of a dream, or satisfactorily account for circumstances which were inexplicable to the conscious self, and which were entirely unknown to me. My friend is much puzzled as to which entity will survive after the dissolution of the body, and the conscious self is by no means pleased at the possibility that its subliminal self will be the survivor.

Madame Blavatsky's Version

Madame Blavatsky* teaches, and the Theosophists accept, a somewhat similar theory; but, instead of saying man has two minds, they say a Higher and a Lower Self, which, again, they describe as Individuality and Personality. Madame Blavatsky, in an article published in *Lucifer* for June, 1890, quoting with approval Professor Ladd's remark* that every region, every area, and every limit of the nervous system has its own memory, thus sets forth what may be regarded as the true Theosophic doctrine on the subject of 'the Two Selfs.'

The Higher and Lower Self

'The metaphysics of Occult physiology and psychology postulate within mortal man an immortal entity, "divine Mind," or Nous, whose pale and too often distorted reflection is that which we call "Mind" and intellect in men—virtually an entity apart from the former during the period of every incarnation. The two sources of "memory" are in these two "principles." These two we distinguish as the Higher *Manas* (Mind or Ego), and the *Kama-Manas*, *i.e.*, the rational, but earthly or physical intellect of man, incased in, and bound by, matter, therefore subject to the influence of the latter: the all-conscious Self, that which reincarnates periodically—verily the Word made flesh!—and which is always the same, while its reflected "Double," changing with every new incarnation and personality, is, therefore, conscious but for a life period. The latter "principle" is the Lower Self, or that which, manifesting through our organic system, acting on this plane of illusion, imagines itself the *Ego Sum*, and thus falls into what Buddhist philosophy brands as the "heresy of separateness." The former we term Individuality, the latter Personality. From the first proceeds all the noetic elements, from the second, the psychic, *i.e.*, "terrestrial wisdom" at best, as it is influenced by all the chaotic stimuli of the human or rather animal passions of the living body.

The Limitations of Higher Self

'The "Higher Ego" cannot act directly on the body, as its consciousness belongs to quite another plane and planes of ideation: the "lower" Self does; and its action and behaviour depend on its freewill and choice as to whether it will gravitate more towards its parent ("the Father in Heaven") or the "animal" which it informs, the man of flesh. The "Higher Ego," as part of the essence of the Universal Mind, is unconditionally omniscient on its own plane, and only potentially so in our terrestrial sphere, as it has to act solely through its alter ego—the Personal Self. Now, although the former is the vehicle of all knowledge of the past, the present and the future, and although it is from this fountain head that its "double" catches occasional glimpses of that which is beyond the senses of man, and transmits them to certain brain cells (unknown to science in their functions), thus making of man a Seer, a soothsayer, and a prophet; yet the memory of bygone events—especially of the earth earthy—has its seat in the Personal Ego alone.'

Dr Richardson's Theory

There is a very interesting article in the *Asclepiad* for December 15th, by Dr Richardson,* on the duality of the mind. He holds that every man has two brains in his skull—separate and distinct brains, which are sometimes so very different that they seem almost to belong to two different men. Dr Richardson quotes a conversation which he had with Mrs Booth, in which she challenged him to study the phenomenon of a sudden conversion in which a drunken reprobate became a changed man.

The Second Brain and Conversion

Mrs Booth, of course, attributed this to the grace of God, but Dr Richardson is ready to account for it on his theory of the duality of the human mind. The following passage gives occasion for much reflection:—

'Her model submerged man appears before me as one governed for long years by an evil brain. So long as that evil brain retained its dominant strength it ruled the man. But there came a time when that excited brain wore out into feebleness, when impressions upon it derived from the second brain began to act with superior force; when doubt and contrition thereupon agitated the man; when he felt that he had in him two volitions beyond his mere animal instincts and passions. At this crisis a strong and earnest external nature fell upon him, roused into action his own better nature, drove his lower nature into obedience of fear, and, temporarily or permanently, transformed him into that which he had never yet experienced—into a man in full exercise of a newly-developed strength. That man, physically and literally, was born again. We need not criticise the means employed for that regeneration; we will not, at this moment, question whether the training that followed the new birth was the best and only best; but we must admit the phenomenon of the change. There was about it no mystery; it was, in scientific definition, an organic mental transformation; the awakening into life and living action of an organ in a state of partial inertia; a physical conversion leading to new action, and, if we like to say so, making a new man. No wonder, from this reading, that the worst specimens of vice should become, under the change, the most lasting specimens of virtue.'

The Oscillation of the Brain

Dr Richardson is full of his theory, which he thinks is one of the grandest expositions ever revealed in the study of mental science. It explains no end of difficulties, especially those which arise in the study of insanity. No man has his two brains exactly balanced; sometimes one is stronger than the other. Occasionally he can get on very well when one of the brains has half gone to water. Sudden changes in the character are due to oscillations in the domination of one half of the head over the other half. Mrs Booth would probably have replied that Dr Richardson's discovery deals more with the mechanism of the means by which grace works than an explanation of the secret by which the domination of the good brain can be secured. Granting that the reformation of the man is secured by securing the ascendency of the good brain over the bad, still his explanation does not give us any clue as to how that desirable alteration can be effected.

Mr A. N. Somers' Speculations

In the *Psychical Review* for May, 1893, Mr A. N. Somers publishes an ambitious paper entitled 'The Double Personality,' and the 'Relation of the Submerged Personality to the Phenomena of Modern Spiritualism,' in which he endeavours to prove that there is a physical basis of double personality and that two sets of factors enter into and constitute the personality of a man.

The Double Circuit of the Nerves

'The cerebral central centres and surface filaments (end-nerves) constitute opposite poles of a circuit of energy (nerve-energy). The two circuits of the neural system are connected in the crossing over of their fibres in the medulla oblongata and fibres of commissures, by which arrangement the entire system acts in harmony with one purpose and will; but if deranged the activity may be double or alternating in acts of double personality (or mediumship).

'The process of ideation may go on doubly, giving us "conscious" and "unconscious" cerebration (double cerebration). These facts are now demonstrable through hypnotism. Twenty years ago, when I discovered them, the only demonstrations known to our crude methods were comparative experimentation (often involving the vivisection of animals), confirmed by a few simple experiments on the human subject.

The Submerged Personality

'The constitution of the body, with its sensations and the tendencies that express it, gives us the physical basis of personality; while the emotions, reflection, and the imagination impart to it the psychological facts that complete it. Although the physical organism that furnishes the primary facts of personality is double in structure and function, under normal conditions of health its parts tend to act in unison, as the apparatus of a single personality, due in most part to hereditary influences and training.

'Under such circumstances the second possible personality is never destroyed. It is simply submerged; and disease, fatigue, or psychical inactivity of the dominant cerebral hemisphere may allow it to come into the ascendency of consciousness, with its stock of ideas wrought out in acts of double cerebration on the part of the least active cerebral hemisphere.

'The strongest of the personalities early in life (usually about puberty) gains the mastery over the weaker, and in a state of bodily health and normal mental habits so continues in ascendency, showing itself in all the states of consciousness. It is by it that we know the individual.

'The most fundamental facts of the dominant personality are those sensations that make us conscious of our bodies ('bodily sense'). When we lose that class of sensations (always absent in trance), through physiological or psychological causes, then the submerged personality becomes dominant in its states of consciousness (sometimes spoken of as states of sub- or semi-consciousness). Ignorance, or low mentality, favours the doubling and intermittence of personality, which takes place with equal frequency from an intellectual gauge of facts not properly comprehended and classified, as with the *mystic* and *visionary*.

A Submerged Sex

'The researches of Darwin, and others after him, have revealed two sets of sex characteristics: the one primary (physical), and the other secondary (psychical). These have been the most prominent factors in the evolution of man.

'In the bodily organism that gives us the primary facts of personality there is a double sex, the one more or less completely submerged from the sight of the uninitiated, yet controlling in one side of the binary neural system the less dominant one. Under abnormal conditions of disease (sexual perversion), or mental infirmity, the submerged sex may become the dominant one, in respect to its secondary characteristics. Although the one sex is submerged, it continues to manifest itself in its secondary or psychological characteristics throughout the entire life of the individual.

'The essential femaleness is conservative (*anabolick*), while the essential maleness is radical (*katabolic*).* These opposite forces contending for the mastery in the physical body stamp their imprint upon the mind.

The Resurrection of the Submerged Sex

'When the dominant sex and the personality that goes with it have run their limits, the submerged sex and its accompanying personality may, and generally do, come into the ascendency with respect to the secondary (physical) characteristics of sex. The ascendant sex and its personality run their limits at the point we call, 'change of life,' which affects males and females; or it may be at an earlier period, through disease or abnormal physical condition. The personality of the opposite sex always controls the secondary characteristics after that change. When these 'changes' take place we always see the personality doubled. This is generally due to a weakness of the physical organism, which diminishes the primary facts of personality and allows the hitherto submerged personality, accustomed to low physical tone, to rise and assert its secondary characters in the ascendency (consciousness).

Two Brains Because Two Sexes

'It is a fact, known even to the lay reader, that the centres of inhibitory motion for one side of the body are located in the cerebral hemisphere of the opposite side; that the nerves cross over from one side to the other in the medulla oblongata. If we recognise the brain as a binary body, as we some day shall, it follows that the left brain controls the right side of the body, and the right brain the left side of the body.

'The brain is binary to meet the neural demands of two sexes resident in one bilateral body, and the parts are as opposite in their psychical characteristics as the sexes they serve. Let us examine this matter a little closer. At the point in the embryological life at which sex differentiation becomes completed, cerebral differentiation becomes more rapid and distinct. The one rudimentary brain (usually the radical, katabolic, left brain) becomes the dominant one, as its early stages of differentiation have been more marked, which gives it the ascendency in speech, right-handedness, and general control over the circulatory and neural systems. Its psychical powers will naturally be in the ascendency, no matter which sex gains the reproductive ascendency.

'We thus have female men and male women. The one sex prevails physically and the other psychically.

The Psychical Personality of the Cell

'We have here, then, the possibilities and source of two sets of psychical facts that give rise to the doubling of personality. The submerged personality is ordinarily more mechanical (automatic) than the ascendent one, though when it comes permanently into the ascendency it loses this feature.

'As all sensibility is psychical, there is personality in all forms of living bodies. Human personality is higher, and doubles because the organism is more perfect in its adaptations to its environment and in its functions. We may accord personality to the original cells (ova and spermatozoa), as their actions can be accounted for on no other grounds. They are psychical bodies, possessing organized bodies of sensations (experiences) that govern their acts. Every added cell derives its psychical powers from its parent cell, and is under its control until developed. Here we have the real basis of the laws of heredity.

'The ascendant personality is the sum of all that consciously takes place in our nervous states.'

EXPLANATORY NOTES

STRANGE CASE OF DR JEKYLL AND MR HYDE

2 *Katherine de Mattos*: cousin to RLS, sister of Bob Stevenson, RLS's early model for the bohemian artist. She married and later divorced Sydney de Mattos.

It's ill to loose . . . north countrie: second stanza of RLS's poem 'Ave!', composed May 1885.

5 *Cain's heresy*: Cain is the Bible's first murderer, killing his brother Abel. Genesis 4: 9, 'And the Lord said unto Cain, Where is Abel thy brother? And he said, I know not: Am I my brother's keeper?' Utterson might be misremembering his Bible, since it is Cain who goes to the devil, not Abel. However, there was an early Christian dissident sect, the Cainites, that regarded Cain as 'possessed of a dignity, power and enlightenment superior to Abel' (as discussed by James Hastings, *A Dictionary of the Bible* (Edinburgh, 1898)). This is an early sign that conventional biblical meanings may be inverted in the tale.

man about town: this is the figure of the urban dandy fixed in the early nineteenth century by Beau Brummell. However, in the dictionary *Slang and its Analogues, Past and Present*, co-edited by RLS's friend and collaborator W. E. Henley in the 1890s, 'man about town' is attached to the 1690 quotation 'Man o'the town, a Lew'd Spark, or very Debaushe'. It can therefore imply certain sexual behaviour.

7 *It sounds nothing to hear*: in a famous letter to Robert Bridges on 28 October 1886, the Catholic priest and poet Gerard Manley Hopkins commented: 'You are certainly wrong about Hyde being overdrawn: my Hyde is worse. The trampling scene is perhaps a convention: he was thinking of something unsuitable for fiction,' Gerard Manley Hopkins, *Selected Letters* (Oxford, 1990), 243. In a poor parody that appeared in 1886, *The Stranger Case of Dr Hide and Mr Crushall* by 'Robert Bathos Stavingson', this scene is made significantly more violent: a baby is kicked down the street. Later described more generally by Jekyll as 'an act of cruelty', contemporary audiences might have had in mind W. T. Stead's journalistic exposé, 'The Maiden Tribute of Modern Babylon', in which he sensationally described the violation of young girls on the streets and in the brothels of London (see Introduction).

Juggernaut: a corruption of the Sanskrit Jagannath, 'The Lord of the World', the name of the Hindu god Vishnu worshipped at a famous temple in Puri, Orissa. There is an elaborate cycle of rituals attached to the temple, with the Car festival the most important: the image of the god is dragged by pilgrims on a carriage. In the nineteenth century, this festival was rumoured (incorrectly) to involve pilgrims throwing themselves under the carriage in self-immolation, and Juggernaut came to be associated with an unstoppable force or fate that crushes the individual.

view halloa: hunting cry made when the fox breaks cover. Enfield's language bristles with the slang of a certain urban, louche class.

Sawbones: slang for medic. Note that in the next few sentences this is the first doctor in the tale associated with murderous rage.

harpies: in Greek mythology, noisome birds with the faces of women who embody violent winds that carry men off to their deaths.

8 *Coutts's*: this marks out Hyde as a man with gentlemanly associations. Coutts's bank has been in London's Strand since 1755, and is banker to royalty and aristocracy. In the Victorian period, the bank was associated with the extensive philanthropic work of Angela Burdett-Coutts.

Black Mail House: that a low, repulsive young man like Mr Hyde has some power of blackmail over Dr Jekyll is the theory held for most of the novella by his concerned circle of friends. This is a knowing wink and nudge from Enfield, who does not need to spell out the various heterosexual and homosexual associations of blackmail at the time: these are discussed in the Introduction. However, this oblique conversation deliberately leaves open many possibilities: Hyde might also be the very product of those blackmailable sins—an illegitimate son. This was a classic 'sensation fiction' plot line, and the relationship of Jekyll and Hyde is repeatedly described in terms of father and son.

9 *Queer Street*: there have been some energetic interpretations of *Jekyll and Hyde* by 'Queer Theorists', who pick up on instances like this and suggest that the modern understanding of 'queer' as a slang term for homosexuality was already in use in the late nineteenth century. Being 'in Queer Street' was in fact a standard phrase for being in financial difficulties, and is a corruption of Carey Street, where the bankruptcy courts were located. The phrase was used by Bulwer-Lytton in *Pelham* (1827) and by Dickens in *The Pickwick Papers* (1837). Henley's *Slang and its Analogues* lists an extensive range of meanings and associated terms, none of which is sexual.

11 *M.D. . . . F.R.S.*: Medical Doctor, Doctor of Civil Laws, Doctor of Laws, Fellow of the Royal Society. Jekyll is therefore qualified as both medical doctor and lawyer, and has done sufficiently pioneering work in science to be elected Fellow of the most influential scientific society in London.

the lawyer's eyesore: Rider Haggard's otherwise glowing review of *Jekyll and Hyde* pointed out that this will would have been impossible to execute under English law, since either proof of Jekyll's death or a period of years would have had to lapse before Hyde could inherit. In the summer of 1885, Stevenson had written to Haggard praising *King Solomon's Mines*, but told him sections of it were 'slipshod'. Haggard's pedantry over the will was perhaps a pointed response to being told by RLS 'to be more careful'.

11 *Cavendish Square*: one of the few places actually named in the book, this situates Lanyon in the heart of the medical world, since the road that houses London's most exclusive private doctors is Harley Street, which leads into Cavendish Square.

12 *Damon and Pythias*: in Greek myth, the ultimate loyal friends. When Phintias (as it should be spelt) is sentenced to death, Damon stands in for him in prison, even at the risk of his own death. Dionysius is so impressed by this demonstration of loyalty and faith that he reprieves Phintias.

14 *Gaunt Street*: no such street existed in London at the time, but Stevenson is including a significant literary reference point here. In William Makepeace Thackeray's *Vanity Fair*, the libertine Lord Steyne lives in Gaunt Square. At the opening of chapter 47, there is a lengthy description of his house which clearly informs the strange houses we encounter in *Jekyll and Hyde*. Gaunt Square is described as on the way down from its aristocratic heights—'Brass plates have penetrated into the Square— Doctors, the Diddlesex Bank Western Branch—The English and European Reunion etc.—it has a dreary look.' In the second paragraph of the chapter, Thackeray begins: 'A few score yards down New Gaunt Street, and leading into Gaunt Mews indeed, is a modest little back door, which you would not remark from that of any of the other stables . . . It conducts to the famous *petits appartements* of Lord Steyne,' and this is where several assignations and celebrations after gambling victories take place. This description echoes the house owned by Jekyll which is described a few pages on, and yet it is Utterson who lives in Gaunt Street. RLS perhaps deliberately elides Utterson with Jekyll here.

16 *troglodytic*: the *Oxford English Dictionary* records that 'troglodyte' was first used in 1555 for 'one of various races or tribes of men (chiefly ancient or prehistoric) inhabiting caves or dens (natural or artificial); a cave-dweller, cave-man'. The Victorian period adds more figurative uses: 'a person who lives in seclusion; one unacquainted with the affairs of the world; a "hermit." Also, a dweller in a hovel or slum; a person of a degraded type like the prehistoric or savage cave-dwellers.' One citation comes from a major influence on RLS, the social scientist Herbert Spencer.

Dr Fell: this refers to the famous rhyme immortalized in a translation by an Oxford student, who was set the task as a punishment by Dr John Fell (1625–86), then Dean of Christ Church, Oxford. 'I do not love you, Dr Fell; | But why I cannot tell; | But this I know full well, | I do not love you, Dr Fell.'

all sorts and conditions of men: phrase from the Book of Common Prayer, but most immediately this is also the title of the 1882 novel by Walter Besant, set in the slums of the East End of London.

17 *pede claudo*: Latin, 'on limping foot'. The reference is to the last lines of one of Horace's *Odes*, iii. 2: 'seldom has Punishment, on limping foot, abandoned a wicked man, even when he has a start on her.'

21 *the horror of these sights and sounds*: one of the most detailed responses to the novella within the first year of publication came from the poet, psychologist, and psychical researcher Frederic Myers, who forwarded his 'Notes on *Dr Jekyll and Mr Hyde*' to RLS, with the hope that RLS would use them to correct a subsequent edition of the book. They form a fascinating commentary (and are reprinted in full, together with 'Further Meditations on the Character of the Late Mr Hyde', in Paul Maixner, *Robert Louis Stevenson: The Critical Heritage* (London, 1981), 212–22). At this point in the novella, Myers objects that 'The cruelty developed from *lust* surely never becomes of just the same quality as the cruelty developed from mere madness and savagery . . . Jekyll was thoroughly civilized, and his degeneration must needs take certain lines only. Have you not sometimes thought of incarnate *evil* rather too vaguely?' (pp. 214–15). This again testifies to the puzzlement the actions of Hyde consistently produce in readers: the actions either seem 'too *maniacal*' for Myers here, or too underpowered, as for Hopkins in the trampling scene.

22 *Soho*: this area of central London south of Oxford Street was a network of alleys and passageways associated with foreign populations, bohemians, and political agitators (it was where Karl Marx lived in his years of exile). In Oscar Wilde's 'Lord Arthur Savile's Crime' (1887), when the Lord needs a bomb, he immediately drives to Soho to discuss explosives with an enthusiastic German anarchist.

many women . . . key in hand, to have a morning glass: the key in hand signals that they are lower-class women, possibly prostitutes. Carrying a key signals a suspicious independence; within ten years, the middle-class women dissidents who were discussed under title of 'New Woman' would adopt the key as a symbol of female autonomy, as in George Egerton's collection of short stories, *Keynotes* (1894). Stead's interviews with prostitutes for 'The Maiden Tribute' suggested that many drank heavily to escape their appalling conditions.

23 *a good picture hung upon the walls*: Myers wrote at length to RLS about this detail in his notes on Hyde's character. Interestingly, he suggests that this picture would be 'unworthy' of Hyde: 'There are jaded voluptuaries who seek in a special class of art a substitute or reinforcement for the default of primary stimuli. Mr Hyde's whole career forbids us to insult him by classing him with these men' (Maixner, *Critical Heritage*, 219–20). Myers's speculations continue for some time. Strikingly, then, Myers admires Hyde and does not wish him contaminated by the decadence of Jekyll—a very different way of understanding the moral meanings ascribed to the characters in the rudimentary 'good versus evil' reading.

27 *two hands are in many points identical*: Myers lectures RLS on this detail of his story: 'Here I think you miss a point for want of familiarity with recent psycho-physical discussions. Handwriting in cases of double personality (spontaneous . . . or induced, as in hypnotic cases) *is not* and *cannot be* the same in the two personalities' (Maixner, *Critical Heritage*,

215). This clue of identical handwriting remains important for the shocking denouement of the story, however.

35 *we'll get this through hands*: we'll deal with this. Poole's language is studded with Scottish turns of phrase.

41 *by the crushed phial in the hand and the strong smell of kernels . . . the body of a self-destroyer*: the smell of kernels indicates the poison cyanide; Jekyll's body is therefore that of a suicide. Sodium cyanide and potassium cyanide are both white powders with a bitter smell; cyanide acts very quickly on the stomach and hence has been a favoured way of committing suicide. The use of the term 'self-destroyer' indicates the strong moral condemnation of the act of suicide, which remained illegal in England until 1961. The act was a source of moral horror and family disgrace throughout the Victorian period.

42 *cheval-glass*: a body-length mirror on a central pivot. Their horror perhaps recalls the long tradition of mirrors in various occult practices, such as scrying. When they peer in and see only their own faces, it inevitably reminds the reader of Wilde's maxims that preface his Stevenson-influenced *Picture of Dorian Gray* (1891): 'The nineteenth century dislike of Realism is the rage of Caliban seeing his own face in a glass. The nineteenth century dislike of Romanticism is the rage of Caliban not seeing his own face in a glass.'

45 *left hand*: the standard idiom talks about the right hand. It suggests Jekyll is already lost to the devil, the left hand being traditionally associated with evil, illegitimacy, and underhand dealings.

47 *version book*: Scottish term for an exercise book, usually used for English and Latin translations, but a peculiarly appropriate term given Jekyll's interest in versions of himself.

bull's eye: a lantern used by police, with a thick lens that helped direct the beam. In Gustav Doré's *London: A Pilgrimage* (1872), one etching shows a policeman using a bull's eye to expose a group of paupers on the street.

48 *incipient rigor*: this is Lanyon's medical terminology for the experience of revulsion others have hinted at, but rarely been able to formulate precisely. He is referring to goose pimples.

50 *to stagger the unbelief of Satan*: again, Myers suggests to RLS, 'Style too elevated for Hyde . . . Surely Hyde's admirable style should be retained for him' (Maixner, *Critical Heritage*, 216). As in note to page 23 above, Myers again shows approval of Hyde. However, the scene is a kind of echo of Doctor Faust's temptation by the devil Mephistopheles (although it is Lanyon who plays the tempted doctor), and therefore requires elaborate rhetorical flights.

under the seal of our profession: the classical version of the Hippocratic Oath, taken by all medical doctors on assumption into the profession, includes the passage: 'What I may see or hear in the course of the treatment or even outside the treatment in regard to the life of men, which on no account must one spread abroad, I will keep to myself, holding such things shameful to be spoken about.' This has been updated to a short statement about respecting privacy; gone also are the elaborate declarations of the fraternal bond that tied all (male) members of the profession together in an unbreakable brotherhood. It explains why Lanyon will not break his silence, even unto death. Why does Hyde say *our* profession? Is Jekyll already speaking to his fellow medical friend through Hyde? These pronoun slippages proliferate further and further as the book proceeds.

52 *I was born . . . distinguished future*: RLS's wife told the story that the first draft of *Jekyll and Hyde* was thrown on the fire by RLS after her criticisms. Some have suggested she was alarmed by how explicit the text was about the nature of both Jekyll's and Hyde's sins, and this is one reason why there are so many critics anxious to fill in the gaps by seeking proof for their speculations in their interpretations of the text. There do exist three textual fragments of earlier drafts of the final published version of the tale, and they have interesting variations at this point. These variant texts have been usefully collected by Richard Dury in the Centenary Edition of *Strange Case of Dr Jekyll and Mr Hyde* (Edinburgh, 2004). Immediately after this asterisked passage, the notebook draft reads, 'From a very early age, however, I became in secret the slave of disgraceful pleasures; my life was double; outwardly absorbed in scientific toil.' The surviving manuscript also includes a version of this extra sentence: 'From an early age, however, I became in secret the slave of certain appetites' (both transcribed by Dury, 139). Later in that same paragraph, the notebook reads: 'the iron hand of indurated habit plunged me once again into the mire of my vices. I will trouble you with these no further than to say that they were at once criminal in the sight of the law and abhorrent in themselves' (Dury, 140). Some look to the excised passages of this opening section of Jekyll's statement as the final clue to the nature of his 'sins'. William Veeder even pins hopes on a *missing page* from the manuscript, which might have held the key to Utterson ('The Texts in Question', in William Veeder and Gordon Hirsch (eds.), *Dr Jekyll and Mr Hyde after One Hundred Years* (Chicago, 1988), 9). Yet RLS's excisions surely suggest he wanted to make the reader project their own ideas of the sins into the vaguer assertions of the final text, thus acting like Utterson and Poole, staring into the cheval-glass in horror.

gaiety of disposition: this is again a deliberately vague description of Jekyll that can be taken straightforwardly to mean general mirth or levity or as an echo the slang of the time. In Henley's *Slang and its Analogues*, gay as an adjective is taken to mean 'dissipated; specifically, given to venery'. All the examples refer to women: 'GAY WOMAN, or GIRL, or BIT = a strumpet', although a 'GAY MAN = a wencher'. The Gaiety Girl was a particular type of young urban woman, taking her name from the risqué shows of the Gaiety Theatre in the 1890s.

the mystic and the transcendental: Doctor Jekyll, then, is not a materialist but an occultist, and this is what has disgusted his one-time friend Hastie

Lanyon. Jekyll is in a long line of doctors in literature who pursue these dangerous lines of enquiry, perhaps the most immediate reference being to J. Sheridan Le Fanu's mysterious German medic and detective, Dr Hesselius, author of '*Essays on Metaphysical Medicine* which suggest more than they actually say' (Le Fanu, 'Green Tea', *In a Glass Darkly*, 1872). This statement also brings to mind Bulwer-Lytton's Gothic and occult novel, *A Strange Story* (1861–2), in which the doctor Louis Grayle transports his soul into the body of the more youthful Margrave. The founding figure for these modern doctors was Frankenstein in Mary Shelley's novel (1818).

52 *war among my members*: biblical echo, from James 4: 1: 'From whence come wars and fightings among you? Come they not hence, even of your lusts that war in your members?'

56 *captives of Philippi*: in Acts 16: 26, Paul and Silas are imprisoned for preaching the gospel, and pray to God: 'And suddenly there was a great earthquake, so that the foundations of the prison were shaken: and immediately all the doors were opened and every one's bands were loosed.' However, Jekyll shows that at this point he has passed well beyond biblical teaching for he fails to remember the point of the story: they do not make their escape, but stay to save the prison keeper's life.

bravos: from the Italian, hired soldiers or assassins; in general, reckless desperadoes.

57 *sloping my own hand backward*: in *A Dictionary of Psychological Medicine*, edited by D. Hack Tuke (London, 1892), the entry on 'Handwriting of the Insane' comments: 'Handwriting must be looked upon as a highly developed method of muscular expression and as such will be affected by any nervous states or conditions which affect the nervous control and the distribution of nervous energy . . . Mirror writing is generally produced by the left hand, and is written from right to left; it may occur in cases of moral perversion' (pp. 568 and 573).

59 *the Babylonian finger on the wall*: Daniel 5. The celebrations of the king Belshazzar are disrupted by a spectral hand that writes a message on the walls of his palace. His astrologers and soothsayers fail to interpret the message, and the Christian Daniel is sent for, who reads the message: 'God hath numbered thy kingdom, and finished it. Thou art weighed in the balances, and found wanting.'

60 *he came out roaring*: in a letter to RLS on 3 March 1886, John Addington Symonds wrote that he regarded *Jekyll and Hyde* as brilliant yet also 'a dreadful book, most dreadful because of a certain moral callousness, a want of sympathy, a shutting out of hope . . . Most of us at some epoch in our lives have been on the verge of developing a Mr. Hyde' (*The Letters of John Addington Symonds*, ed. Herbert M. Schueller (Detroit, 1969), iii. 121). This bestial image of the long-caged devil was clearly in Symonds's mind when he described in his memoirs ' "the wolf"—that undefined craving coloured with a vague but poignant hankering after males.' He

describes one moment soon after his marriage in these terms: 'Now the wolf leapt out: my malaise of the moment was converted into a clairvoyant and tyrannical appetite for the thing which I had rejected five months earlier' (*The Memoirs of John Addington Symonds*, ed. Phyllis Grosskurth (New York, 1984), 187). That suppression of instinct only makes the impulse stronger and more animalistic is a definitively Victorian conception of desire.

morally sane: the idea of a specifically *moral* insanity was first proposed by James Prichard in *A Treatise on Insanity* (1835): 'a morbid perversion of natural feelings, affections, inclinations, temper, habits, moral dispositions, and natural impulses, without any remarkable disorder or defect of the intellect or knowing and reasoning faculties.' Mary Rosher cites numerous parallels between *Jekyll and Hyde* and psychological studies of apparently rational and orderly patients concealing perverted, criminal, or murderous moral dispositions: ' "A Total Subversion of Character": Dr Jekyll's Moral Insanity', *Victorian Newsletter*, 93 (Spring 1998), 27–31.

61 *the veil . . . was rent*: biblical echoes multiply as Jekyll's statement proceeds. Here, one echo may be at the death of Jesus: 'And it was about the sixth hour, and there was a darkness over all the earth until the ninth hour. And the sun was darkened and the veil of the temple was rent in the mist' (Luke 23: 44–5).

65 *emptied by fever . . . the horror of my other self*: in 1892, RLS wrote to Myers about the division of his mind during fever in strikingly similar terms. 'From the beginning of the evening *one part of my mind* became possessed of a notion so grotesque and shapeless that it may best be described as a form of words. I thought the pain was, or connected with, a wisp or coil of some sort; I knew not what it consisted nor yet where it was, and cared not; only I thought, if the two ends were brought together the pain would cease. Now all the time, with *another part of my mind*, which I ventured to think was *myself*, I was fully alive to the absurdity of this idea, knew it to be a mark of impaired sanity, and was engaged with *my other self* in a perpetual conflict' (Letter 14 July 1892; *The Letters of Robert Louis Stevenson*, ed. Bradford A. Booth and Ernest Mehew, 8 vols. (New Haven, 1994–8), vii. 331–4). Myers used the text of this letter in full in his major psychological study, 'The Subliminal Consciousness', in 1894.

THE BODY SNATCHER

RLS began writing this tale in 1881, but wrote to Sidney Colvin on 3 July 1881 that it was 'laid aside in a justifiable disgust, the tale being horrid'. He returned to it in November 1884, when casting around for a story to fill a commission for the Chrismas *Pall Mall Gazette* after his first choice, 'Markheim', proved to be too short (see next story). 'The Body Snatcher' fitted the bill perfectly: this Christmas special was advertised in London with 'six pairs of coffin lids, painted dead black, with white skulls and cross-bones in the centre for relief . . . Six long white surplices were purchased from a funeral establishment. Six sandwich men were hired at double-rates' but were eventually told to desist by the Metropolitan Police (report reproduced in J. A. Hammerton's *Stevensoniana* (Edinburgh, 1907), 318). RLS chose not to reprint this tale, and although he argued its case for inclusion in the collected 'Edinburgh Edition', it was excluded by Sidney Colvin. It was not reprinted in Stevenson's lifetime.

The tale takes many of its details from the most notorious nineteenth-century case of 'body snatching' that took place in Edinburgh, 1827–8: the Burke and Hare story. RLS may have dropped this work because of this reliance, but it shows his fascination with the gruesome side of Victorian popular culture. Robbing graves to sell bodies to anatomists and medical schools was a weird economy that developed in the late eighteenth century because the only legal human bodies made available were a tiny number of executed criminals, where dissection was named as part of the punishment. With the growth of medical schools, many wealthy doctors paid for gangs of so-called 'resurrectionists' to steal bodies from graves. In the 1820s, fresh corpses sold for between £10 and £20, a large fee (the fee could be higher for unusual bodies: the corpse of an Irish giant was bought for £500 by the famous surgeon and collector John Hunter, and was openly displayed at the Royal College of Surgeons in London). The practice was a source of popular anger, given firm religious beliefs about bodily resurrection, and grave robbers utterly despised.

Burke and Hare took the practice to its logical conclusion: they cut out the risk of being caught at graves by murdering fifteen people in Hare's lodging house, plying them with drink and then smothering them (a practice that became known as 'burking'). They then sold them to the private anatomy school of the highly respected lecturer Dr Robert Knox. One of the students employed at Surgeons' Square to receive bodies at night did recognize one of the corpses as a well-known prostitute, but Burke persuaded him she had died of alcoholic excesses. The murders continued until fellow lodgers raised the alarm, and the last body was discovered in Knox's teaching rooms. With only one body and little firm evidence, the police gave Hare immunity from prosecution for his confession; Burke was found guilty on Christmas Day 1828, hanged in January, and then publicly dissected, some 40,000 people queuing to see the dismembered corpse. After Hare was spirited away to England by the authorities, popular agitation to have Knox prosecuted included riots and dismemberments of the doctor's effigy, and his reputation was destroyed. Anatomists remained a source of popular suspicion, the debates revived again in campaigns against animal vivisection in the 1870s and 1880s, just when RLS was composing 'The Body Snatcher'.

This story was told over and over again in various broadsheets and ballads. William Roughead's collection of documents, *Burke and Hare* (Edinburgh, 1921), lists 22 broadsides, 21 ballads, and 20 pamphlets and books on the crime in the immediate years following the trial. As RLS shows throughout his Gothic tales, the author had an intimate knowledge of this popular tradition.

67 *camlet cloak*: a name originally given to costly eastern fabrics, mixing silk and camel hair.

68 *Voltaire might have canted*: Voltaire (1694–1778), a key figure in the French Enlightenment, associated with free thinking and anti-clerical attitudes. The phrase suggests that even Voltaire might have turned to religion.

69 *fly*: a one-horse carriage.

71 *Mr K—— was then at the top of his vogue*: as the introductory note above explains, many details of this tale are derived from the case of Burke and Hare, who provided recently murdered bodies to the anatomy school of Dr Robert Knox in Edinburgh in 1827 and 1828. Knox became a demonized figure in popular culture, but eventually a figure of some sympathy for being a scapegoat. After the *Pall Mall Gazette* published RLS's tale, it received a letter of complaint from Professor John Goodsir, trained by Knox in anatomy. He dismissed the tale as 'vulgar': 'a pleasant piece of fiction, certainly, to attach the stigma of cold-blooded deliberate murder to the name and memory of a man who has relatives and friends and admirers amongst the few still living of his many thousands of pupils' (cited Isobel Rae, *Knox the Anatomist* (Edinburgh, 1964), 150).

72 *wynd*: Scottish term for a narrow street or passageway off a main thoroughfare.

quid pro quo: Latin tag, used in legal language to mean a reciprocal exchange.

73 *ghouls*: the term is used precisely: it derives from the Arabic 'to seize', and refers to evil spirits who prey on human corpses in graveyards. This paragraph also identifies the robbers as Irish: both Burke and Hare were Irish migrants.

74 *the girl he had jested with the day before*: Burke and Hare were nearly caught over their murder of the prostitute Mary Paterson, since the senior student at the Surgeons' Hall recognized the body: see introductory note.

75 *Great Bashaw*: variant spelling of Pasha, a Turkish ruler or figure of rank, and transferred into English to mean any haughty or imperious figure.

77 *cras tibi*: Fettes is thinking of gravestones, where he would have read the common inscription *hodie mihi, cras tibi*: 'It is my lot today, yours tomorrow.'

80 *precentor*: the person who leads or directs a singing choir or congregation.

83 *let's have light*: an echo of Shakespeare's *Hamlet*. When Claudius can no

longer bear the play that restages his murder of Hamlet's father, he stops
the performance and commands 'Give me some light' (III. ii. 263).

MARKHEIM

This story was originally submitted to the *Pall Mall Gazette* in
December 1884 for a Christmas special. It proved to be too short for the
commissioned length, and RLS had second thoughts about this version
of the tale. He therefore submitted 'The Body Snatcher' instead.
'Markheim' was revived for the 1885 Christmas market, where it first
appeared in *Unwin's Christmas Annual*.

This story bears many resemblances in terms of plot and even phras-
ing to Fyodor Dostoevsky's *Crime and Punishment*, which also begins
with the murder of a pawnbroker, explores a battle with conscience, and
ends with an eventual surrender to the authorities. These parallels are
examined by Edgar Knowlton ('A Russian Influence on Stevenson',
Modern Philology, 14 (1916), 449–54). *Crime and Punishment* appeared in
Russian in 1865–6, but had been translated into French in 1884. RLS had
read this translation, passed on to him by Henry James. RLS commented
in a very revealing letter to J. A. Symonds in early 1886: 'Henry James
could not finish it: all I can say is, it nearly finished me. It was like having
an illness. James did not care for it because the character of Raskolnikoff
was not objective; and at that I divined a great gulf between us, and, on
further reflection, the existence of a certain impotence in many minds of
today, which prevents them from living *in* a book or a character, and
keeps them standing afar off, spectators of a puppet show.'

85 *Markheim*: in German, *Mark* has meanings that include 'medulla',
'bone', or 'essence' and *Heim* means 'home'. Some critics have suggested
the name might be translated roughly as 'seat of the soul'.

91 *Brownrigg . . . Mannings . . . Thurtell*: this shows a good knowledge of the
ballad, broadside, and Newgate traditions of popular accounts of famous
murderers and their public hangings: exactly the kind of 'chamber of
horrors' that would have been shown in the travelling fairs Markheim
remembers from his youth. Elizabeth Brownrigg was hanged in 1767 for
the violent and abusive treatment of her female apprentices at the work-
house in St Dunstan's-in-the-West. The *Newgate Calendar* record of her
crimes lovingly described the beatings and whippings that eventually
killed Mary Clifford. Maria and Frederick Manning killed Patrick
O'Connor in 1849, burying him beneath the flagstones of a kitchen. A
manhunt for the Mannings tracked Maria down to Edinburgh and
Frederick to Paris. Both were hanged on the roof of Horsemonger Lane
gaol, before an estimated crowd of 50,000. Some two and a half million
broadsides were distributed with details of this crime. Charles Dickens
attended the hanging and expressed disgust in a letter to *The Times* about
'the wickedness and levity of the crowd'. John Thurtell murdered
William Weare in 1823, allegedly for cheating at cards. The body was

buried at Elstree, but Thurtell's accomplice turned king's evidence and Thurtell was hanged in January 1824. He remained famous through the waxwork made of his corpse and displayed at Madame Tussaud's.

That this is Markheim's childhood recollection prompts Ann Gossman to suggest that RLS is deliberately echoing *Macbeth* here, when Lady Macbeth tries to calm her husband's horror over the murders he has committed by stating: 'the sleeping and the dead | Are but as pictures: 'tis the eye of childhood | That fears a painted devil' (Shakespeare, *Macbeth*, II. iii. 53–5).

92 *halbert in hand*: a weapon that is a combination of spear and battle-axe.

93 *pier-glasses*: a large, tall mirror, originally fitted to fill up the pier or space between two windows, or over a chimney piece.

95 *bravos*: See note to p. 56 above.

96 *or to sow tares in the wheat-field*: tares is a grain that looks like wheat while growing, but when full and ripe has ears which are long, the grains being black and poisonous; a biblical reference to Matthew 13: 24–5 and 30: 'Another parable he put forth unto them, saying, The kingdom of heaven is likened unto a man which sowed good seed in his field: But while men slept, his enemy came and sowed tares among the wheat, and went . . . Let both grow together until the harvest: and in the time of harvest I will say to the reapers, Gather ye together first the tares, and bind them in bundles to burn them: but gather the wheat into my barn.'

OLALLA

RLS briefly discusses the origins of this tale in a dream in 'A Chapter on Dreams'. He grew to dislike the tale intensely, complaining to his mentor Sidney Colvin in January 1887 that 'it somehow sounds false' and lamenting the closing pages for their overwrought style. Contemporary critics have revived an interest in the story, due to its treatment of the degeneracy theme.

101 *get you out of this cold and poisonous city . . . pure air*: one of Stevenson's earliest published essays, 'Ordered South', described wintering on the Riviera on doctor's orders, an essay that helped establish RLS's persona as a fragile literary invalid. Although describing France in 'Ordered South', RLS explores in general 'the indefinable line that separates South from North' in the essay, and 'Olalla' further overlays this with the Gothic distinction of Protestant North and Catholic South. In the first wave of Gothic literature in the eighteenth century, events were often set in Italy, less often in Spain. The other opposition in play is between diseased city and pure countryside.

wounded in the good cause: likely to refer to the Second Carlist War (1872–6). Since the death of Ferdinand VII in 1833 rival royal factions had fought over the Spanish throne. RLS was likely to identify with the Carlist side: like the failed Scottish forces behind Bonnie Prince Charlie, the Carlist line had been defeated, crushed, and largely driven into exile.

101 *tatterdemalion pride*: 'a person in tattered clothing; a ragged or beggarly fellow; a ragamuffin' (*OED*). Pride is the first Christian deadly sin to be associated with the family.

102 *degenerate both in parts and fortune*: degeneracy, a steady decline in a family through successive generations, was both a biblical idea of punishment for the 'sins of the fathers' and, in the late Victorian period, a contested pseudo-scientific idea that deviancy in parents produced off-spring lower down the evolutionary scale (for more details, see Introduction). Degeneration was often associated with the dense populations of the urban poor. Interestingly, in his lecture *Degeneration amongst Londoners* (1885), James Cantlie uses the example of Spain for the instance of general racial decline: 'From Spain, the sons of labour sailed forth to the utmost ends of the earth, civilising, conquering, and adding to their wealth. So monetarily wealthy grew they that in time labour ceased to be a necessity, the sons of the active spirits grew up to laugh at labour, and in no long time degeneracy succeeded . . . and now the sons of the mighty Spaniard are content to play a second-rate part in the affairs of the world. Thus it is that luxury in families or nations begets sloth' (37). That RLS's tale pursues precisely this trajectory suggests this was a general view of the Spanish 'race' in Britain at the time.

103 *Felipe*: Felipe is portrayed throughout the tale as an atavistic throwback, physically strong yet mentally and morally imbecilic. A little like Hyde (some of whose physical characteristics echo those of Felipe), this was also how many theorists of degeneracy regarded the general class of agricultural labourers and peasants. The literary model for Felipe is Donatello in Nathaniel Hawthorne's *The Marble Faun* (1860), a Gothic tale of blighted inheritance set in a sensuous Italy: 'Olalla' consistently borrows from Hawthorne, as several critics noted at the time.

104 *Kelpie*: 'a water demon haunting rivers and forests, generally in the form of a black (or white) horse, which lured many human beings to death by drowning' (*Scottish National Dictionary*).

106 *a picture on the wall*: the device of the portrait features extensively in Gothic literature, often for revealing fatal family resemblances or gener-ational repetition. Reference points might be Horace Walpole's *Castle of Otranto* (1765) or Charles Maturin's *Melmoth the Wanderer* (1820), which also has an embedded tale set in Spain. Ann B. Tracy's *The Gothic Novel 1790–1830* has an 'Index of Motifs' that lists many lesser texts from the era that use portraits and miniatures as key plot devices. In tales sub-sequent to 'Olalla', obvious points of reference are Oscar Wilde's *The Picture of Dorian Gray* (1890) and Conan Doyle's *The Hound of the Baskervilles* (1902), where the identity of the killer is revealed by his resemblance to the portrait of an ancestor.

107 *frieze*: a coarse woollen cloth.

philtre: a potion or drug supposed to be capable of producing love.

110 *bartizan*: a small, overhanging turret on a wall or tower.

112 *sunk in sloth and pleasure*: this lengthy description of the Señora, and all of her subsequent behaviour, is written from a deep religious knowledge of the sin of sloth or 'acedia'. There are some Old Testament references to sloth, associating it with sleep and laziness, leading to ruin and decay (Ecclesiastes 10: 18: 'By much slothfulness the building decayeth; and through idleness of the hands the house droppeth through'). Sloth, however, became one of the seven deadly sins only in the medieval church, when acedia acquired a very specific set of meanings as a specific sin of the spiritual life, a kind of boredom or dejection that leads to the desertion of spiritual duties and due reverence for God and thence to further sins of sadness, wrath, and lechery. RLS seems to be very aware, in this tale of moral descent, about the causative links between ever-worsening sins, played out across the generations. For full discussion of the origins of sloth in Christian doctrine, see Siegfried Wenzel, *The Sin of Sloth: Acedia in Medieval Thought and Literature* (Chapel Hill, NC, 1960).

113 *hebetude*: dullness or stupidity.

117 *port of noble offices*: dignified carriage or stately bearing.

118 *They were of all sorts . . . Latin tongue*: this room, and its contents, describes someone trying to resist the sin of sloth by devotion to study and worship. Sloth was originally considered to be a particular risk of monastic life; hard work and constant devotional meditation were the suggested treatments.

119 *a foreigner, a heretic, and yet one who had been wounded for the good cause*: it is common in the Gothic romance to place an upstanding English man from an implicitly Protestant tradition among the superstitions of southern European Catholicism (think of Jonathan Harker in Transylvania on the approach to Count Dracula's castle). The narrator's honourable role in the Carlist Wars can only confuse this typical representation of a craven Catholic priest.

124 *El Dorado*: in the Renaissance era, this was a fabled gilded city of unimaginable wealth, thought to exist somewhere in the New World. Explorers like Walter Raleigh and Gonzalo Pizarro hunted for its gold.

128 *bitten me to the bone*: this scene inevitably suggests a kind of vampiric act, and is meant to mark the Señora's final descent into animalism. In 'A Chapter on Dreams', RLS claims this scene derived from a dream. Yet, as Claire Harman observes in her biography, Fanny Stevenson had bitten RLS's hand in Paris in 1877 to try to prevent *his* outburst of uncontrollable hysterical laughter (see Claire Harman, *Robert Louis Stevenson: A Biography* (London, 2005), 151 and 308–9).

catamount: short for catamountain, a common name for a big cat such a puma, cougar, or tiger. It was then transferred to refer to the 'wild men' of mountainous regions.

132 *to be forgotten*: Olalla's whole speech here would appear to be an abneg-
      ation before God for the sins of her fathers, but it is also entirely in
      keeping with the pseudo-scientific language of degeneration theory. Her
      advocacy that dangerously corrupted inheritance should not be allowed
      to reproduce conforms to the views of Francis Galton. Galton wished to
      ensure good breeding ('eu-genics') to bolster the best elements of the
      English race; the attendant logic was a negative eugenics that sought to
      control the reproduction of those he regarded as undesirable and unfit.

133 *kirk-town*: the village in which the parish church is erected.

134 *crossed themselves on my approach*: the peasants are defending themselves
      against someone they regard as a devil. English folklorists and anthropo-
      logists measured civilization according to the progressive elimination of
      such superstitions: in textbooks like Edward Tylor's extremely influential
      Primitive Culture (1871) instances of such superstitious practices surviv-
      ing in the 'backward' places of Europe formed the bulk of the anthropo-
      logical evidence.

136 *basilisks*: a fabulous reptile, widely held by classical sources to have a gaze
      and a breath that could kill.

A GOSSIP ON ROMANCE

This essay first appeared in *Longman's Magazine*, 1 (November 1882),
and was then reprinted in *Memories and Portraits* (1887). This gives a
helpful sense of RLS's literary reference points. More widely, it is an
early essay in the debates about the late Victorian 'romance revival'. A
number of writers and critics worried that the novel was becoming too
analytic and interior; the romance was an older and more vigorous and
kinetic form. The influential critic Andrew Lang would use RLS's
Treasure Island (1883) as an example of the renewed form, and the success of that book would pave the way for the success of authors like Rider
Haggard, Arthur Conan Doyle, and others. When Henry James composed 'The Art of the Novel' in 1884, RLS restaged his defence of the
romance in 'A Humble Remonstrance'.

139 *A Jacobite would do*: Jacobitism was political movement dedicated to the
      restoration of the Stuart kings in England and Scotland. It developed in
      response to the deposition of the Catholic James II and the arrival of the
      Protestant William and Mary. In Scotland, the movement was also
      marked by a resistance to English imperialism. The first rising was in
      1715, the second in 1745, which was defeated by English forces at the
      Battle of Culloden in 1746. This was an era RLS frequently returned to
      in his historical romances, for acts of desperate and doomed heroism.

      John Rann or Jerry Abershaw: more evidence of RLS's fascination with
      the *Newgate Calendar*, the popular record of the crimes and executions
      of London criminals, and popular ballad traditions of famous executed
      criminals. Rann was known as 'Sixteen-String Jack' (for his ostentatious
      style of knee breeches), and was hanged as a notorious highwayman at

Tyburn in 1774. Abershaw refers to Lewis Jeremiah Avershaw, a high-wayman hanged in August 1795. Avershaw survived in popular legend long into the twentieth century, was the subject of many penny dreadfuls and referred to by Dickens in *Nicholas Nickleby* and Frederick Marryat in *Jacob Faithful*. Whilst at work on *Treasure Island*, RLS sketched out the idea for 'Jerry Abershaw: A Tale of Putney Heath', and wrote to his friend W. E. Henley: 'Jerry Abershaw—O what a title! Jerry Abershaw: d—n it, sir, it's a poem.'

What will he Do with It: novel by Edward Bulwer-Lytton (1865).

140 *horrors of a wreck*: when collected in book form, RLS added a footnote to this description: 'Since traced by many obliging correspondents to the gallery of Charles Kingsley.'

141 *miching mallecho*: the reference is to Shakespeare's *Hamlet*, III. ii. When Hamlet is asked about the meaning of the dumb show he has staged for the king, he responds: 'Marry, this is miching mallecho, it means mis-chief' (probably from *mich*, to lurk + Spanish *malhecho*, meaning malefaction or mischief).

Antiquary: Walter Scott's romance, *The Antiquary*, opens at this inn in Queensferry, on the Firth of Forth.

142 *Crusoe . . . Achilles . . . Ulysses . . . Christian*: the references are to Daniel Defoe's *Robinson Crusoe* (1719), Homer's *Iliad* and *Odyssey*, and John Bunyan's *The Pilgrim's Progress* (1678–84).

143 *Trollope*: Anthony Trollope (1815–82) was famed for his Barchester Chronicles series of novels, exemplary of mid-Victorian realist depiction of small town life. 'Chronicling small beer' is borrowed from Shake-speare's *Othello*, II. i, where Iago suggests marriage is 'To suckle fools and chronicle small beer'.

If Rawden Crawley's blow . . . art: reference to chapter 53 of William Thackeray's *Vanity Fair* (1847–8), where Crawley strikes Lord Steyne in the face.

here borrowed from the . . . French thief: William Thackeray's *The History of Henry Esmond* (1852) is here praised for its debts to the work of Alexandre Dumas, author of *The Three Musketeers* (1844–5) and *The Count of Monte Cristo* (1844–5), and one of RLS's favourite authors. Note that RLS here praises such borrowing, something he did extensively in his own fiction: it is seen as part of the romance tradition.

Clarissa Harlowe: Samuel Richardson's *Clarissa: or, The History of a Young Lady* (1747–9), an eight-volume epistolary novel, and central to the formation of the English novel of character.

144 *Arabian Nights*: the *Arabian Nights' Entertainments* is a collection of Arabic tales, framed as a succession of tales told by Scheherazade to save herself from death by spinning out her husband's curiosity through storytelling skill. English translations had been available since the eight-eenth century, with the most risqué bits excised. A full translation by

John Payne appeared 1882–4, succeeded by the notorious edition by Sir Richard Burton (1885–8), which associated the text with Oriental sexual perversity. At exactly the same time, RLS issued his *New Arabian Nights* collection of stories, and again later evoked the title with his *Island Night's Entertainments*.

145 *Lucy and Richard Feverell*: George Meredith's novel *The Ordeal of Richard Feverel* (1859). Meredith was another, rather incongruous, RLS favourite.

Haydn and Consuelo . . . incident: scene from George Sand's novel *Consuelo* (1861).

146 *Clark Russell*: William Clark Russell (1844–1911) had served in the British Merchant Service as a boy and young man, these experiences providing the material for his prolific career as a novelist. *The Sailor's Sweetheart* appeared in 1877.

that dreary family: J. D. Wyss's *Swiss Family Robinson* (1812) was hugely successful in the Victorian era, but clearly already on the wane.

Mysterious Island: Jules Verne's novel appeared in 1874, part of his cycle of scientific and technological adventures commonly held to anticipate the science fiction genre.

147 *Rawden Crawley or with Eugene de Rastignac*: references to central characters in Thackeray's *Vanity Fair* (1847–8) and Honoré de Balzac's *Père Goriot* (1835).

Walter Scott is out and away king of the romantics: these last pages constitute RLS's serious attempt to come to terms with the legacy of the Scottish writer that most overshadowed his own literary endeavours. References are principally to *The Lady of the Lake* (1810), based on Malory's *Morte d'Arthur* (the quotation, 'The stag at eve had drunk his fill' is line 28 of Canto First). *The Pirate* appeared in 1821, *Guy Mannering* in 1815. He later refers to 'the character of Elspeth of the Craigburnfoot', a reference to *The Antiquary* (1816). Later editors, like Edmund Gosse, silently erased RLS's last sentence of the essay, considering its judgement on Scott too harsh.

148 *Mrs. Todgers's idea . . . expounded*: in chapter nine of Charles Dickens's *Martin Chuzzlewit* (1843–4), Mr Pecksniff reflects: 'The legs of the human subjects, my friends, are a beautiful production. Compare them with wooden legs, and observe the difference between the anatomy of nature and the anatomy of art . . . I should very much like to see Mrs Todgers's notion of a wooden leg, if perfectly agreeable to herself.'

A CHAPTER ON DREAMS

When RLS arrived in New York in September 1887, he was to discover that *Jekyll and Hyde* had made him a celebrity author. He was asked continually about the origins of the story by journalists, and the New York *Critic* reported RLS's account of the dream origins of the tale:

'At night I dreamed the story, not precisely as it is written, for of course there are always stupidities in dreams, but practically as it came to me as a gift, and what makes it more odd is that I am quite in the habit of dreaming stories' (cited J. A. Hammerton, *Stevensoniana: An Ancedotal Life and Appreciation of Robert Louis Stevenson* (Edinburgh, 1907), 85). The essay became an extension of these comments, one of twelve contracted essays for Charles Scribner's monthly journal. It is another suggestive account of the divided self, this time in the autobiographical register.

152 *He was from a child . . . dreamer*: towards the end of the essay, RLS reveals that this person is of course himself. The account of the division between waking and sleeping selves is therefore further split by displacing 'I' to 'he'.

hell and judgment . . . nightmare: much has been made of the impact of RLS's childhood nanny and nurse, Alison 'Cummy' Cummingham, who filled the boy with the stern doctrines of hellfire and damnation of the Scottish Covenanters (Presbyterian extremists who became a persecuted minority in the Restoration era). In 'Memoirs of Himself', RLS recalled: 'I would not only lie awake to weep for Jesus, which I have done many a time, but I would fear to trust myself to slumber lest I was not accepted and should slip, ere I awoke into eternal ruin . . . I remember repeatedly . . . waking from a dream of Hell, clinging to the horizontal bar of the bed, with my knees and chin together, my soul shaken, my body convulsed with agony' (cited Harman, *Stevenson*, 23–4).

153 *Jacobite conspiracy*: see note to p. 139 above.

G. P. R. James: James (1799–1860) was the most prolific and successful novelist of the early Victorian era, who wrote reams of historical romances and popular histories after the manner of Walter Scott.

a tall land: Scottish term for a building divided into flats for different households.

154 *whereupon . . . he was restored*: RLS was a student of engineering and then law at Edinburgh University, although 'The Body Snatcher' reveals a fascination with the gruesome details of the independent anatomical schools of the city that served the medical students. His divided self is dreaming of a city that RLS himself said in *Edinburgh: Picturesque Notes* 'leads a double existence . . . half alive and half a monumental marble'.

155 *the little people*: for readers after the complex models of mind developed by Sigmund Freud and others, RLS's metaphor of the 'little people' in the 'theatre' of the mind may seem very simplistic. In fact, it relies on a long tradition of philosophical thought stretching back to the Greeks. These were the kind of resources available to RLS before the language of the 'unconscious' and 'dream-work'. Philosophers have since debated 'the homunculus fallacy', what Anthony Kenny called the mistake of 'the postulation of a little man within a man to explain human experience and behaviour' (in 'The Homunculus Fallacy', in Marjorie Grene (ed.),

Interpretations of Life and Mind: Essays around the Problem of Reduction (London, 1971), 66).

156 *like Claudius in the play*: in Shakespeare's *Hamlet*, the guilty conscience of King Claudius is pricked by Hamlet's restaging of the murder of his father. Claudius orders the play stopped midway through. This is also echoed at the end of 'The Body Snatcher', suggesting a key reference point for RLS.

sleepless Brownies: Jamieson's *Scottish Dictionary* (1879) defines a Brownie as 'a spirit, till of late years supposed to haunt old houses, those, especially, attached to farms. Instead of doing any injury, he was believed to be very useful to the family, particularly to the servants, if they treated him well; for whom, while they took their necessary refreshment in sleep, he was wont to do many pieces of drudgery.' Brownies are small, hairy, or often clothed in a dogskin—acting rather like a dog to guard the house from strangers. Jamieson adds, however, that the Shetland version is not benign, but has a rather malign reputation, and the Brownie must be propitiated with offerings of food and drink.

158 *Dennery or Sardou*: Adolphe D'Ennery (1811–99) wrote over 200 melo-dramas and comedies from 1831 onwards; Victorien Sardou (1831–1908) also wrote scores of light comedies and historical dramas, and had written two successful plays for Sarah Bernhardt in the 1880s. The two dramatists are invoked as the quintessence of 'jobbing' authors.

159 *pineal gland . . . Descartes*: French philosopher René Descartes famously located the soul in the pineal gland. In *The Passions of the Soul* (1649), he wrote 'on carefully examining the matter I think I have clearly estab-lished that the part of the body in which the soul directly exercises its functions is not the heart at all, or the whole of the brain. It is rather the innermost part of the brain, which is a certain very small gland situated in the middle of the brain's substance . . . From there [the soul] radiates through the rest of the body by means of the animal spirits, the nerves, and even the blood' (*The Philosophical Writings of René Descartes*, vol. i, trans. John Cottingham *et al.* (Cambridge, 1985), 340–1).

160 *my garden of Adonis*: the phrase refers to anything disposable or short-lived: it derives from the Greek festival of Adonis, when fast-growing plants were placed in pots as offerings to the god but allowed to die off, being ritualistically discarded after eight days.

aping Bunyan: John Bunyan's *The Pilgrim's Progress* was published in two parts in 1678 and 1684. It was presented as a dream, and was an allegory of Protestant spiritual life. This is an ironic suggestion, given that RLS's Brownies have no conscience or sense of morality.

161 *A Chance Acquaintance*: novel by American writer and editor, William Dean Howells, published in 1873. Howells was associated with the trad-ition of social realism in the novel, and was therefore a literary opponent of the 'romance revival'. At the end of RLS's essay 'A Humble Remon-strance' (1884), his rejection of realism contains an explicit attack on

Howells as 'the zealot of his school'. Defending the kinesis of the romance against the analytic stasis of the novel, RLS ends 'the danger is lest, in seeking to draw the normal, a man should draw the null, and write the novel of society instead of the romance of man'.

APPENDIXES

164 *ens unum et semper cognitum in omnibus notitiis*: Latin: 'the being which is one and always understood in all things as one.'

167 *pro tanto*: 'only to that extent', a phrase usually used in legal language to restrict precisely a particular order of the court.

168 *savants*: French term, usually used to refer to eminent thinkers.

169 *Félida X . . . Louis V.'s case*: the study of the apparent multiple personalities of the hysteric Félida had been undertaken by the French doctor Eugène Azam, his case study being published in 1876. Louis V. (or Vivet) had been published as a case history in July 1885, again in France. As Ian Hacking records in his history, *Rewriting the Soul: Multiple Personality and the Sciences of Memory* (Princeton, 1995), cases of multiplex personality were so rare that these individual instances were endlessly circulated and discussed across Europe. Louis alone was the subject of studies by over twenty psychologists (for more details, see Introduction).

   epilepsy: in the nineteenth century (and some way into the twentieth), epilepsy was regarded as a biological marker of mental weakness and insanity, rather than as a neurological disorder.

   mauvais sujets: literally 'bad subjects'; one might be tempted to translate this more freely as 'strange cases'.

170 *transfer of hysterical hemiplegia from one side to the other*: doctors had been experimenting with the effects of magnets on hysterical patients for a number of years, claiming that hysterical symptoms could be moved from the left to right side, and vice versa, with the application of a magnet. This 'metallotherapy' received the support of the most famous Parisian psychologist of the time, Jean-Martin Charcot, in 1882. Although clearly a product of suggestion (patients become much more susceptible to direction in trance states), the use of magnets had long been part of the occult tradition of Mesmerism, where the 'animal magnetism' of humans could be channelled and redirected if the patient was in 'rapport' with the Mesmerist.

172 *Wesen*: German for nature.

173 *Juvenis quondam . . . revoluta figuram*: the citation is from Virgil's *Aeneid*, vi. 449–50: 'Here too is Caeneus, once a young man, but next a woman | And now is changed back by fate to his original sex.' This is a figure from Greek and Latin mythology, encountered by Aeneas in the group of lost souls in the Underworld.

   Esquirol's: Jean Etiénne Dominique Esquirol (1772–1840), an important asylum doctor, who famously exposed the violent abuses of the insane in the asylum system of France, and set about new treatments that involved forms of therapy rather than punishment and physical restraint.

174 *J'existe . . . réelle*: 'I exist, but outside real life.'

Teiresias: androgynous prophet and seer, who lives immortally and endures his role as witness to human suffering.

état bête: bestial or stupid state.

175 *Galahad's cry*: reference to Alfred, Lord Tennyson's *Idylls of the King* (Myers was a member of Tennyson's social circle). In 'The Holy Grail' section of Tennyson's epic, Galahad recalls Merlin's warning against loss of selfhood. 'Galahad, when he heard of Merlin's doom, | Cried, "If I lose myself, I save myself." '

177 *The process . . . by which some of my friends constantly report to me*: the magazine *Borderland* had been set up by Stead upon his claim that he had discovered that he was able to receive communications from others at a distance simply by entering a light trance state, and letting his 'subliminal' mind take dictation from them through a telepathic link. This is why he calls himself a 'two-legged telephone'. This 'automatic writing' had been used by some spiritualist mediums for decades as a way of contacting the dead, but it had also been taken seriously by psychologists as evidence of the existence of a subliminal or subconscious part of the mind that could be accessed during hypnosis. Psychical researchers publicly upheld the view that automatic writing was the communication of one part of the mind with another, and disdained the view that these were spirit messages. Stead reported the science breathlessly, but also firmly believed that he was in communication with the dead.

Miss X: the identity of Stead's co-editor and principal writer was kept secret until the journal closed, allegedly to protect a gentlewoman from disapproval. She began to publish under her own name in the late 1890s: Ada Goodrich-Freer. Freer was a woman who claimed she had been born into a Scottish family gifted with second sight and many other psychical powers. She was active in London's occult circles and became involved in psychical research, where she worked as a 'sensitive' investigating allegedly haunted houses. There is a rather savage assessment of her career as an occultist by Trevor Hall, *The Strange Story of Ada Goodrich Freer* (London, 1980).

178 *Madame Blavatsky*: Helena Blavatsky founded the major late Victorian occultist grouping, the Theosophical Society, which had established lodges in Britain, America, and India before her death in 1891 (people interested in her teachings included the poet W. B. Yeats, the political agitator Annie Besant, and Gothic novelist Algernon Blackwood). The Society continues to study her occult writings, such as *Isis Unveiled* (1877) and *The Secret Doctrine* (1888), which promise a complete synthesis of all scientific knowledge and religious beliefs, revealed to Blavatsky by a group of immortal wise beings, the Mahatmas, who posted letters to her from the mysterious (and then inaccessible) land of Tibet. Amongst

the skills a training in Theosophy offered was the ability to project psychic doubles across the 'astral plane'. Psychical researchers declared she was a fraud in 1885; the ecumenical Stead was happy to take information from any occult source.

Professor Ladd's remark: George Trumbull Ladd (1842–1921) was the first president of the American Psychological Association (in 1893), and wrote textbooks on what he termed 'physiological psychology'. He also published on biblical history—exactly the sort of combination of theology and science favoured by Blavatsky.

179 *Dr Richardson*: Benjamin Ward Richardson was the editor of the occult journal *Asclepiad*, which ran from 1884 to 1895.

182 *anabolick . . . katabolic*: these terms are derived from the influential and formative book of sexology by Patrick Geddes and J. Arthur Thompson, *The Evolution of Sex* (1889), which biologized cultural differences between the sexes using these terms.

	Late Victorian Gothic Tales
JANE AUSTEN	Emma
	Mansfield Park
	Persuasion
	Pride and Prejudice
	Selected Letters
	Sense and Sensibility
MRS BEETON	Book of Household Management
MARY ELIZABETH BRADDON	Lady Audley's Secret
ANNE BRONTË	The Tenant of Wildfell Hall
CHARLOTTE BRONTË	Jane Eyre
	Shirley
	Villette
EMILY BRONTË	Wuthering Heights
ROBERT BROWNING	The Major Works
JOHN CLARE	The Major Works
SAMUEL TAYLOR COLERIDGE	The Major Works
WILKIE COLLINS	The Moonstone
	No Name
	The Woman in White
CHARLES DARWIN	The Origin of Species
THOMAS DE QUINCEY	The Confessions of an English Opium-Eater
	On Murder
CHARLES DICKENS	The Adventures of Oliver Twist
	Barnaby Rudge
	Bleak House
	David Copperfield
	Great Expectations
	Nicholas Nickleby
	The Old Curiosity Shop
	Our Mutual Friend
	The Pickwick Papers

WALTER SCOTT	Rob Roy
MARY SHELLEY	Frankenstein
	The Last Man
ROBERT LOUIS STEVENSON	Strange Case of Dr Jekyll and Mr Hyde and Other Tales
	Treasure Island
BRAM STOKER	Dracula
JOHN SUTHERLAND	So You Think You Know Jane Austen?
	So You Think You Know Thomas Hardy?
WILLIAM MAKEPEACE THACKERAY	Vanity Fair
OSCAR WILDE	The Importance of Being Earnest and Other Plays
	The Major Works
	The Picture of Dorian Gray
ELLEN WOOD	East Lynne
DOROTHY WORDSWORTH	The Grasmere and Alfoxden Journals
WILLIAM WORDSWORTH	The Major Works

ANTHONY TROLLOPE

A SELECTION OF **OXFORD WORLD'S CLASSICS**

ANTON CHEKHOV

About Love and Other Stories
Early Stories
Five Plays
The Princess and Other Stories
The Russian Master and Other Stories
The Steppe and Other Stories
Twelve Plays
Ward Number Six and Other Stories

FYODOR DOSTOEVSKY

Crime and Punishment
Devils
A Gentle Creature and Other Stories
The Idiot
The Karamazov Brothers
Memoirs from the House of the Dead
Notes from the Underground and
     The Gambler

NIKOLAI GOGOL

Dead Souls
Plays and Petersburg Tales

ALEXANDER PUSHKIN

Eugene Onegin
The Queen of Spades and Other Stories

LEO TOLSTOY

Anna Karenina
The Kreutzer Sonata and Other Stories
The Raid and Other Stories
Resurrection
War and Peace

IVAN TURGENEV

Fathers and Sons
First Love and Other Stories
A Month in the Country

HONORÉ DE BALZAC	Père Goriot
CHARLES BAUDELAIRE	The Flowers of Evil
DENIS DIDEROT	Jacques the Fatalist The Nun
ALEXANDRE DUMAS (PÈRE)	The Count of Monte Cristo The Three Musketeers
GUSTAVE FLAUBERT	Madame Bovary
VICTOR HUGO	The Essential Victor Hugo Notre-Dame de Paris
J.-K. HUYSMANS	Against Nature
PIERRE CHODERLOS DE LACLOS	Les Liaisons dangereuses
GUY DE MAUPASSANT	Bel-Ami Pierre et Jean
MOLIÈRE	Don Juan and Other Plays The Misanthrope, Tartuffe, and Other Plays
ABBÉ PRÉVOST	Manon Lescaut
ARTHUR RIMBAUD	Collected Poems
EDMOND ROSTAND	Cyrano de Bergerac
JEAN-JACQUES ROUSSEAU	Confessions
MARQUIS DE SADE	The Crimes of Love
STENDHAL	The Red and the Black The Charterhouse of Parma
PAUL VERLAINE	Selected Poems
VOLTAIRE	Candide and Other Stories
ÉMILE ZOLA	L'Assommoir The Kill

The Oxford World's Classics Website

www.oup.com/uk/worldsclassics

- Information about new titles
- Explore the full range of Oxford World's Classics
- Links to other literary sites and the main OUP webpage
- Imaginative competitions, with bookish prizes
- Articles by editors
- Extracts from Introductions
- Special information for teachers and lecturers

www.oup.com/uk/worldsclassics

American Literature

Authors in Context

British and Irish Literature

Children's Literature

Classics and Ancient Literature

Colonial Literature

Eastern Literature

European Literature

History

Medieval Literature

Oxford English Drama

Poetry

Philosophy

Politics

Religion

The Oxford Shakespeare

A complete list of Oxford World's Classics, including Authors in Context, Oxford English Drama, and the Oxford Shakespeare, is available in the UK from the Marketing Services Department, Oxford University Press, Great Clarendon Street, Oxford OX2 6DP, or visit the website at www.oup.com/uk/worldsclassics.

In the USA, visit www.oup.com/us/owc for a complete title list.

Oxford World's Classics are available from all good bookshops. In case of difficulty, customers in the UK should contact Oxford University Press Bookshop, 116 High Street, Oxford OX1 4BR.